Born in the UK, **Becky W**
interminable wanderlust
She's lived and worked all over the world, from London to Dubai, Sydney, Bali, NYC and Amsterdam. She's written for the likes of *GQ*, *Hello!*, *Fabulous* and *Time Out*, a host of YA romance, plus three travel memoirs—*Burqalicious*, *Balilicious* and *Latinalicious* (HarperCollins, Australia). Now she blends travel with romance for Mills & Boon and loves every minute! Find her on X @bex_wicks and subscribe at beckywicks.com.

Sue MacKay lives with her husband in New Zealand's beautiful Marlborough Sounds, with the water on her doorstep and the birds and the trees at her back door. It is the perfect setting to indulge her passions of entertaining friends by cooking them sumptuous meals, drinking fabulous wine, going for hill walks or kayaking around the bay—and, of course, writing stories.

Also by Becky Wicks

Finding Forever with the Single Dad
Melting the Surgeon's Heart
A Marriage Healed in Hawaii

Buenos Aires Docs miniseries

Daring to Fall for the Single Dad

Also by Sue MacKay

Fake Fiancée to Forever?
Resisting the Pregnant Paediatrician
Marriage Reunion with the Island Doc
Paramedic's Fling to Forever

Discover more at millsandboon.co.uk.

TEMPTED BY THE OUTBACK VET

BECKY WICKS

HEALING THE SINGLE DAD SURGEON

SUE MacKAY

MILLS & BOON

First published in Great Britain 2024
by Mills & Boon, an imprint of HarperCollins*Publishers* Ltd,
1 London Bridge Street, London, SE1 9GF

www.harpercollins.co.uk

HarperCollins*Publishers* Macken House, 39/40 Mayor Street Upper,
Dublin 1, D01 C9W8, Ireland

ISBN: 978-0-263-32171-5

09/24

This book contains FSC™ certified paper
and other controlled sources to ensure responsible forest management.

For more information visit www.harpercollins.co.uk/green.

Printed and Bound in the UK using 100% Renewable Electricity
at CPI Group (UK) Ltd, Croydon, CR0 4YY

TEMPTED BY THE OUTBACK VET

BECKY WICKS

MILLS & BOON

Dedicated to Paul and Campbell,
two handsome excuses to visit Australia for real.

CHAPTER ONE

SAGE STEPPED CLOSER to the paddock gate cautiously, the scraps bucket held tight in her hands. Storm was all action and nervous energy, rearing up and bucking violently at the sight of her.

'Steady, boy!' She flinched as the horse's hooves slammed to the sandy ground, his eyes wild with distress. This was the third week in a row that Storm had been inconsolable, refusing to let anyone near him. Ellie shuffled just behind her, twirling a strand of her sun-bleached blonde hair around one finger, as her young veterinary assistant often did when she was thinking.

'I just don't know what to do, Ells.' Sage's voice came out strained. 'I mean, look at him. I can't even get close enough to examine him! If anything he's getting worse. The mayor is going to want answers soon and, right now, I don't have any. Zero.'

Sage's heart ached. Feeling helpless never had sat well with her, especially where animals were involved—it brought back too many bad memories—and Abigail's husband, Amber Creek's beloved Mayor Jarrah Warragul, had brought Storm to her, convinced she could apply her years of veterinary expertise to help convert the wild animal into the doting pet his eleven-year-old wanted. Lucie, Sage's favourite of her best friend's three crazy kids, was beyond excited for rides through the outback on her very first horse, and at this rate Sage was going to have to let the whole family down, hard.

Ellie gave her shoulder a gentle squeeze, still quite understandably hesitant to step her petite frame much closer. 'Did you think any more about what the mayor said, about that vet we saw on TV last month? The one who calmed that uncontrollable racehorse?'

Sage nodded slowly as the image of the equine vet's face flashed back into her brain, throwing her off track for a moment. Rugged, handsome, built like a soldier in a sunhat… the kind of man who lived a life outdoors and could wrestle a croc with one arm. The mayor had suggested she call him; in fact, when she hadn't taken his advice, he had told her just today that he would go ahead and arrange things, which she hadn't told Ellie yet. It was more than humiliating, knowing she hadn't been good enough for the job.

'Ethan Matthews. Yes,' she said on a sigh. 'He used some kind of pressure-point massage to relax that horse.' She frowned as his features grew clearer in her mind's eye. The equine vet was bordering on being the sexiest man alive and not just because of the way his muscles rippled beneath his shirt like a sculpted masterpiece. He radiated the kind of magnetism that could stir something primal in a corpse, even through the TV screen. There should have been nothing more attractive to her than a guy who'd devoted his entire life to caring for animals, the same as she had, but this was her territory. She'd never had anyone else come in and take over before.

'Yes, him,' Ellie said with a dreamy sigh. 'I kind of wanted to *be* that horse.'

Ellie giggled into her hair and Sage rolled her eyes. The two of them had watched the vet in action intently for about ten minutes before realising they were both admiring a lot more than his horsemanship.

'He's supposed to be the best you can get when it comes to problematic horses. And Storm is definitely problematic. Look at poor Karma!' Ellie pointed out.

Sage looked at her newest gelding, Karma, who snorted obstinately from the corner of the paddock. He was doing better after his surgery, but she had her suspicions the healing horse just didn't want to provoke Storm in the same space.

Sage finally told Ellie that Ethan was flying in tomorrow, and Ellie pretended she wasn't excited about it, even though her eyes practically bugged out of her head. Ethan lived in Queensland, and he was known for some pretty weird holistic practices, which felt more infuriating the more Sage thought about it. She'd been used to handling things her own way for the best part of six long years, and now they were just supposed to let some TV celebrity come in and take over?

'Maybe some of his methods might actually work?' Ellie suggested cautiously, eyeing Sage's fierce scowl.

Sage crossed to Karma, careful not to spook the wide-eyed Storm, who watched her every move suspiciously. 'Don't mind us, buddy,' Ellie told him, keeping close behind her.

She didn't have a choice about Ethan's so-called methods, she thought gloomily. Jarrah wanted him here, and, besides, the horse was too dangerous and unpredictable to have around his growing family. Abigail was five months pregnant with their fourth child and what if this unruly beast got a little too wild, a little too close to her? It didn't bear thinking about! Everyone here adored the mayor and his family, Sage most of all. She would be eternally grateful for the soft cushion they'd given her to land on six years ago when she'd driven into town, looking for work. Abigail knew everything about her past, too: the bushfire that had rendered her an orphaned child at ten years old, the fact that she might have prevented it if she hadn't been such a silly, disobedient kid, and that weird, sudden break-up with Bryce too, just weeks before she'd rocked up here.

Abigail had unbottled Sage years ago, along with the wine they had taken to sharing most Friday nights, and Sage was incredibly thankful that she'd been able to talk to someone about it all. It wasn't as though she went around telling just anyone *why* she'd grown up in the care of a foster family in Perth. Just the thought of all the animals that must have died that night when the fire had spread and killed her family, and Juni too—the best dog who'd ever lived—devastated her.

Keep on moving, keep busy, be a good vet, be good to your community, help the animals.

That was her strategy for life. It seemed to be working most of the time, except for when she saw a dog in distress. That always brought all the trauma rushing back, along with the overwhelming guilt.

Sage squinted against the sun. Why exactly was the thought of Ethan Matthews coming here unsettling her like this? He might well be an arrogant showbiz equine expert, but so what?

Maybe it was something about the look on his face when the camera had panned in, she thought. As if he was carrying some kind of close-held secret he only ever shared with his horses. Something that reminded her of herself.

The morning sun warmed her tense shoulders as Sage stood with her arms folded over the fence, chewing her lip distractedly under the wide-brimmed hat. She called out to Storm, who ignored her. He'd been restless all night again, snorting and pacing as if an invisible phantom were on his tail. It had taken even longer than usual to coerce him between the stall and the paddock with a broom handle.

The rumble of a truck caught her ears. Turning around, she felt her breath catch as the door of the red pickup swung open and then she was watching Ethan Matthews jump to the dusty ground. All six-foot-something of him.

The sunlight streamed across his broad shoulders, forcing her gaze to the contours of his biceps and the dark, almost jet-black thickness of his hair. He wore it scraped back into a rough, manly ponytail at the nape of his neck and he moved with a quiet confidence that made Sage's pulse quicken. She took him all in as he strode towards her in jeans. A forest-green T-shirt moulded to his sculpted torso, muscular thighs visible through every stretch of denim.

Holy hell...

'Dr Dawson?' He was in front of her, extending a big hand, fixing her with the most piercing blue eyes she'd ever seen. They were striking, rimmed with a deep green, and were more bewitching the longer she looked at them. She was suddenly aware they were roaming her face inquisitively, turning her cheeks into beetroots. 'Great to finally meet you.'

Finally? She bit back a grimace. So, he'd been anticipating showing up here for a while, then. Knowing the mayor as she did, he'd have waited at least two weeks out of the three before making the call. It wasn't as if he didn't trust her. He'd probably just realised she clearly didn't have the right experience for this task.

Sage adjusted her hat, willing her heart to calm down. She wanted to stay annoyed, but Ethan Matthews was so good-looking it was almost too much to take in—how were they not constantly doing close-ups of his eyes on TV? He was brooding from a distance, but this close the effect was devastating.

Maybe they were afraid of hypnotising the nation. At any rate, nope. Such charm and charisma would *not* work on her.

'Dr Matthews, thanks for coming on such short notice,' she said after a rather awkward silence.

His grip was strong. That green shirt was doing strange things to her insides too; he either hit the gym every single day for an hour or so, or he'd honed his physique purely from wrestling wayward horses. Either way, he was likely all style over substance; he probably had a huge ego too, having everyone telling him how great he was all the time. Why was she feeling considerably hotter than she had been five minutes ago?

'Ethan, please,' he said, catching her eyes and holding them in a way that made her feel as though she'd forgotten to put on clothes this morning. This was nothing like when she'd first seen Bryce with his shaggy hair and oversized backpack, she thought, agitated all over again.

Wait...why was she comparing Ethan to Bryce?

'Ethan. I appreciate you being here. It's a long way from Queensland,' she said, forcing herself to be polite.

'I go where I'm needed,' he replied with a trace of a smirk. 'I'm sure I can help the mayor get this horse into shape in no time.'

'Well, good luck with that,' she said, more snippily than she intended. Oh, to be that confident and self-assured! 'Three weeks in and I've barely been able to meet his eyes. The only way I can get him to move anywhere is by waving the broom at him. I feel like an evil witch.'

At that, Ethan stifled a laugh, which annoyingly, rather pleased her to hear. Then his eyes trailed the whole length of her body from her boots right up to her face. Sage had never felt so exposed in her life. Even more than before, she certainly did not want this cocky man all up in her business for longer than he had to be. But still, the way he was looking at her made her swallow hard…

'I'll take you to Storm,' she said, flustered.

CHAPTER TWO

IN THE PADDOCK, Sage watched Ethan's eyes lock onto Storm with sharp focus. Keeping his movements slow and steady, he followed her to the stall of their troubled animal patient, ignoring the creature's indignant snorts and holding up both his hands. Sage stood at his side, casting secret glances his way, taking in the decisive slope of his nose, the sharp angle of his cheekbones. What would it feel like to have those big man hands on her own skin? His forearms were so thick with muscle, she half expected to see him pick up Storm with one arm…

'I'm going in,' he said.

'What?'

She watched aghast as Ethan flicked the latch on the stall door, causing the horse to stop in his tracks and stare straight at him.

'What are you doing?' Panic coiled in her belly as her hand went out to his arm. It was hard as a rock and she withdrew it almost instantly, embarrassed. But he didn't even have the broomstick to move him with, or to use as defence.

'I wouldn't go in there. I just told you, he hasn't let anyone close…' she started. Was this really the right approach, so soon? But Ethan didn't appear to be listening to her. He took one step into the stall and Sage held her breath, waiting for the horse to bolt, or, worse, lunge for them both.

'Easy, boy,' he said, almost under his breath. The horse eyed him warily from the corner. Ethan started lowering himself at a snail's pace to his haunches, murmuring gentle words of reassurance. Storm was still looking at him suspiciously down the length of his long nose, and Sage's heart was banging like a drum. What was he doing? Surely, this tactic would not end well! Still, whatever he was doing, her eyes couldn't help but trace the rugged lines of his biceps, their well-defined curves hinting at the raw strength of this man before her.

'I reckon we should start with some quiet talking,' he said. 'He's scared, and we need to be the ones to show him his fear isn't necessary.'

Sage almost snorted despite herself. 'Quiet talking?' She had already tried that, as well as begging the horse fervently with her dignity firmly squashed beneath her own muddy boots, all to no avail.

Ethan nodded, eyes still fixed on Storm. 'Horses understand everything about our tone and intentions. We have to speak to his spirit first.'

OK...maybe this was a mistake.

'This isn't some Hollywood movie, Ethan. It's not that simple,' she heard herself say, agitated by both his words and the way he was looking at her, as if he was drawing her out of herself and everything that up to ten minutes ago had been quite comfortable, thank you very much.

Ethan gave a short laugh. 'Trust me, he's waiting for someone to understand him.'

Sage just looked at him. What was she supposed to do with this? She hadn't actually heard much of what Ethan had said to that horse on TV; the focus had been on his actions, his strong, confident energy. He had all the right qualifications, a background in veterinary care that stretched back more than a decade; he'd even been on an episode of *Vets in the Wild*, where he'd tamed a stallion that had already stomped a man down and left him fighting for his life in hospital, but this was just...well—not quite what she'd expected. This was supposed to have been her issue to handle, her problem to solve, yet she was more confused now than she'd been before.

She bit her tongue as he held out a hand slowly, cautiously. Surely it was only a matter of seconds before he regretted this too; Storm was wilder than she could handle with her experience alone and, she'd assumed, Ethan's too, despite being the star of the nation. To her shock, though, the horse took a tentative step towards him.

'He's listening to you, he's responding,' she said in awe, covering her mouth with her hand. OK, so maybe he wasn't just all mouth and muscles as she'd assumed. She'd gone as far as assuming the camera had lied, or they'd at least done some clever editing. But here he was. In the flesh. Succeeding where she'd failed. So infuriating.

Ethan continued to murmur soft words of encouragement from his lowered position on the ground and soon the horse was sniffing warily at his outstretched hand. Sage watched, afraid to move for what felt like at least an hour but was probably only three minutes.

'So, are you a wizard or something?' she asked him eventually, feeling silly instantly.

Ethan finally tore his gaze away long enough to chuckle at her under his breath. No sooner had he flashed her a half-smile, however, than Storm was scrambling backwards and rearing up on his hind legs, spooked by something all over again.

'Move!' Ethan's reflexes were as fast as the horse's. He rose to full standing and before she had a chance to react he was throwing himself between her and the snorting, wild-eyed animal. Sage gasped for breath as Ethan yanked her against him, holding out his other hand to Storm as they backed away slowly through the stall door.

'Steady,' he implored quietly. Did he mean her, or the horse?

Her whole body tensed with shock as he shielded her from the threat of Storm's powerful hooves and she didn't know whether to be impressed by his quick reaction or annoyed with her own slow one as he latched the door behind them. Storm hoofed at the floor repeatedly, kicking up the dirt. Sage's back was still pressed hard against Ethan's chest, his flexed arm like a giant safety belt across her abdomen. For a moment she couldn't even move. Then, embarrassed and maybe more than a little undermined by this man who was still a stranger on her turf, she uncoiled herself.

'I told you, he hasn't let anyone close, so *why* did you do that?'

Ethan fixed his blue gaze onto hers. 'And I told you, Dr Dawson, he's waiting for someone to understand him. He'll only know that we do if we back off now.'

His tone was gruff and assertive and somehow managed to both irritate her and turn her on at the same time. She smoothed down her overalls and was about to tell him that maybe this hadn't been the mayor's best idea when he cut her off by extending a hand, straight at her face. She blinked as he swiped something from the rim of her hat, and a wisp of straw floated to the ground.

'This will take a while. But I'll take the case,' he said. 'No broom necessary.' Then he tilted his head at her in a brief, courteous bow before turning and leaving the stable. Sage followed him out into the sunlight, squinting, heart still racing. Ethan didn't bother opening the gate to the paddock. He simply scaled the five metal bars with one jump like a two-legged show pony in jeans. Then he swung it wide open just for her to walk through after him.

Sage bit down on the inside of her cheek. How dare he just stroll in and make everything look so easy? OK, so this man had made more progress with Storm in a matter of minutes than she'd made in three whole weeks, but the magic show had to end at some point. Storm was unpredictable at best. He could take many weeks, even months of training. Ethan's confidence would likely wear off just as hers had, but she still might be stuck with him for ages until that happened!

Why was she suddenly wondering how close he'd be sleeping to her? Of course, he'd stay at Yukka Guest House, just like everyone else!

Leading Ethan into the clinic, Sage was acutely aware of his tall, muscular frame behind her. She glanced back at him as he looked around, taking in the examination rooms and medical equipment, the poster of the horse with the kookaburra on its head that hung over the reception desk, and the row of slightly dusty cactus plants in the window. He exuded an aura of quiet intensity that charged the room.

'Nice place. How long have you been here, Dr Dawson?' He ran a finger over one of the cacti as if daring it to prick him.

'Call me Sage. And it's coming up for six years now,' she told him, just as Ellie appeared from the back with an owner and her rabbit, its leg freshly bandaged from its brush with a snare. She introduced them and watched Ellie and the rabbit's female twenty-something owner flush. Both women actually fluttered their eyelashes! Ethan fielded questions from them with brief replies, while casting his gaze first to her, then back to them, causing her to roll her eyes, as well as smooth her frizzy hair from her face so many times it went static.

Ruffled, she called Yukka Guest House in Amber Creek to ask about a room, warning her eyeballs to stop roving over his face from across the reception. But she couldn't help it; he was probably one of the most striking men she'd ever laid eyes on. Not that a TV star with an ego the size of the moon would look twice at someone like her, covered in dust and straw on the outside…a bit of a mess on the inside most days, too.

She tutted to herself. That wasn't entirely fair; she wasn't ugly. And she wasn't always covered in dust and straw either. It was just that she was…well…what man would want to deal with all her baggage? The orphaned child, fostered by a wealthy miner, given all the privileges and advantages she could've dreamed of: a caring new family who weren't her own, but who loved her anyway, an education at one of Australia's most prestigious veterinary institutions, money, freedom…yet who still couldn't date a guy without the same profound sense of hopelessness swallowing her senses, reducing her to an undatable weirdo, incapable of forging an emotional connection. She hadn't slept with more than three people since that doomed relationship with Bryce, six whole years ago. She probably had cobwebs. Not that those three men hadn't all tried to pursue her afterwards; she just had a habit of keeping her heart locked up where it couldn't be broken any more. They all got tired of her emotionally stunted self eventually.

'I've booked you my regular room at Yukka Guest House for tonight,' she told him when they were alone again, as an image of him lounging in bed forced her eyes back away from him. 'After that you can decide if you want to stay there or move…'

He quirked an eyebrow. 'Your regular room?'

'The room I reserve for locums and visitors,' she corrected herself. Could he read her mind or something? He laughed softly. The sound of it made her skin prickle and she cleared her throat.

'That was pretty remarkable, back there,' she said before she could stop herself. 'I've never seen anyone calm any horse so quickly. Even if it didn't last.'

Ethan gave a modest shrug. 'Just takes patience. And reading their body language.'

The way he said 'body language' while looking at her…

Oh, my.

Sage started quickly tidying up some scattered papers on the front desk. In her hurry, a sheet fell to the floor and it floated in the draught against his leather boot. He bent to retrieve it just as she did, and their hands brushed over the piece of paper. Sage sucked in a sharp breath. On reflection, it was so loud she could've sworn Ellie heard it in the exam room. It must have spoken volumes about the way he was tangling up her insides already in this confined space, but if Ethan noticed, he said nothing.

'So, Mr Famous,' she said bluntly, shoving the papers back onto a pile on the desk and finally retrieving Storm's file. 'I've seen you on TV. How long have you had this gift with horses?'

'Gift?' He smirked, placing the file under his arm as he made a thing of eyeing her exam certificates, framed in a row on the wall. Bachelor of Veterinary Science, Member of the Australian Veterinary Association, and also a specialised postgraduate qualification highlighting her advanced training in veterinary surgical procedures.

'You seem to have some kind of qualification that I don't,' she said pointedly. 'I don't even think you can study for what you can do. Therefore it's a gift, isn't it?' Sage hoped the comment didn't inflate his ego any further. But she'd said it now. His eyes met hers, and her pulse quickened. He was so intense. She'd just caught his bergamot-like scent too: citrus and wildflowers and horses and man. The smell stirred something in her, made her heart start to beat even faster. Maybe she was just a little starstruck, she reasoned, because of the whole TV thing. How irritating.

Ethan rubbed his neck self-consciously. 'I wouldn't call it a gift. Just skills I've picked up over the years. Helps that I'm as stubborn as most horses,' he said wryly.

Sage sensed his humility was genuine and felt a momentary stab of guilt at her prickliness. 'Still, your techniques are quite different from how we practise around here,' she followed.

'I hope that won't be a problem.'

For a moment, she glimpsed a flicker of rebellion in his eyes and she fought the instinctive desire to tell him there was a way of doing things around here—*her* way. Her way hadn't worked so far, had it? Not with Storm. And the *mayor* wanted him here.

'We open at seven a.m.,' she said instead, motioning for the door. She walked him across the dusty forecourt to his vehicle, simultaneously flustered and intrigued. 'I understand you'll want more time with Storm tomorrow…'

'And the other horses,' he said, opening the car door and leaning on it, eyeing her over his crossed arms. 'I need to see how he interacts with the others. I'll be here early, if that's OK.'

She fished around in the giant pocket of her overalls, then handed him a key. 'Sure, that's the key to the back. You'll find the coffee machine there. If it doesn't start, just give it a firm kick.'

'I'll be sure to do that.'

'Any problems, I live just over there.' She pointed to her humble cabin beyond the tree line, where she'd been shacked up since arriving. It was modest to say the least, but it had become somewhat of a home while she tended the small native plant garden around it and kept the wildlife from moving in. Better than paying rent in town.

'You live here too?' he asked, seemingly surprised.

'Yeah, I'm still trying to figure out the irrigation system so we can grow more than cacti but…'

'Can I see?'

She watched as Ethan closed the car door again and made for her cabin. Following him, she prayed she hadn't left any undies out to dry. Thankfully she hadn't, but he seemed curious about her rock garden, and the compost pile she'd constructed to recycle organic waste. Before she knew it, they were discussing the plans for the drip irrigation system, which would eventually deliver water directly to the base of plants, minimising evaporation. He told her he lived on a homestead with his dad that included an equine centre for troubled horses and prime grazing that she knew they only had in Queensland. His late mother had been adamant they turn it into the most climate-conscious place they could for the whole community to enjoy, before she died.

'I'm so sorry you lost your mother,' she told him as the awkwardness snaked around her like a living thing. How could her own mum's smiling face not come back to her, the second he shared that information? Ethan simply nodded at the ground, ending the conversation by making for his ute again.

Suddenly Sage was wondering if he had a wife, or a girlfriend, waiting at this homestead, and found herself looking at his left hand. No ring. That didn't mean anything though, really. And why should she care? Still, they stood there at the vehicle for just a second too long for it to be comfortable. And as his ute rumbled away, she felt the strangest sensation that her entire world had just shifted completely on its axis.

CHAPTER THREE

ETHAN SCANNED THE horizon over his coffee mug. The landscape beyond the borders of the clinic seemed endless, hugged by jagged dunes and rugged, red-earthed wilderness. It was beautiful around here, even at six-thirty a.m., and remote. It wasn't as if he didn't know remote, though.

He and his dad lived this way themselves for the most part in Queensland, just them and the horses and dogs, away from the noise and traffic and…memories, but this was something else. The nearest town, Amber Creek, was four miles away. Babs, the funny and kind woman at the guest house, hadn't been able to stop staring at him when he'd first arrived; was he that much of a celebrity here? The thought was grating.

He could tell Sage wasn't particularly keen to have him here either. He would get her on board, show her it wasn't all camera magic and celebrity draw that kept people calling him where other vets failed, but still he probably shouldn't have agreed to all the TV stuff in the first place. It was just that they'd offered him a lot of money. And with everything he and Dad had wanted to do with the land to honour Mum's dream, their plans for the self-sufficiency workshops, the rainwater-harvesting system and solar panels she'd started implementing before the cancer stole her mobility and mind—well, they'd needed a significant injection of funds. But there was still so much to do. And the mayor of Amber Creek had offered him a significant amount of money to treat Storm. Almost as much as the network.

Clutching his coffee, he rested a boot on the gate of the paddock and sipped the scorching black brew. Dr Dawson… Sage, had been right. He'd had to kick the machine pretty hard to get a decent cup of coffee out of it. He'd also relocated a redback spider more than once over the last few days. Little guy had made a home for himself, nestled amongst the filters.

'I'm almost done, Ethan!' The stable hand, Billy, had shown up ten minutes after him. The lanky kid, dressed in denim shorts and a baseball hat, was mucking out the stalls now, neatly avoiding Storm. Ethan raised his cup at him, ready to address the situation when the kid was out of the way. The horse was snorting again, not as angrily as he had done on day one, but Storm's sweat-soaked coat was reflecting the morning sunlight in a way that concerned him. This was one unsettled animal. The problem was, he didn't know why yet.

He was just placing his chipped mug back by the kickable coffee machine in the back room, wondering yet again why there was a giant NO NAKED FLAMES IN THE KITCHEN PLEASE! sign on the wall, when a shadow appeared behind him in the doorway.

'Morning, Ethan.'

The light cast a warm golden glow over Sage's wavy chestnut hair, loose again today, falling around her shoulders from the same wide-brimmed hat. For a moment he just stood there, and she stood opposite, smiling from one corner of her pretty mouth, seemingly taking in his clean checked shirt and jeans, and the brown leather boots he'd stormed across a thousand paddocks in.

'I like the boots,' Sage quipped.

'Thanks. They were a gift,' he said. Sage nodded from

the doorway as if waiting for him to tell a story. Of course, he wouldn't. Carrie had bought him these boots eight years ago, right after they declared themselves an item. If only he'd known back then that the footwear would last longer than their relationship; that she'd wind up with his best friend while he was blinded to it all by grief, reeling from losing Mum.

Sage blinked, offering a slightly nervous laugh before skirting around him. 'I just need a…'

'Right, a coffee.' He moved quickly, but not before catching the scent of her: freshly showered, maybe a splash of fragrance, something floral. She went about putting a new mug under the ancient contraption and hit the button under 'flat white'. Then she pulled her phone out, scanned it unseeingly and slid it straight back into her pocket while his eyes fixated on her movements.

So, here it was again. The same unsettling attraction to her that he hadn't known exactly what to do with on day one. It had probably made things a little awkward, all the little silences between their exchanges. Sage Dawson kind of reminded him of Carrie. And that wasn't exactly a good thing. They were the same slight build, the same height, five-foot-five-ish, with eyes that unpicked you. There was something about her intelligence and determination that had caught him off guard and put him in his place, and she never seemed starstruck like the woman at the guest house. Having her remind him of Carrie wasn't ideal. His ex-fiancé was probably just waking up to another Brisbane sunrise in the fancy penthouse apartment she and Cam had bought after their wedding: traitors, both of them.

'So, how's Storm this morning? Did you get a chance to examine him yet?' Sage was still staring at the empty coffee cup, and the silent machine.

'I was waiting for Billy to finish mucking out. We don't want to startle him.'

'Oh, so Billy showed up.' Sage frowned and raised a knee at the machine. He grinned as she gave it a hearty kick from below, sending the mug flying. Deftly he caught it mid-flight and handed it back, and she pulled a face behind her hair as their fingers brushed. There. Again. She'd started out all spiky but after they'd talked in her garden the other day, he was almost sure he'd detected a spark of something else. That *spark* was something he hoped he'd been imagining. The last thing he needed was another woman looking at him all googly-eyed because of how the network portrayed him—they'd cut out most of his words and focused instead on long shots of his body and close-ups of his muscles as if he was nothing more than a gym rat—which he was, to some degree, he supposed. Keeping strong was imperative, plus it kept his mind from going into dark corners it would do best not to revisit.

But there was something different about Sage, too. As if she was looking beyond all that. As if she had the capacity to reach places he'd barriered shut for a reason. Good thing he wouldn't be here long; he'd fix up this horse and be out of here in no time. Back to his father, who needed him.

Sage took her coffee outside, and this time he didn't leap over the fence as he had a few times now. Force of habit. It was just what he did back home. She seemed as conflicted as Billy when he walked towards Storm's stall. They both stood behind him as he flicked the latch again, but soon they disappeared somewhere into the silence on the periphery, as people usually did when it came to the horses.

He'd always been this way, so deeply connected to the animals in a way most others couldn't understand. Except Dad, who'd done it all his life, too. This horse had been growing increasingly restless. He heard Billy whisper as much to Sage, but Ethan hoped his presence would offer some kind of solace to the creature. As it had the first time, right before Storm had reared up and almost taken their eyes out.

'Easy, boy,' he said, holding out a steady hand so the horse could see he meant no harm. Slowly he approached Storm, and noticed the animal's ears flicking back and forth, his nostrils flaring with every breath.

'What made you this way, boy? Or who?' he murmured softly, stepping closer. He allowed Storm to sniff his palm before gently stroking the horse's velvety muzzle. Sage held her breath behind him, but this time he didn't break his focus. That was what had happened before, he realised. It had kept him awake for a good hour extra that first night. For the first time in a long time while dealing with a distressed horse he had looked away, distracted. By Sage. She'd asked if he was a wizard.

There *was* something about her that unsettled him, more than just her likeness to Carrie. He'd seen it increasingly these past few days, watching her going about her business, a faraway look in her eyes. They had as much pain locked behind them as this horse sometimes. Like looking in a mirror, he thought, not looking away from Storm. He was still stroking his snout—this was some form of success at least. To his relief, Storm's eyes softened further at the touch, and he let out a quiet nicker as if to say thank you.

'I can tell he trusts you. At least he's starting to, mate,' Billy said behind him. Sage immediately asked him to be quiet.

It wouldn't be smart to push things, he thought. This was enough for now. 'The exam can wait,' he told them, backing out of the stall again. Billy left to answer a call. Sage watched intently as Ethan reached an arm over the railing and gave Storm another soft stroke, along his chestnut neck this time.

'How do you...?' Her voice, before she cut her question short, was tinged with a kind of begrudging respect that tickled him.

'I don't know, Sage, you tell me,' he said, biting back a smile. He led her back outside. It was getting warm already and he removed his hat to tighten his hair in the band at the back of his sticky neck. He didn't miss Sage's eyes trailing down the front of his shirt, all the way to his belt, where they hovered for just a moment too long.

'My dad, his father, and his before that,' he said, by way of further explanation as her gaze flicked back up to his. He locked his eyes to hers as he adjusted his belt. He didn't need to. It just felt tighter after having her look at it. 'They're communicating with us in their own way. We just have to tune in to what they're saying, like finding the right frequency on a radio. They harbour fear and pain just like we do. And they can be blissfully peaceful. So calm and tranquil. Which humans are not, generally speaking.'

'You're intuitively understanding their pain from the signals they transmit.'

'Kind of.'

Sage studied his face again thoughtfully, waving a fly away from her face, then fanning her white shirt, which was open just enough at the neck to reveal sun-tanned skin and freckles. There was a flicker of hurt in her voice now, a hint at whatever pain she harboured herself deep below the surface. 'Well,' she said quickly. 'Whatever it is you're doing, it's working.'

Ethan watched her run a brief exam on Karma. There were five horses here, considerably less than his herd of twenty-plus, give or take, depending on the equine patients who stayed for variable lengths of time. Billy had explained this morning how three of them were his, including Karma. He worked in the stable and grounds here to subsidise their upkeep. Sage was the chief vet and, as far as he could see, she had a limited staff on the rota. Ellie and…that was it. It seemed like a lot of work for a skeleton crew but he wasn't about to question or judge.

He had got the impression, that first day in her garden, that she had poured all her efforts into this place because it was more than just a job to her. This was her entire life. No wonder she hadn't wanted some strange vet waltzing into what she'd built and upending it all. He also got the feeling that this was her whole life for another reason too. He knew better than to push, though. There was the matter of his own internal scars; he'd hate to be forced to discuss all those. Losing Mum to cancer three months after her diagnosis was one thing…two years on and Dad was only just starting to come out the other side. Then there was the ultimate gut-punch on top, knowing his best friend and his ex-fiancée were probably happier than they'd ever been now that Ethan's own grief and his horses were no longer in the equation, living their city dream in wedded bliss.

He could still hear Cam's words to Carrie. It was far too easy to picture himself standing right outside the door of that hotel suite all over again, the blood from the cat he'd just done emergency surgery on still fresh on his shirt.

'How can you stand Ethan when he does all that weird horsey stuff? You know he'll never love you as much as his animals, right, Carrie? You won't ever come first for him.'

'Don't be so mean. His mum just died!'

'Is that why you don't want to tell him about us yet?'

Catching himself, he snatched up a bridle from the hook on

the wall and threw it to her. 'Tack him up,' he said. Thirteen months and three weeks since the day he'd found out about their affair, and it still had the power to stab him in the gut, as if it had happened only yesterday.

'Now?'

'He's healing just fine.'

Sage stared at him, incredulous. 'I don't ride Karma. He's Billy's horse. And are you sure he's ready? He's not long been castrated.'

'He's fine,' he said. 'It'll probably be good for Storm to see you riding him, too. Show him what *his* role's supposed to be. You said the mayor bought him for his daughter, over the phone?'

Sage shook her head at her feet a moment, and he realised that despite her growing tolerance to his presence, and their undeniable attraction, she still harboured a little scepticism over his so-called unconventional methods. It wasn't as though he was the only qualified veterinarian in the world who knew horses and their minds, but for people like Sage, who'd gone down a more traditional path with all her certificates from top establishments…well, sometimes they needed convincing. Not that he had the time for all that. If people didn't trust his 'weird horsey stuff', that was their problem. The results spoke for themselves. Karma was clearly well and could do with a ride after his time off.

A call came from beyond the fence. Ellie, Sage's veterinary assistant, was waving a phone at them. 'Sage, it's Lance, down at Redgum Ridge. A kookaburra just crashed into his glass door, and it's in pretty bad shape. He doesn't want to move it.'

'Lance's place is beyond the bridge, the one that's closed,' Sage explained to Ethan, chewing her lip. 'I can't get the ute through.' She cast speculative eyes at him. Before he could even suggest it, Sage was striding back over to Billy.

'Do you mind if I take Karma out?' she asked him, pressing a gentle hand to Karma's silky forelock.

'Not at all. I think he's ready, too.'

'Great. I'll have to take more supplies than I can carry. We're going to need a cage to bring it back.' Then she looked at Ethan again, her gaze filled with the question.

'I'll go with you,' he replied. 'Billy, can you saddle up one more while I grab my bag?'

CHAPTER FOUR

'DR DAWSON?' LANCE, an older guy, maybe late fifties, stood in the doorway of the old run-down house, clutching their injured kookaburra protectively in his hands. 'I was watching TV. Then I heard the crash at the back door,' he explained. 'I thought someone was trying to break in, but when I went to check I found this poor fella just lying there all…wonky.'

'No worries, Lance, you did the right thing, calling us,' Sage said. 'This is Ethan Matthews, by the way. He's working with me for a while over at the clinic.'

Ethan stuck his hand out, noting the dishevelled hair, the crumpled shirt and the beer cans littering the porch. His own dad had gone this way for a while, after Mum died. Luckily Ethan and his sister had pulled him out of it. Jacqueline had been a total rock through the whole thing, though she'd suffered the loss in her own way. She always said she had to be strong for her husband, Mack, and she'd had the kids to think about when their mum had passed, too. He'd always maintained it was better to experience the full spectrum of emotions that orbited grief. Then Carrie had done what she'd done, and he'd blocked the whole damn lot of it out.

'You rode all the way out here,' Lance said, nodding towards the horses tied up out by bushes in the shade.

'The bridge is still out of action, remember?' she said

kindly as he directed them inside. Lance furrowed his brow, as though he had actually forgotten.

'He doesn't leave this place much,' Sage whispered to Ethan in explanation as they followed the man inside. 'Not since he lost his wife.'

Ethan nodded. So he'd been right. Poor man.

Despite its old tin roof and weathered exterior, the house seemed quite cosy and well maintained on the inside. A cat unfurled itself lazily from the sofa and crept around Lance's legs as Sage instructed him to place the bird carefully on the small round table in the kitchen.

Together, they examined the kookaburra, gently probing it for signs of injury. Sage inspected its wings and feathers, murmuring softly to it under her breath as she did so. As they worked side by side, her green eyes seemed to glow even more with determination. Her loose chestnut hair fell in soft waves around her face, framing her delicate features. When she wasn't wearing the hat, she looked younger for some reason. She couldn't have been much younger than him though, and he was thirty-five. So much like Carrie, he thought again… only, the more he looked at Sage, the more he could see how different they really were.

Sage had a look that was entirely her own. Besides, being a city girl, Carrie wouldn't be seen dead in overalls. Looking back, she probably never would have ended up moving from Brisbane to the homestead as they'd planned to after they married. It was far too rustic out there, with way too many snakes and spiders for her to feel completely comfortable. Besides, she wasn't all *that* into horses really. They'd been an odd match from the start. She was an actress, fresh from Sydney. He'd met her the same night as Cam in the pub next to the theatre. The three of them had chatted for four solid hours, till Cam had murmured that he felt like a third wheel and left them to it.

Carrie used to love how he and his family had turned the old family cattle station into a successful equine centre and homestead, with plans for an eco-conscious community that would eventually, with all of their help, thrive around it. Mum had always dreamed of off-grid living, creating a hub for sustainable ventures and permaculture initiatives. Carrie had seemed so into it at first, talking about 'learning the bees', as his sister, Jacqueline, had done. His sister's honey was still the best for miles around, and she still came over every Saturday with Mack and his niece and nephew, who buzzed about the place more than the bees.

Carrie had helped Mum and Jacqueline with the bees a lot for the first couple of years, or just read her books and studied her lines in the hammock while he worked with the horses. She'd seemed happy, and it had shaken his world up when Dad had taken him aside one day and asked if everything was OK between them.

Dad had noticed Carrie was spending more time on her phone than she was engaging with them; more time out and about in the city with her friends than honouring plans she'd made to do things with *him*. She'd missed three farmers' markets in a row.

He'd thought if he proposed, things would get better. She'd always said they could wait for marriage—who knew when her latest show would go on tour? He'd agreed; after all, he'd been so busy being a vet, and working out in the fields with Dad and the horses. There had been plenty of time to plan a wedding, really, but he'd figured they would be doing it eventually so he'd asked her anyway.

For a while, things had got better; Carrie had got excited

trying on dresses, sending him photos of vineyards and beaches and wine glasses and platters of cheese. Then Mum had died. And afterwards, when neither of them could agree on a date for the wedding—probably because she'd already started seeing Cam—she'd stopped coming to the homestead at all, saying he spent *too* much time with the horses, and that she found it all increasingly boring being with someone who didn't seem to enjoy the same things any more. Maybe she was right. But after several years together, she should have gone to him with all this. Instead she'd gone to Cam.

'Looks like a broken wing,' Sage was saying now, carefully holding the bird still.

'But there must be some internal damage too,' he mused. 'He's not moving much. We can take him back with us for further tests.'

Their hands touched briefly as he helped apply a splint and Sage seemed to be looking at him with a strange look on her face as he wrapped a towel gently around the bird, motioning for her to open the cage they'd brought with them.

'What?' he asked.

'You're good with the animals,' she said, and he frowned.

'Did you think I wouldn't be?'

'I don't know...you never know if what you see on TV is real or not any more,' she answered as he took over settling the kookaburra inside the cage on another fresh towel. 'And I'm not used to having a qualified partner for things like this.'

'Well, I'm here. And I'm totally real.'

'I see that now.'

The vulnerability in her eyes caught him off guard, and he found himself wondering if she'd had any partners at all lately, all the way out here.

'We should get this little guy back to the clinic, make

sure he's OK,' she said, breaking whatever moment that had just been.

As they were leaving, Ethan got a glimpse of the bedroom through the hallway. Two broken windows. Peeling paint everywhere. He made a mental note to talk to Billy later about them possibly helping out with some repair work. It wouldn't take long to fix a few new glass panes and run a brush around. Unless that wasn't his place, he thought as he lifted the cage out carefully to the horses, telling Sage he'd carry it back. He'd only been here five minutes—of course it wasn't his place! He just wasn't the kind of guy who could stand around knowing someone might need help, as his dad had needed help; not when he could be doing something about it.

The vast outback surrounded them on all sides as he rode with the cage in front of him against the saddle. The silence seemed charged. 'Is he OK?' Sage asked stiffly.

'He's doing fine,' he replied, hoping it was true. The sun beat down on his back and the horses plodded along steadily, their hooves creating a comforting rhythm that was broken only by the occasional soft whinny. Ethan couldn't help but marvel at the beauty of this wilderness: the rolling hills, the majestic gum trees reaching for the sky. It wasn't home. He could never leave Queensland permanently—his dad relied on him, and his mum's living legacy was still under construction—but despite its ferocious heat and unforgiving terrain, there was something inherently peaceful about it.

Then Sage spoke.

'Does your wife or girlfriend mind all the travelling you do?'

Ethan hesitated, caught off guard by her personal question. How much did he need to reveal?

'Or your husband, or boyfriend, perhaps?' she added with a rare smile.

He bit back a laugh. 'I don't do relationships at all,' he said, keeping his tone light. Neither of them mentioned the kangaroo that bounded away into the distance from behind a bush as they passed.

'Ah, I see,' she replied softly, her gaze focused on the path ahead. Was that a small smirk on her face? Did that sound like a 'typical bloke' thing to say? It wasn't as if he could blurt out why he didn't do relationships, and probably never would again. 'I'm single. And I like it that way…for now.'

He'd only added 'for now' so he wouldn't sound too miserable. That wasn't how he felt most of the time; in fact, he was starting to see a little light through the fog of confusion and anger that had seen him confiding only in his horses, and pouring his grief into working out in his makeshift home gym for the last year. But he'd never get over it completely—who would? His best friend and his fiancée…such a cliche.

'So, what brought you to Amber Creek?' he asked her, realising an awkward silence had descended again.

Sage blew air through her nose and kept her eyes on the horizon. She told him how she'd floated around a lot before landing on this place, working with aboriginal tribes, and cultural and conservation programmes across various indigenous protected areas. She'd even worked at a koala reserve for a while. 'Guess I didn't know where I wanted to be, till I found this place.'

'Why's that?' he pressed, picturing how cute she'd look with several koalas clinging to her.

She told him about her friend, Abigail, the mayor's wife. How she'd helped her a lot. How she'd found it nice to be able to talk to someone about anything and everything. He told her how he used to have a friend like that. Ethan couldn't read the look on her face, but Sage was starting to drift somewhere in her mind again.

'How did she help you?'

'I guess I grew up pretty reserved after…well, after losing my parents. I mostly talked to the animals about it all, you know, like a weirdo.'

He flinched. Being a weirdo who talked to the animals. He knew all about that, too, but all he said was, 'I've met bigger weirdos, trust me.' They had the horses walking slowly, so as not to disturb the kookaburra, but he could feel his shirt starting to stick to his back. This Abigail had probably heard more about Sage's life than she'd ever share with him and it wasn't his job to pry.

'I'm so sorry you lost both your parents,' he couldn't help saying, picturing his mum again, how she'd used to wear a silly hat around the homestead, as Sage did around the clinic grounds. 'How old were you?'

That was OK to ask, right?

'I was ten when they both died,' she replied curtly, pulling Karma to a stop and leaping off. 'Anyway. It's all ancient history, right? Here we are.'

Ancient history? She'd lost *both* her parents at the same time?

Ethan hadn't even realised till now that they were back at the clinic already, and she was unlatching the front gate, sending a dust cloud up around her that swallowed her boots. She reached up for the cage, blowing her hair from her sticky face.

'I'll carry it from here. Can you take the horses back to Billy?' She squinted up at him. Her tone had turned strictly professional again now, with no room or time for personal stories.

'Yes, ma'am. I'll examine Storm now.'

'If he lets you,' she said drily.

Ethan opened his mouth to reply that he was sure Storm would, but decided against it. If she was so determined to be surprised every time he was good with an animal, let her be surprised when Storm let him in.

Ethan watched her walk purposefully up the path, where Ellie met her on the front steps. She stopped, then gave a quick glance back at him over her shoulder, and even from a distance he could see the apprehension in her body language. Sage already felt as though she'd told him too much about herself, but if it really was ancient history, why didn't it explain the lingering sadness he could feel ebbing out of her? What else had she endured? Now he needed to know more.

CHAPTER FIVE

SAGE WATCHED AS Ethan's fingers drummed rhythmically on the wooden fence, his blue eyes narrowed in concentration. He had those damned boots on again. He looked so hot in them. Last night she'd dreamed about them—weren't they on her kitchen floor, along with that denim shirt he was wearing the other day? The details were kind of blurry. In fact, the blurry and not so blurry dreams about Ethan Matthews were getting out of hand now, the more he seemed to crawl inside her skull.

They had retreated to the shade of a nearby tree, allowing Storm some space after his first semi-exam. It was a semi-exam because Ethan had so far managed only to lift one front leg. Three days ago, after rescuing the kookaburra together, which thankfully was now doing a lot better, Ethan had tried to examine the unruly animal and failed. He'd spent an hour on the phone to someone afterwards and later she'd found out it was his father. He seemed to speak with him every day, actually, and she envied that a little. Obviously they were close after losing his mother; they lived together at the homestead. What she wouldn't give to be able to pick up the phone to her biological dad—not that Ken wasn't there for her when she needed him. Her foster dad was amazing.

Even after showing some semblance of normality and trust towards Ethan in the stall, when it came to an exam, Storm just wasn't having it. Almost as if the horse didn't *want* anyone to see inside his head. 'Doesn't it bother you that he's still being so…hostile?' she said now, surprised at herself for actually being concerned that Ethan's methods weren't working—wasn't that what she'd expected, before he showed up? Ethan huffed a laugh, still drumming his fingers as Storm trotted around the perimeter of the paddock, sweeping right past them like a tease.

'We'll get to the bottom of it. I'm not worried yet. It just takes time.'

'Well, I admire your confidence,' she said, pulling her phone out to check the time. Ellie was supposed to be at the clinic by now, but she had called in sick, and there was a long list of animal patients still left to see today. A no-show was not ideal.

She looked up from the screen, feeling his eyes on her face. 'Everything OK?' he asked, sipping from the chipped mug, which by now was pretty much his mug. She had taken to arriving at the stables earlier than usual the last few mornings, just to have a coffee with him. It amused him whenever she kicked and cursed at the machine. The tension between them simmered just below the surface, a palpable undercurrent that seemed to charge the air with electricity every time there was a second of silence between them. Unless, of course, she was imagining it because of her dreams, and *he* hadn't noticed at all.

She explained that she was a little stressed because of her veterinary assistant's absence. 'Could it be something in his diet?' she then asked, steering the subject back to Storm so as not to appear entirely unprofessional. People got sick; it wasn't fair to be annoyed at the inconvenience.

Ethan nodded. 'It's possible. I've seen horses become more anxious when their feed is too high in sugar.'

'Exactly,' she said. 'Only, we've been careful what we fed him.'

Ethan shrugged. 'I doubt diet alone would cause such severe symptoms. I'd bet it's purely psychological but…'

'Until we can get close enough to rule anything out, we can't say for sure,' she finished, and he nodded, pulling out his shirt slightly. Even in the shade, it was hot, and she forced her eyes away from the fine chest hairs peeking out above the neckline. What was wrong with her? She almost wished he'd leave and take his sexy chest with him, but the mayor was paying for him to be here, and here he would stay until he succeeded.

Still, her wild dreams about him weren't helped by the fact that he was so good with the animals, when she'd actually assumed his so-called gift had been staged! He was also a good man in other ways, too. Ethan had rallied Billy to help repaint Lance's place, down at Redgum Ridge, once he knew the man had lost his wife. She knew she'd do well to keep things professional with Ethan, not to get too close, and definitely not let on how he was affecting her! The last time she'd let her barriers down with a man enough to truly make a connection—Bryce, ugh—he'd just disappeared on her, and while she most certainly was not going to be forging any kind of meaningful connection with Ethan in the brief time he was here, how could she not be intrigued by him?

Sage's thoughts drifted back to their conversation out on horseback the other day. She'd told him her parents died when she was ten, which in retrospect wasn't a whole lot of information, but the whole self-deprecating thing about being a weirdo who'd grown up talking to animals... Why had she said that?

He was beyond perceptive. He could probably see by now that she was more than a little broken, but she'd gone and admitted her confidence, outside her veterinary skills, was in the toilet.

Still, why didn't he 'do' relationships? She was dying to ask him. Something about his tone and general secrecy had implied there was a pretty interesting reason behind that decision.

'I can help out,' Ethan said after a moment, his gaze not leaving Storm. 'I can't paint today anyway; Lance is expecting a delivery.'

Sage's heart kicked at her ribs. He would do that for her? Could she even handle working so closely with him?

'If you're sure,' she said nonchalantly, realising she sounded quite unsure of herself. He'd already moved in on her own responsibilities with Storm—not that she'd had a choice, and not that he wasn't making more progress than she ever had, annoyingly.

He turned to her, deadly serious, his voice low and gruff. 'Am I really so unconventional that you don't trust I'd obey your every command, Doctor?'

'I do trust you,' she heard herself say, a little too quickly. Gosh, why was she getting so hot again?

Later, Sage was wrapping up the last examination of the day—a cat who'd been struck down with the feline calicivirus—when she heard Ethan greeting someone who'd walked in. She would know that voice anywhere. Abigail, and her kids too by the sounds of it.

Waving off the lady and her cat, Sage felt unease coil in her belly as Abigail, gorgeous as ever in a long pink sundress, hair in a standard messy bun, raised her eyebrows out of Ethan's eyeline. Sage knew exactly what that look meant. It meant that Abigail also found him astonishingly attractive and was already pairing Sage up with him in her head!

'It's nice to meet Ethan here,' she said, beaming. 'I brought you some of that pineapple cake you like. Mum made too much again and you know it makes Daisy go doolally. Daisy, don't touch things, please, darling.'

Sure enough, Abigail was clutching her toddler, Charlie, over her bulging pregnant belly. Her five-year-old, Daisy, was already assessing the blue teddy bear in the box of toys by the window. Ethan crouched beside her, holding up a fire truck while throwing them both a look of his own that said he'd watch her a second.

'We should, uh, get this to the kitchen,' Abigail said loudly, holding up the cake tin. Quickly, Abigail pulled Sage by the sleeve towards the back room and shut the door. 'Oh, my God!' she murmured at her, eyes comically wide.

'Shh, Abi!'

'He's gorgeous!'

'He'll hear you!'

Abigail snorted and deposited Charlie onto the table, stretching out her back for a second before hoisting him back up onto her belly. 'So he's the one who's fixing our Storm?'

'Storm is not a car, Abi, but yeah, he's trying.'

'Maybe he can fix you too, if you know what I mean?' Abigail laughed and dodged Sage's play slap, then rummaged in the cupboard above the sink for mismatching plates. 'Seriously, the mayor didn't tell me he was this hot; I would've come by sooner.'

'I still think it's weird you call your own husband the mayor.' Sage sighed, slicing up the delicious-smelling cake, only just realising her stomach was growling. Abigail often fed her here when she worked long shifts, and the kids enjoyed meeting any animals she had in the healing room. Sometimes the thought sneaked in that some day she might like to have kids of her own. It wasn't entirely an unpleasant notion, the thought of raising a little animal-loving tribe to run around here with Abigail's, teaching them the ways of the world. A fresh start, she supposed.

Then she had to remind herself that in order to have kids, she'd actually have to meet a man…which meant opening herself up emotionally. Something she could never quite manage. Her life was the exact opposite of Abigail and the mayor's. It was so adorable how crazy they were about each other, how easy their relationship was. They trusted each other implicitly. When they bickered it always evolved into laughter. It felt inconceivable that she might some day find the same. There were things she probably shouldn't share with a man, and more that she couldn't laugh off. She'd never heard from Bryce again after he'd disappeared on her, and she'd liked him. A lot.

He'd shown up at the koala reserve, all smiles and stories, a bright light, a shiny distraction from Canada. He'd already done another three-month stint at an orangutan sanctuary in Borneo. A real nomad animal activist. They'd bonded, and for a while it had felt pretty real. More real than anything she'd known till then, at least. She'd slept with him, trusted him. He'd even promised to take her to Canada to meet his dog.

He'd vanished one morning. Left without so much as a 'this was nice but I'd better be on my way'. She'd always assumed he couldn't handle learning how and why her family had died. He'd looked horrified when she'd told him, literally the night before she'd found him gone! She'd taken the leap and confided in him, and straight away he'd brought the facts and newspaper articles about it up on his phone. As well as feeling wounded all over again by her parents' death, she'd had to relive the shame of hearing how many dead koalas the environmentalists had found in the following weeks. All the birds.

The story about the bushfire and her parents had done the rounds for months. She remembered her foster parents whispering about it, trying not to let on what they were talking about—but she'd grown to trust Bryce in their short time at the reserve. She'd revealed everything, the way she had disobeyed her parents' request that she leave her phone alone for a whole night while they got back to nature as a family and camped outdoors in their yard. She'd been such a stubborn ten-year-old, waiting till they fell asleep, then sneaking back into the house to grab her phone and text with her friends. She'd completely failed to notice that their smouldering fire was in danger of spreading into their makeshift camp. By the time she'd come back outside, the fire was raging beyond control. A neighbour had called the fire brigade, but it had been just…too late. The bush had burnt for a mile in all directions, taking her sleeping parents, their dog, and their tents with it. Sage had never forgiven herself.

'The mayor hired Ethan for up to six weeks,' Abigail commented now.

'Did he?' she said casually, forcing her focus back onto the cake. 'That's helpful. Ethan has offered to help me out while Ellie's off sick, too.' She realised from the look on Abi's face that, despite her efforts to appear unaffected, she must still sound quite put out about it.

'Listen to you! You sound like you don't want a stupidly handsome and incredibly buff guy walking around looking hot all day, helping you out.'

'I don't!'

'Liar.' Abigail took a huge bite of cake before Charlie swiped at it, sending it flying to the floor. 'Oh, God. Sorry, babe.'

'Leave it,' Sage told her, as the slice slid behind a floor cabinet. Charlie giggled in delight. 'Anyway, he might be hot, but it's not like he'd look twice at someone like me…a lonely spinster who spends most days hiding in a clinic in the middle of nowhere.'

Abigail cocked her head and scowled in the way she often applied to her kids. 'Stop that. You're a rock-star vet and a pillar of the community, Sage. Now, be a good spinster and deliver your hot new assistant some cake.'

Before Ethan could take his third bite of pineapple cake, having been accosted by Daisy and swept up in a game of teddy-bear-driving-fire-truck-over-cushions-and-books, the main phone shattered the playful reprise, during which Sage had firmly implanted the image of Ethan's future 'Greatest Dad' trophy in her brain. She answered the call, trying to ignore the looks Abigail kept shooting her whenever Ethan wasn't looking.

'Camel sanctuary?' she repeated. 'What's wrong with the camel?'

She could feel Ethan watching her intently throughout the call, his curiosity piqued as he finally got to finish his cake.

'OK,' she said, ending the call and looking up at him. His eyes remained fixed on hers despite the blue teddy bear being swept across his head. 'There's a camel in distress at the sanctuary down by Cable Beach. They think it might be colic, but they aren't sure. Ellie's still out sick, obviously, so I'll be going alone.'

'Why don't I come with you?' Ethan offered, oblivious to Abigail pulling another dramatic face behind him as she swept up the toys and ushered Daisy through the door, waving goodbye.

'No, thank you, I'll be fine,' she said.

'I've dealt with colic before, and it might be good for you to have a second opinion.'

'Are you sure?' Sage asked, realising she didn't actually have a good reason to refuse him, even though she really could have done with some distance to fight this mounting and deeply unsettling attraction. 'It's been a long day already, and I don't want to impose.'

Ethan just stood with his empty plate, then deposited it dutifully back into the kitchen. 'We should get going,' he called back. 'My ute, or yours?'

CHAPTER SIX

'PRETTY INTERESTING PLACE, isn't it?' Sage remarked, feeling her boots sinking into the soft white sand outside Camel Ride HQ. The afternoon heat shimmered over the beach ahead of them, casting an almost ethereal glow over the surroundings.

'Emphasis on the pretty,' Ethan replied, glancing at her quickly—too quickly to know if he was referring to her or not—before taking in the scene with a mixture of curiosity and amusement. They could already see people on camels, heading out from HQ onto the sand. This company ran tours all day, every day, as well as rescuing camels and orphaned calves and giving them a new loving home.

As he joined her on the path from the parking lot, she picked up on his scent again, the earthy musk of it, almost animal. He hadn't had to join her out here, but he'd volunteered, which felt more exciting than it should; this was getting silly now. Abigail had got into her head too. As if anything was going to happen outside her hot, sweaty dreams.

'Dr Dawson!' A woman in an orange skirt with long strawberry-blonde hair pulled back in a ponytail was holding her hand up, exiting the main building ahead. This was Marleen, the woman who'd called her. Soon they were both being ushered into the long corrugated-iron shed, where twenty or so stalls were bulging with hay and healthy-looking camels. A small crowd was already gathered around one of the enclosures, which Marleen dismissed as they approached. The camel was lying on the ground, its breathing laboured and shallow. Ethan got to his knees in his jeans, back muscles flexed as he murmured to the sick animal, rolling up his sleeves.

The poor creature looked so vulnerable and helpless. It stirred a wellspring of empathy inside her as she knelt beside Ethan with the stethoscope, running her fingers gently along the camel's side. The soft groaning sound the creature made caused her heart to ache as Ethan gently lifted its heavy head, his strong hands cradling it with tenderness.

'Could be dehydration, or even anaemia,' he suggested, and she pressed her fingers to the camel's neck next, feeling for any swollen lymph nodes. The scent of hay and animal musk hung heavily in the air, mingling with the salty breeze drifting in from nearby Cable Beach, and Ethan's scent too. She couldn't get enough of it. He was close now, leaning even closer, feeling along the camel's back as she ran the stethoscope over the smooth fur of the creature's belly and sides. Sage couldn't help but steal glances at him as he concentrated, admiring his strong hands and the way the sunlight was streaming in through the door and dancing off his dark hair.

'Her gums are pale,' Ethan said after a moment. He was peering into the camel's mouth now.

'And her heart rate is elevated,' Sage confirmed. 'Anaemia seems unlikely though, given her diet and environment. She doesn't appear to have any external wounds or lesions.'

Ethan reached for the thermometer and she watched as he slipped it under the camel's tongue. She could feel the animal tremble beneath her touch.

'Temperature's normal,' he announced after a moment, his

brow furrowed in concentration. Then he pressed his ear to the creature's neck. He appeared to be listening intently as if trying to discern some other subtle clue from the animal's laboured breaths and she wondered...did this gift he had with horses extend to other animals?

'We'll run some blood tests,' she said to him, worried for a moment that she might be starting to believe he could diagnose an animal without any modern tools at all. He helped her collect the samples, she asked Marleen a few more standard questions and arranged some pain meds, while Ethan mumbled something indecipherable to the camel, still stroking her tenderly. By the time they left the stall, the poor thing was definitely calmer.

On the way out, Ethan stopped promptly at another stall, where a smaller camel was grazing. The gentle creature looked up, focusing its doe eyes on him. Then, to Sage's surprise, it stepped forward and promptly placed its head in Ethan's waiting hands.

What is happening?

Ethan seemed to study the camel in silence, caressing its big soft head, before a smile flashed across his lips. 'I think she's pregnant,' he announced.

Marleen, who was watching in equal fascination, shook her head. 'Nah, mate. No way. We just got her—she's a newbie.'

'It happened before she got here,' Ethan murmured. Sage felt her pulse fire up as he guided her hand to the camel's belly, his warm fingers lingering just a moment too long on hers. 'Do you feel that?'

'Is that...a heartbeat?' Sage looked at him in shock as she felt the unmistakable rhythm of life beneath her fingertips. 'Ethan, you're right.' A quick exam with her stethoscope proved it.

'Really?' Marleen looked confused as he showed her how to feel for the heartbeat, too, without the stethoscope. 'But she's not even showing. How did you know?'

Ethan just shrugged his shoulders and dragged a hand through his hair. It was loose now, free of its usual ponytail, and Sage had to admit she really liked it. It looked wild. Marleen was looking at him in awe. 'How…?'

'It's a gift,' Sage heard herself whisper.

Marleen's eyes widened.

Of course, Sage had looked all this up online, and there were lots of animal communicators out there, lots of proven cases of people diagnosing mystery problems. It still didn't make it any more conceivable to her scientific brain…but it was definitely hot when Ethan did it. She'd known, since before he even drove onto her dusty forecourt, that he had a special gift with horses, but to see it *did* in fact appear to transfer to other animals actually left her speechless.

It wasn't right to feel jealous of him. This was not a competition. But she'd had to work so hard for her qualifications and here Ethan Matthews was, doing everything as easily as breathing. Her envy was quickly merging with admiration, however, the more she witnessed him in action. The attraction she felt to him in this moment was so far off the charts there was hardly a measure for it, she thought, forcing her feet to walk her back outside while Ethan and Marleen discussed the pregnancy. What if he could see inside her head, too? Lord, the shame of what he'd see!

He found her by the ute, watching the ocean. Its gentle lulling waves, the sound of the gulls, all of it was a balm to her frazzled senses.

'Marleen asked us to join the sunset camel safari.' Ethan opened the door and dropped the bag back onto the back seat.

'I said I'd ask you. Are you as confident on camels as you are on horses?'

'They don't tend to move as fast,' she replied coolly, instantly aware of his manly presence beside her; the way her skin and cells stood to attention. 'Sure, we can ride, if you like.'

On the beach, Marleen and her staff were greeting the returning riders and guiding the camels to water. They'd have to wait a few minutes for their turn. The ocean glistened and a fishing boat bobbed in a path of sparkles as she dropped to the sand, letting the warmth travel up through her feet to her bones.

'This reminds me of my dad,' she said aloud without thinking. 'We used to visit the ocean a lot when I was little.'

Ethan was quiet a moment as they studied the sky on the horizon. The sun was already sinking, a huge ball of fire casting peach-amber streaks across the water. 'Losing your parents, at just ten years old, I can't imagine. What happened to you after that?'

'I got lucky,' she said, turning to him. 'I landed on the *good* side of the foster system. Ken and Arielle treated me like their real daughter, and I love them like one. But you never forget a loss like that. It only takes a little thing, like this view, or a smell, or a song to bring it all back.'

'I know,' he said on a deep exhale that came right from his heart. Of course he knew.

'Were you close with your mum?' she asked.

'Very.'

She bit her lip. There were so many questions she wanted to ask him, still, but he wasn't staying long, and the last thing she should be doing was sharing her feelings, or catching more feelings for someone who'd simply disappear back into the TV in a few weeks…or wherever else he was called to next.

Soon, the sunset tour group was gathered on the sand, and Marleen had Ethan stepping on a small stepladder up to the seat on the camel, which made Sage laugh. Just the way the bulky beige animal lowered to its knobbly knees to let the equally awkward humans on its back was hilarious.

'You next,' Marleen said, gesturing to her. Sage paused. Oh, so they were riding in twos, on the same camel?

OK, then.

Ethan held out his hand and she clasped it tight, allowing him to hoist her up into the seat. She sat in front, with barely a centimetre between her back and his chest, just like the other 'couples' in the group. Maybe Marleen had misinterpreted their relationship…not that she was complaining, exactly.

Just enjoy it for what it is, she told herself, settling into his safe, strong proximity, letting out a thrilled shriek as their camel stood up slowly, as if it was actually being careful not to drop its heavy load.

Ethan's hands landed on her shoulders, steadying her. He kept them there as he pointed at a young couple attempting to coax a stubborn camel into posing for a photo further down the beach. As the sun dipped lower in the sky, painting the horizon and people with deeper shades of orange, Sage found herself relaxing, even though the camel's plod was bumpier than any horse she'd ever ridden. Every now and then her back would brush Ethan's chest and sparks of adrenaline flooded her belly from behind. The salty breeze tugged at their hair and hers was more than likely landing in his mouth from time to time, but he wasn't complaining. Was it weird that she'd never ridden a camel before? She was just about to ask Ethan this question when he spoke over her shoulder.

'You know, I haven't been to the beach in a long time.'

She swivelled her head back to him and bumped his nose with hers by mistake. He laughed, as did she, but his eyes quickly fixed on the setting sun. He'd felt it too—when their noses touched—and he clearly didn't want to address it.

'Why not?' she said, feeling a flash of heat to her groin as her back slid another couple of times against his torso. She should focus on the magnificent view, but the effects of Ethan's muscles swiping her flesh with just flimsy bits of material between them were impossible to ignore.

'I had a pretty big bust-up with a good friend on the beach not so long ago and it brings it all back.' He stopped talking abruptly, his mouth a thin line. Sage's heart was already hammering. She knew she shouldn't ask but it was way too intriguing. This was more than he'd ever said about his life.

'A bust-up?'

'More like a heated argument.'

'What about?' she dared to press. He didn't seem the type to engage in arguments of any kind. But Ethan stayed silent. Then he sighed so hard she felt it ripple through her hair, leaving a trail of goosebumps on the back of her neck.

'You don't even want to know,' he said, finally. His tone silenced her, right until their group came to a stop and they were ordered to dismount for a break and a drink. This was more vulnerability than she'd expected from some supposedly arrogant hotshot celebrity vet. Maybe she'd painted him as that quite unfairly. It was becoming clearer every day that there was more to Ethan Matthews than she'd seen…maybe more than anyone watching him on TV had ever seen. He had layers, and some of those were still tender, still painful, as hers were. She was so caught up in her thoughts about his mysterious bust-up on the beach that she almost missed what was going on around her.

Oh, no.

Already, everyone was settling down around a huge, spitting, burning, roaring fire.

CHAPTER SEVEN

SAGE SLID OFF the camel after Ethan and stepped onto the sand, inhaling air deeply into her lungs. Their guide was handing out small cups filled with sweet tea and she took one gratefully, breathing in the aromatic scent; anything for a distraction. Ethan was taking a seat close to the fire already, where someone had scattered cushions in anticipation of the tour group. This was basic tourist stuff, and she willed herself to calm down as laughter and conversation filled the air, along with the giant sparks from the crackling logs and driftwood.

Don't be a baby. Don't be an idiot, Sage.

Despite her internal pep talk, fear and panic welled up inside her as she closed her eyes. The memories were slamming her now from all directions. Her cup almost crumpled in her fierce grip. She'd stood just like this that night, helplessly overwhelmed in front of the raging bushfire, watching the tents ablaze beyond a flaming row of bushes. She'd stared, unable to move, feet glued to the floor. It was only when the neighbour had arrived and swept her up in his arms and carried her away that she'd been able to comprehend the magnitude of what had happened, what she'd failed to try and prevent, but by then, everything was gone. Everyone had died.

'Sage?'

Ethan was in front of her suddenly. His curious gaze made

her shuffle in embarrassment as he studied her distance from the fire. 'What's wrong? Don't you want to sit closer?'

'No, I'm fine here,' she replied, her heart pounding in her chest at the thought of revealing her vulnerability to him, as she had to Bryce. 'I just, uh, I don't like fire a lot. At all.'

'You don't like *fire*?'

She would have to say something. 'There was a bushfire,' she said finally. 'Around our property. That's how I lost my parents.'

Ethan was quiet. Maybe it was the fact that she'd sensed his own vulnerability back there, about the argument with his friend, that had forced her guard down just a little, but his eyes were filled with such empathy and sadness now, she almost felt sick.

'I lost my dog that night, too,' she added. Might as well get it all out. In fact, she was quite prepared to carry on, suddenly, to tell him everything about how she'd failed to save them all, how the fire had spread beyond control past their little makeshift campsite, designed to get the family back to nature and away from all technology for the night, how the house had burned to the ground next along with all their possessions, but her voice got lodged in her windpipe till she could barely breathe, let alone speak.

'Sage.' Ethan was looking at her with such horror now, she was glad she'd stopped talking. 'What happened?' he asked. 'I mean, how did you—?'

'I still think about Juni, my dog,' she interrupted, nervously. 'Maybe that's why I do what I do, you know? If I can save just one animal's life, then I can still make a difference.'

'You make a big difference here every day, everyone knows that,' he said. 'But, Sage, I'm so sorry to hear about your family.'

'Doesn't matter. Enough about me, what about you, Mr Secretive? What was your big argument with your friend about? Does that have anything to do with why you don't *do* relationships?'

Her blurted questions hung in the air like a lead balloon. The laughter around them seemed to fade into the background as her heart slammed in her chest. Abigail would have punched her in the arm right about now; that eager question made her seem way too interested in deep diving into his life history than was acceptable, or attractive, but better to talk about him than her, and all the stuff that she couldn't discuss.

Ethan's eyes met hers again and she swallowed. Suddenly she forgot what she'd been thinking. There it was, plain as day: layers of hesitation and discomfort flickering within their ocean-blue depths. She'd hit the nail on the head. Whatever had happened on that beach was exactly why he didn't do relationships. Taking a step back again, she watched the group over the rim of her cup, desperate for some distance between herself and this burning reminder of her own trauma, and the feel of his eyes burning equally hot on her face.

'I'll get us some cushions,' he said, and she wrestled with the guilt as she watched him collect two from beside the fire, his muscular frame a solid silhouette against the flames and the fading sun. He motioned for her to take a seat beside him away from the flames, and watched her closely, as if she might combust with her grief.

'You sure this is OK?' he asked.

'I'm fine here,' she replied. 'So, you were saying?'

He shook his head and adjusted himself on the cushion. 'It's...complicated,' he muttered as she put down her cup.

'Isn't it always?' she said. It felt as if her cheeks had absorbed the flames as he took her in, as if committing her freckles to memory. Then he cleared his throat and dropped back onto the sand, resting back on one thick, toned arm. The firelight played on the rock of his biceps, a thin sheen of sweat making her lick her lips despite herself. Maybe fire wasn't so bad under the right circumstances. She was fully attuned to him now, and there was no way he didn't feel the same; the air between them was buzzing, even though he was clearly deflecting. Something complicated had stomped on any wish he might have once had for a relationship with someone special and he didn't want to talk about it.

'Look, I didn't mean to make you uncomfortable,' she said softly, hoping her eyes were filled with sincerity as much as the questions that were still jumping about in her brain. 'I understand if it's something you don't want to talk about. I know what that's like.'

Ethan pressed his lips together a moment. 'You're right, I don't normally talk about this stuff with anyone.' His voice was strained with the effort to find the right words. 'I was with someone for a long time. We were engaged to be married, and I very much *wanted* to be in that relationship with Carrie, until she…'

Carrie?

Sage gripped his hand without thinking, feeling the warmth of his skin beneath her fingertips instantly. 'Oh, no, Ethan. Did Carrie die?'

Ethan's eyes grew wide. Mortified for him, she squeezed his hand. It should have been obvious, of course, the pain she'd seen in his eyes, the way he was reluctant to talk about it, just as she still was. It hurt too much. It would always hurt.

'No one died,' he blurted, biting back a humourless laugh.

'Oh. Sorry.' Sage pulled her hands away and hugged her

knees to her chest. Great, now he thought she was a total drama queen. 'I just always assume…'

'No one actually died,' he said again, gruffly. 'But I have two people in my life who are pretty much dead to me now and maybe that's the saddest thing about what happened. I miss them even though they're still alive. I miss what we all used to be to one another. We won't ever be that way again.'

'What did they do? I assume the one who isn't Carrie is the person you argued with.'

'On the beach, yes. Palm Cove to be exact,' he finished. 'His name's Cam.' The name came out through slightly clenched teeth before he continued. 'Cameron. I've known him my whole life, since we started school together.'

Sage realised she was staring at him with her mouth open as the pieces started fitting together in her head. Ethan had been engaged once, and then his fiancée did something, and now there were two people he couldn't see. Cam was one. What did his buddy Cam do to cause a bust-up…? Oh, no. He'd stolen Ethan's fiancée! She knew it without him saying; it was written all over his face.

'They're married now,' he confirmed, still looking at the fire. She shook her head, touching a hand to his quickly as he sat back up beside her, cross-legged. 'I hear it was a beautiful wedding.'

Sage pulled a face, and he mirrored it. 'Look at us,' he said, wrinkling his nose. 'We only came to help a camel, and now we're on a beach, which I hate, near a fire, which you hate—'

'Well, at least we're alive.' She smiled, nudging his shoulder with hers. 'And beaches aren't that bad, are they?'

'Not when you're with me, they aren't.' Sage felt the shivers from her fingers right through to her feet as he took her hand and held it tight over his knee. 'I like talking to you,

Doctor,' he murmured, without realising he was stealing all the breath from her body.

'How long were you together?' she asked as the heat of his hand seared through her, hotter than the fire.

'A long time,' he replied, looking at their fingers. 'Seven years.'

'And how long ago did you split up?'

'Thirteen months ago. That's when I found out about it anyway.'

'Some friend,' she heard herself say, before she could hold it in. The injustice of it all left a nasty taste in her mouth, and a tsunami of empathy for him threatened to have her say more, but she didn't, equally occupied by the drumbeat throb of her heart now that he was holding her hand. Even as their group reassembled around them, ready for the ride back up the beach, Sage felt suspended by some strange new gravity holding her right here.

So she'd had a messed-up start herself as a ten-year-old orphaned girl, but at least no one had betrayed her as Ethan had been betrayed; not that she'd let anyone close enough to try. She'd started to think she wouldn't know how to be someone's long-term partner anyway, that maybe it just wasn't in her destiny. At the heart of it, she supposed—and as Abigail often reminded her—was her raging guilt. It slammed shut every door she'd ever tried to open, till she'd eventually given up. Why should she be happy when her family never would be again, because of her selfishness?

The silence between them grew heavier, punctuated only by the sounds of the camels' footsteps and the distant laughter of the other riders. The sun had fully sunk now, but the moon was huge and the magnetic pull from Ethan only seemed to intensify every time he looked her way. It didn't subside in the ute either. The whole way back to Amber Creek, it felt a lot as if an unspoken desire to unpick the other's past was simmering between them. Unless it was all her, she considered, stealing another glance at his profile in the moonlight. What was his ex-fiancée like? Was she pretty? Of *course* she was pretty. Ethan wouldn't have been with anyone *not* pretty for all those years.

'Look,' Ethan said suddenly, gesturing towards the paddock. They were back at the clinic already, where they'd planned for him to drop her off before he drove on back to the guest house. She turned to where he was pointing, but he was sprinting from the ute already, making for the gate. Sage's heart swelled as she watched him vault over it with one leap again.

A momentary reprieve from the intensity of her thoughts was promptly replaced by slight alarm. Storm was lying down in the grass, cool as a cucumber under the moon, calmer than she'd ever seen him. He was lying right next to Karma and, contrary to all of their previous encounters, the two horses seemed entirely comfortable with each other.

She gasped as she reached the gate and watched Ethan kneel slowly in front of them. Karma snorted and got to his feet, trotting off merrily, but Storm, to her total surprise, stayed put, and lowered his head, as if bowing to him. Even from where she was, she could tell that this was progress. Storm had never been this welcoming or appeared this placid before, and he barely flinched as Ethan started running his hands gently along his neck and back.

'He's going to let me examine him,' Ethan said, and the look of victory on his face made her grin, it was so infectious. 'I'll wait till the morning, first light,' he followed, striding back over to her. He met her on the other side of the gate.

'It was only a matter of time,' she heard herself say, through her own smile. Why did he have to be so gorgeous, on top of being a bona fide equine wizard?

Maybe it was having the gate safely between them, but a quiet confidence overruled her common sense. Before she knew it, her fingers were reaching out for his face, brushing off a small fleck of ash from his left cheek that had been bugging her since the beach. He caught her fingers deftly, and held them against his face, and for a moment neither of them moved as he scanned her eyes. An almost tortured expression hovered in his gaze that made her pulse thud, before he reached across the gate and cupped the back of her neck. Butterflies exploded in her belly.

Oh, my Lord...he's going to kiss me.

Sage closed her eyes and prepared herself as her heart started bucking like an unbroken horse in her chest.

Don't move, she willed herself. *You do deserve this, just one kiss. One little kiss to keep you floating from someone who's just passing through. That would be OK, wouldn't it? That would be enough.*

He was inching closer over the gate, she could feel his breath warming her face, smell his earthy scent mingling with heat and hay. He was going to kiss her, she knew it. Any second now…

Ethan pressed his lips to her cheek, and then dropped her hand. In a beat he scaled the gate, landing with a thud beside her as she blinked her eyes back open, mortified.

Her senses screamed in unison—*What about the kiss? The proper kiss!*

'I should go. We have an early start tomorrow,' he said, striding ahead of her towards the car.

Reeling, Sage hugged her arms tightly around herself as

he gave her a final look over his shoulder, then drove away. OK…so that was weird, she thought, straightening up and composing herself. They'd been so close to kissing, but he'd backed off. Probably for the best, she thought with a wince, seeing as there was no point starting up anything with someone who was leaving as soon as Storm's issues were fixed, but still…hmm. Something must have been going through his mind to have pulled away like that, though. Was it Carrie? She frowned down the drive, now devoid of any sign of him. Perhaps he wasn't over Carrie.

CHAPTER EIGHT

ETHAN KEPT HIS hands steady as he aligned the splint against the koala's fragile leg. All the while his heart thrummed an erratic beat that betrayed the calm of his practised movements. Sage was close, too close, her own hands mirroring his with a deftness that spoke volumes about her compassion and skill, both of which he'd had the pleasure, and the torture, of observing up close since volunteering to help her out at the clinic. He'd almost pressed his mouth to hers last week. What the hell was wrong with him?

Ellie had come in briefly to share some patient files, despite her sickness, and before Sage had sent her away again to rest she had eyed him in that usual awestruck way. He was used to women like her, looking at him as if he were something amazing, something to be devoured with a gaze alone.

A woman like Sage, however, who grasped at the broken shards of his soul and loosened the reins on his heart, and made him want to talk about things he would rather usually not talk about...that was something else entirely. He had never felt so drawn to anyone so inexplicably before. It was as if her wounded soul called out to him—and it was why he'd almost kissed her. But also why he'd swiftly backed off. There was no way he was going down the road Carrie had taken him on again, where a woman had bent his universe so out of shape that the loss had altered his DNA for ever.

Still, with Ellie still sick, here he was. How could he have kept his distance knowing they were running out of hands to attend to all these animals? There was so much to do. And now that Storm was finally responding to him without galloping off a mile each time, it was imperative he stay close, vital he make sure the horse didn't do a one-eighty and backtrack on the progress he'd made in the week since conducting that first physical exam.

'Good, just like that,' Sage murmured now, her voice soft but authoritative as she secured the bandage. The air between them was charged, thick with the words they hadn't spoken since that…what had it been? A mistake. It *should* have felt like a mistake, but every time he watched her mouth move now, the slow burn for her went from a smoulder to a full-on inferno till all he could think about was pressing Sage Dawson up against the stable wall, running his hands over the curve of her hips and claiming her lips and…healing her, like one of his horses? As if he could. He hadn't even been able to heal *himself* enough after his mother had died to notice Carrie was slipping away.

'Ethan?'

'Yeah, it's secure,' he said.

Focus, man. What was it now, just seven days? A week of wondering if he just should've kissed her and been done with it.

Ethan kept his attention on the tasks at hand, trying to ignore how the scent of her—wildflowers and something uniquely Sage—overwhelmed his senses. His ego didn't quite know how to handle looking in a mirror like this, seeing someone else so fragile, someone else he didn't know how to fix. She'd been keeping her distance, too.

'Steady there, mate, we're almost done,' he whispered to

the fidgeting koala, who blinked up at them with trusting, glassy eyes. The animal's quiet resilience struck a chord with him. In the face of its obvious pain, it was clearly letting them help. If only his own efforts to maintain his composure weren't so flimsy around Sage. Every time he so much as brushed against her accidentally, that moment in the paddock the other night flew back into his brain, as well as the way he'd exited stage left as if she'd threatened him with a cattle prod!

But after everything he'd spilled to her on the beach, after showing that level of vulnerability it was hard to place the feelings he was starting to experience for someone who didn't even live in the same Australian territory as him. Why start up anything with someone like her, who'd be incredibly hard to get over? The dreams he was having were torture enough.

He used to have regular dreams about walking in on Cam with Carrie. They had tortured him for months, and he'd barely dared to think about sex as anything other than something *they* were doing together, which had repulsed him. Now, though, his suddenly revived libido was roaring back in spades, taking those dreams to new places, mostly steamy midnight rides with Sage, and not always on horseback...

Sage stood back, running a gentle hand over their brave koala. 'Thank you, Ethan,' she said on a sigh, brushing a wisp of hair from her forehead. 'I couldn't have done this without you. We're so short-staffed.'

Ever the professional attitude now, he mused.

'Any time,' he replied gruffly as she snatched her gaze away again and turned to the sink, visibly flustered by his closeness. She'd told him some pretty personal things on the beach, and he'd reciprocated. At least, he'd told her the necessary details. And then he'd turned away from her. She hadn't brought it up since, or the almost kiss, and neither had he, but it still hung between them in the silence.

'What's next for today?' Sage's question cut through his inner reverie.

'I'm just thinking about Storm out there,' he lied, offering a tight smile. He *should* be thinking about Storm—he and Billy were planning to try and saddle him later—but now he was thinking about Sage, yet again.

'He's already doing so much better; the mayor said so this morning, didn't he?' she said, before going on to the subject of the new food and troughs Ethan had suggested, and then the weather. Her brow creased slightly, and she diverted her eyes the whole time, as if she was just filling the air with words for the sake of saying something, anything. He watched her shift the koala gently on the table, motioning for him to open the cage. 'Could you bring it a little closer?' she said.

Ethan picked it up easily and placed it closer. Her sleeve caught for a second on the cage door, and he freed her deftly, then drew his hand back quickly this time, before she could retreat from him again. 'Sorry,' they both muttered simultaneously. Then they shared an awkward smile over the koala's head. Why did he feel like a fake all of a sudden? As if he was lying about not wanting to rip off her clothes, press his mouth to hers and kick the door shut behind them.

'Looks like our friend will be OK,' he said about the koala. It seemed to be quite comfortable now, if a little dozy.

'We're a good team,' Sage replied. More words to fill the silence, from both of them this time. Then she busied herself folding up some towels while he filled in the animal's file. The little marsupial's leg was neatly splinted now. She was right, their team was a good one for the most part. He watched her cross the room, putting significant distance between them again as she put away instruments and bottles.

'What?' she said, somewhat nervously from near the window, brushing another tuft of fallen hair from her eyes.

The air between them was charged with that thick, hot, electric buzz he knew should be defused. Every rational thought screamed at him to keep his distance, yet his hands and his body seemed entirely disinclined to obey right now. Sage was the first person who'd made him forget the extent of the pain Carrie and Cam had inflicted on him, but at the same time, this thing had just as much potential to mess with his head, more than it already was. Talk about being blindsided! The very last thing he'd expected to find when accepting this gig was a woman like Sage bringing his libido back to life, most inappropriately!

'What?' she said again as he looked at her. She sounded so conflicted, as though his eyes on her made her feel things she didn't know what to do with. Same as him, then.

'You…' he started.

Sage lowered her head slightly, then looked up at him through her eyelashes. This mad chemistry was not going to go away. Maybe he should just address it? Drag it out into the open so they could laugh about it.

As if he would laugh about it.

'Me?' she said, finally, searching his face through narrowed green eyes.

He opened his mouth. The words formed on his tongue: *You are driving me crazy.*

He stepped forwards, all efforts to resist this gone, out of the window.

As if on cue, the shrill ring of the clinic's phone shattered the bubble. Sage cleared her throat, lifting the receiver. 'This is Dr Dawson.'

The caller's frantic voice spilled through the line; something about a bird, rare and injured, found miles away. With each detail, Ethan's professional focus snapped back into place. What was he thinking, almost letting that craziness consume him again?

'Got it. We're on it.' Sage hung up and turned to him, her expression grave. 'It's a black-throated finch. Someone up at Koorabimby Nook's found one, but it's badly hurt.'

Ethan frowned. He had no clue where Koorabimby Nook was, but the black-throated finch species was in a precarious state, almost extinct, in fact.

'What's the plan?' he asked, and she bit her bottom lip thoughtfully, pacing the room while the koala looked on.

'It's too far by road. We won't make it in time,' she calculated quickly, making his mind race through alternatives. But Sage was already on the phone again, dialling someone.

'Mayor Warragul, it's Sage Dawson. We've got a situation with a black-throated finch,' she said. 'I need a huge favour.'

Ethan watched, admiration warming his chest as they talked. Her decisiveness was one of the hundreds of things he admired about her—her ability to switch modes and take action under pressure, her drive to save any creature, no matter the odds. It had started with losing her dog, she'd told him that, which made sense if it died in the bushfire, but there was so much he didn't know; not that he would be asking. Getting too personal had never been part of his plan when he got here… In fact he'd made up his mind to get the job with Storm done as fast as he could and get back to rebuilding the second beehive with Dad, the one his niece and nephew wanted to keep as their own. And he was losing his train of thought about what mattered most, more often than was safe. He'd almost kissed Sage already. Twice.

'We should pack a field kit,' she said now, and he helped her gather supplies.

'How are we going to get there?' he asked her on their way out. He'd failed to hear exactly how Amber Creek's mayor was planning to help them in this situation.

Sage turned to him, her expression a blend of determination and hope. 'The mayor's going to fly us out there in his chopper.'

The whirr of the helicopter blades grew louder as they approached, the rhythmic chopping sound slicing through the air.

'Thanks for doing this, Mayor,' Sage said as they climbed aboard, her voice barely audible over the din. Ethan watched them make brief conversation, admiring this multifaceted mayor who clearly had a soft spot for Sage. She'd been close with his wife Abigail since she moved here, he remembered as the helicopter lifted off and Billy and the horses and Sage's rock garden grew smaller and smaller below. In fact, Sage had been to their house a few times since he'd joined their small team at the clinic. They loved her, and she loved those kids. It was nice to see. He wasn't so great with kids himself, with the exception of Jacqueline's kids, Kara and Jayson—the horses had always been easier to understand, and quieter too—but sometimes he imagined a tribe of his own: little people who he could teach to ride and read and take over the plot some day. Carrie had wanted all that, initially. She'd probably get it too, with Cam.

'I hope we're not too late,' he heard Sage say, and he stopped himself saying anything. There was no point in giving her false hope. Who knew the extent of the bird's injuries? It was moments like these, however, that reminded him why he'd become a veterinarian himself—to save and protect animals in their natural environment, to give a voice to the creatures who couldn't speak for themselves. The rare finch had been mentioned in a lecture at a conference, just the other month, about endangered species, and now here he was, with Sage in a chopper, on a mission to save one. Dad would get a kick out of this story.

Sage sat next to him now, her face pressed against the window as she scanned the terrain below. Her eyes filled with concern, and maybe a little annoyance too as the massive coal mines started dominating the landscape below. The stark contrast between the untouched wilderness and industrialisation was even more unsettling from up here. So many creatures had perished and would perish with all this overdevelopment. It only strengthened his resolve to do everything in his power to protect and preserve this fragile ecosystem, as well as get the homestead running as sustainably as they could back in Queensland.

He found himself staring at her mouth, thinking again about their almost-kiss, when she turned to him and found his eyes on her. It was too late to turn away. Busted. She quirked an eyebrow and shook her head.

'It's not a good idea, Ethan,' she murmured over the rotors. Ethan's pulse spiked but he kept his expression in neutral.

'What isn't?'

'You know what,' she said, sweeping her hair back to a rough ponytail and holding it to the nape of her neck, like his. He said nothing; what could he say? It was not a good idea, and of course he knew it.

She released her hair, letting the chestnut waves loose till they were catching the gusts from the open door and billowing around her face. Wild strands whipped against his cheek, daring him to question the validity of these claims.

Oh, so that's how she's playing this.

She was freaking out, because, yes, it had almost happened again, and she knew it shouldn't because they were colleagues? Who knew why, really? But she was making excuses. She wanted him as much as he wanted her. Just by saying *this* she was confirming it. He couldn't fight the smile from his mouth at the look of pure tortured desire in her eyes.

'Stop it,' she said again, pretending to thump his shoulder.

'Stop what?'

'Looking at me like…that.'

Then her face seemed to scrunch up in front of him before she pressed her face into her hands quickly, as if she was trying to erase her last words. 'I shouldn't have said anything, should I? You weren't going to. Forget I said anything?'

'I can barely hear you anyway,' he lied loudly, pointing at the roof, mouthing, *The blades are too loud.*

She pulled another face and shook her head at the window, and he busied himself with double-checking the contents of the field kit, pulling it between them on the seat, creating a necessary distance between them. OK…so the small talk was killing him, but if she thought him kissing her for any reason was a bad idea, he'd respect that, of course. He was here to work, after all. There was no point getting swept up in this… thing. She'd obviously been thinking about their situation as much as he had, so much in fact that she'd blurted out an attempt at resistance, to push him away. He almost asked her why she'd done it, but did it matter, in the end? What could come of it? Best to keep things professional, however hard it was going to be.

The noise of the chopper felt like a fitting match for the turmoil he could feel building inside him though, every time he considered how much he was kidding himself, trying to imagine it would be fine for the rest of his time here ignoring the obvious sexual tension between them. They should talk about this. It would hang over them otherwise. He'd promised to work the weekend on the drip irrigation system outside her house and she'd agreed. Why had she done that, if she didn't want him getting too close?

She wasn't looking at him now, she was talking to the mayor again, and he weighed up his options, watching the curve of her shoulders in her billowing white shirt. He could simply tell her there was no room in his life for romance either. In truth it wasn't what he was looking for at all, at least, not a *relationship*. But anything else would end badly, not just because of the distance between their home lives. He could never leave Dad, and the horses, and all of Mum's memories, the same as she could never leave her practice. This was probably just his libido rebooting after months of being dead and dormant, that was all.

Also, Carrie and Cam had a point. His work would always come first, he would always be considered a solitary enigma, and any good self-respecting woman would tire of that eventually, as Carrie had. And Sage's life was here. It was hard to measure how much he admired her for pulling her life together, for providing this selfless service to others. How could anyone go through losing both their parents in a bushfire and come out so strong and seemingly self-assured?

On the *outside*, he reminded himself quickly. Sage appeared strong on the outside, to most people. But now she was showing him her vulnerabilities too. He was one of them. For that reason, he would stay well away from her.

* * *

'It's over here!' The towering, big-built lady in knee-high rubber boots raised a trowel at them as they reached the path, metres from the chopper. The mayor had landed in a eucalyptus field and Ethan noted the Koorabimby Nook sign by the slatted house. Ah, so it was part of a farm. Llamas and a solo horse were looking at them curiously. There, beneath a scrubby bush, lay the finch, its delicate plumage ruffled, one bloodied wing hanging at an unnatural angle. They crouched down beside it and Sage held a hand up, instantly protective of the rare bird.

'Careful,' she instructed, as if she needed to, as he gently scooped up the injured creature, cradling it in his big hands. Blood soaked his fingers. Sage's gaze turned sad. 'It doesn't look good,' she told him. She was right, it didn't. Some kind of animal attack? It was definitely a predator of some sort that had done this much damage.

'I think it probably had a disagreement with a cat,' Sage said with a frown, confirming his thoughts.

'I think he had a run-in with one of mine, yes,' the woman told them sadly, blocking the sun from their faces with her generous frame. Sage communicated her sorrow with him via another look, her fingers gently probing as he held the bird steady. It was hot, still, in the afternoon sun. Its low-hanging intensity scorched the back of his neck as he watched a bead of sweat trail down Sage's cheek. Why did he want to touch her so badly, even in moments like this? It was completely unprofessional and unnecessary, and it was damn well not helping his resolve to keep his emotions out of working with her.

'Fractured wing, possible internal injuries,' Sage was noting now. 'We'll get some pain meds ready. We can't do a proper analysis until we get it to the clinic.'

'Will it survive that long?' the woman asked in concern. 'They're rare, you know.'

'We know,' Sage said after a lingering pause, flashing her eyes to his. Ethan got the distinct impression she wanted to tell the woman to lock up her cats. There wasn't much you could do about natural instinct, though. He should know; his was building the longer those beads of sweat trickled down Sage's cheek…and onto her neck. All he wanted was to touch her, wipe them away with his lips, as if that were likely to cool her down. Or him.

Back in the chopper, the mayor was ready to take off the second they'd both buckled up their seat belts. Ethan carefully laid the injured bird on the foldable table and prepped a bandage, while Sage pulled out a syringe and vial from the field kit for the meds. Neither of them spoke but he could read her face. She was determined to save this bird.

Everything she did lately, after what she'd told him on the beach, spoke volumes about why she'd chosen this profession. She was obviously haunted by losing her parents in that fire, and her dog too. What the hell must that have been like? Unimaginable. Her love of animals ran deep, her need to care for them and save them when no one else could. He would do everything he could to make her job easier, he realised as she raised the syringe and the chopper bumped around midair. And that involved not kissing her.

'Sorry, guys, the wind's getting up,' the mayor's voice echoed from the radio.

'Steady now,' Ethan murmured, holding the bird gently on both sides of its fragile body as Sage administered the medication slowly.

'I'm always careful,' she said through gritted teeth, taking the bandage from him and getting to work while he continued to steady the finch and ease some water into its dehydrated mouth. The medication had to be enough, but what if it wasn't? Its breathing was laboured, its eyes were closed, the poor thing could barely move.

His gaze lingered on Sage, the furrow of concentration between her brows. He itched to tell her that it would be OK, but it wouldn't be fair, so he didn't. In truth, the bird didn't look at all good now. Each breath from its fluffy chest seemed more difficult than the last, and the towel on the table was blood-soaked, its colour growing increasingly darker. The mayor was doing his best to avoid more bumps, but Ethan's instincts were on red alert; none of this was making much of a difference.

'That cat did a real number on him,' Sage cried. This time he didn't pretend he couldn't hear her. They were both watching the bird's chest rise and fall with less vigour, even as he held the oxygen to its beak. Sage's hands faltered slightly.

'Come on, little one,' he encouraged, hoping to be a mantra of hope against an encroaching shadow of inevitability. This bird's life was ebbing away between them. Sure enough, all too soon, the heartbeat beneath his fingertips stilled. Sage's shoulders slumped and her fists clenched.

'Damn it,' she muttered, not looking at him. Her voice was a heavy growl of anger and sorrow that tightened Ethan's throat. When he put a hand to her shoulder her green eyes brimmed with resignation and sent a chill up his arm—they'd failed. They hadn't even made it back to the clinic.

'I'm so sorry, Sage—'

'I suppose it was a long shot, considering the injuries,' she said, swiping her damp forehead. Any sparks he'd felt before felt smothered by the finality in her tone. He'd seen death before in a hundred innocent creatures, the end of suffering, the quiet exit from pain that was often as beautiful as it was distressing for those left behind, but somehow the loss of this rare bird felt personal, tied to the woman beside him and everything she had already lost. Sage turned to the mayor and told him what had happened. Ethan wrapped the delicate bird carefully in a clean towel, watching her body language. Her posture was telling him more than words ever could; she was definitely taking it personally.

'Hey,' he said. 'You did everything you possibly could.'

Her gaze flickered to him. For a second, Ethan thought he saw the walls she'd built around herself tremble, but she squared her shoulders and sniffed. 'Sometimes it's just not enough though, is it?'

The silence returned, heavy and oppressive as they descended over Amber Creek. When the helicopter touched down in the adjacent field and the blades wound down, Sage didn't even wait for the rotors to stop turning before she thanked the mayor and disembarked with the bird in the towel, her steps hurried as she made for the clinic.

Ethan made to jump out after her but the mayor was faster. 'Ethan. Make sure she's OK, yeah?'

He paused with the supplies, his gaze tracking her as she made for the gate to the property. He was about to ask the other man what he meant, but he decided it was pointless. You could tell a lot about Sage Dawson by how she walked or held her head, the things she wasn't saying. He'd picked up on that already but the mayor had known her longer. She was putting on a brave face now, but they could both tell she was shaken.

'She goes out of her way to do these things, and we all want to help her, knowing what she's been through, you know?' the mayor said, looking over his sunglasses at him, as if inviting him to reveal he knew exactly what she'd *been through*.

Again, Ethan almost asked how he was supposed to know what Sage had been through, but again, it would have been pointless. Sage was best friends with this man's wife—she'd probably told Abigail about their conversations…and their almost kiss… The mayor would likely know he'd been getting closer to Sage than to Storm since taking on this project.

'I'll keep an eye on her, make sure she's OK,' he reassured him.

'Good man, take her out or something, make her laugh. She needs it.'

Ethan nodded resolutely. 'Yes, sir,' he said, remembering this man was the one who'd hired him, and trusted him, and who'd *also* dropped everything to try and help save a rare bird. He would do it for the mayor as well as for Sage, he decided, because taking Sage out, feeling the way he was starting to feel about her, was the last thing he should be doing, really.

CHAPTER NINE

THE RHYTHMIC KNOCK on the flimsy wooden door of her cabin startled Sage from her reading. She glanced up at the clock—six minutes past eight. She moved the plate of half-eaten toast from the duvet, her heart racing as she folded the corner of the page in her book, and flicked the needle off her vintage record player. She wasn't expecting company.

'Hey, Sage? You OK in there?'

Ethan's deep voice carried through the thin barrier with an undercurrent of concern at the sudden absence of her jazz music, and she stood up too quickly. She'd seen him through the windows before settling down to read, his muscular silhouette moving around the paddock with Storm. He and Billy had finally managed to saddle him but she'd forced herself not to watch, to mind her own business. The day's events had taken their toll, another almost-kiss that had freaked her out, an unpreventable death, all of it confusing and sad and now she wanted to hide away from it on her own.

She opened the door to find him standing there. The moonlight cast long shadows across his angular features. His blue eyes searched her face.

Oh, Lord, why do you have to be so gorgeous, Ethan, and why did I tell you this wasn't a good idea...?

'What can I do for you, Ethan?' she said instead.

'It's been a tough day,' he confessed with a weary smile

that melted some tiny frozen-over part of her. 'I could use a drink. What do you say we go out somewhere?'

Sage clutched her book to her chest. That look in his eyes was unnerving. The way he'd said *'You...'* earlier at the clinic, before they'd been interrupted by the call about the finch, had been playing on her mind. *'You...'* As though he'd been about to confess something she was doing to unnerve him. It had turned her inside out.

This chemistry between them was undeniable, and after their first almost-kiss it had started to affect her concentration—it was why she'd done her best to undo it all in the chopper. Why start something up that would just go wrong and leave her worse off than she was, thinking even *worse* things about herself? He'd pretended not to hear her.

'Actually, I was about to go see some friends.' Sage stepped aside, inviting him in anyway. How could she not? The walls felt as if they'd closed in tighter with Ethan's broad shoulders moving past her in the confines of her small living quarters. His scent caught her nostrils, mixed with soft hay, and she tried not to groan.

'Some friends?' he asked now, with a small smirk. She rolled her eyes at him.

'Yes.' Did he think she didn't have many friends, except Abigail? He was right, though. She really needed to get out more.

'You can come too, if you like,' she said, trying to keep her tone even while her mind buzzed with questions. Why did she just invite him to the only place she ever went at night besides Abigail's? What did he think of her home? Too humble, too cluttered with all her veterinary journals and second-hand furniture? 'Sorry about the mess, by the way.'

'This isn't a mess,' he said, casting an eye over her record collection before perching on the corner of the tattered leather couch and picking up the book she'd just put down. 'You should've seen the chaos at Jacqueline's house last Christmas.'

'Jacqueline?'

'My sister,' he said, flicking absently through the pages. 'My niece and nephew, little terrors… Kara's six, Jayson's eight, they're like a tornado of toys. One day when I was there, they decided it was the perfect time to test out their theory that the ceiling fan could carry their weight and help them fly.'

Sage raised an eyebrow, her earlier tension giving way to a grin. 'And you stopped this…experiment?'

'Caught them red-handed, chairs stacked on tables, tinsel everywhere. I had to channel my inner negotiator to get them down.' His laughter was infectious, so rare from him, but clearly coming from a place of deep love and affection and, for a fleeting moment, Sage felt a lightness she hadn't known she'd needed. He had come here on a mission to make her smile, she realised. Because of the dead bird. Or maybe he just felt sorry for her, she thought suddenly, now she'd told him how her family died. Did he think she couldn't cope when things got tough? She frowned. Maybe she was overreacting… Ugh—too many confusing emotions, it was hard to know what to think around this guy, but she'd invited him out with her now, so she was stuck with the consequences, whatever those might be.

She crossed to the corner where her shoes lay scattered, her well-worn slippers now seeming embarrassingly inadequate. 'Just need to change out of these.'

'I've got a pair just like them,' Ethan told her, with a nod to her slippers. 'Comfiest things ever.'

Sage smiled, feeling another shard of ice thaw inside her at the thought of sharing something so trivial with this man.

She couldn't really imagine someone so masculine and active sitting about the house wearing slippers, stopping kids from attaching themselves to ceiling fans. And she hadn't known he had a sister, and a niece and nephew. Seeing how comfortable he'd been with Abigail's children, she'd bet he was a great uncle to them.

Beneath this new warmth and appreciation, tension coiled tight in her belly. The proximity of him in the small room magnified every breath, every shift of movement. As she bent to slip on her boots, she felt him watching her, but, standing up, she caught his gaze lingering on an old photograph of her with her mum and dad. The pride in her parents' eyes was immortalised right there in the picture, all three of them standing by the swimming pool after she'd completed her one-hundred-metre race and come in first place. The medal around her neck was so huge it covered her stomach.

'I was nine,' she said, looking at the photo with him. Then she felt his eyes on her again. Did he see the way she ached so badly to turn back time? She waited for him to bring it up, to ask more questions about her parents, but he didn't.

'Ready?' He broke the silence that had stretched too thin between them and she opened the door for him to walk ahead.

'Sounds like you're quite the uncle,' she remarked as they stepped out into the balmy evening air. Somehow she hadn't pictured him with anyone else from his family besides his dad. He always seemed so solitary, as if all he did outside working with his horses was hang out even more with his horses.

'I love the little monsters,' he quipped, making her laugh. He was pretty good at dissolving tension when he wanted to, she thought, gratefully. Also pretty good at making her forget she should be staying away from him.

The sky above was a canvas of ink around the moon. It

hung like a solitary lantern amongst the stars as Sage clutched the straps of her backpack. Thank goodness it was cool out now. They walked side by side along the dusty path that curled behind the clinic, and she tried not to think about the fact that his presence out here in the silence was already sending a stampede of horses to her chest in place of her heart.

The mayor had almost certainly put him up to this, told him to check on her, and stupidly she'd invited him further than her doorstep, where she probably should have just thanked him for his well wishes and closed the door. It was hard, though, to resist this softer side of him. To think she had once assumed he was more style than substance, only good for posing for the cameras! The more she got to know him, the more he proved he was actually a really decent guy and a great vet.

The crunch of gravel underfoot was the only sound now, and the rhythm seemed to pulse with unspoken words. She was already turning this into something it wasn't.

So silly! Just calm down, Sage.

She glanced at Ethan, his handsome, way too kissable profile etched against the night sky, and felt that familiar pull, the one that tied her stomach in knots. He was close enough that she could see the contours of his face soften in the moonlight, but he wouldn't try to kiss her again, she'd made sure of that. Surely she had done enough to keep him at arm's length, at least as far as a romance was concerned. He was only here now because of the mayor, anyway.

The possibility that he might not be interested in her after all caused her thoughts to spiral, her confusion mingling with the cool night air.

'So, where are we going?' Ethan's question sliced through her reverie.

'You'll see,' she told him, but her voice came out distant

and distracted. She wrapped her arms around herself. Why had she invited him along? This was something she always did alone. Maybe she *did* want a fling…maybe she should just stop being a wuss and kiss him! But flings led to feelings and she knew her heart couldn't handle someone else she admired and cared for disappearing on her.

She stopped just short of the familiar tree, her eyes tracing the constellations in the sky above them as she slid the backpack from her shoulders. Ethan stifled a smile.

'I thought you were seeing friends?' he said, his voice low and curious.

'And here they are.' She didn't look at him as she pointed skyward. 'Up there,' she whispered, spreading out the soft pink blanket she always brought with her, and dropping to the ground. He was here now, so she might as well reveal her secret.

'That bright one, that's my mum, Caroline,' she said. 'And next to her, that's my dad, Anthony. The little one that sparkles a bit differently? That's Juni, my Australian Shepherd.'

Ethan lay beside her, his body a solid presence. His silence instantly comforted and unnerved her at the same time. He probably thought she was completely crazy. 'What do you talk to them about?' he asked instead and she felt the heave of relief lift her heart. Of course he wouldn't judge her; he knew what it was like to lose loved ones.

'Everything. You mean to say *you* don't talk to the stars yourself?'

He smirked, shook his head. 'No, but I might have to start. At least they don't talk back.'

'Neither do animals,' she reasoned.

'Which is exactly why we like them, stars and animals. Peaceful beings. Mostly unargumentative.'

'Exactly.'

She stole another glance at him, at the strong line of his jaw, the faint stubble that was growing on him, and her too. He was more than what people saw on TV. So much more than what she had expected to see, when he'd first shown up in his sexy jeans and boots with enough charisma to charm a nation. With her he was both open and closed, revealing these small parts of himself to her piece by piece, only to withdraw again, protecting himself.

A lot like she was doing, she realised now. He'd been through enough himself to warrant him being a little cautious when it came to their obvious chemistry. But he did feel it, with her—it was pretty much undeniable when the panic and confusion around her own feelings subsided. Should she kiss him now? It would be so easy.

No. Sage, what are you doing?

'So you come here all the time?' Ethan said.

'I do. Always alone,' she added.

He nodded. 'Well, thank you for introducing me to your family.'

His gaze followed hers as she stared at all the sparkling celestial bodies she'd assigned to her loved ones, and various other animals she'd lost over the years.

'What happened that day?' he ventured gently after a moment. 'The fire?'

Oh, man, here we go.

Sage drew a shuddering breath as her chest and every bone seemed to tighten inside her. 'I should've helped them...' Her voice trailed off, choked by the weight of it like always, heightened by the loss today. That poor bird.

If she said too much, he'd find an excuse to leave, he'd link her to the stories that had done the rounds when they were kids, that still resurfaced now sometimes, thanks to the Internet. Bryce had loved all animals, just like Ethan. Bryce had turned his back on her and Ethan would, too.

Ethan shifted, propping himself up on his elbow to look at her. He seemed to see the battle in her eyes and for a second the whole story formed on her tongue, but she willed herself to keep quiet.

'What do you mean, you should have *helped* them?'

She bit her tongue.

'Sage?'

She released a small sigh through her nostrils. 'I was looking at my phone, in the main house,' she said eventually. 'That night. We were camping out front—my dad loved us all to do that. Campfires, stories, hot dogs on the flames, no technology. I needed the bathroom in the house, so I went inside, and then of course I sneaked a look at my phone and got distracted chatting with my friends, and when I came back, the wind must have changed direction and…the fire was… everywhere. I hadn't noticed on my way into the house that our campfire was starting to spread outside the pit we'd dug.'

Ethan was still studying her closely. Sage's mind spun. Any moment now she would stop talking, if only her head weren't processing it all over again and sending it straight out of her mouth into his understanding, way too hypnotic eyes.

'They couldn't get past it. It just kept spreading,' she continued. 'My phone was back in the house. I *could* have just run back there but I didn't. I completely froze.'

'You were just a kid,' he said, putting a hand over hers softly.

She sighed. 'I wasn't a *stupid* kid, Ethan. I could have done something. Instead, my family died, and the fire spread out of control and all those poor animals in the bush… I can't ever forgive myself for any of it. If I hadn't been so selfish, and absorbed in my phone, if I just hadn't gone behind their backs to check it in the first place, I would have got there in time to—'

'Sage!' He sat up straighter now, reached for both her hands. She was looking at him through a blur of tears, as if it had all happened yesterday. Great, she was already way too emotional because of the bird's death. It had brought everything roaring back to the surface. 'What happened wasn't your fault,' he pressed. 'Please don't tell me you've been carrying this guilt around all this time. Fires spread, that's what fires *do*.'

Sage's throat tightened around her next words. She turned away, ashamed of the tidal wave building up in her chest, and the tears he was bringing out of her.

'Tell me, sweetheart,' he urged gently, stroking the backs of her hands with soft thumbs.

'Everyone says there was nothing I could have done,' she confessed, her breath hitching, 'but I failed them all, I know I did. I should have seen—'

'You didn't fail anyone,' Ethan insisted, his tone firm and compassionate all at once. 'You were only a little girl.' He squeezed her hands in reassurance and she watched his hands tightening around hers, big hands, safe hands. Did he even know how she had wanted someone to understand all this, to talk to someone other than Abigail about it?

'You're making a difference every day, Sage. That counts for something. I'm inspired by you. Look what you've done here, for the people and for the animals. And for yourself.'

Sage's fingers curled around his now, grounding her in the present, in Ethan. It was such a relief, feeling as though someone truly saw her. Then… 'Did you just call me *sweetheart*?'

The word cut through her suddenly. Bryce had called her that once, before he'd changed his mind about her and disappeared from her life completely.

Ethan was studying her mouth now in silence, tracing the lines of her face with those all-seeing blue eyes again, and she swallowed, drawing strength from him. He was still here, he wasn't getting up to leave. 'The last person I told about the animals couldn't handle it at all,' she said before she could think straight. 'It was a guy, actually.' She glanced up at him, checking for a reaction, but he was unreadable. 'He broke things off with me. Well, actually he didn't even do that. He just disappeared without ever speaking to me again.'

Ethan shook his head gravely, and gave her hands a final reassuring clasp before rolling to his back again. 'Well, maybe he had a different reason for going,' he said, looking up towards the southern cross while her heart continued to pound at his closeness and everything she'd just spilled out after telling herself she wouldn't. What was it about Ethan that made her want to talk? She was just like one of his horses already, responding from a place deep inside her that she couldn't fathom.

Then he turned his head to her. 'Did this man actually *say* he was breaking things off with you because some animals died in a fire that wasn't even your fault?'

Sage opened her mouth to talk, but nothing came out, so she closed it again.

'Who was he?' he demanded gently.

Sage swallowed, measuring the seriousness in his eyes. 'A Canadian man I was seeing, called Bryce.'

'And Bryce just *disappeared*, right after you told him about that night?'

She nodded slowly, cringing. 'It was the morning after,'

she admitted. 'And nobody else knew why he left the koala reserve, because he didn't tell anyone he was leaving.'

Ethan was nodding to himself slowly, still looking at the sky. 'Which koala reserve was it?'

She told him, and his eyebrows drew together. 'I've heard about that place. It's notorious for not paying people who show up without work visas and still expect to be paid.'

Sage combed back through her memories. Come to think of it, Bryce had once said something about not getting the money he'd been promised for the work he'd done there. Being an Australian citizen herself, she had never had a problem getting paid, so she'd forgotten about it. Also, she'd had a lot going on at that point, namely opening herself up to a man for the first time since vet school. She'd been a recluse, pretty much, till Bryce, aside from a couple of brief flings that had gone nowhere. Her work had been far more important to her, and she'd let everyone know it.

Her mind reeled; she must have zoned out because when she came back to herself, Ethan had changed the subject already.

'Did you know that Alpha Centauri is actually three stars, not one? And it's the closest star system to our own,' Ethan said, nudging her out of her reverie. 'And over there, that's the Carina Nebula...'

'The Carina-Sagittarius Arm of the Milky Way galaxy, I know. Almost nine thousand light years from Earth. Can you imagine how long it would take to get there?'

'Or what we'd find?' he added. 'I see I'm not about to impress *you* with my star facts.'

'You can try?' She shrugged. Was she flirting now? How did they get here from what they'd just been talking about?

Sage's heart pumped furiously as they talked about the

stars and veered onto the subject of the cosmos and the probability of aliens and the intricate connections that bound humans to each other and to the world. For a while she forgot about Bryce entirely—who cared why he'd left at this point, anyway? She was distracted by the fact that she could talk to Ethan about anything, she realised as they lay there on the ground, side by side. But then, she couldn't quite muster the courage to ask any more about what had happened with his ex-fiancée and his best friend, and he didn't bring it up. Had he had a relationship since Carrie, of any length? A fling, maybe? If she asked him now, would he think she was sizing him up as more than a colleague and friend? Were they even *friends* now?

They were barely touching but somehow they were still travelling the world together tonight. It had been so long since she'd had a conversation like this with a man. Being friends with Ethan would be OK. A friend like him was welcome. If only she didn't still want to rip his shirt off and get inside his bed as well as his head!

In no time at all two hours had passed and they were both fighting back their yawns mid conversation. Ethan walked her back to the front door, told her it had been a pleasure meeting her friends, and Sage waited a few seconds longer than she should have, gazing into his mesmerising eyes before realising he most definitely was not planning to kiss her this time. He seemed different, as if he'd drawn a line under the whole idea, and once again she cursed what she'd said to him in the chopper.

'Goodnight, Sage,' he reiterated.

I liked it when you called me sweetheart more, she wanted to say.

But she let him go.

She groaned to herself as she listened to his ute pulling away. Who was she kidding? She could never make Ethan her friend. She'd never wanted to be with *anybody* as much as this in her life, but she couldn't have him. He was going to disappear out of her life, just as Bryce had, eventually. And there was no way she was going through that again, whatever the reason.

CHAPTER TEN

The ute's engine roared, cutting a furious path through the dense bushland. Sage clung to the dashboard, her knuckles white as the vehicle lurched over another unseen dip in the rugged earth. Beside her, Ethan's hands were steady on the wheel, his jaw set with determination. 'How much further?' he asked her.

'Should just be over this ridge,' she said, squinting at the coordinates on her phone against the glare of the sun. It was doing its best to blaze through the canopy overhead.

'Are we sure it was caught in a trap?' Ethan asked, his voice mirroring the unrest inside her, not least because they'd left the clinic at the speed of light after a local hiker had sent co-ordinates to them, telling them a dingo was stuck. Sage replied, her gaze not leaving the rough track ahead.

'Yes. She said the poor thing didn't look too good, but she couldn't stay with it, because she was out of water herself, and then she had to search for a phone signal.' As she said it, she noticed the bars on her own phone were fading from five right down to one. 'It's all alone right now, the poor thing.'

'We'll find it,' Ethan assured her, pressing his foot to the gas again.

Sage tried to focus on the dusty path, hatching a plan to help free the dingo whatever state it might be in, but her thoughts kept drifting back to the other night, last week, the last time they'd sat alone talking, under the stars. He'd helped her at the weekend with the irrigation system as promised, stopping only to answer a call from his dad. They'd chatted as they'd worked, but only on the topic of sustainable gardening practices. Nothing deep. Nothing personal. It was killing her.

It was almost as though that whole night alone with him under the sky had been a dream, and he'd closed off again, deeming her too broken maybe, as Bryce probably had? Ethan had made her think for a moment that maybe there had been another reason why Bryce had disappeared on her, but she couldn't figure out what that might have been. Why hadn't he just talked to her about it before he'd left?

The stars had been the only witness to her and Ethan's conversation that night. Now, as they drove deeper into isolation, surrounded by the twisted trees and sprawling scrub, the memory of Ethan's hand in hers that night, how nice it had felt, how safe and reassuring, wove itself so stubbornly around her heart she knew she'd be able to recall it fifty years from now, even if they never saw each other again once Storm was healed. Was it wrong that she was starting to wish Storm would never recover fully, that Ethan would have to stay here for ever and start doing more than just holding her hand?

'Here!' Ethan braked hard. The ute skidded to a stop. As they stepped out into the dust, the silence of the bush greeted them both like a living entity. They found the dingo just beyond a thicket of mulga bushes.

'Oh, you sweet thing, look at you.' The creature's furry leg was firmly caught in the grip of a rusted steel trap. 'The farmers just don't know what they're doing when they set out to get kangaroos,' she told Ethan. The dog-like animal's eyes were wild with pain as it lay panting, its coat matted with dirt and blood.

'Don't get too close,' Ethan warned her as she got to her knees. 'He's scared.'

'I know,' she told him, approaching slowly while he grabbed the bag from the ute. She crouched over the wounded creature, murmuring soothingly, even as it snarled in self-defence. Its teeth were tiny razors and Ethan put a hand to her shoulder, warning her to let him try something. At first, she ignored him, determined to do things her way. It was still so frustrating that he was here, on her turf, working his methods with more success than she was having with hers…but when the dingo snapped at her again and she narrowly missed a sharp bite she stood back in resignation and let him take over. She watched him lay his hands on the animal, how it immediately stilled beneath him.

'Easy there, mate,' he whispered, his voice low and soothing as he slipped a muzzle over its mouth as a precaution. The dingo had already stopped trying to bite. Sage just swiped her hot forehead and let him assess the damage to its hind leg. Their closeness, with bare arms and knees in their respective T-shirts and shorts, shot bolts of awareness through her bloodstream, though she tried to concentrate on the mission at hand.

That night, after she'd told him about Bryce…after he'd got her thinking about what really might have happened to make Bryce leave… Ethan had walked her back to her door like a gentleman, and left her to think about it some more. Only now, the more she thought about why Bryce left, she couldn't help but think that maybe he just hadn't been that into her…not in the way she'd wanted him to be, after trusting him with all her secrets. Maybe she'd just been a brief holiday romance for him, and she had turned it into something more. He'd seen his chance to make a break for it, and like a coward he'd taken it without even talking to her first. For whatever reason, Bryce was long gone, and now Ethan was here. For a while at least. She could have invited him into her home. This time, if she got the chance, she would accept it for what it was, a fling, a bit of fun, and she wouldn't get attached.

I should have just invited him in...

'Pass the bolt cutters,' he requested. Sage did so without a word and he concentrated on the task with fierce intensity, his muscular forearms glistening with sweat. With gentle, precise movements, they worked in tandem to free the dingo and soon the nasty trap was cast aside. She tossed it into the back of the ute, where it couldn't harm anyone else, and felt Ethan's gaze on her as she carefully applied iodine to the animal's injured leg. She continued with her soothing words, although it had stopped trying to lunge for her too now, as if it knew they were trying to help. She was even able to apply dissolving stitches and an antibiotic shot and she knew that together they were giving it the best shot at survival they could.

Ethan's admiration for her—or for her work, at least—was evident even without words. It felt nice when he looked at her so approvingly and worked with her like this. It made her feel guilty for not wanting him here at first and for not trusting in his methods. His methods worked for him, and by proxy they were working for her too. Ethan knew that every creature was of equal importance to her: a dingo was no different from a rare, endangered bird. Losing either was another heartbreak, to her at least. He knew that now and he knew why she felt that way, because she'd told him everything. And now the air around them crackled with an electric charge as another shared mission brought them closer, beyond the physical.

Sage allowed herself a fleeting glance up at him, her pulse quickening as the sunlight played across the angles of his handsome face. He'd shone a new light on the whole Bryce thing, making her wonder if she should gain closure by looking him up and finally *asking* him what had happened. Ugh, why couldn't she just get over it? It was as if, as soon as she decided to try, the guilt crept back in and stopped her. Despite Ethan's reassurances, nothing would *ever* make her feel differently about the way she'd let her family down. How could she ever shake the guilt over what had happened? How would she continue to live if she lost anyone else she cared about? That was the biggest reason she hadn't initiated anything with *this* man.

Ethan told her to stand back and she obeyed, watching him unclasp the muzzle. The dingo limped away, and a rush of pride blocked everything out for a moment. She turned to him, and before she knew what she was doing she'd held her hand up ready for his. Their palms met in an awkward high-five that somehow morphed into something resembling a clasp.

'Nice job, boss,' Ethan said.

'I'm not really your boss,' Sage huffed, swigging from her canteen, trying to ignore the hum of awareness that zipped along her nerves as his thumbs brushed the back of her hand. 'You're on the mayor's payroll, remember.'

Ethan's eyes held hers, and she found herself lost in their vivid blue depths for a heartbeat too long, trapped as the dingo had been. She knew why he called her boss, really. Because it was better for him to see her like that, an illusion of safety.

'It suits you, being a boss lady,' he said, thoughtfully, motioning her back to the truck.

The drive back began in silence along a different route. Sage focused on the landscape unfurling outside the window—a tapestry of greens and browns all punctuated by the brilliant blue sky above. None of it was enough to distract her from the fact that Ethan knew everything about the night of the fire, which had formed the very backbone of her existence, yet she still knew next to nothing about him really; not when it came to matters of the heart. Maybe it was too soon after Carrie for him to feel right about initiating anything with her, someone who would soon be operating tasks like this alone, thousands of miles away from him. Torture. Maybe he really did still have feelings for his ex, despite how she'd betrayed him with his best friend?

The pull towards this man, who hadn't judged her in the slightest, was getting impossible to ignore.

'Watch out for the—' Sage's warning came about three seconds too late. A jolt threw her against her seat belt as the ute's front wheel caught on something. Ethan wrestled with the steering wheel, his jaw set in determination as he tried to manoeuvre out of whatever was ensnaring them, but it was no good. Each attempt only seemed to dig them deeper into the earth. He cursed under his breath, throwing the ute into reverse. It still wouldn't move.

'Here, let me try,' Sage said, unbuckling her seat belt. As she stepped from the vehicle with him the issue was immediately apparent. They were ensnared in a network of tree roots that would be a pretty impressive work of nature if it didn't mean their vehicle was totally stuck. They swapped places and she gripped the steering wheel with the familiar surge of adrenaline that came with a challenge. The engine growled as she tried to manoeuvre them out, but the roots held fast.

'Stubborn thing,' she muttered in frustration.

'Like someone else I know,' Ethan teased through the window, a half-smile softening his features.

'Ha-ha, I had to try,' Sage shot back, though secretly she appreciated the lightness in his voice. It was rare to see this side of Ethan—the same one he'd revealed when he'd been talking about his sister and his niece and nephew that night under the stars and, later, all the speculation about aliens and the cosmos. It was impossible to think there was nothing else out there when you lived under skies like this. The thoughtful philosopher was yet another facet to him that wasn't at all like the larger than life, sometimes arrogant personality the TV had portrayed, but still, the revelation did nothing to free the trapped tyre.

'Looks like we're going to be stuck here for a bit,' he said, his gaze meeting hers.

'Seems so, yes.' The tension flew back in between them and wove itself through her frustration like a fine thread, till she stepped back out of the ute into the dust, shutting the door behind her with a sigh. Her thoughts were in a frenzy, trying to come up with a solution while also avoiding the intense energy that seemed to surround them as he approached. She nervously watched him move around the car opposite her as they circled it together, inspecting the tangled mess of roots once more. Sage fumbled for her phone, her heart sinking as she swiped the screen. No bars. Not even a flicker. She met Ethan's expectant eyes and shook her head. 'Still no signal,' she reported. The isolation enveloped them like a second skin.

'Maybe if we dig around the tyre?' Ethan suggested, and she shrugged. They might as well try.

Sage's hands were caked with red dust as she clawed at the earth, her fingers aching from the effort. Ethan was beside her, his body bent in exertion as he dug around the trapped tyre with a piece of sturdy wood. The sun bore down on her shoulders, relentless in its late-afternoon fury.

'Almost there,' Ethan grunted, his voice threaded with

dogged resolution. 'Just a bit more leverage and we should be able to rock it out.'

Sage wasn't so sure, but she didn't like to say it. She watched him swipe at his brow with the back of his hand, leaving a smear of dirt in its wake, and continued digging. She knew she really shouldn't be looking at Ethan's muscles bunching under his sweat-dampened shirt at the same time; her mouth was already dry enough as it was. But who would be able to help it?

'Ready?' he called out as she finally positioned herself behind the wheel yet again.

'Ready,' she echoed, finding him in the mirror. He braced himself against the ute's frame and started to push, straining against the metal beast, willing it to break free. The vehicle groaned, a low, protesting sound, and soon it lurched, once, twice, and again before settling stubbornly back into its earthen prison. Ethan swore softly, kicking at the stubborn root that was holding the wheel captive. Checking her phone again, she felt dread settle in.

'Still nothing. We're completely cut off.'

A heavy silence settled over them. It felt compounded by the vast, lonely wilderness that stretched endlessly in every direction. It was just them—the bush, the fading light, and all their unfinished business hanging in the air like ripe fruit. The thought of spending the night out here in the open wild sent a shiver down her spine despite the heat.

'Someone will be along soon. If not, it could be worse,' Ethan noted, scanning their surroundings. 'At least we've got that one water canteen, and some supplies…'

'We have trail mix,' she said, and he pulled a face, making them both smile for a second.

'It'll be fine.' She sighed, clinging to the practicality of the moment. But the sun wouldn't be up for much longer, its descent already painting the sky orange and pink. Maybe *someone* would realise they weren't home yet, and be along soon?

Ethan's silhouette cut through the dwindling light as he stooped to pick up another branch. 'We don't *need* a fire, you know,' he called over his shoulder, but the growing heap of wood beside him belied his words. She wished she could be as enthusiastic and as useful as he was, but they'd been out here an hour and a half already with no hope of rescue and she was hot and exhausted.

'Are you going to keep the wildlife away with your bare hands, then?' she retorted, and he flexed a biceps at her playfully. It was meant as a joke, but instead it made her insides flutter. He had no idea what his strength and physique, on top of his talents—not to mention his *eyes*—could do to a woman.

'Seriously, I've seen your "no naked flames" signs,' he said, tossing a bunch more sticks onto the pile. 'And now I understand why.'

'I'm fine with it, really,' Sage said quickly, gathering a smaller, more manageable stack for herself. The scent of eucalyptus rose from the bark and mingled with the earthy fragrance of the cooling ground. 'We need to save our phone batteries,' she added, trying to ignore the thrum of her heart that had started along with his concern. They were pretty close to the bush. But Ethan was here, and she couldn't let her old fears control her for ever. More to the point, she couldn't act like a fool in front of him when it was her fault they were stuck out here anyway. There had been warnings on the radio and from locals about the tree-root system. It was because of the drought—the ground was just too dry. What with the dingo, and her head being full of Ethan, she'd clean forgotten.

Ethan located the cigarette lighter from the ute and coaxed the first flickers of life from the dry wood. Sage forced her feet not to take three steps backwards, instead inching closer. He shot her a look, as if to ask if this was *really* OK with her, and she nodded her silent consent. Thank goodness he was with her, really. Being out here alone would have been terrifying, and there was no way she'd have lit a fire on her own.

They'd pulled bags and a couple of spare towels from the ute to sit on, and soon the last of the dusk had faded from above them and the flames were curling up into the sky, spitting at the stars. What would her parents think if they could see her now? she mused, feeling Ethan's eyes on her again. He was picking at the last of the trail mix, which was all they had to eat.

'I'd murder a bowl of pasta right now,' he said, scrunching up the empty packet.

'Are you a good cook?' she asked curiously. She had never seen him cook a thing in the clinic's small kitchen.

Ethan nodded slowly. 'I can heat things up in saucepans, put pizzas on a rack, boil water in the microwave… That's what you mean by cooking, right?' he teased.

They started to talk about their favourite foods and Sage realised she was imagining him in a silly apron with boobs or something on the front, in a cosy kitchen with sunshine streaming through the windows. She was there too in this imaginary kitchen, stirring something in a pan on the stove. He was coming up behind her, coiling his arms around her waist, nuzzling her neck…

She chastised herself silently. *Sage, you are being totally ridiculous.*

'Here, drink some of this water,' Ethan said, handing her the canteen.

'Thanks.' Her fingers brushed against his as she took it, and a timely, inappropriate jolt attacked her core. She took a sip, busying herself with arranging the towel underneath her, trying to focus on the practicalities of settling into a night out here in the bush, rather than the warmth that lingered from his touch, or how much she wanted to sleep pressed against him. They talked about their favourite restaurants, his in Brisbane, hers mostly in Perth, and she tried to ignore the ache to ask him anything too personal, even though she was dying to.

'The fire feels nice,' Sage murmured without thinking. Ethan just raised his eyebrows and smiled, resting back on his elbows. It had actually grown a little chilly now that the heat of the sun was completely gone. She hugged her knees, the silence around them deep and full of unvoiced thoughts the second they stopped talking. Ethan swigged careful rations of the water, muscles shifting under the fabric of his shirt, shadows playing on his cheekbones. Sage couldn't concentrate any more. She also really had to pee.

'I have to go…' she told him, making to stand up.

'Need me to come too?' he asked her, sitting up straight. She laughed and shook her head, looking around for the non-existent bathroom.

As if.

'I can manage, thanks.'

'Well, take your phone for the torch, at least.'

'OK.'

The second she left the heat of the fire, the vastness of the sky and the shadows closed in. Silently she wandered to the nearest line of trees and crouched down close to the earth. What a situation this was. People were probably wondering where they were by now, but it was highly likely that no one wanted to take the path they'd all been warned about in the dark.

Sage was just doing her business when something sleek caught the corner of her eye. She turned her head slowly, her heart rate quickening as she flashed the phone's light around.

Where are you? What are you? Oh, my God.

Suddenly, she was frozen in a crouch. Just a couple of metres away, coiled among the underbrush, was a huge snake. It was hard to see its length exactly, but its scales glistened under the faint moonlight, reflecting a dangerous mix of black and deep red. She knew this one—a red belly. Highly toxic.

Sage's breath caught in her throat. This was not ideal—she'd been mere steps away from this creature while she'd just relieved herself! The gravity of the situation sank in, right as the creature decided to move again. A scream instinctively clawed its way up her throat, but she bit it back, not wanting to alarm Ethan. She had to stay composed.

Calm, calm, calm...

Careful not to make any sudden movements that might provoke the snake, she rose slowly from her crouched position, her heart pounding against her chest like a trapped bird.

Calm, calm, calm...

Her mind raced as she weighed her options, right as Ethan appeared from behind the tree. She almost jumped out of her skin as she fumbled to do her buttons up, eyes darting from him to the snake. She couldn't see it any more, it had moved. 'Ethan...'

'Sorry, sorry,' he said, shielding his eyes. 'You were just gone too long and I was worried.' He went to move towards her but she held up her hands.

'Snake,' she hissed.

He froze on the spot, just as she had. 'Where?'

'It was just here!'

'I don't see it. You must have scared it off.'

Even so, he shone the torch around as a warning as he led them both back to their makeshift camp. The fire was blazing now, its crackle deafening in the hush of the evening. The flames leaped and twirled and she forced herself not to move further back, to embrace it. It was a good thing tonight, keeping all the bad things at bay. Ethan's features had hardened, the lines of strain around his eyes more pronounced as he sat closer to her than he had before, shoulder to shoulder, alert and aware, as if he'd assumed guard duty on the lookout for snakes on attack.

Sage had dealt with snakes her whole life, but she'd let him protect her, she decided. Ethan was quiet for a few moments, contemplating the fire. Then he turned to her and out of nowhere he asked: 'So, that guy Bryce. Was it serious between you two?'

CHAPTER ELEVEN

ETHAN WAITED FOR her reply, studying her lips close up in the firelight. Maybe he shouldn't have asked such a personal question but, after hearing everything about the fire that killed her family, he was still putting the pieces of the Sage puzzle together. She'd tortured herself over what had happened that night, completely unnecessarily he was sure, and that guilt had affected so much of her life. As it had with Bryce; the way she'd just assumed he'd left because of something she'd done or hadn't done as a child.

She chewed her lip, looked at him sideways. 'It was just a little fun, I suppose,' she told him warily, fidgeting on their makeshift blankets.

'How long did you have fun for?' He looked over her shoulder for the snake, before focusing on her eyes again.

'Why do you care?' she asked, digging a stick into the dirt between her feet.

He studied her brown boots, the way one of the laces was coming undone, and nodded quietly. He'd asked for that.

'You're right, it's none of my business.'

She sighed. 'It was just a few months, and, looking back on it now, it was nothing serious. I mean, I'm like you, I guess. I don't really *do* relationships.'

'Is that right?' He couldn't help the smirk that crossed his mouth.

'I'm pretty good at self-sabotaging my own happiness, in case you hadn't noticed,' she said tartly, straightening her shoulders. 'I suppose I always just assume...'

'That you don't deserve anyone's love or attention,' he finished. 'Which isn't true, by the way. I've said it before and I'll say it again. What happened to your family was not your fault. I really hope you know that.'

She pursed her lips but didn't answer.

'You were just a child. Would you really still be blaming anyone else for something that happened when they were ten? You're thirty-five, right? I saw your driver's license.'

Sage's eyes widened, before her brow furrowed into a deep frown, and he had to wonder whether anyone actually ever reminded her of this, whether she even talked to anyone about it, besides Abigail. She looked as if she was going to argue with him for a second, but then she tossed her stick into the fire and deflected away from her family. 'I don't know if I was ever really in love with Bryce anyway. I don't think I've ever really been in love with anyone.'

He didn't ask why, even though her quick glance at him made him acutely aware she was attracted to him. Her survivor's guilt, and her fear of letting someone in, only to lose them as she'd lost her parents, had dictated her whole life... the same way losing his mum, Cam and Carrie had dictated his. This was all dangerous ground, but here they were, and he wasn't just going to sit here in this weird silence.

'The more I think about it, I know I haven't,' she followed. 'I've certainly never wanted to marry anyone.' Sage's voice caught as her fingers twisted the edge of the towel. Ethan stared into the flames. Her hesitance to continue plunged them into another heavy silence.

'I proposed to Carrie because things hadn't been that great

between us for a while,' he admitted after a moment. Sage pulled a face, and he grimaced. 'I know, I know. I just thought maybe it would keep us together—we always said we'd do it one day. It was the longest engagement anyway. Four years…'

'Four years?' Sage looked incredulous.

'We got engaged three years in, but we could never agree on a wedding date,' he explained, realising how silly it sounded now, even to his own ears. 'Looking back, I guess neither of our hearts had been in it for a long time. Carrie even stopped wearing the ring. It started when she lost interest in my life, in my horses and my family, everything I loved, you know? Everything she used to love about me…or said she did. Then I lost Mum and had to care for Dad and I guess it all just got too much for her. I was blindsided…or just blind, I suppose. I let my grief take over everything for a while, and I didn't even see her slipping away till she was gone.'

Sage listened closely, not interrupting. It felt strangely therapeutic to talk about it, even with her. 'How did you find out about the affair with Cam?' she asked.

Ethan scowled into the flames. He was saying things he'd never said to anyone but Jacqueline, but then, keeping it all stacked up inside him was toxic and he loathed small talk more than anything. Their crumbling communication had been the death of him and Carrie.

'I booked a hotel on the beach for Cam's birthday,' he said eventually. He explained how it was something they always did for each other on their birthdays, a guys' night away somewhere. Fishing, motorcycling, surfing, all that stuff. That year Carrie had really wanted to come, and he frowned to himself as he recounted it all, remembering how much Cam had advocated for her being there that year. 'We had dinner booked for seven, but a cat was knocked down by a car outside. I went to see if I could help. By the time I got back from the local vet I'd missed dinner. I heard Cam and Carrie talking in the suite…'

'They went to a suite together?'

'I'd booked the suite for Carrie and myself,' he said, explaining how he'd thought it was a little strange that they'd gone there instead of staying in the restaurant, or the bar. 'I was about to walk in but then I heard what they were saying.'

Sage touched his arm gently, her expression gently inquiring.

'It doesn't matter,' he said, his voice a low rumble. It really didn't matter; besides, there was no way he was telling her the exact conversation he'd overheard about his 'weird horsey stuff', and about how Carrie had dragged the wedding plans on because she didn't have the heart to break things off after his mum had died. How he'd then heard them kissing, convinced they were doing great at keeping their secret. 'I heard all the proof I needed that I was about to be given the boot, one way or another,' he said instead.

'What did you do?'

'Nothing, for a while.' He poked at the smouldering logs with a stick. 'I took myself down to the beach to clear my head. That's where Cam found me,' he said. 'I had it out with him, but Cam went on the defensive, telling me I hadn't been paying enough attention to Carrie, how she'd come to *him* and he'd fallen in love with her, and he hadn't been able to control it. I went and faced Carrie next,' he continued. 'She was angry…but more angry that I'd found out, I guess. Then she said she just didn't love me any more. That she'd tried to, but I wasn't the same person any more. Simple.'

'Seven years together—that doesn't sound simple.' Sage looked furious on his behalf all of a sudden, and while his own burning anger had turned to a mild, albeit perpetual simmer months ago her solidarity made her all the more attractive, all the more deserving of the truth that had driven him away from wanting another relationship.

'You lost your mother; how could you be the same person after that?'

'I'm fine,' he said quickly, even as the humiliation tore through him like a lightning bolt. It was true, he'd retreated, but Carrie hadn't been there for him either. 'It wouldn't have lasted anyway, me doing what I do, her doing what she does.'

He told her about Carrie being an actress, travelling city to city, party to rehearsal to late nights on the town with different casts and crews. His head and his heart had always been at the homestead, and now he was working towards making his mum's dreams a reality and making sure his dad never felt alone.

'You were just doing what you love, what you were born to do,' she reasoned kindly, and he ran his eyes over her lips, wondering why he was saying all this to her, while he could barely imagine Carrie's face any more.

'They're not like us,' he said. You're not a city girl, Sage, no more than I'm a city guy.'

'That is true.' She sighed. 'Cities have way too many people in them.'

'And you can't always see your friends when all those other lights are blinding you.'

'My friends?'

He pointed up at the sky and she smiled. 'Oh.'

The silence had shifted now into something comforting. 'I'd be lying if I said I didn't like it remote and quiet. Even though, tonight, I would have planned more of a dinner if I'd known we'd be out here *this* long.'

Sage was still smiling to herself. 'Sounds like a date, Ethan.'

Their eyes met and he knew they both felt this unspoken acknowledgment of the bond between them growing stronger, and tighter. It was a kind of quiet understanding he hadn't felt with anyone human in a long time. Only the horses.

'She'll never know what she's missing, you know,' Sage said next. Her tone was laced with so much sympathy and longing it drew the flames from their fire into his blood. He'd been cleansing himself of the pain of what Carrie and Cam had done to him just by talking about it with Sage and now he couldn't stand it any longer.

Ethan reached out, his hand brushing hers tentatively. She turned her palm upward, allowing their fingers to entwine as they'd done before, and his body responded in the exact same way, as though her touch was grounding any swirling emotions, pulling all his focus back to one place—her. He leaned closer, slowly, checking if she'd push him away.

The kiss was soft at first, exploratory, but it soon deepened as they both gave in. His heart thundered in his ears as he drank in the sweet taste of her mouth, and he let out a low moan that was swallowed up by the crackling of the fire. She felt so good in his arms. Sage's heart was racing against his chest as she pressed closer, her knees in the dirt as she straddled his lap, hips to his. Moving the way she was now… It turned him on so much he could hardly think. Their tongues danced together, teasing each other's mouths eagerly.

'Sage,' he heard himself groan, before she silenced him with another kiss. Her hands travelled up his chest and wrapped around his neck, holding him tightly as she deepened the kiss even more. Her breath was warm and ragged against his skin when she pulled away slightly.

'You taste like trail mix.' She smiled against his lips before sliding her tongue back into his mouth again. Their bodies swayed together with every passing second. He was lost in her now, they were lost in each other, and the rough bark digging into his backside as she writhed on top of him only seemed to add to the intensity of it all. It was almost as if nature itself were encouraging them onward and he groaned again with anticipation.

He lay back on the ground and brought her with him; they were wrapped up in each other, still kissing furiously. Every touch, every taste of Sage consumed him. The warmth of her breath against his skin, the sound of the crickets, the heat of the flames and the sensual urgency of her touch all made his blood rush around his body. He couldn't actually remember an encounter that could match this one. This woman was made from something different. He'd sensed it the first day they'd met. So what if this was a bad idea? It didn't have to be serious or complicated...just a fling. She didn't do relationships either—wasn't that what she'd said before?

'Ethan,' she moaned against his mouth, clearing his head again of everything but her.

Just enjoy this, he told himself, allowing his fingers to travel softly down around the curve of her waist, circling her navel. It was so hot when she shivered underneath him.

Sage's body was on fire. Ethan's tongue claimed her mouth over and over, dancing with hers as though he was trying to bury every thought that might be advising him against this, as though she was already his. His big, strong hands stroked her skin, sending shivers of butterflies round her belly and down her spine despite the fire. She gasped his name, pressing her eyes shut, losing herself again in the sweet sensations so her brain wouldn't get the better of her.

Stop worrying too much, she told herself. *Focus on the now a bit more, the things about this that are so good.* Right now, she felt more alive than she ever had.

'Ethan...' Her voice came as a breath against his mouth.

Just enjoy this, be in the moment, feel him...his fingers on your waist, curling around your hair, so soft, so gentle... God, I am shivering...

They'd rolled over and her back against the roughness of the ground felt deliciously wicked. The blankets and towels they'd set out were somewhere else entirely now, they'd pushed them away, and the root system dug into her flesh as if it wanted to keep her there too, with their vehicle. He lay on top of her, propped up on his elbows, arching into her, letting her move them both together.

Every tiny touch and caress and kiss drove her deeper into him. *So* connected, even without him inside her. This connection was everything, she thought to herself as her skin warmed at the friction, at his kisses.

'Do you want this?' Ethan whispered against her neck, his breath hot against her skin.

Yes, yes, yes, never stop, she said in her head, but any vocal response was lost the second his lips were on her throat, kissing softly, sensually up the column of her neck.

The trembling started again, from her toes this time, right up through her core. His kisses grew more focused, more passionate, harder against her mouth, harder and harder, and harder.

His thighs around her waist pinned her, till she felt herself biting back a laugh at the sheer absurdity of herself like this, being here with him, pinned between these legs, deep diving into his soul, feeling with a non-refutable certainty that he wanted her despite what he knew she'd done. His fingers traced the line of her shoulder blades, following the gentle curve to the small of her back, then back up again.

His hands on my body feel so good. I love the way this feels when he's pinning me down.

Her eyes raked his muscled chest as he lifted his arms and slid off his shirt, tossing it aside to refocus all his attention on her, arching beneath him, locked between his rock-hard thighs, like a trapped animal. She sat up beneath him, letting his hands slide down her body, catching her breath as he slowly unbuttoned her blouse while trailing more soft kisses along her exposed skin. She had never felt this way before, completely and utterly surrendered to the kind of desire that was consuming them both in this moment.

He pulled away then, his gaze still burning with intensity as he looked down at her, his eyes searching hers for any sign of hesitation or uncertainty.

I want this, she confirmed with her eyes, and her hands, and another urgent kiss that felt as if it were binding his soul to hers.

Seemingly satisfied with her silent consent, Ethan trailed his fingers down to the waistband of her shorts, and he inched it down slowly, savouring every bit of skin that was revealed with another stroke of his thumb, or a groan that made her feel like more of a woman than she'd felt since…since when? It was actually hard to remember. Sage moaned into his mouth as he moved back between her thighs. She tangled her fingers in his hair and arched against him, wanting even more, all of him.

How is this happening?

His eyes were dark, full of desire and longing, making her start to perspire in places she hadn't been too aware of for a while. The firmness of him against her thigh was insistent, and huge.

Oh, my.

She could feel every inch of him now, with only their underwear between them, and the trembling, the anticipation, was too much to take. She made to reach a hand into his boxer shorts, preparing herself.

Ethan stopped suddenly. Pure torment took over his face as he groaned in dismay and pulled away, sitting up on the ground beside her. Her heart lurched at her ribs as if a truck had slammed on the brakes a millisecond before hitting her.

'What's wrong?' she asked him breathlessly, sitting up beside him, suddenly self-conscious. She was more exposed than she'd ever been, and not just physically—her brain had just been somewhere else, dancing in a whole other universe, and they hadn't even had sex yet! If that was foreplay with Ethan, what the heck would the real thing be like?

Ethan looked at her with regret, making her insides swirl with dismay. 'We shouldn't do this, not right now,' he said with a growl.

'What?' Sage was confused, more than a little disappointed, and also… *What the heck?* 'Why not?'

Ethan shook his head. 'We don't have any protection,' he told her, tying back his hair that had come loose in their fit of passion.

'I have a coil,' she explained tightly, suddenly feeling silly. It was true, it helped calm her ridiculously heavy periods, but she hadn't expected to have to spell it out; she wouldn't be initiating sex if she wasn't protected against pregnancy, would she? Especially out here. He must know that.

'I'm sorry, I don't know what I was thinking. It's not you, OK? I just, I got carried away in the moment, but it's not fair to you.'

Sage nodded again. Not fair? This felt an awful lot like

rejection. In fact right now she didn't trust herself to even speak. Her soul could not retract that fast, even if his could. Maybe sensing her disappointment and confusion, he took her hand again and kissed her palm gently. 'It doesn't mean I don't want you, trust me,' he followed, tracing a finger across her cheek in a way that made her breath catch.

OK...so he seems like he's telling the truth.

'I want you, Sage, more than you know.'

That same tortured expression came over his face again, and her heartbeat felt like a thousand kicking kangaroos all over her body.

But?

He was wrestling with emotions he was not going to talk about. Was it too soon for him after Carrie? After seven years of being with the same woman? How could she not think that, after everything he'd just told her? But she wouldn't mention her name, not after everything they'd just done.

Ethan shook his head at himself, and she couldn't help it, she reached for him again and kissed him, and for a moment, as he responded, all traces of uncertainty disappeared as she melted into him again. All right, so they didn't have to have sex right now, it was probably smart not to, what with there being a snake and God only knew what else on the loose that might bite them...but when they were home again, somewhere safe, she was not going to allow any excuses. They'd started so they'd finish. Seriously, it had been so long since she'd felt this good, there was no way she'd deny herself an extension of this...so to speak.

Sage pulled back and turned over on the ground. Ethan draped a protective arm around her body, pulling one of the giant towels over them both. It felt like a shield against the night, and everything else she'd been carrying around that had been keeping her in this bubble of self-defence and denial. Why on earth had she been denying her own needs, her right as a woman to feel this way, even if it was only for a little while?

She had to remember what he'd been through with Carrie though, she thought, watching a shooting star scurry across the sky so fast she didn't even have time to mention it to him. It was hard to believe he'd just shared all those awful memories with her, and that he was here, holding her close, leaving her in no doubt that he wanted her. Maybe there was a side of Ethan only *she* had been able to coax back out into the open. Imagine that.

The thought made her smile as she snuggled into him as his little spoon. The warmth of his body curled around hers, his heart beating steadily against her back, the scent of the outdoors mingling with the lingering, delicious scent of his own personal sweat… This was enough for now. They lay there, wrapped up together, as Ethan's hand moved gently over her hair, his fingers trailing along her scalp in a soothing touch.

Ah, that feels so wonderful... I wish this night would last for ever.

'Sage, wake up!'

Ethan's voice broke into her dreams. Sage blinked her eyes open to the light of dawn creeping through the trees behind him. He'd already started scrambling for his clothes and she caught a brief glimpse of his impressive muscles before he yanked his jeans back on over his boxers. The sound of an engine hit her ears. How long had she been asleep?

'Oh, no!'

'Hurry,' he urged her, half laughing as he threw her shorts at her. The engine had been distant at first, but now it was growing steadily louder. Sage buttoned her top up wrong, and then hurriedly rebuttoned it, scanning the horizon.

'I think rescue is on its way,' he said, folding the towels up haphazardly and then much more carefully scattering the remains of their fire across the dirt. He'd left his shirt open and now she was fully awake, looking at the flexing of his six-pack in the early morning sunshine, all she wanted was to kiss him again.

CHAPTER TWELVE

THE UTE EMERGED over the ridge, and she recognised it instantly. 'Abigail!' Her friend's dusty old truck had seen more of the bush than most locals combined; she and the mayor knew these roads and everything off-grid around them for miles. The sight of her best friend coming for them should have brought unadulterated relief, she thought as Abigail and the mayor pulled to a stop and got out, but as Ethan shook the hand of the mayor, who quickly assessed the situation and started pulling tools out, Sage's emotions were a train wreck. She drew a deep breath, then another and another, closing her eyes, trying to find her equilibrium.

Abigail took her aside, her deep blue sundress swishing around her ankles, her giant sunglasses hiding her expressive eyes.

'Did you do this on purpose to get him alone out here?' her friend asked with a wicked smile.

'Of course I didn't,' she replied, a little too haughtily, watching Ethan sliding under the stuck ute with the bolt cutter. She rolled her eyes at herself, turning her back to him and facing Abigail head-on so her eyes wouldn't be forced to linger on Ethan's sexy body.

'I think I'm in big trouble,' she admitted with a sigh.

Abigail pushed her shoulder playfully. 'Have you gone and done the unthinkable, Miss Dawson?'

Sage cringed at the ground. 'Not quite. Almost.'

Abigail just grinned. 'I don't blame you,' she swooned. 'I mean, have you ever seen such a stunning specimen of a man?' Her gaze followed Ethan as he expertly manoeuvred the cutter around the tree's roots. 'I love my husband, but, really, possessing those arms and abs should be a criminal offence.'

Sage merely nodded. What could she say? Her head was still full of the warmth of his touch, the comforting rhythm of his heartbeat, everything they'd shared in the quiet darkness. Her heart ached at the thought of losing that connection with him so soon after she'd discovered it. Sage couldn't help the pang of loss overriding her thrill at having spent the night in his arms. Sex or no sex. The intimacy of it, all that shared vulnerability. It had felt so right, and so real. But now it seemed as though it was slipping away from her already. He'd said something like it wasn't fair to her. It wasn't fair of him to sleep with her? That had to mean he still had feelings for Carrie, didn't it?

'You're beating yourself up over this, I can tell,' Abigail observed quietly.

'He didn't want to, you know, he didn't want to have full sex with me,' she muttered, creasing her nose.

'Sage, look at where you are!' Abigail gestured around them as a tumbleweed floated past. 'It probably wasn't the time or the place. Maybe he's got some stuff going round in that big old handsome head of his, too. Am I right?'

She was pretty spot-on there, actually. 'Don't say anything, Abigail, keep it quiet, OK?' Before Abigail had a chance to say anything more, a holler from the guys told them the mission had been a success. The adventure was over; finally she could get home, and take a shower…with or without Ethan in it with her. Already she was flushed just thinking about what might happen next.

* * *

Sage and Ethan unloaded the gear from the back of the ute, while Abigail hurried inside to the bathroom and the mayor padded over to the stables to see Storm. 'I'm hoping I can saddle him up again, show the mayor how much better he's doing,' Ethan said as his hand brushed hers over the empty water canteen. The move sent a trail of sparks right up her arm and she gripped the canteen, its cool metal a stark contrast to the scorching morning sun. Or was she hotter because of Ethan, and last night? She took a deep breath, resting for a moment against the back of the truck.

'Everything OK?' Ethan's ocean-deep eyes searched her face. The intensity in them left her feeling more exposed than she had last night. She'd had to do a quick check in the ute to make sure she hadn't buttoned anything else up wrong—not that Abigail didn't know exactly what had gone on. Why had she told her what had happened…or what had almost happened? Now the mayor would know, and there were no secrets in Amber Creek, ever. The last thing she wanted was for poor Ethan to think everyone was talking about them.

'Of course I'm OK,' she said anyway, tucking a stray curl behind her ear. The memories of what they'd shared last night were clinging to her harder than the dust on her boots and he was throwing her thoughts off track the more he looked at her.

Ethan took the canteen from her hands gently, his gaze not leaving hers. 'You've been quiet since we left. If I crossed a line—'

'I wanted us both to cross a line, Ethan. I thought I made that perfectly clear.' The words were out before she could stop them. Again. She watched his eyes widen in amusement a second before they narrowed in speculation.

Oh, great, so now he thinks you're desperate for sex, Sage. How attractive, well done.

Ethan scratched at his chin. 'I'm sorry if I made things weird,' he said finally. 'I guess I got lost in my head after everything we were talking about and seeing you so...'

'So what?'

He growled to himself, low in his throat, and shook his head and she willed her hands not to reach out and touch him. 'I did think that maybe you're just not ready for that level of intimacy with someone else after—I mean, you were with her for years until pretty recently. And that's OK,' she lied.

'It's definitely not that,' he confirmed, and the incredulous look on his face made her cringe inwardly.

'Then, what is it?'

'You're making me kind of nervous here, Sage.'

Her heart lunged right for her throat again. She swung her head around. No one was watching or listening. Ethan's eyes were fixed on hers. 'You do the same to me,' she confided.

He sniffed, glanced sideways. 'The things I told you, I've never told anyone other than my sister.'

'Well, that makes two of us, only in my case it was Abigail,' she said.

Oh, Lord... Sage swallowed against the tightening of her throat as it threatened to choke her. He just kept looking at her as if he were scanning her brain, his jaw moving side to side as if he were chewing on his next words. Was the fact that she made him nervous a good thing, or a bad thing?

When he spoke, his voice was laced with a kind of knowing that sent shivers along her arms and between her thighs. 'I don't think we had a choice anyway, back there. What happened between us was always going to happen.'

Gosh, it was hot already. Sage reached for the bundle of

towels to stop her hands from touching him again. The fabric unfurled slightly in her grasp. In an instant, the smile fell from her face. 'Yeow! What was that?'

Snatching her hand away, she sprang back from the ute, clutching her arm against her chest.

'What happened?' Ethan asked, his eyes flooded with concern.

'Something sharp, I don't know…' Her wrist was turning red already and the markings sent her blood cold. Two tiny punctuations, set close together. Then she saw it; a flicker of black and red slithering out from the folds of the towel she'd just dropped to the ground.

'Snake!' she cried out, stumbling backwards again. Her heart pounded against her ribs as if it wanted to run even further, but she sank to her knees in shock. 'It got me.'

Oh, no...no, no, no! This isn't happening.

Ethan leapt over the snake as it writhed on the ground as though it wasn't sure what was going on either, and he was at her side in a heartbeat, his hands examining her wrist with urgency. 'We need to get you into the clinic—now.'

Too late. A flash of pain seared her arm. The red-bellied black snake's poison was already doing its job, working its way into her system. Soon it would paralyse her. She watched, horrified as the creature slithered away and vanished into the brush. Shock morphed into ice-cold fear as reality sank in. It was the same snake that had watched her pee last night; it must have sneaked past their warm fire and up into the stationary ute while they were sleeping. And now it had sunk its fangs into her.

'Can you walk?' Ethan asked, his brows knitted with concern.

'Y-yes,' Sage stammered, fighting the dizziness that was threatening to consume her already. Could she? She wasn't sure. They had to move fast. The world was already swaying around her.

Seeing her rapid deterioration, Ethan scooped her up into his arms as if she weighed no more than a new-born foal and stepped up the pace. Cradled against his chest, she felt herself shrinking as somewhere in her periphery she saw the mayor sprinting towards them. Everything was moving in slow motion. Sage gritted her teeth against the pain, willing herself to stay conscious.

Do not pass out, Sage, do not pass out.

'Stay with me, Sage,' Ethan urged as if he could read her mind, and she held onto his voice like an anchor, fighting for something to make sense in the chaos of her thoughts.

That stupid snake...what did it want with me? Why did it do this? Oh...everything's so floaty...

'Sage, you're fine,' he stated with a confidence she couldn't quite believe. She was clutched tightly against his chest for all the wrong reasons, and a part of her mind that felt as though it existed outside herself replayed the warmth of him last night, as she'd snuggled into the protective circle of his arms.

It would be worth it, if she died like this, she thought groggily; at least she would go knowing nights like that could happen to her. And he'd just admitted he still wanted her... that he'd been processing everything, how nervous she made him feel because...because why? Had he actually given her a reason?

They burst through the door of the clinic. Abigail was on the way out from the bathroom. The mayor was right behind them now and somewhere she heard Ellie, back from sick leave, hurrying a customer out with their animal patient. She vaguely heard Ethan barking out orders, his years of experience evident even to her, in her state, in the way he took charge.

'Antivenom, now!' he commanded, sweeping whatever was on the long metal table to the floor with one hand and laying her down gently. It was hard to force herself to focus on him, but he squeezed her hand and she clung to him like a lifeline, her body trembling with shock and pain. Searing pain. It was snaking from her arm to her lungs, and her blood, it was on fire. How was this happening? One moment everything had been fine, and the next, she was here on her own cold, hard operating table, fighting for her life.

'Ethan,' Sage said hoarsely as her eyes focused in and out on the vial of antivenom he now had in his hand. Abigail clutched her other hand, while the mayor hovered behind on his phone. Who was he talking to? Their childminder?

It doesn't matter, Sage. Am I really dying?

'You're gonna be OK, my darling, just hold on.'

Ethan took her arm, which she couldn't even really feel at this point. He injected the serum and Sage winced, waiting for another sharp sting that never came. From somewhere that might have even been from outside herself again she saw Abigail's eyes flash to Ethan, then back to her, and she had the distinct impression one of them had just said something she'd do well to remember. But she was woozy…so woozy…

He mumbled something and soon she was fluttering in and out of a dreamy sleep. Moments later, or maybe it was an hour, it was hard to tell, she could feel the effects of the antidote taking hold. The world around her began to sharpen into focus again, and she realised with a start that Ethan was still holding her hand, his piercing narrowed eyes searching her face for any sign of distress.

Gosh, you're so handsome.

'Is she going to be all right?' Abigail's voice was laced with genuine worry beside her.

'I won't let anything happen to her,' Ethan replied with a conviction that made Sage's heart thud erratically all over again. It wasn't just the snake venom causing her pulse to race now. What was it she should be remembering? She tried to sit up on the table, causing a makeshift pillow under her head to fall to the floor. This was so embarrassing.

'Easy, Sage,' Ethan ordered, supporting her weight suddenly and urging her back down with an arm that felt like an iron band around her waist. Her senses slowly righted themselves, and she felt the warmth of his breath against her temple, real and intimate.

'Thank you,' she whispered into his eyes. Her voice was barely above a whisper. Her head was light, a residual venom-induced haze clouding her perception. But even through the fog, the expression on her best friend's face was clear as day. Abigail and Ellie had both seen Ethan's unguarded emotions out on show, his raw concern totally stripped of any professional facade. And so had she.

'We should get her to her cabin,' Ellie said just as Mrs Dalloway, one of their regular clients, walked in with a cat basket.

'I'll take her,' Abigail and Ethan said at the same time. Then Abigail relented, placed a soft hand to her cheek. 'Fine, you're stronger than me, Ethan. You can carry her.'

Embarrassment flooded her veins like a new serum. 'Thank you, Ethan, really, but…' She paused in her efforts to get up again, swallowing hard against a tidal wave of nausea. 'You need to be out there, helping with Storm. I'll be fine.'

'I'll see to Storm later.' His eyes were brimming with an emotion she couldn't quite name. Concern, yes—but there was something more now, something deeper.

'If you're sure,' she said with a feeble smile.

Ellie ushered a bewildered Mrs Dalloway and her cat through to the other room, insisting *she* would help with the patients and that the mayor could come back tomorrow. The short journey to Sage's quarters behind the clinic was a blur. All Sage could register was the rhythm of Ethan's movements and the sound of his voice reassuring her.

'Here we go, this is better than last night's cold, hard ground,' he said as he located her bedroom, and gently laid her down on her bed. The cool pale-blue walls and bedsheets were a small comfort against the heat that was radiating from her skin. She still hadn't showered. This was a nightmare… Was her bedroom tidy? Had she put her laundry away or were her clean knickers still in a pile on the armchair? Was any of this suitable for a guest to see? It wasn't exactly how she had envisioned bringing Ethan here, or why.

'Please, Ethan, the others…' Sage began, her voice trailing off as another wave of dizziness hit her.

'All right,' Ethan conceded, though his blue eyes darkened with worry. 'I'll check back in with you really soon.' He put her phone down on the dresser. 'Call if you need anything.'

'Will do,' she managed to say, though the words felt like stones in her mouth. Maybe the snake bite had been fate stepping in, telling her not to get ahead of herself, not to sleep with him the moment he was ready, not to make whatever this was between them into something that would destroy her once it ended and he went home.

Ethan stood up, hesitating for a moment as if torn between duty and desire. He looked as if he was about to say something, but decided not to. Then, with one final, lingering look from the doorway, he left, closing the door quietly behind him.

Alone now, Sage closed her eyes, trying to steady her

breathing. Then she opened them and checked her chair for the laundry pile. Small blessings, she had at least put her knickers away. But Ethan's big, steady presence in her humble, small home still lingered like a tangible thing, wrapping around her in the quiet.

Now that the drama was over, she had had time to consider other things. *Ethan.* What was blossoming between them was real, wasn't it? Everyone had seen it now. He hadn't said it in so many words, except for when he'd called her darling… yes, that was it, that was what she'd forgotten! He'd called her darling, in front of everyone. Not Doctor, not even just Sage. *My darling.* Did that mean Ethan truly cared about her? She already cared about him, and that was even scarier than the thought of that snake, still out there somewhere, lying in wait for its next target.

CHAPTER THIRTEEN

ETHAN'S FINGERS TRACED the coarse hair of Storm's mane. The animal was standing calm and collected beneath his touch in the early hours and he'd watched the dawn break like this, the air cool and the paddock quiet, save for the occasional snort from the horses. His eyes locked with Storm's, a silent conversation flowing between them. Trust was not given freely in this world, he mused, especially not by an animal with a past shadowed by mistreatment like he suspected this one had dealt with. The more he worked with Storm, the more he figured the guy the mayor had bought him from had not been completely honest about his history. But Ethan sensed another definite breakthrough. They'd been coming more frequently. He and Billy had even managed to saddle him the other day, though Storm hadn't liked that much and had taken off around the paddock pretty quickly afterwards, snorting angry little snorts from his nostrils while the other horses looked on in amusement.

Ethan's eyes moved over Storm's back to Sage's quarters, just visible beyond the tree line. Her small cabin wasn't much but she'd made it her home and he'd been to visit her over the last few days, while she'd been resting. He'd forbidden her to work, as had Ellie, and as such he'd taken on more responsibilities around the place. The grass had even been mown, the irrigation system was well under way, and a new surprise would be arriving soon that he was pretty excited to share with her. He didn't mind the work, but the way he cared about it all with ever-increasing depth and passion was starting to unsettle him. He was doing it for Sage. It was all for her, and that indicated that he was starting to like her more than even he thought he did. But he had been down this road before and it scared the living daylights out of him.

'We can't help our feelings, though, can we, boy?' he said to Storm, who grunted indifferently, making him smile. He wanted that woman so badly. He'd wanted her that night out in the bush, but seeing her so vulnerable, after letting himself be so vulnerable in front of her, had pushed a barrage of what ifs into his brain that no amount of kissing or burying himself inside her would ever diminish. She was making him extremely nervous, and that was the truth. Terrified, in fact. This was a dangerous road to go down, but he couldn't deny that he wanted to, even more now.

'Morning,' a voice called out, pulling Ethan from his constant thoughts about Sage. She was walking towards him in the flesh, her footing steady but cautious. The vibrant green of her eyes seemed muted in the early morning light. It was a testament both to the ordeal she'd been through with that damn snake bite, dulling her light in general and keeping her laid up for the last few days, and to how he made her feel, which was clearly equally nervous. They wanted each other. And they were going to have each other.

And then he was going to miss her for a very, very long time, because, even if she came to Queensland for a visit and loved it, this was her home. After everything she'd lost, she'd bravely built a new life here with her practice and her small staff, the local community, and her found family—Abigail, the mayor and their children—and she wouldn't want to give it up any more than Carrie had wanted to give up her life for him. Grasping for a future with Sage would probably end the same way as *that* had, with him feeling less than what she really wanted or needed, and her chasing after something better.

'Hey,' he replied, watching her come closer. 'How are you feeling?'

'Better, thanks.' She stopped at the fence, leaning against it. 'I've been going stir-crazy in that bedroom.'

'Can't keep a good vet down, huh?' He smiled, but he could hear the undercurrent of concern in his own voice, even as he fought the sudden uncharacteristic urge to make an ungentlemanly quip about what he could do to make her bedroom more exciting.

Not the time, not the place.

Sage's snake-bite incident had been drifting into his mind unasked-for ever since; the way her body had gone limp in his arms, her face ashen, the terror that had gripped his heart like an iron vice. Just seeing her like that had been hell. Pure torture. He was surprised his mind hadn't gone completely blank, that he'd managed to somehow stay calm and administer the antivenom, but in that crystallised moment he'd understood the depth of his feelings for her. The revelation was still churning around in his mind, as worrying as it was exhilarating.

'Those flowers you brought me, they're beautiful, Ethan. And the vinyl records…' She trailed off, her gaze flicking back to him. 'I didn't realise you knew I liked vintage jazz.'

'Your record collection gave you away,' he confessed, feeling his cheeks colour just slightly as he caught the hint of a smile on her lips. 'I figured you could use some company, even if it was just more Coltrane and Fitzgerald.'

'Just some of the most influential voices of their era,'

she replied. 'Very thoughtful.' Her voice came out slightly strained, her eyes narrowed at the floor for a beat, as though she was struggling with the meaning of his gifts, as he was, he supposed. He'd gone to the tiny cafe in town, which doubled as a record shop, and the guy in there had known Sage, of course; he'd shown him what she didn't already have in her collection.

Ethan's hands stilled on Storm's mane, the weight of his thoughts growing heavy as haybales on his shoulders. He hadn't kissed her since their rescue from the dingo adventure. The urge had almost overwhelmed him, especially when he'd come by with the gifts, rearranged her pillows, made her tea.

They'd been pretty safe while she'd recovered. Her weakness and vulnerability had been every excuse not to lean in and pick up where they'd left off, but they were still perilously close to the edge. Whatever was growing between him and Sage was something that would not just go away, he knew it, as certain about that as he was about the trust growing in Storm's eyes. Even as he warned himself not to pursue it.

'Thank you, for everything you've done around here too. It means a lot to all of us,' Sage said now, breaking the quiet tension.

Longing and reminiscence tormented his senses as he nodded and pulled his eyes from her legs in those jean shorts—legs he remembered wrapped around him on a night that was probably best left forgotten. She was so near now, he could hear the soft rustle of her shirt against her skin as she moved. How could he forget how her shirt had come off that night, how she'd revealed herself so willingly? Sage was beautiful, inside and out. He cleared his throat.

'Any time,' he replied, before turning to study Storm's eyes. The horse's ears flicked back suddenly as Sage inched closer.

The ghosts of this horse's old fears were still there. He could totally relate, he thought ruefully.

'You can tell, can't you?' Sage asked, stepping backwards again, her voice low and steady beside him. 'You know what's wrong with him.'

'Every time I touch him. It's like he's decided to let me in,' Ethan said, his fingers tracing a faint line along the horse's flank as he met her eyes. They were standing close enough to feel the warmth of each other's bodies without touching, and he willed himself not to move even closer or he'd have to give in and make love to her right here. 'He's been traumatised by humans. It's in the way he flinches at sudden movements, how his eyes constantly dart around searching for an escape.'

Ethan caught a glimpse of pride on her face as she looked at him, which was not how she'd looked at him before, when she'd clearly been wishing he'd never shown up at all. She ran a hand over Storm's soft neck. 'Is there anything we can do to help him recover fully?' Her question held hope, but the shadows beneath her green eyes told Ethan she understood their limitations. 'Or will he always be like this?'

'Time and patience,' he murmured. 'He's getting better. Trust doesn't come easy, not when it's obviously been shattered before.'

'Like with some people we know,' Sage agreed, and Ethan felt her words like a gentle accusation. He knew she was talking about him. Or maybe both of them?

'Sage, listen—' he started, stepping around the horse. But the moment was interrupted by a call from his dad. Oh, man. Dad had the kids and Jacqueline over. He quickly explained to Sage how Kara and Jayson were collecting honey and probably wanted to show him on a video call, and she nodded encouragingly, though he didn't miss the flash of despondency in her eyes as he spoke to his family, *oohing* and *aahing* over their finds, pretending he'd never seen any of it before, to amuse the kids. No sooner had he hung up than the sharp ring of the clinic's emergency bell sounded out. Without another word, both of them broke into a run.

Ellie was still caught up with their first patient in the treatment room, and Ethan recognised the kindly Barbara from the guest house, or Babs as everyone in Amber Creek called her, standing over her terrier. The dog lay whimpering on the examination table. His paw was swollen, and a thin line of blood seeped worryingly through his fur as Sage hurried to pull a white coat over her shirt and shorts.

'Marley jumped off the porch again,' Babs explained as Ethan pulled on his own coat. The woman who had been so kind to him at the guest house was wringing her hands, her usually warm face etched with worry.

'Let's check for fractures,' Sage directed. Her professional demeanour had kicked in again, full throttle. She went for the X-ray machine as Ethan moved to calm Babs.

'Marley's strong, Babs. We're going to take good care of him,' Ethan assured her, his hand firm on her shoulder. He didn't miss the look on Sage's face as she looked up; was that an expression of slight despondency on her face, the same as he'd seen outside? No time to think about it now.

Ethan helped Sage manoeuvre the terrier onto the radiography table. The machine hummed to life, casting a pale blue light over Marley's form as they positioned him gently. Ethan watched the rhythmic rise and fall of Sage's chest as she leaned over the operating table, her focus unwavering. The marks on her wrist were uncovered, healing well just as she was, but the sight of them only reminded him of how it had felt when she'd been lying so weak in his arms. She operated the controls while Ethan held the dog still, his hands firm yet comforting against the terrier's quivering body. So small and defenceless…as Sage had been that night, when he'd rushed her into the clinic after the snake had got its fangs into her.

'Good boy, Marley,' Sage whispered now, eyeing the animal as the X-ray did its silent work. Sage couldn't stand to see any animal in pain, especially dogs. It was like this for her every time, he imagined. And it would be after he was back home with Dad, and the bees, and his own horses.

The image soon appeared on the screen, revealing a minor fracture. Sage discussed the treatment plan with Babs, explaining the need for a cast and pain management. Ethan prepared the syringe with expert precision, his movements conveying the quiet confidence he knew would help ease Babs' distress.

'Will he be okay to walk on it?' Babs asked, her voice concerned.

'Absolutely,' he answered, before Sage narrowed her eyes slightly and continued before he could.

'But he'll have to take it easy for a few weeks. No more jumping up, or chasing sheep.'

As Sage applied the cast, Ethan observed the gentle way her fingers smoothed the edges, and how she spoke softly to Marley, reassuring the animal with every touch. Even so, she was annoyed about something now. It was plain to him, even if Babs wasn't picking up on it. Was she starting to resent him again, for befriending all her clients? he wondered suddenly. Amber Creek was so small, of course he'd got to know a lot of people here, and he'd showcased methods that had worked as well as hers, if not better sometimes. It didn't mean he was trying to take over.

'Thank you, both of you,' Babs said, relief flooding her features as she finally scooped Marley into her arms, the newly applied cast a stark white against his ruffled brown fur.

'Any time, Babs,' Ethan said, offering her a smile that he hoped had reached his eyes. When she left with Marley cradled close against her chest, he turned to find Sage watching him, a set of unspoken grievances lingering between them.

'You called her Babs,' she said, perching on the edge of the desk, pulling off her gloves slowly finger by finger.

'That's what everyone calls her,' he reasoned. What was the problem?

'Well, Babs loves you. Everyone knows you round here now,' she said. 'They all know you're leaving again soon, though. Once Storm is better. Which he is...he's almost better.'

He felt his eyebrows knit together. 'So *that's* what this is about,' he said sharply. 'Me leaving.'

'Well, you will be, won't you?' she said, standing up and tossing her gloves into the bin a little too hard. He heard her voice crack. The tension hummed between them like a charged circuit. 'Storm is like a different animal already.'

She crossed to the sink and turned the tap on full, as if she was trying to drown out the noise in her head. Ethan watched as the water cascaded over Sage's hands, the droplets splashing against the stainless steel. He knew she was struggling, her emotions churning beneath the surface as his had been for days. He stepped forward, the linoleum floor creaking quietly beneath his boots. With each step, he felt his heart beat louder in his chest, till he was right behind her. He reached out and turned off the tap, silencing the rushing water.

'Sage,' he said gently. Slowly she turned in his arms and looked up at him. Her green eyes held a mix of vulnerability and sadness that tore at his heart. Without hesitating, he closed the distance left between them and gently cupped her face in his hands. To his surprise she turned her head away, even though her lips trembled at his touch.

'No. This has to stop,' she said, her voice weak and shaky. She drew a hand across her mouth, as if she was intent on stopping him from even so much as looking at her lips.

'We didn't do anything,' he replied, feeling the weight of his unvoiced confession heavy on his tongue. God, he wanted her so badly, even if it was only one time. One delicious, thrilling, beautiful time. The guilt over these exact thoughts didn't sit well—she would never go for a one-time thing, and nor should she be expected to. But he had stopped what they'd started before this. And yes, he had then gone on to buy her gifts, sat at her side, folded her clean towels, ordered her a new coffee machine…which still had not arrived. No wonder she was as confused as he was.

'Yes, we *did* do something,' she said, running her fingers over her lips, meeting his eyes. 'It's not just about sex to me, Ethan. You've made me feel things I haven't felt before…for anyone.'

She screwed up her nose then, and stepped out from between his arms, moving to the other side of the room. 'You bought me books, and flowers…'

'OK, well, sorry?' This was confusing as hell. And ridiculous. He needed to confront this, whatever 'this' was between them. He couldn't leave with regrets, with what ifs haunting him across the miles.

'I don't know what's going on either,' he admitted, crossing to her again. She inched against the closed door, pressing her back to it, and he placed his hand gently on her arm, feeling the warmth of her skin beneath his fingertips, even through her lab coat.

'You know what you do to me—you've seen it. But I don't want to hurt you,' he said.

Which was true, even though the voice in his head was screaming, *Liar! It's you who doesn't want to get hurt.*

'I'm not staying here. I can't—my life is in Queensland,' he heard himself say anyway. Maybe it *was* too soon after Carrie to trust someone else with his heart.

'And mine is here,' she said sadly, so close to his mouth he could feel the heat of her breath on his lips. 'So I guess that's that. It goes no further, Ethan.'

He studied her mouth in silence. Stuff that. It had nothing to do with Carrie being the last woman he'd been intimate with. It had everything to do with falling for Sage, plunging him straight back into a deep, dark funk that he'd only just climbed out of. *Coward.* Fear should not, and would not, dictate his choices any more.

Ethan closed the remaining distance between them, this time with an urgency that made her gasp as he finally captured her pink lips with his own. Their breathing grew heavier as they lost themselves. Moving one hand to his neck, Sage trailed it down to his chest as their tongues danced, no doubt feeling the pounding of his heart beneath his skin. Tugging her coat undone with one swipe, he pressed his body against hers, pinning her to the door with a new urgency that sprang from nowhere.

Sage folded against him in surrender, moaning softly into his mouth. Her breath hitched with anticipation and he leaned into the kiss, cupping her backside, squeezing it gently, then possessively. Her kisses and lips rained over his face, exploring every inch, and his hands roamed to her thighs, pushing them further apart as he grasped at her shorts, pulling them gently but firmly down to allow him access…

A knock on the door behind them made him shudder. Sage sprang out from under him, pulled up her shorts, and started buttoning up her coat. 'Coming!' she called, sounding delightfully flustered.

He felt himself grin. 'Really? I wasn't even close,' he whispered. She pretended to slap him, casting her eyes to the bulge in his jeans. He caught her hand and pressed his mouth to hers again hard, and she laughed under his kisses before letting her tongue dance seductively around his once more.

'I have to go,' she whispered frantically, pressing both palms flat to his chest. 'You should get back outside to Storm. The mayor will be here again soon.'

She made to open the door, first smoothing down strands of her hair that had fallen from her ponytail in their passion.

'Hey, Sage,' Ethan called after her, his heart hammering against his ribs with the adrenaline. Sage turned, a question in her green eyes as she touched a finger to her lips. There was no stopping this thing now, judging by the hope that flickered in her gaze, and the way he heard his own voice soften whenever he spoke her name. He was gone. A lost cause.

'Come riding with me, this evening,' he said. 'There's a place I found the other day I want to show you.'

He watched her expression shift through surprise, joy, and something akin to fear, before she took a deep breath. 'Sure, Ethan,' she answered, her smile finally reaching her eyes. 'Why not?'

CHAPTER FOURTEEN

THEY GALLOPED IN SILENCE, apart from the thundering hooves that broke the stillness of the night, sending up mini dust clouds that threw Ethan into a sandy blur ahead of her. Sage couldn't help grinning as the world was reduced to the wind's rush in her ears, and the magnetic pull of this incredible man riding beside her. She tightened her grip around the reins as her horse picked up speed, racing alongside Ethan on Karma.

The pale glow of the moon bathed the land around them in a silver sheen, turning the rugged landscape into an ethereal dreamscape that felt all the more surreal because she knew, at the end of this, that she would be making love to Ethan, if they still had the energy after last night. They'd shut themselves into her cabin, listening to the rain again, and he'd reached for her, pulling her closer as the jazz filled the air in her tiny living room, his hands moving with the gentleness of someone who was treating a wild animal with care. His touch still made her shiver, sending goosebumps spreading across her skin. She could feel the desire for him coursing through her veins every time, as if she could never get enough.

Night-time rides had become their unspoken ritual for the past couple of weeks, even in the recent rains. It could have been something to do with being out with him in particular, but Sage felt that the wild pulse of the land had started to call her: *Don't work so hard, get out of your head, come and be happy!*

The way he looked at her, the softening of those guarded blue eyes, told her she had helped take a battering ram to some of the walls he'd built around himself, and he had definitely brought something else out in her.

The part of her that had always been so captivated by nature and these beautiful, rugged landscapes had been shaken fully awake. There were new reasons to breathe now, more space in her tired lungs to sync with her surroundings, and Ethan Matthews. Less time to tie herself to the past, and fewer reasons to feel trapped in the cage she'd locked herself into all this time. In Ethan's arms she was discovering parts of herself she hadn't even known existed.

'Where are we going?' she called to him now.

'You'll see. If you can keep up.'

Sometimes she could feel her heart swelling, as though it were learning how to adjust to being so full after so long. She caught another glimpse of Ethan's profile, determined as they started to race. When the moonlight hit him just right she could have sworn he was from another planet. Oh, Lord, this was completely crazy. This big, huge, all-consuming feeling for him had sprouted from a tiny seed of reluctant admiration into something she couldn't even define. There weren't enough words to express how she felt.

'Too slow!' he teased her now, kicking his heels to Karma and speeding on ahead, even faster towards the horizon, daring her to follow. Their first ride, he'd taken her to a waterfall she'd known about for a while, but she'd pretended she'd never seen it before. He'd known she was pretending, of course. So the next night, she'd shown him a special place she'd known he wouldn't have seen: a circle of earth-red rocks still boasting aboriginal art in red and black markings. After each escapade they would have sex…a lot of sex, everywhere, anywhere. It had started out as just sex anyway. The last couple of nights had definitely felt more as if they were making love.

The word felt so strange, even as it grew in her own head. Love. It was more like a kaleidoscope, constantly changing colours and patterns in her mind, leading her thoughts down different paths she hadn't dared to travel in a long time. It was overwhelming, but the world seemed different now, as if with Ethan at her side in work, and pleasure—a lot of pleasure—she was seeing everything through a different lens. Colours were heightened and vivid, details were clearer, her patients seemed to smile more around her because she was smiling more at them, and everything was tinged with a sense of wonder and magic.

With Ethan, she felt truly seen, and not just for the compassionate veterinarian she had come to be known as in Amber Creek's small community. He made her feel as if she could do anything. This profound connection they seemed to share had almost stitched the fragmented pieces of her heart back together. If only she could summon the courage to tell him she wanted him to stay.

If she said that, she might ruin it all, she thought now with a stab of fear, watching his broad shoulders as he took the lead again, the way the trees seemed to bend in the wind to welcome him. She would probably hear, 'I can't stay,' or, 'Don't talk about that now, let's just enjoy the moment,' and those words would cement the end of the spell for good. Obviously, this was too perfect to last. She knew he'd have to go back to Queensland. It was just something she was trying not to think about right now.

The fear of people disappearing without notice from her

life had kept her life pretty small. Yes, she'd been successful with her career, but life had to be about more than making money; what was it for if you couldn't share any of it? She'd blocked out her need for companionship, stubbed it out like a cigarette by keeping herself busy, but the loneliness and emptiness had a habit of sneaking up on her anyway. Her empty home had echoed with it, till now. Now her humble cabin at the back of the clinic was filled with laughter and all the secrets she and Ethan shared in the dark.

Because of it, and because of him, she had even found the courage to reach out to Bryce. Wouldn't it be good to get some closure after all this time, confirmation that Ethan was right—that he'd left so suddenly because of some discrepancy or altercation over outstanding pay, or purely just because he wasn't into her, instead of because he'd taken offence over all those animals that had perished because she hadn't put the fire out in time?

'Woah!' Ethan's deep booming voice broke through her thoughts. They'd ridden to where the sands met the rainforest, but she couldn't quite figure out where they were exactly. Good thing she trusted Ethan, although since the last time they'd found themselves stuck somewhere for the night she had been careful to bring a spare two-way radio, just in case.

'We're here,' he announced as the horses slowed without another word from either of them. Sage realised her heart was pounding from more than just the exhilarating ride. In awe, she drank in the sight before her. The relatively hidden glade seemed to pulse with an alien glow under the moon. A ribbon of water reflected its beams, creating a desert oasis that felt as though it had been created just for them.

'I've never seen this place,' she said in wonder, following

him forwards on her horse. It was as if they'd stumbled upon a secret that had somehow been kept for centuries.

'Welcome to Star Creek,' Ethan announced, his voice brimming with pride as he slid off Karma with ease. 'I found it when I was tracking that herd of wild horses the other day.'

Sage dismounted, her legs shaky not just from the ride but also from the pure beauty of the place. How was it possible she had never seen this before?

'I've never even heard of Star Creek,' she confessed as they both moved to tie up their horses, giving them a rest and a chance to drink from the creek. He looped his arms around her and pulled her close, dropping a soft kiss to her forehead that still sent sparks flying from her head down to her feet.

'That's because I named it myself. I think the recent rains must have helped it form,' he said. And she kissed him again because she could, and because, of course, this hot wizard had managed to find something out here in the nothingness that she'd never seen before. Together, they explored along the bank of the creek, their footsteps quiet on the soft earth. The air was alive with the sound of crickets and cicadas, and other nocturnal creatures. The serenade to the night was a living pulse, and her heartbeat matched its thrum as Ethan's hand found hers, their fingers intertwining naturally.

They settled near the edge of the oasis and Ethan pulled a bottle from his saddlebag. It was wine, he told her, aged and apparently special, saved for a moment such as this. 'Where did you get it?' she asked.

'Babs brought it over, to thank us for looking after her dog. You were with another patient so I thought I'd surprise you somewhere special.'

It felt as though she was the only woman in the entire world he'd ever looked at like this. Then he leaned down and drew her into a kiss that made her insides fill with balloons that threatened to float her up into the sky. He uncorked the bottle with a flourish and whipped out two glasses that he'd carefully wrapped in towels, handing her one so she could take the first sip. The wine was rich and full bodied, and as the taste of it filled her mouth, she let her head rest softly on his shoulder, looking up at the stars. This was perfection. Having him here with her was perfection. Maybe she should risk it and ask him about his plans after this—ask him to stay longer? Or would that seem too needy? Maybe she should just relax and leave it to fate and the stars, and see what unfolded naturally?

'Look at that,' he said, pointing upwards, and she smiled as she caught the particularly bright star he meant, twinkling above them. 'That one seems new to me, what do you think?'

'It could be a UFO,' she teased.

He smirked. 'Take me to your leader.'

'Let's name it anyway,' Sage said, caught up in the moment. There were lots of them like this, filled with a kind of child-like excitement that Abigail declared was disgusting, even though she said it with the utmost affection. They suggested different names for the star as Ethan's fingers trailed softly along the back of her neck in slow movements that made her shiver with desire. They kissed for a long time before refocusing on the star.

'I want to call it Hope,' she said after a while.

'Hope,' Ethan echoed, his thumb brushing over her knuckles. 'I like that.'

'It used to be a pretty alien feeling to me,' she added with a sigh. There was no way she was going to tell him, but she really *hoped* he wouldn't decide he'd had enough of her company once Storm was fully recovered. She was filled with so much hope she was bursting with it some days, but somehow she couldn't bring herself to put him on the spot and ask him what this was exactly. What *were* they? It felt like more than just a fling, more real than anything she'd ever experienced in her whole life. It was unprecedented and had sprung up from nowhere and now that it was here, she couldn't imagine living without it. No one had ever made her feel like this, as if she could face anything.

With the taste of the wine lingering on her lips, she felt the confession bubbling inside her. It was no good, she couldn't keep it from him. 'I reached out to Bryce the other day,' she said finally, her words coming out slowly as she gathered up the courage.

'Bryce?' Ethan's hand stiffened around hers. Suddenly his expression turned impenetrable.

'I felt I needed to know why he really left the sanctuary, why he left…me. To give me some closure.' She watched him carefully, searching for any sign of understanding in his deep blue eyes.

Ethan released her hand and looped his arms around his knees, picking up his wine glass again and twirling the liquid in it around. 'And did he reply?' he asked neutrally, his voice level but distant. He was acting as though he'd retreated behind a wall all of a sudden.

'Not yet,' she admitted, a twinge of regret making her shuffle her boots. Did he think she was a bit silly for doing this, for reaching back into the past like this, looking for an affirmation that probably wouldn't even come? The silence stretched between them, her unspoken thoughts turning into heavy weights.

'Closure is important,' he said quietly, though his eyes didn't meet hers. 'Unless you want him back, of course.'

What? Sage snorted in indignation. 'Why would I want him back? That was just a fling. It was nothing like what we have…'

Ethan tightened his lips.

Oh, no. Why did I say that?

She heard him release a deep breath through his nose as he studied the water, as if he couldn't risk meeting her eyes now. The words had just fallen out of her, she'd blurted them at him before she'd even had a chance to rein them in. Great, now she'd gone and admitted how obsessed she was with him, that she thought being with him was more than a fling, when he'd never mentioned it being anything at all.

'Do you need him to remind you that what happened to your family and the bushland around your home wasn't your fault, or are you ever going to start believing that for yourself?' he cut in quickly.

What? Sage's heart dropped into her boots. Why was he changing the subject away from him, and them?

'Because I've been telling you that for weeks,' he continued, 'and I'm sure Abigail has reminded you of it too. I would hope that, even if I'm not here, you'll at least remember that, Sage.'

Even if I'm not here... OK, then. Now she knew.

She chewed on her lip, rocking on the spot as she hugged her knees. The words sounded so final, like a message he'd been waiting to clarify at the first chance he got. The silence grew louder and louder, until it rang in her ears and made her head hurt.

'I don't know what I want Bryce to say,' she said finally, realising it was true. She'd found the confidence to reach out, but she supposed it really didn't matter what Bryce said or did in response. His opinions of her had ceased to matter a long time ago. It was herself she'd always had issues with; her crippling fear of people entering her life and then leaving her again with nothing but ashes.

Ethan drank his wine quietly, and she wanted so badly to ask him what was on his mind, to ask if this was a fling or if it *could* possibly be more, if they both found the courage. But no…the mood was totally ruined now. He looked as if a storm was going on between his temples. Like Bryce, he *was* going to leave her. It was probably what he'd been thinking ever since they'd started whatever this was: that they'd just have sex and keep each other warm at night until he finished the job with Storm.

He'd never deceived her; he didn't do relationships. He'd told her that himself. He also had to go home; he'd warned her about that, too. He had a successful, thriving equine centre on prime, lush land, a million memories of his mother, and a father who still counted on him. She'd been so wrapped up in him, she'd conveniently forgotten all that…or more like chosen to ignore it.

Don't say anything, you'll just make it worse, she warned herself.

Instead, she took another sip of wine, letting the flavours distract her momentarily from the questions that had started to claw at the edges of her new-found confidence. This was going to end badly, so it would probably do her good to back off a bit, before it really was too late.

CHAPTER FIFTEEN

ETHAN STOOD, ARMS CROSSED, in the shadow-dappled stables, the sound of hooves stamping softly against the hay-covered ground blending with the distant hum of the bush. Mornings were quiet, peaceful. He was starting to enjoy them too, especially the part where he woke up with Sage in her bed. He watched her now, unboxing the delivery. It was finally here; it had taken ages to arrive. Mind you, he thought, everything did out here.

'Ethan, what did you do?' Her brow furrowed in puzzlement that quickly melted into surprise as she pulled off the last of the brown paper and got down to the giant square box.

'Is this…?' She trailed off, pulling the sleek new coffee machine from its cardboard confines, gasping in surprise.

'Don't drop it,' he said, swiping it from her quickly, biting back a smile. He loved nothing more than seeing this woman happy, even though he should probably get used to not seeing her smile, and not hearing her laugh, and not waking up next to her hair tickling his face on the pillow next to him.

'Figured we could use a decent shot of caffeine around here that we didn't have to kick something to get,' he managed, his own voice sounding gruff with attempted nonchalance.

'You're the best.' Sage's green eyes met his, and he caught them with his gaze. He knew her eyes by now, in every kind of light. He knew when she was genuinely happy, like now, and when she was retreating, holding something back, as she had been for the past few days, since he'd taken her to Star Creek.

'Thank you, Ethan. This means more than you know. The rest of the staff will be so thrilled!'

I did it for you, he wanted to say, but he didn't because she already knew. Well, she *should* know. Things had been a little weird recently, though, and if he was honest, her gratitude, simple and sincere, was perforating the tension that had been hanging between them like a heavy curtain.

They'd been close in the most physical of ways over the past weeks, their bodies moving and talking without words, and that had started to make him feel infallible. But even as their mouths and hands and limbs found their way under the sheets, or in the hay right here—clichéd as it was—he knew it would soon be his last night here, and the longer he tried to delay the inevitable, the more painful saying goodbye would be.

He couldn't move out here, he was too embedded in his homeland, in his business and his family, and why would any feelings she might have for him override her need to be where *she* belonged? He was not enough. As he hadn't been for Carrie.

'I thought you'd like it,' he said, stuffing his hands in his pockets to keep from reaching out to her. 'It's a good one, right?'

'Definitely a good one,' she agreed with a smile that didn't quite reach her eyes.

She turned to examine the machine, and Ethan's gaze lingered on the wavy chestnut hair falling like a sleek horse's tail down her back. There were so many questions now. They'd been coming at him for days like barbed hooks waiting to tear open the worst of his wounds.

Maybe she would find someone else soon—possibly even Bryce, if she listened to his explanation for leaving, understood it and forgave him. She'd have every right to, seeing as he himself didn't do relationships. This was the rock and the hard place.

He just didn't know if he could ever trust another woman with his heart. Carrie had been so thrilled when he'd slipped the ring on her finger, as if nothing could ever be more important than them or their relationship and their plans, and look how *that* turned out. Carrie could be barefoot and pregnant with Cam's baby by now, for all he knew.

The past kept clinging to him like a ten-tonne koala, strangling any ounce of courage he mustered when it came to really talking to Sage about what came after this. Dad and Jacqueline had both said he should ask her to come and visit Queensland, to try it out, to see if she might like it there. But his walls had shot back up that night at Star Creek, brick by emotional brick, and he still hadn't really let them down. The second she'd clammed up on him, he'd done the same. What he wanted, what he needed, really, was to not get in any deeper.

Damn it, man, you're always overthinking things. Just ask her to visit Queensland!

'Hey,' he heard himself say, the word slicing through the silence. 'So, I've been thinking…'

'About?' Sage prompted.

'Queensland.' The word felt like a stone in his mouth, heavy and hard.

She flinched. 'Ethan, I—'

The moment shattered with the jarring ring of her phone. Sage glanced at the caller ID, her expression shifting into something unreadable. 'Hold that thought,' she said, before she excused herself and stepped outside to take the call.

'Right,' Ethan murmured to no one, watching her go. His heart thudded in his chest. He had only managed to utter one word, with no context around it at all, and already his insides felt as if they were being mauled by jackals. Later, he would just put an end to this misery and initiate the conversation. He would ask her to come and visit him in Queensland. Maybe some form of long-distance relationship might work, while they figured this thing out?

'Please! She's been attacked by a croc!' Ethan's hands clenched at the sound of frantic footsteps rushing into the clinic. He turned from the guinea pig he was placing back into its basket as a middle-aged man burst through the doors, his face etched with panic. He was cradling a bloodied Blue Heeler in his arms.

'Help my Belle,' the man cried again as Ethan hurried with the guinea-pig cage. Sage was close behind him and he caught the flicker of panic on her face as the man gasped with fear and exertion. The dog, a sturdy, strong animal built for the terrain of the outback, lay limp, its breathing shallow and laboured. Deep gashes marred its side and leg. Raw flesh on show made a stark contrast to the dog's dusty fur, which was matted with blood.

'Get her to surgery!' Sage barked, and Ethan led the way, the man following close behind, their footsteps echoing down the small corridor and into the next room. Ellie met them at the door, her eyes widening at the sight of the wounded creature.

'This is an emergency, cancel my next appointment,' Sage directed, her voice steady but her eyes betraying the swell of emotions he knew must be breaking inside her. Another badly injured dog. There were a lot of dogs coming in and out of here, they were the most popular pets, of course, but he'd never seen one this badly injured before.

'Easy, Belle,' he muttered, catching for the briefest second a look of such profound fear and pain in her eyes that he had to swallow back a cry of his own. Together, they transferred the dog onto the stainless-steel table. Its surface seemed extra cold and unwelcoming, even to him, as the traumatised owner stood back, wringing his hands. Gloves snapped against skin, and tools clinked as they were laid out with careful precision despite the pounding hearts in the room.

'We have multiple puncture wounds and lacerations,' Sage observed, her brow furrowing as she assessed the damage. 'We need to stop the bleeding, fast.'

Ethan helped elevate the animal. With deft fingers, he began applying gentle, steady pressure to slow the bleeding while Sage worked to clean around the wounds so they could judge the severity of the attack. The dog whined softly, her body twitching with pain despite the sedatives they had quickly administered. At least she was alive, and breathing on her own.

'Easy, Belle, you're going to be okay,' Sage murmured soothingly, working on another deep cut with a concentration that bordered on reverence. Her hands moved with an expertise honed across her years spent dedicated to healing animals. He could feel how each of her movements and whispers and treatments was a silent promise to end the suffering before her, and, as it always did, his mind went to Sage as a kid, watching the flames of the bushfire, knowing her parents and her dog were dying right in front of her.

He'd been through hell, but nothing compared to what she

had… How could he inflict any more suffering on her, asking her to come to Queensland, starting something he already knew would probably end badly, one way or another? Was that the kind of life she'd want, living off-grid with him and his dad, and the horses? Without the small support network she'd gathered around her? He could move here, he supposed…but then it wouldn't be fair on Dad, Jacqueline and the kids, or his mother's legacy, which they'd vowed to honour at the homestead. The equine centre he'd established wouldn't thrive here either, not on this dry soil. His heart sank.

'Scalpel,' Sage requested, without looking up. Ethan placed it firmly in her waiting palm and watched as she carefully excised a piece of embedded tooth from the dog's hind quarters. 'Got it,' she announced, holding up the jagged remnant triumphantly before dropping it into a metal tray with a clink.

How the heck did the crocodile's tooth end up there? he wanted to ask. It must have been an old croc, or maybe a really young one? The man didn't know, he'd been so panicked at the sight of his dog in its mouth that nothing else had really registered.

'Well done, boss,' Ethan said, and her eyes softened at the genuine admiration that laced his tone. 'Let's flush these wounds and get her closed up.'

Sage reached for the saline. Together, they irrigated each and every wound meticulously once more, making sure that no trace of infection would remain and put this creature on course for any more suffering. It was a dance they knew well by now, moving around each other with a synchronicity that made him wonder sometimes if he'd ever work with another vet this well again.

What might they do if they did make something work, if she wound up moving to Queensland with him? They could open a surgery there, as his father had always planned. Dad had been pretty disappointed initially, when he'd ended up with an actress from Brisbane as a future daughter-in-law instead of a qualified veterinarian who could help mould the family business into something beyond horses. Mum's dream of a self-sufficient life, and eco-conscious activities for the community, had only just started, really. There was so much still to do, and he would do it there, with Dad, while Sage remained here, honouring her own commitments.

They continued to work seamlessly, anticipating each other's needs, passing instruments back and forth without needing to speak, and the man looked on from the corner, his face a shade of grey Ethan recognised. A special shade that seemed to be reserved for the owners of beloved animals who were fighting for their lives.

Belle's breathing steadied as they worked. As Sage finished the very last suture, a palpable sense of relief flooded the room and he removed his mask. It felt as though he hadn't drawn a breath this whole time.

'She's going to be OK,' Sage said, peeling off her gloves and giving Ethan a tired smile.

'I can't thank you both enough.' The man's voice choked as he ran his hands along the dog's head and ears, tears glistening in the corners. They told him they'd have to keep her in to monitor her, and as the man slunk off in relief and exhaustion Ethan watched Sage watching Belle. Her dedication to her work, the way she fought for each life as if it were the only one that mattered, still stirred something in his soul. It was more than professional admiration; it was a growing affection and appreciation and happiness he felt around her that he couldn't compartmentalise. It was so soon after Carrie, though, how could he trust this was even real?

'So, that was Bryce on the phone in the stable, earlier,' she said suddenly into the silence.

He turned to her, feeling the muscles in his jaw tightening. Her attention was already shifting to the paperwork that needed to be filled out.

'What does he want?' Ethan asked, guarding his tone. He should feign indifference; besides, he had nothing to be jealous of.

'He wants to visit me,' she said coolly.

'Right.'

He watched as Sage's shoulders stiffened, her body language telling him how much she hadn't wanted to divulge this information, but had decided to anyway.

'It's OK, if you really still need him to visit you,' he said. 'But what do you want from him?'

Meeting her eyes, he encouraged her silently. She was free to tell him the truth, if she wanted. She could tell him how she still deemed herself responsible for the fire that killed her parents and all the animals, and that despite everyone reminding her it wasn't her fault, including him, she was rewriting the story in her own head where she was still guilty and undeserving of forgiveness.

'Why do you still need reassurance that the bushfire wasn't your fault?' he probed. Her eyes clouded over as she looked to the side and sniffed. 'Why didn't you talk to me before you contacted Bryce?'

'I don't know what you mean.'

'Talk to me, Sage, I'm right here,' he urged. Then he realised how it sounded and backed off as her eyes narrowed. She was like Carrie right now, refusing to talk to him, or even acknowledge that she wasn't happy, despite him asking her to just be honest with him. How many months, even years, had

Carrie been sleeping with Cam before he'd found out? Their communication had broken down so slowly he'd barely noticed, till she was admitting the affair.

This was supposed to be different. He'd thought, despite the challenges they faced, that what he had with Sage was a world away from anything he'd had with Carrie. But right now Sage was shutting him out on purpose, edging him off the cliff while he was blind, and he was right back where he'd started.

CHAPTER SIXTEEN

SAGE CHOPPED CARROTS with rhythmic precision, watching the sky cloud over. Each slice was pretty much a futile attempt to silence the cacophony of shrieks and laughter that were echoing through Abigail's kitchen. The kids darted around them like wild spirits, their energy the total opposite to that of the quiet, calm horses the mayor was tending to outside the window. Bad weather was coming, and already she could feel the tension in the atmosphere…although maybe some of that was of her own creation.

'Bryce called me,' Sage confessed over the din, her knife pausing mid-motion. She'd been storing up this information since that phone call and yes, OK, she was nervous. Abigail always told her things how they were, no messing. 'He wants to come to Amber Creek, to talk.'

Abigail glanced up from where she was seasoning the chicken, her brow furrowed in confusion under her fringe. 'Are you going to let him?'

'I don't know,' she said, pulling a face.

Abigail tutted. 'Why would you even consider it? Didn't he walk out on you, never to be seen again?' She made a 'poof' motion over her own head with the oregano jar.

Sage sighed, pushing a loose strand of hair behind her ear. The weight of her thoughts pressing down on her was worse than last night without Ethan in her bed. At least she'd had

Belle. The Blue Heeler was good company, and it was also easier to keep a close eye on her there. She'd have been pretty much alone in the kennel in the clinic.

'Ethan's been...different since I told him. He didn't even stay over last night. He just went back to the guest house.'

'*Why* did you tell him?' Abigail said, skewering a chicken breast with a sharp look in her eyes. 'What are you doing here, Sage?'

Sage let out a long sigh as her hands faltered. Setting the knife down, she turned to face her friend, admitting she wasn't even sure. Abigail accused her of trying too hard to protect her heart, and also of thinking she didn't deserve something real, like she seemed to be building with Ethan. She said Sage was deliberately inviting in drama that would push him away. That drama, of course, being Bryce.

'You're also freaking yourself out over the chance that something will happen to Ethan and he'll leave you one way or another. Sage, these are old demons of yours—we know them well.'

'Wow.' Abigail was so wise, as well as pretty beyond measure, and successful. For a moment Sage had to laugh at how much they must have shared during all those nights they were getting to know each other, drinking wine, confessing their sins and their darkest moments. Abigail was right, of course.

'Let it go,' Abigail said, clutching her hand and pressing it to her heart. 'Let all of that go, Sage, please.'

'I know I should...'

'Please. Ethan might be guarded, but you two have something special. I've seen it. When that snake got you, I swear I saw that man's heart working overtime. Ethan is head over heels in love with you. How did you do it, by the way?'

Sage absorbed her friend's words as Abigail stirred pots and picked up shoes and reminded her kids that this wasn't a zoo and that they were not animals. Whether she was right or not about Ethan's feelings, Abigail saw through all Sage's excuses, the crazy stuff inside her own head that had been holding her captive since the fire. It was true, she sabotaged everything that threatened to bring the slightest trace of upheaval into her life, the good as well as the bad, sometimes.

'Would you move to Queensland if he asked?' Abigail's question pierced through a fresh round of screeching by the kids.

Sage held the knife suspended as the gravity of the question sank in. 'But he hasn't asked. He did once briefly mention Queensland but then dropped it.'

'Ah.' Abigail hummed, reaching for the pepper grinder, adding a twist to the pan. 'Well, this could get awkward pretty fast. He'll be here any minute.'

Sage almost dropped the knife. 'Ethan's coming?'

'Jarrah invited him, to say thanks for everything he's done with Storm.'

Sage drew a breath that was mostly pepper. A twinge of annoyance at the mayor's impromptu decision flitted through her mind—this was supposed to be a quiet, no-stress dinner between friends—but then she couldn't blame Jarrah; Ethan had charmed him as he had everyone else. Before she could probe any further into the sudden dinner arrangement, the sound of hooves on gravel told her he was here already. Her chest tightened on the spot as she saw him through the window and Abigail gasped.

'He's riding Storm!'

Sage took a moment to process that Ethan was actually here, arriving on the back of the horse that up to this point hadn't let anyone ride him. Storm was finally healed? She wiped her hands on the apron tied around her waist, suddenly more than conscious of her flour-dusted jeans and basil-scented fingers. Not that anyone was looking at her. Ethan was the man of the moment now, Charlie and Daisy, and even the eleven-year-old Lucie were all busy cheering and whooping at his arrival.

Finally, the back door swung open. Ethan stepped inside followed by everyone else. Sage held her breath as his eyes found hers immediately.

'Hi,' she said. The intensity of his gaze magnetised her. Her feet somehow moved across the floor without her knowing. She leaned in for a kiss, her cheeks warming just attuning to his presence. It was almost instinctive now, this greeting they had shared countless times in private. She almost couldn't have helped her body's reaction to him, even standing in her best friend's kitchen, covered in flour. But as the family scattered around her, all talking at once, Ethan's hand came up gently and rested on her shoulder.

'Best not,' he said softly, so only she could hear. 'I'm still working for the mayor, remember?'

Sage stopped short. 'But Jarrah knows about us,' she protested quietly, searching his face for clarity. Was this because of what she'd said before, about inviting Bryce here?

Ethan's jaw tensed. A flicker of something unreadable passed through his eyes before he composed himself. 'It's about keeping things professional in public,' he explained, his words measured but firm.

'Right.' Sage stepped back from him, panic gripping her heart. Abigail asked her to get the plates out and help her set the table and she got to the task, head whirring. She'd helped serve a hundred meals in this house, but now she felt clumsy, opening all the wrong cupboards. He was being weird. Because of Bryce, probably. She needed to apologise, tell him how ridiculous she was being, still needing any kind of closure from her ex. Abigail was right. Bryce was just another barrier she'd erected quickly to make sure Ethan couldn't hurt her. What if they made something work, she and Ethan, something incredible, but then Ethan decided he wasn't over Carrie, and that *she* had always been a rebound? Or what if he was thrown from a horse and died… God, it was just too much for her heart to cope with, all these boomeranging emotions.

'We made chicken,' she heard herself say as she placed a plate down in front of him at the table. Her fingers knocked a fork and Ethan caught it in his lap. His eyes went to hers for a brief hot second and the look in them made her hands tremble more. Wanting him. More, now he was being so different around her. More, now that she could lose him in a hundred different ways. Storm was finally healed and he was back where he should have been weeks ago, with his family, ready to be the horse Lucie had dreamed of. Which meant Ethan would be leaving.

Sitting next to Ethan, she tried to compose herself, feeling his body heat meld with hers even though he wasn't touching her. She could be the professional veterinarian she was, the one he wanted her to be right now, but he knew her now, he knew how to tune in. He could probably tell that just by doing what he'd done, refusing a kiss, he'd made her long for him all over again…

'So, bees, huh?' Abigail started talking about the honey he'd told them about, asking Ethan all about the permaculture project and the rain-collection system he and his dad had built.

What was Ethan's father like? Sage wondered. Would she ever know? What they were trying to achieve in Queensland sounded interesting too. More than interesting, it sounded like building a sustainable future in every sense of the word. There was no possibility of anything like *here*, it was too dry and dusty for most things to thrive, whereas her practice could, in theory, be moved anywhere. OK, she would have to start again, make new friends, new relationships, new clients, but she could do that, couldn't she?

Yes. You would move to Queensland if he asked you to. You would go anywhere with him. Because you love him with your whole heart!

She watched as Ethan sliced through the tender meat, his movements deliberate and controlled. He could barely seem to look at her, except for the occasional sideways glance, like a wolf checking in on its prey. Sage's mind was drifting now, zoning out, stealing more glances at Ethan. Maybe he *was* over Carrie, but he was worried about their whirlwind romance. He just didn't want his world to be smashed to smithereens again, any more than she did.

'Ethan,' she whispered, trying to catch his hand under the table.

He pushed her away gently, but firmly.

The longer they sat there, talking about horses and bees and farmers' markets, the further away she drifted, and the more she felt him letting her. It was like a light going out between them, with Ethan operating the dimmer switch. He was tired of her already, all of these emotions that she was only half sharing. If she didn't start being totally honest with him, as his ex hadn't been, he would go and he wouldn't come back, and who would blame him?

Sage heard a toy drop to the floor above their heads. Abigail and the mayor were now upstairs, doing their best to put the kids to bed, and the warmth had all but evaporated from the room. Ethan's eyes were on her, watching her when he thought she wouldn't notice. They were alone.

'Great dinner,' he said, leaning against the doorframe across the room.

She nodded, unsure how to articulate the feeling of being on the edge of a confession that could turn her life around. He had no idea what he was doing to her, all these emotions buzzing through her, but she'd invite herself to Queensland if he didn't do it first.

'Your parents would be so proud of everything you've achieved here, Sage,' he said, his voice low. 'But, look, I didn't come here looking for anything serious.'

What?

His words hit her ears first. Everything felt hotter as the statement hit her brain, and then got at her heart, stones hurled onto glass. Ethan watched her, his expression guarded.

'What do you mean?' she stammered.

'I mean, I'm not here to start a relationship with you,' he said plainly.

His face was so dark now, and he wouldn't look at her.

'Is this because of Bryce?'

'No. Let's not forget our reality,' he said. 'This was always going to be temporary.'

The word 'temporary' echoed through her and hollowed out her belly. Temporary felt the same as worthless, as if he was off to better things already. Her heart clenched tightly, as if his actual fist had squeezed it.

'Is that truly what you want?' she asked numbly. Ethan's eyes would still not find hers. The ground felt as if it were opening up beneath her, as if everything he'd given her physically till now, the safety, the comfort, the reassurance, the love, was being retracted slowly but purposefully, as if he were pulling what was left of the snake right out of her. 'Is this because you're scared I'll run away with someone else, like Carrie did?'

'It's for the best.'

'I don't believe you.'

His face was set, his cheek turned slightly, but she stood there in silence until he was forced to look at her. Holding his gaze, she projected what she hoped was loathing and anger and disappointment, but the more he held her stare and worked his jaw, and curled his fingers to his sides, the more she knew she was only telling him she loved him. Daring him to break first. Daring him to tell her he wanted her. The more he ignored her silent confession, the harder she projected it, and the harder he rejected her.

Then he turned his head away and the slight almost sent her collapsing to the floor.

'I read you all wrong, Ethan.'

'I just wanted to make it clear, before I go,' he murmured. 'I don't want there to be any misunderstandings between us.'

Sage nodded, walking to the window and fixing her eyes on Storm, chomping on grass in the floodlit yard. There was no way in hell he was getting the satisfaction of seeing her break down and beg him to take her with him.

'Sage… I'll be leaving first thing tomorrow.'

'Go,' she said, her back still turned, where he could only see her legs shake, and not her face. Her eyes had crinkled into wet slits and her stomach was threatening to make her sick. 'Go then, Ethan. I'll tell Abigail and Jarrah you had an emergency.'

She heard his feet shuffling on the floor for a moment.

Do not turn around. Do not give him the satisfaction. Do not call out that you love him.

He left without another word. The sound of the front door closing behind him punctuated the end of their conversation, right as Abigail appeared on the stairs.

'The mayor's doing story time—' she started.

Sage slumped into a chair. Abigail rushed to her side, urging her to explain what had happened. How could those words have just come from Ethan's mouth? Abigail told her all the right things, like he was probably just freaking out and pushing her away because men were incapable of processing their emotions in a way that actually included open communication. She told her to go after him and tell him how she felt.

'I tried to, already!'

'Did you? Did you say those actual words? I love you, Ethan?'

Sage growled into her hands. He knew, he knew what she felt without her saying it. So why couldn't she just say it for real?

'You don't think you deserve him,' Abigail observed. 'But what if you're what *he* needs, Sage?'

This was ridiculous. She needed to be brave for once. Ethan had as many walls up and blind spots as she did. She'd been so focused on her own woes that she'd forgotten his. Just being around Ethan had been like opening a door she hadn't even known was there—one that had all the happy things hiding behind it. There was no guarantee that Ethan would reciprocate her feelings, or even talk to her if she followed him to the guest house and sat on his suitcase to stop him packing it. But there was no peace left in the 'what ifs' and 'maybes' any more. Things had gone well beyond that.

CHAPTER SEVENTEEN

ETHAN STOOD AT the window, his gaze fixed on the horizon as the first drops of rain on the guest-house balcony started tapping against the plants. Telling Sage he didn't want a relationship—why had he done that? Even the word relationship did not sum up what he'd imagined he'd have with her. It had been the same story the entire time he'd been here, knowing he wanted her, but knowing what had happened the last time he'd felt like this. Going through that again could hollow a man out.

He glanced at the caller ID on his buzzing phone. Jacqueline. 'Hey, sis.'

'Ethan—did you book your return flight yet? The kids are asking when you're coming to finish that game of Jenga with them. You know, they haven't touched it since you left.'

His tone was nonchalant, bordering on dismissive as he told her about the flight delays and the storm, but she saw right through it. 'OK, what's wrong?'

There was a softness to Jacqueline's prompt that loosened his tongue. He explained what he could, how he'd blown something small out of proportion in his head. She asked if he was feeling overwhelmed because it was happening so soon after Carrie, and he stopped himself saying, *Yes, everything is because of Carrie,* because what was the point? He said nothing and Jaqueline, who knew him, told him he wasn't giving things a fair chance, because Carrie was not Sage.

He bristled at the comparison, unsure how to articulate the fear of being vulnerable again that had rooted itself so deeply in his bones. Instead he paced the wooden floorboards and kicked at a fallen coat hanger.

'It was just a bit of fun, you know, and I took it too far, and now… I have to forget about her.'

'Ethan. Why don't you just give her a chance?'

'I don't want to give her a chance.'

Jacqueline sighed deeply and he almost felt her eyes roll. 'Well, you're an idiot, even though I love you. Sounds like you love *her*, too. Just remember the love, brother, and you'll be fine. I gotta go.'

Ethan clenched his fist as she hung up, the phone still tight against his ear. His breath hitched. 'It's not love,' he muttered into the emptiness, as if he could possibly convince the walls—or himself at this point. 'I do *not* love Sage.'

The words fell flat. The lie felt like a physical ache in his chest as he paced the cramped space between the bed and the window. 'Sage doesn't need someone like me. She's better off alone.' Even as he said it out loud, he was picturing her laughter, all the times she'd caught him kicking the old coffee machine. When Sage forgot herself and the pain and guilt she wore like a badge of honour, she had the kind of laugh that stopped time. *All you want to do when you hear a laugh like that,* he thought, *is keep it going, and lose your own dark thoughts in the light.*

As long as he lived he would never stop seeing the way she'd looked just now when he'd hurt her with his words. She'd looked as if she'd never laugh again, as if he'd stolen something new and precious and irreplaceable, something maybe he'd gone some way to providing, right out from under her. And he loved her even more after he'd done it, because no one had ever looked at him with that much love, especially when he was taking it away.

All the times he'd told himself he didn't want a relationship bucked at his insides; it wasn't true, not when it was Sage. It was just…impossible…to know for certain that she wouldn't come to his home and be with him, and his father, and his horses, and promise him for ever, and make him want to have her babies, and then do the same thing Carrie had done. Not that she would do that—she wasn't Carrie—but how could he really be sure something else wouldn't go wrong, and take him right back to square one? He just had to trust that she wouldn't. He *could* trust her not to hurt him, he realised. But now he'd gone all out to ruin what they had on purpose. If she never forgave him, he wouldn't be surprised.

He tried to call her. It rang off. Of course, why would she pick up the phone to him now? She was probably fuming. He knew she didn't really want Bryce here. And instead of sympathising with her attempts to protect herself, and giving her the reassurance that she still needed, or fighting for *them* and telling her to forget Bryce and come and see his home in Queensland instead, where she could make love to him in the study, and the cabin and the greenhouse, meet his horses, meet his sister…instead of doing any of that, he'd shut her down.

Dialling her again, he bit his nails and waited. And waited. *She's clicked off again!*

'Tomorrow,' he growled, eyeing the fierce storm. The word felt like less of a promise to himself and more like a lifeline right now, some remaining tiny tether to the kind of life he could have with her if he'd just get out of his own damn head and reach for it.

Tomorrow he would find Sage and mend what he'd smashed to pieces—or, at the very least, try and explain to her why he'd felt the need to break it in the first place.

Sage was seething. She'd been seething when she'd gone to sleep after getting back home in the rain, and now, waking up after only an hour to the ominous skies overhead, she was even angrier.

How dare he humiliate me like that? But I still love him.

'Come here, girl,' she said to Belle, putting a plate of kibble down close to the Blue Heeler on the bed, so she wouldn't have to walk for it on her bad leg. Realistically it probably wasn't right to have the dog on the bed, but she'd been such good company last night after what she'd overheard from the other side of that guest-house door.

'It was just a bit of fun, you know, and I took it too far, and now I just have to forget about her... I don't want to give her a chance.'

Sage pressed her face into the pillow. It smelled of him, his scent, the animal and the gentle lover, taking turns to savour and worship her, giving her space and time to explore him in return. She'd seen inside him. Let him inside her.

How could I have been so stupid over this man, so many times?

'I went there to make things right,' she said, tossing the pillow to the floor. Belle swiped her hand with her hot tongue in understanding. 'I mean, I actually thought I would hear him say he wanted me to at least go with him to Queensland. I thought he was going to say we should try. As if men just change like that!'

Thinking back to the tone of his voice through the door, it had struck her more than his words. He'd made it very clear that whatever had been between them, it wasn't what she'd thought. '*I do* not *love Sage*,' he'd said, definitively.

To think how determined she'd been, marching to the guest house earlier this evening…then realising she didn't know his room number. And she didn't have a key. And she'd left her phone at Abigail's. It was still there, probably tucked down the sofa on silent mode. She'd set it that way in case Bryce called back; she would have to let him know she didn't want him to visit any more, but it was too much to deal with now. What a mess.

After Babs had let her into the guest house and pointed to Ethan's room, which weirdly she had never been to this whole time, she'd raised her hand to his door and prepared herself to show him exactly why it would be a crime not to see if this connection could be something worth salvaging… and expanding…for a little bit longer. Or for ever. This kind of emotional roller coaster was a sign that the path was right for both of them, but obviously the way there was always going to be rocky, considering the challenges that faced them.

But then, Ethan had been on the phone, probably to his father or sister. Oh…what an idiot she'd made of herself going over there. He was probably at the airport now, counting down the minutes till they started rescheduling the flights. Her heart burned till the anger turned to tears that threatened to soak poor Belle's head.

A crash of thunder. Sage sat up and blinked in shock. Great, a storm was definitely on its way. 'Stay here,' she ordered Belle. 'I have to go check on the other animals.'

The isolation pressed in on her as she checked on the few animal patients they had—a tortoise, a cat and a wallaby. It wasn't unusual for her to be alone in the clinic, her patients often kept her at work long after the others had gone, but now, on top of everything with Ethan, the solitude felt a lot like abandonment. The air was thick with electricity, too, a tangible intensity that put her even more on edge.

Another crash, closer this time, sent a jolt of dread to her bones. It sounded too close for comfort. She whipped around, her eyes landing on the window. The sight rooted her to the spot.

No, no, no, not again!

A bolt of lightning must have struck her cabin. Smoke was curling out from somewhere she couldn't see. Fear knotted in her stomach. Not again, she couldn't face this again!

Then… 'Belle! Belle is in there.'

Somehow, Sage forced herself to the phone and called in the emergency. They'd take too long to get here, though. The flames were erupting from the roof now, greedily devouring shingles and wood with an insatiable hunger as her legs propelled her outside. The cabin was fully ablaze and poor Belle was still trapped inside. The world seemed to pitch and toss as Sage took a step forward on trembling legs.

'Belle!' she called out, as if the dog might appear through the closed door. The flames before her eyes were dancing with an eerie familiarity. She was back to that night again, when the same orange tongues of fire had greedily licked at the tents and trees and sky and robbed her of everything she'd known and loved. The sheer magnitude of what she was about to do settled in her chest like lead. The same terror rendered her immobile as a frightened child, clawing at her insides and threatening to paralyse her again.

But… Belle. The thought of the poor dog, trapped and afraid, spurred her forward. She wasn't a child any more. And she could finally see, through adult eyes, that what had happened back then had never been her fault. She had let the guilt and fear eat her up, and now she'd lost the love of her life to Queensland. But there was no way she was letting Belle die today. Belle needed her.

Sage dashed towards the cabin, the heat radiating off the structure, pushing back against her advance. Miraculously the front door was still clear; the lightning must have struck at the back.

Come on, Sage, you can do this.

The door was a barrier of heat, but she forced it open with both hands. Smoke billowed out to greet her and met with the dust in the wind. Her vision impaired, she coughed, her eyes stinging as she searched for the bedroom door through the haze. The glow of the fire crept under the door to the kitchen and painted monstrous shadows on the walls like a gallery of all her worst fears coming to life.

You can do this.

'Belle!' Her voice was a desperate plea, hoarse and cracking. Smoke cloaked her as she staggered over the threshold, her lungs screaming for clean air. She could barely see a thing, but she wasn't backing away this time. She would not let history repeat itself. There was no way the fire was taking anything else from her, not if she could help it.

But before she could move any further, a firm hand clasped around her arm, wrenching her back. Ethan stood there on the porch, solid and unyielding, his deep blue eyes boring into hers with an intensity that matched the heat. His ute was behind him, the engine still running.

'Sage, what are you doing?'

She shook her head, wild and frantic. What was he doing here? 'Belle is in the bedroom, Ethan! I have to—'

His expression shifted as he coughed, something like understanding softening the hard lines of his face. 'Stay here,' he ordered her. Without another word, he released her and sprinted past her, the muscles in his back flexing beneath his shirt as he propelled himself towards the bedroom.

'Ethan!' she screamed after him.

Her heart lurched into her throat as she watched him disappear into the smoke. She screamed his name again, but it turned into a cough. Reluctantly she stood back. Sirens wailed somewhere in the distance and her hands clenched into fists at her sides. The possibility of losing him strangled her with every second that ticked by with her pulse hammering in her ears.

Why had he come back here anyway, after everything he'd said to whoever it was on the phone? Unless she'd missed a piece of the puzzle somehow. She'd been rattled and upset; she could have been creating another narrative, as she'd probably done about Bryce! That fortress Ethan had built around his emotions—he'd just smashed that completely to pieces by coming back here despite the fierce storm, obviously to see her. And now he'd dived into the blaze for her, for Belle.

'Ethan!' Her voice was a raw, guttural cry as she sank back into the depths of terror. The clinic behind her felt like another world, safe and sterile, while she stood here, heart thundering against her ribs, literally on the precipice of her worst nightmare. He had gone after Belle, for her, without a second thought. What if he didn't come out? His selflessness was a blade to her heart suddenly—what if she lost him, too?

The sirens grew louder. She imagined him struggling against the smoke and heat in there and desperately tried to hold onto her belief in his strength and resourcefulness. He was the strongest person she knew! But doubt crept in just as fast, whispering that maybe she was wrong. Maybe he wasn't strong enough. Fire took everything away and she knew it. Seconds felt like hours. Her mind conjured images of him overcome by smoke, succumbing to the heat, and she shook her head fiercely, trying to dispel the thoughts. No, he *was* strong, he could do this.

'Please, Ethan,' she whispered, her voice breaking. 'Please.'

How long had he been gone? Thirty seconds? It felt like a lifetime. The heat pushed against her as if warning her back, but she took a step forward, then another, her body moving with a will of its own. She couldn't let fear paralyse her again, not when it mattered most. She was about to go in after him, when a silhouette forged through the smoke. 'Ethan!'

He was grey from the ashes, arms cradling the limp Belle. 'Get back!' he commanded, his voice rough with smoke but edged with an iron-clad resolve as he urged her away from the door, back to the forecourt. Sage turned to see firefighters jumping out of their truck, unravelling hoses and yelling commands to each other as their battle with the blaze consuming her home began. The urgency of the scene, and the fact that her home and everything in it were being destroyed, barely registered with Sage; all that mattered in that moment was the man in front of her now, leading her through the doors to the smoke-free clinic. The phone was ringing off the hook.

Belle squirmed in Ethan's grip, coming to life as the fresh air filled her lungs. The relief was overpowering as he laid the dog down carefully. With the chaos unfolding outside, Sage reached up and pulled him into a kiss that she hoped held all the words she'd left unspoken, and could barely have uttered if she'd tried.

'Ethan,' she choked out eventually, hands in his ash-filled hair, her voice croaky from smoke. 'I would never have survived losing you! What are you doing here?'

Ethan's expression softened as he put one large hand to the back of her neck and drew her against him. 'You were about to run into the fire,' he said in awe, stroking her cheek with his thumb. 'You! Sage, do you realise what could have happened to you?'

'I couldn't let Belle die.'

'And you would have done the same thing for your parents, if you could have. If you hadn't been a terrified child back then. Do you see that now?'

She closed her eyes, pressed her forehead to his. 'I know, I do know that.'

'I was talking to my sister about you,' he admitted, his voice carrying over the tumultuous sounds of gushing water and men shouting, and the phone still ringing off the hook. 'She kindly reminded me I was in denial…but I love you, Sage. I do. I've fallen in love with you.'

Sage's heart hammered against her chest as he kissed her again, and Belle sat up, confused but perfectly fine apparently.

'I overheard you talking,' she said, her lips still an inch from his. 'In the guest house… I came to talk to you after you left Abigail's. I thought—'

'You thought what?' Ethan's brow furrowed, his concern palpable.

'I thought you said you *didn't* love me. That we were just having fun or something.' A bitter laugh escaped her lips, and she shook her head. 'But I only caught part of it, didn't I?'

Ethan cupped her face, his thumbs gently wiping away the ash that must have been coating her cheeks as much as his. 'You heard the fear talking, Sage. My fear of admitting what I really feel for you. But I want you to always talk to me, always tell me everything, OK? We can work anything out, as long as we talk about it.'

She saw it then—the way his eyes shimmered with intensity, the way his hands trembled ever so slightly as they held her. It was raw vulnerability, and it struck at the very core of her being. She hadn't been honest about why she'd really considered asking Bryce here—as if she needed to hear anything from him at all when she had Ethan right here, painting a picture of the truth, plain and simple.

'I've been pushing you away, Ethan, I have, because I was scared,' she confessed, 'of losing someone I love all over again. And you—'

'Guilty as charged,' he said softly, tipping her chin up to meet his gaze. 'I think you should come to Queensland. What do you think?'

Sage felt a shift inside her that felt like chains falling off. She could hardly help her smile as his hands found hers. 'I hope you're not just saying that because my house just burnt down,' she teased.

'I'm saying it because I've fallen madly in love with you,' he replied, a grin tugging at the corner of his mouth. 'How many more times do you want me to say it?'

'As many times as you like, don't ever stop,' she said, kissing him again. In that moment she knew she would go anywhere with him, and for him. Everything was going to be just fine.

EPILOGUE

SAGE PERCHED ON the edge of the veranda, her feet barely grazing the sun-warmed wood beneath them. She took a slow sip of the honey lemonade they had made together yesterday with Kara and Jayson, and some of the other kids from the local school, loving how the sweetness of it danced on her tongue. Ethan sat beside her, his gaze scanning the horizon where the new horse with the limp would soon appear.

'When does it get here?' Sage asked, breaking the comfortable silence that had settled between them as he sat at the long wooden table, addressing a file of paperwork.

'Soon. I'll have my work cut out with this one, but we'll get there,' he replied, his tone reflecting the calm certainty that always surrounded him when it came to his equine patients here at the homestead.

'You always do,' she told him. There was always a steady stream of horses coming in and out and most days Ethan spent his time outside with them. Occasionally he would fill in at the small clinic they'd just opened on the property, but that was her project really. Setting up a whole new practice in Queensland hadn't been too complicated in the end. Of course, she missed her regular patients, but Ellie and Billy had a new chief vet now, with the fees coming out of Amber Creek's budget, and the community was thriving even without her. And now she had a growing rota of even more regulars and wonderful connections, with both the local animals and people. She had also joined a book club and a swimming club in an effort to socialise outside work; something she hadn't dreamed of doing before, when she'd been too busy judging herself in her own head to make many friends.

The dogs, a ragtag crew of rescue mutts, were sprawled out in contentment around their feet. Their tails thumped in lazy acknowledgment any time one of them was addressed. Their presence was a comforting constant to Sage these days, a reminder of the simple pleasures that life on their little homestead had brought her since the move, although, as hard as they tried, they would never add as much comedy value as Joey.

Sage glanced over to the paddock, where their rescue kangaroo was engaged in his own brand of morning exercise. With each buoyant leap, Joey seemed to defy the very notion of gravity, and a chuckle escaped Sage as she watched him dart after a bird. It was impossible not to find him funny; the kids all loved him.

'You know, he can hop off anywhere, whenever he wants,' Ethan said, catching her eye with a shared sense of amusement. 'But he chooses to hang out around here. Because you rescued him as a baby. You're his mother now.'

'I hope he never leaves,' she told him, her laughter fading into a softer smile. Her hand drifted instinctively to her stomach, resting gently on the curve that had only just begun to show. Three months along, and already the life within her stirred a protective love she hadn't known she possessed.

Ethan stood, and in seconds his big hand was covering hers, the strength in his fingers a reassurance. 'How are you feeling? Any more morning sickness?'

'Better today,' she admitted, more than grateful for his unwavering support in what would have been a somewhat jarring experience without him, feeling her body grow and change day by day. His fierce protectiveness had been a surprise at first, especially when he'd refused to let her ride anywhere alone, but now she knew it was all born from his love for her.

'Remember, no overdoing it,' he said, his thumb brushing across her skin in a tender caress. 'That includes worrying about our new arrival.'

Sage smiled. 'Promise,' she whispered, watching a bee hover over the plants she'd just potted along the edge of the veranda. The new irrigation system was a success, and they'd even given a workshop the other day in town, teaching others how to harvest greywater and rainwater, as she and Ethan had done in Amber Creek before bringing the new skills here with them. Sometimes she thought about that place, how it had all been rebuilt after the fire. Only her record player had been salvaged. Abigail and the mayor had brought it over when they'd come to visit, and she kept it here now, in what was going to be the baby's nursery.

She inhaled the scent of eucalyptus from the surrounding trees, letting it steady her nerves. Ethan looked up, his deep blue eyes reflecting a curiosity that told her how attuned to her he was. 'What's going on?' he asked.

'I've been thinking,' she began, 'about names for the baby.'

'Have you, now?' His lips curved into an expectant smile, lemonade forgotten.

'Actually, I already have one in mind.' She watched his face, seeking assurance, needing to know if he agreed with her. 'I was thinking…about naming him after my father if it's a boy. Or my mum if it's a girl.'

Ethan's reaction was immediate, his happiness sending butterflies swooping through her. 'Anthony or Caroline. I love that. Your parents would be honoured,' he said, and the excitement in his tone gave way to a warmth that wrapped around her heart.

'Really?' The doubt in her voice was a whisper of her old fears, but she let it wash away as he dashed his hands through his hair, grinning before kissing her and lifting her from her feet.

'Absolutely,' he affirmed, pulling back just enough to meet her gaze again. 'It's perfect.'

The creak of the veranda gate made them both look up. Ethan's father, John, emerged from his part of the homestead, a basket of eggs in one hand. He offered a knowing grin as he caught the tail end of their intimate exchange.

'Morning, you two,' he called out, approaching with a stride as familiar as Ethan's. 'Fresh eggs for breakfast.'

'Thanks, Dad.' Ethan shifted his stuff to make room for his father at the table.

Sage studied John's face. It was etched with the wisdom of years and the kindness that he always seemed to bestow on her when she needed it most. Living with Ethan's father on the property was great. Not only did the two of them seem to have endless topics to discuss whenever it was just them, but he'd brought an unexpected kind of solace too. While her adopted father and mother had visited several times already and always made the place feel more like home, in a way, John was filling a void left by her own biological dad's absence. It wasn't the same, of course—nothing could be—but it was a comfort that further dulled the edges of her loss, and she knew without a doubt her own parents would have loved him too. They would have loved this whole place.

'Any special plans for today?' John asked. The twinkle in his eye suggested he knew more than he let on.

'Just taking it easy,' Sage replied, sharing a glance with Ethan. Sometimes she wondered if they'd ever been caught making love; it was impossible to always keep quiet, and John had a habit of pottering about the place on his chores in the yard. Luckily he was pretty relaxed about that sort of thing. Ethan had said before now that his dad was different now, less shrouded in grief, and more like he used to be. He insisted they had Sage to thank for bringing a new lease of life to the property, but Sage knew Ethan was probably different too. They were both a work in progress, but somehow they made things work. Communication was everything. And their love.

'I was thinking I might make some calls today, tell people about the baby,' she said.

'Good, good.' John nodded. He glanced at Ethan, his voice softening. 'You know, I'm so proud of the family you're starting, son. It's going to be good for you, for all of us.'

Sage's heart swelled. Ethan reached under the table and gave her hand a squeeze. 'Let's call Abigail first,' Ethan suggested. His blue eyes sparkled with the kind of anticipation that made Sage's heart do a somersault. The news they were about to share was big, life-changing and, oh, so gossip-worthy. Abigail was going to flip out, not least because this had happened so soon after the wedding.

Sage had only just come off birth control when the faint blue line on the pregnancy test had had her weeping with both joy and fear in the toilet cubicle of a Brisbane shopping centre. Fear because she hadn't the faintest idea how to be a parent. Ethan had soon taken that fear away though. He always liked to say that they could handle anything together, and she knew just by looking around this place that he was right.

Sage watched him dial, her fingers absently tracing the rim of her lemonade glass. 'Abigail? It's Ethan. Could you put me on speaker? Sage has something to tell you.'

The line crackled slightly before Abigail's familiar voice

filled the air, bubbling with warmth. 'Hey, you two! To what do I owe the pleasure?'

'Hi,' Sage chimed in, her pulse quickening. She took a deep breath, feeling Ethan's supportive gaze upon her. 'We wanted to tell you first… I'm pregnant.'

There was a moment of stunned silence before Abigail erupted into squeals that could have woken the entire countryside. 'No way! Are you serious? Oh, my goodness, congratulations!'

Sage laughed, relief flooding through her. Sharing this secret with her best friend had just lifted a weight she hadn't realised she'd been carrying. 'We're over the moon,' she confessed.

'I wish I could hug you right now!' Abigail cried, and the longing in her voice travelled across the miles, making Sage blink back a sudden tear.

'Us too,' Ethan agreed, his strong hand finding Sage's again.

'Remember the wedding, Sage? When the kids chased the chickens around the coop and collected eggs like they were treasure? They'll have a little cousin to teach them all the farm tricks too, soon,' Abigail mused aloud, sending Sage's mind drifting back to that day five months ago.

'It was a great day.'

'It was magical,' Abigail agreed as they reminisced. 'They've been asking to help sort the recycling and throw coffee on the compost heap ever since. I don't know how you did it. They want to visit you again soon.'

'They're always welcome.' Sage smiled, picturing her friend's children's faces all lit up with wonder…dirt smudged on their cheeks despite their best smart outfits for the wedding.

'Speaking of warm welcomes, we should let you go. We've

got a new horse coming in today that needs some love and care,' Ethan interjected, mindful as always of their responsibilities.

'Of course, you busy bees,' Abigail said playfully. 'Take care of yourselves, and that little miracle too. Love you both.'

'Love you too,' they echoed before hanging up.

Sage leaned back in her chair, the lightness in her chest spreading through her entire being. She glanced at Ethan, who was already lost in his thoughts, watching the gates for the horse. She could barely believe she'd got so lucky. How had it happened to her? Soon they'd be nurturing more than just animals here; they'd be raising a child of their own.

'Are you going to be OK here for a while, Mrs Matthews?' Ethan asked as the horse and its owner appeared ahead. He reached across to tenderly brush a strand of hair from her face, then bent to drop a kiss to her belly.

'Always, Mr Matthews,' she replied, her eyes locking with his. Sage knew without a trace of doubt that she was home, and safe, and for as long as he was with her, she always would be.

* * * * *

HEALING THE SINGLE DAD SURGEON

SUE MACKAY

MILLS & BOON

This is for my writing group,
without whom I'd go crazy at times.

Love you all.

CHAPTER ONE

'ELI, YOU MIGHT want to hand over the final suturing to your sidekick. Your son's had an appendectomy and been taken to Paediatrics.'

'What?' Surgeon Eli Forrester stared at his friend Duncan. 'Why wasn't I told earlier?' Jordan had had surgery and he knew nothing about it? Of course, he didn't have his phone with him in Theatre so his sister Liz could've rung or texted in that time. 'Who did the op?'

'I did. I was between a rock and a hard place knowing you'd want to be with him and that you were in the middle of a very difficult surgical procedure. I couldn't dither though, as the appendix was close to bursting.'

Eli shuddered. His boy had had surgery and he hadn't been there for him. He couldn't blame Duncan for his decision. He'd been doing a three-hour op that had taken all his focus and could not have been interrupted without serious consequences for the patient. But Jordan had been under the knife and he hadn't even known. It would've been a huge distraction. He knew that and respected his friend's decision. But he was a dad first and foremost. His gut squeezed painfully. 'I'm glad it was you,' he conceded. If he'd had a choice of surgeon, Duncan would've been the man.

'Jordan came through it fine and is recovering as he should. So get out of here, and go be with him.'

Already peeling his gloves off shaky hands, Eli turned to the surgeon who'd been with him throughout the procedure. 'You okay with finishing off?' He had no concerns that the guy wouldn't do a good job.

'Try stopping me. Your son needs you.'

He was already halfway out of the room and answered over his shoulder. 'Thanks.' Why hadn't Liz called him the moment she suspected something? She didn't work Mondays and would've been giving Jordan her undivided attention. When had she noticed Jordan had abdo pain? She'd had him at her place since seven that morning so surely there'd been some indicators? Though with Jordan having Down syndrome it wasn't always easy to understand what he might be carrying on about, or if he even was.

The lift up to the children's ward took for ever. 'Should've taken the stairs.' If Jordie was anything like his usual self he'd be restless and demanding to get out of bed, but hopefully he'd be half asleep from the after-effects of anaesthetic.

'Leanne, how's Jordan?' he asked the nurse sitting at the main desk when he raced into the ward.

'He was grizzly and yelling for you, but Anna's calmed him down so he's happy at the moment. And fighting going to sleep.'

Anna. The nurse everyone adored. Jordan wouldn't be any different. Hell, when she wasn't being sharp with him, he was attracted to her and that was saying something. Sometimes he had to turn his back on her before he came out with something like, 'How about joining me for lunch?' Keeping his head on straight and squashing any random feelings for a woman was imperative to protecting his son—and himself.

'Anna's stayed on after her shift ended to sit with Jordan as we're one nurse down at the moment.'

No wonder she was so popular. Didn't she have a family to go home to? 'What room?'

'Three.'

'I'll be with Jordan from now on.' He spun around and headed to room three. He had to see Jordan, hold him, to reassure him—and himself—that everything was all right, though it sounded as if Anna had beaten him to it. He'd stay the night as his son would likely wake up and panic when he found he wasn't in his own bedroom. Now he really and truly understood the fear his younger patients' parents went through.

Striding into room three, Eli took in the scene before him. Nurse Anna was sitting on the edge of the bed reading a story in a soft, seductive voice, her deep red hair in its usual neat plait lying down the centre of her back. He felt a tingle of something alien. Lust? Attraction? Hardly. Though he'd often felt the same sensation when he'd been too close to this particular nurse while discussing a patient. So far he'd always managed to move on and ignore the way she did that to him, but it was getting harder by the week.

Jordie appeared mesmerised by Anna, taking in every word as though she were handing him his favourite chocolate biscuit. Eli's heart stumbled. This was getting too much. Without knowing it, Anna was pushing too many of his buttons to ignore. But he had to. It was the only way to be safe. Approaching the bed from the opposite side to where Anna sat, he found a smile. 'Hey, Jordie. How's my boy?'

'Daddy,' Jordan shrieked. 'Nurse Anna's reading my favourite story.' The words tumbled out of his mouth in such a hurry Eli wouldn't have understood them if he weren't used to the speech challenges that came with his son's Down's.

'Aren't you lucky?' Hunching down, he carefully wrapped his arm around Jordan's tiny frame and hugged him as close as he dared, mindful of the abdominal wound, while desperate to hold him in tight against his chest. Brushing a light kiss on top of his head, he felt the tension he'd been carrying from the moment Duncan had told him about the op start to fade. 'Thank you for staying on, Anna. It means a lot.' She really didn't have to. 'Jordan can get distraught when confronted with a new situation and this in particular would've been very scary for him.'

'No problem. He was quite wound up and calling for you so I figured I'd see what I could do to help settle him down. Seems he likes stories about puppies.'

'His favourite at the moment.' Eli sat on the bed, arm still around Jordan, trying to ignore Anna's caring smile directed at Jordan and not succeeding. He focused on his boy. 'You probably need to get some sleep now, matey.'

'No. I've been sleeping lots.'

True, but the last thing the staff wanted was Jordan when he got overtired and refused to sit still for even a minute. So far he had the room to himself, another perk of being a surgeon's son. 'I'm going to stretch out here with you.' He'd have to try and sort out some time off tomorrow. It wouldn't be easy with a full operating schedule but hopefully his colleagues would step up as they usually did for each other.

'He's calmed down a lot and there've been a few yawns he's tried to hide so you might get lucky with the sleep idea.' Anna smiled at him this time, and his stomach knotted tighter.

No wonder she was so popular around here if she smiled at everyone like that. Half the male staff must bend over backwards to get her attention. Was she single? Funny that he hadn't considered that before. No wedding ring in sight, but that didn't mean a thing. Most of the staff didn't wear jewellery on duty. Anyway, she could be in a steady relationship. Why was he even wondering about her status now? He wasn't interested. He had Jordan to think about, and that meant protecting him from any woman he got close to who wouldn't give his son all the support he needed. 'Right. Thanks again. I'm sure you want to get home now.' He spoke brusquely in an attempt to cover what he was really feeling.

Anna gave him a sharp look before standing up. 'Goodnight, Jordan. I'll see you tomorrow, buddy.' Then she strode out of the room without a backward glance.

'Jerk,' Anna muttered as she strode to the main desk. Eli Forrester came with a reputation for being blunt. More like rude in her book. They'd had a few run-ins over his terse manner with the nurses. He was a superb general surgeon, especially with children, but he'd never read the manual on being friendly with staff. He seemed to think everyone should toe the line when he was around. Not that that stopped her from taking second glances at him when he was on the ward. Not only was he drop dead gorgeous, but there was something about his aloofness that caught at her and had her wanting to know more about what made him tick—when he wasn't being rude, that was. Though he did thank her for staying on to be with Jordan. *'It means a lot.'* That was a small step towards being friendly, which was probably a one-off.

A picture of his face as he held Jordan and kissed the top of his head made her blink, and filled her with a softness for him she wouldn't have believed possible before now. He'd been abrupt with her, but when it came to his son he was a marshmallow in hiding. He obviously loved that boy totally. As any parent did, or should.

Another image tapped her mind. Eli looked shattered. His face was drawn and his body unusually slumped. According to Leanne, Eli had been doing a complicated operation when Jordan was admitted so it would've come as a shock to learn his son had had urgent surgery for appendicitis. No wonder he looked beyond exhausted. He'd have been in a hurry to see Jordan and make sure his boy was doing okay so he wouldn't have stopped to grab a coffee or something to eat.

How come Eli was on his own with his son? There had been no mention of a mother coming in to be with the boy. Was Eli a solo dad? She didn't know the guy other than as a general surgeon qualified in paediatric surgery who sent a lot of patients to the paediatric ward. Plus the fact he was super sexy—when he wasn't being remote, which wasn't often.

'Hey, you'd better get out of here while you can.' Leanne looked up from the computer on her desk.

'I'm on my way. Mr Forrester says he's staying the night with Jordan.'

Leanne's eyes twinkled. 'Why did you call him Mr Forrester and not Eli as per normal?'

'Because he annoyed me.' His blunt manner when she'd been taking care of his son had got to her. She wasn't asking herself why when it was nothing out of the ordinary.

'I know that's not unusual but he is pretty upset about Jordan having surgery when he didn't know.'

Anna let out a long sigh. 'Yeah, I get it.' Well, she would if she were a mother with a young child. Mother to her son. Stop it. The pain from having to give her son up for adoption always hovered just below the surface, raising its head at all sorts of moments to distress her. 'Does Eli drink tea or coffee?' She was going to be nice. It wouldn't hurt and who knew? He might be nice back.

Leanne's eyes widened. 'You're going to get him one?'

'Might as well do the decent thing.' As a reward she'd take another look at that long, sexy shape no doubt now sprawled the length of the bed, then go home and forget all about him. Ha!

'I think the answer's coffee, white with one. While you're at it, can I have a black tea? Pretty please?'

'No problem.' Might as well also heat up the pie she'd brought in for lunch and not got around to eating. Eli probably wouldn't be heading out to grab a meal any time soon, if at all. There was a supermarket handy where he could grab something but she'd save him the bother. She laughed to herself. She was stretching the 'be nice to the jerk' thing, but then she was known for helping people out. Today Dr Eli was no different when it came to needing a helping hand.

Ten minutes later, after she'd given Leanne her tea, she walked into room three carrying a tray.

Eli looked up from the story he was reading to Jordan, who appeared to be two breaths away from sleep. 'Thought you'd be long gone by now.' His voice was barely above a whisper, probably hoping not to wake Jordan. His tired gaze went to the tray. 'What've you got there?'

'Coffee, as well as pie and salad. I figured you probably haven't eaten in a while,' she answered just as quietly, handing over the tray.

'What's in the pie?' He was staring at the plate as though stunned. Maybe he was. Did no one do anything as simple as offering him something to eat?

'Are you allergic to any foods, or is there anything you prefer not to eat?' she asked. It was her version of bacon and egg pie with mushrooms, tomatoes, cheese and parsley thrown in.

'No.'

'Then eat and enjoy. It was my lunch I didn't get time to have.' She got the feeling he didn't want to accept her generous offer. Why had she bothered?

'Anna.' He hesitated, which was so unlike Eli that she had to swallow a smile.

She looked directly at him, her heart tightening at the sight of that gorgeous face. 'Yes?'

'Thank you so much. I do appreciate this. I haven't eaten for hours and since I'm staying here for the night I was going to go without till the morning.' No hint of remoteness now. Instead it had been replaced with something akin to friendliness in his face and steady gaze.

Her heart loosened, letting him a little closer than she liked. 'It's nothing fancy, but it'll fill a gap.'

Eli glanced down at Jordan and then back to her. 'Jordie thinks you're the bee's knees, by the way.'

That was one way to get to her, for sure. She adored children. If only she— *Stop right there.* Nothing could ever change the past, or bring her son back to her. 'He's gorgeous.'

'I think so, but then I am biased,' Eli said with the softest, most caring smile she'd ever witnessed from him.

Blimey, if he smiled like that more often he'd have the whole hospital at his beck and call. He'd certainly have her in the palm of his hand, and she didn't like being at the end of anyone's leash. Working alongside him, she often felt a tingle of longing slide under her skin. He was good-looking in an outdoorsy way, with tanned skin and slightly too long dark hair, and legs that ate up distance in a blink. But then he'd say something in his take-no-prisoners tone and the tingle would disappear in a flash, replaced with annoyance that she'd been aware of him as more than a doctor.

'Aren't all parents?' Stupid thing to say. Hers hadn't been. They'd thought she should do absolutely everything their way when she'd screwed up big time by getting pregnant when she was fifteen. But then they'd always put themselves first. Unfortunately she'd had to do as they'd insisted because there'd been no other option if she wanted her child to have a decent life. One that she couldn't have provided by herself.

A shadow crossed his face. 'Most are, I suppose.'

Ouch. Something, someone, had upset him. Had she put her foot in it? She wasn't asking. That'd only lead to another abrupt comment. 'I'm off. See you both tomorrow.' If Eli was spending the night with Jordan then most likely he'd be here when she started her shift at seven. As for bringing him breakfast, forget it. She'd done her good deed for this man. He could fend for himself tomorrow when he'd be in a better space. Wouldn't he?

'Goodnight, Anna.' Her name sounded like molten chocolate on his tongue, something she could all too easily get used to.

Waving a hand over her shoulder, she left the room without a word. It was enough to have him waking her up more than usual. He was certainly a different man around his son—loving and vulnerable. The vulnerability was a surprise. At least, Eli showing it was. Who knew what else lay behind that intriguing face?

So much for thinking she was immune to a sexy man. Immune, or worn down to the point she'd given up trying to find one to fall in love with and have the family she longed for. It hadn't happened so far and she'd just turned thirty-four. Now, whenever she got close to a man, she started getting nervous about sharing what she'd done with her son because twice she'd told the man in her life and been called a selfish bitch and worse. That made it so much harder to be open about her past and upped her insecurities about being good enough for any man who wanted to have a family with her. She *had* given up her son when he was twenty-four hours old. There'd been no choice. Not that that made her accept what she'd done. If she could go back to that day, she knew she'd do it all over again. For her son's sake, not hers.

It had been the right thing to do. Or so she'd kept telling herself ever since, because how else could she get up every morning to face another day? Barely sixteen years old when he was born and with her parents saying they'd disown her if she kept him, she'd had no choice. She was still at school and even if she'd got a job it wouldn't have paid for accommodation and supporting her son. Her heart had been smashed into so many pieces as the nurse took her baby out of her arms. Not all those pieces had found their way back into place. This was why she got so much from being a paediatric nurse. She could care for children, make them smile, and then let them go home to their families knowing she hadn't let them down. She could never make it up to her son, but she could do her damned best to look out for other children.

With an unusually heavy heart Eli watched Anna go. She got under his skin so effortlessly. No denying it. She'd often had him looking at her twice, or feeling out of sorts around her, but exposing his feelings wasn't possible when he had so much to protect. If his boy's mother could walk out of their lives then how could he trust another woman to stay around for them both? He'd always been able to pull on his neutral face and carry on regardless. Not tonight. He could put it down to exhaustion after a difficult day and Jordan keeping him awake half the night before. But really he'd been shocked to learn Jordan had had surgery. That had knocked him off his feet.

He did like how Nurse Anna had made Jordan happy. Anna, the woman off duty, had worked out he wouldn't take the time to get something to eat because he desperately wanted to be with his son so had brought him food and coffee. He liked her very much for that. But that was where it stopped. He wasn't looking for a lifetime partner.

Not true, Eli.

It really wasn't. For him, falling in love with a wonderful woman to share everything with seemed impossible. Share being the operative word here. Melissa hadn't known the meaning of it. Her pregnancy had been unplanned as they had both still been studying in their respective careers and Melissa had struggled to cope with being pregnant. She'd found it even harder accepting Jordan had Down syndrome. Just before his second birthday she'd asked for a divorce, saying she needed to go offshore to finish her studies in fashion design and that it wouldn't be fair to expect Eli and Jordan to go with her. In other words, she was bailing on her wedding vows *and* her son. One of the upsides was he'd got full custody of Jordan. The other was he'd learnt to be super careful when it came to falling in love. As in it was not happening again while his boy still lived at home, which would be for many years.

He leaned close to Jordie. He loved the little guy so much it hurt. How Melissa could give up her son was beyond him. How could any mother? Or father, come to that. He knew too well how it felt to be abandoned by the one person who should never be able to sever ties with their child. His mother had handed him over to the welfare system when he was six months old because it took too much effort to keep him happy and she had better things to do. He'd been extremely lucky when Jackie and Kerry adopted him. They loved him as much as their two daughters, his adoptive sisters, who'd taken to him just as quickly. He'd grown up knowing he was loved without any boundaries, and always would be. But it still rankled how his birth mother didn't want anything to do with him even now. It wasn't as though he was asking anything of her except to be accepted as a small part of her life.

'That pie's getting cold.' Leanne stood at the end of the bed. 'You won't want Anna to find out you didn't eat it.'

He glanced up at her. 'I was miles away.'

'I could see that. Why don't you sit in the chair while I check Jordan's temperature and vitals?'

Carefully sliding off the bed so as not to disturb Jordie too much, he did as suggested. Savouring the flavours humming across his tongue, he gave a happy sigh. 'This pie's to die for. Did Anna make it?' He'd questioned what was in it and she'd got annoyed. He owed her an apology.

'Probably. She loves cooking. Shh, Jordan. Lie still for me or I'll tickle your chin.'

Jordie's eyes were open and he was staring around as though he'd forgotten where he was. Putting the tray aside, Eli got up and went to hold his hand while Leanne finished the obs.

'All good. I'll give him some more antibiotics when he's due in an hour.'

'Thanks, Leanne. For everything.'

Her eyes widened as though she was unused to him being quite so friendly which, he admitted, was true. He didn't do becoming buddies with his colleagues other than a couple of surgeons he'd known since specialising. He came to work to help patients and then went home to be with Jordan. There wasn't a lot of energy left for anything else.

She said, 'Just doing my job. If you're staying the night then we'd better get a bed in here for you.'

'I'll be fine in the armchair that's across the hallway. I'll haul it in later.' One thing learned along the way to becoming a doctor was sleeping on any manner of furniture. Though it had been a few years since he'd last done that.

'There's a bed that should be in here that the orderly hasn't returned. I'll get it brought up and you cross your fingers we don't get another unexpected wee patient during the night.'

'Can I finish the pie first? Crossed fingers could make for awkward eating and I don't want to waste a crumb.'

Another surprised look came his way before Leanne laughed. 'As I don't want to be the one Anna blames for you not finishing it, I think you'd better get on with the job.'

He couldn't imagine Anna being cross with anyone—other than him. Experience had taught him how it felt when she took offence to his curt instructions. Settling into place beside Jordie, his legs stretched to the end of the narrow bed, he relaxed and enjoyed his meal while thinking about Anna Passau—because it was too easy. She was gorgeous.

Today she'd got under his skin more than ever with how she'd calmed Jordan down, how she'd got him something to eat. Not to mention those damned smiles. He couldn't afford to lose his heart and yet she was making it difficult to remain aloof. He struggled with being let down again after his birth mother and Melissa had each done their number on him. He owned half the marriage break-up because surely if he'd been a good husband she wouldn't have gone? He shouldn't feel like that when his adoptive family had never once let him down, always gave him all the love and support anyone should get from their family, but it was hard to forget how those other two women hadn't cared enough. They'd undermined his belief in himself.

Anna, with her crazy red hair that made his fingers itch at the thought of running his hands over it and her suck-me-in smile that caused his gut to tighten, was a complete turnaround in women for him. Did she have what it took to be that certain special woman? The fact he was even wondering had his toes twitching. He'd have to get back to his usual remote persona tomorrow. Except that felt wrong now. Anna had been nothing but kind and friendly. Even Leanne had laughed with him. Getting onside with the staff could make for happier days at work. He'd learned to be aloof with everyone he worked with after two nurses had continually pestered him for dates and more when they'd heard

Michelle had left him. Neither of them had understood the meaning of no and he'd changed his approach to all staff, especially the females.

Putting aside the tray, he turned to study his little man and his heart expanded as Jordie smiled in his sleep. He was a tough wee fella, took the teasing some kids gave him on the chin. He had some good friends who attended the same preschool. Preschool was his dream come true with lots of games to play, books to read, and other kids to run around with. His teacher aide was exceptional in teaching him basic skills with a pen and paper. With lots of help from his family, Eli worked hard to give Jordan the same loving environment he'd grown up in.

The sound of a bed being wheeled along the corridor diverted him. Something he probably needed about now. All this thinking didn't achieve anything but too many questions he had no answers for. Standing up, he went to help the orderly put the bed in place, even though the guy had done it a thousand times before and he was probably getting in the way. Seemed everyone was stepping up to help him. Especially Anna. A grin spread across his face, stretching his lips further than they were used to. Anna was getting to be a pain in the backside with the number of times she popped into his head.

Quite a gorgeous pain though. One he was happy to put up with for now anyway.

CHAPTER TWO

'MORNING, EVERYONE.' Anna bounced into the ward before seven the morning after Jordan's operation feeling chipper. She loved this job *and* she'd had a good night's sleep despite the exciting interruptions from her brain bringing up images of Dr Forrester. Make that *Mr* Forrester. He wouldn't be pleased with her for calling him 'doctor'. Some specialists couldn't care less, but she didn't intend to find out how Eli felt about that. The fewer grumps from him the better. 'How was the night?' she asked the nurses crowded around the main desk ready to hightail it out of the place asap after the night shift finished.

'Not too bad considering the afternoon you had yesterday,' Debbie answered for everyone. 'No new patients and apart from the girl in the car crash yesterday morning the rest were relatively quiet. Jordan Forrester did wake a couple of times grizzly as all be it, but his dad quietened him down in no time at all.'

'The father's touch,' Anna said. 'You can't beat it.' Except maybe with a mother's touch. *Stop it, Anna. Jealousy won't get you anywhere.* 'Is Eli still here, or has he gone to get some breakfast?'

'I'm showered and dressed for work, which is a lightened workload thanks to my colleagues pitching in to take over some of my minor cases so I can be with Jordan on and off during the day. I'm about to go to the café along the road for a full breakfast,' answered the man himself as he appeared in front of her. He looked a lot more relaxed this morning. Gone were the lines around his eyes and those shoulders were back in place filling his shirt to perfection.

Her heart did a little skip. 'You obviously slept all right despite where you were. How's Jordan doing this morning?'

'Ready to get up and tear the place apart.' Eli laughed. Laughed, as in really let it out.

Unheard of. By her, at any rate. 'I'll be with him shortly.'

'He's asking where you are, and why can't he go to preschool today.' The laughter faded from Eli's eyes. 'Do you have any answers for that one? It must be a question you hear often in here.'

'I'll come up with something. If I'm working with him, that is.' She turned to Leanne, who'd just arrived, looking flustered. 'You okay?'

'I'm good. Luca didn't want to go to kindy and we had a bit of a battle when I tried to get him out of the car.' She shook her head. 'I won in the end. Bribery works wonders sometimes, though now I've got to remember to buy a book about policemen at the end of the day.'

'Sometimes there are no other choices when it comes to getting them to do what's necessary,' Eli said.

Crikey, the guy *was* opening up. Could be due to the fact he'd spent a night in the ward with his son and got to see first hand how hard they all worked and the endless care they gave the kids? But he'd know that. It was more likely that he had a kind, soft side that his son brought out too easily. Another side to him that lifted her already happy spirits and made her take another, longer look at him. He really was something else. 'What do you bribe Jordan with?' she asked, fully expecting him to not answer.

'Chocolate fish.' He smiled, then shrugged. 'Hey, it works at those times I've run out of patience and want to get on with preparing dinner or running his bath.'

'I bet it does. I'd probably behave for a choc fish. No, make that a bag of them.'

Another laugh came her way. It was as though they were the only ones here, but they weren't. Looking around, she drew a breath. Everyone was watching them as though something funny was going on. So she laughed because, damn it, if this wasn't funny then what was? Eli acting relaxed with her was new. Face it, being relaxed with all of the nurses was new.

'Okay, everyone, let's get the day under way.' Leanne had pulled on her sensible hat but there was a cheeky glint in her eyes as though she thought there was more going on between Anna and Eli than was anywhere near close. 'Fill us in on the night and get out of the way. Eli, you're not needed for this. I take it you're up to date with Jordan?'

'I am. He'll be restless now that he's feeling a little better. Just warning you,' he added with a look of worry in those grey eyes that Anna knew never missed a thing.

'We've dealt with similar situations. We'll manage with Jordan,' Anna told him. 'Though his abdomen will be tender for some time to come he'll be fine, promise.'

'I'm sure he will.' Eli didn't look as though he believed himself.

She'd make sure the boy was happy and comfortable in between looking after other wee patients. Moving closer to

Leanne, she listened as their patients were assigned to various nurses, and sighed happily when Jordan was given to her. The little guy had tweaked something that had her wanting to spend more time with him. Just like his dad. Careful. That couldn't happen. Any sort of relationship with a surgeon she worked with could only lead to problems as far as she could see.

She'd dated a paediatrician once and when he'd called it quits after learning she'd given a child up for adoption he'd made sure everyone knew that she wasn't good enough for him. Another nurse who'd also had a similar nasty experience with the jerk about something in her past soon made it known who wasn't good enough and it wasn't Anna or her. Anyway, she wasn't going to dive into anything more than a possible friendship with Eli, and even that was unlikely as everything would settle back to normal once Jordan was discharged and Eli wasn't worried about him.

'Anna, Louisa Crane's coming up from ED shortly. I'd like you to take her too. We'll put her in with Jordan as there aren't any other beds available until the specialists have done their rounds so it works quite well for you.'

'No problem.' Louisa had cystic fibrosis and was a regular here. On past experience they knew she'd be quiet until the treatment kicked in to help her breathing and then she'd want to read stories to Jordan. Though that could take a while, depending on how sick she was. 'How bad is she?'

'Lung infection causing strain on her heart.'

So she wouldn't be reading any stories today. Hopefully Jordan wouldn't be too active or they'd have to look at shifting one of them to another room. 'I'll go see Jordan.' Get the day started.

* * *

'Nurse Anna, I'm all better,' Jordan shouted when she walked into his room.

'Jordie, stop shouting. You're in hospital and other kids are sick,' Eli said sternly from the other side of the room.

Anna wasn't prepared for the sudden flash of heat in her veins. Looking across to Eli, she was confused. He made her light-headed and still she was wary. What was going on? 'Th-thought you were going to breakfast.'

'On my way. Jordan has been talking to his grandmother on my phone.'

'Granny's coming to see me today.' Jordan bounced up and down on the bed, then cried out. 'Ow, that hurts.' His hand went to the surgical wound on his abdomen.

'You have to stop moving around so fast.' Anna took his hand away and lifted the pyjama top. 'If you don't, you'll hurt yourself some more.'

'I don't like hurting.'

'I bet you don't. I'm going to put a new bandage on here and then you can have some breakfast.'

'What do I get?'

'Let's wait and see. It's a surprise.'

'Careful,' warned Eli. 'He's a picky eater.'

Like his father? she wondered, thinking how he'd asked what was in the pie she gave him last night. 'I'll sort it.'

'By the way, that pie was delicious. Thank you for sharing.'

She hadn't had a mouthful of that particular pie. 'You got the lot.'

'I know.' His mouth twitched. 'What did you have instead?'

She'd been having him on. 'The second pie I made at the same time. No point in only making one.'

'You enjoy cooking?'

'I get a kick out of it. So many different recipes to follow—or not.' Though not having someone to share the results with often made her efforts seem pointless. She was popular around here for the cakes and biscuits she brought in for them to try whenever she had a cooking spree, which was quite often. Luckily her hips didn't seem to mind being loaded with yummy treats.

'I'd better get a move on or there won't be time to check up on Jordan before I scrub up for surgery.'

Why did that sound sexy? Scrubbing up in preparation for going into Theatre had to be the most tedious process out there, nothing to do with heating blood or super-active heart rates. But still, the thought of Eli doing that was winding her up something terrible. Focusing on her little patient, she waited for her heartbeat to return to normal. 'Let me have a look at your tummy, Jordan.'

He'd pulled his top down. 'No. It hurts.'

'That's why I want to see it.' She didn't think there'd be anything wrong but there was only one way to be certain. Gently extricating the pyjama top from Jordan's fist, she lifted it up and pulled his bottoms down enough to expose the covered wound. 'I'm going to remove this,' she reaffirmed as she tapped the dressing.

'Why?'

'You need a clean one.'

'Why?'

'So you get better faster.'

'How?'

Did this kid ever stop with the questions? 'There's a cut in your tummy. It will be getting back together and we need to help it by keeping the dressing clean.' Glancing around, she saw that Eli had left them. Or left her to the list of questions. He'd probably known they'd been coming. Back to Jordan, she grinned. 'You'll have a little line there to show your friends. They'll be jealous.'

'Yes.' He fist-pumped the air. 'I like that.'

Hopefully she'd talk him into eating his breakfast just as easily.

When he returned from breakfast, Eli found Jordan sitting up in bed looking at a picture book, a wide smile on his face. 'Hey, man, you look happy.'

'Nurse Anna got me this book out of a cupboard. She told me it's the best one about elephants.'

Again Nurse Anna to the fore. 'What else did she tell you to do?'

'I had to eat the cornflakes and peaches first.'

Good for you, Anna.

Bribery wasn't off her list any more than his, he thought with a grin. Of course, if she were a parent, she'd be a dab hand at getting the result she wanted. Did she have any kids of her own? 'And you did.' Jordan wouldn't be holding the book otherwise.

'I have to look after my tummy. Dad, did you know I've got a line on my skin? Nurse Anna told me. I'm going to show it to everyone when I get to school.'

The things that made kids happy. 'It's called a scar.' Hopefully a very small one. Though at the moment, Jordan would no doubt be happy if it was large. Nurse Anna had a way of making everything come up smelling of roses when it came to his son. Something to be aware of. He didn't want Jordan to think she was becoming a part of their lives, as he often did with people he liked a lot. Sometimes that caused problems when he realised they weren't going to stay around. With a bit of luck and all going to plan, he'd take Jordan home tonight and then Anna wouldn't feature in Jordan's life any more. Except *he'd* have to accept she'd still be here, working with some of his patients, filling the air with the scent of vanilla and reminding him of the cookies his mother baked for him as a kid.

'Can you read to me?' Jordan asked, hope in his face.

He hated to disappoint him, but he had no choice. 'Sorry, Jordie, but I've got to start work. I'll be back to see you later.' First up was a thyroidectomy, then, because Duncan had taken his next patient, he had a break to be with Jordan before his next scheduled op at eleven.

Jordie's face screwed up with disappointment. 'That's not fair.'

'You know I have to help people get better.' He was always explaining how he had to work and that not all his time could be spent with Jordan, but, like most kids, Jordie always tried to persuade Eli to hang around for a bit longer.

'Like Nurse Anna does?'

Time to get out of here. 'Yes.' Nurse Anna had certainly turned his son's head. He hoped she didn't do the same to him. He hadn't been able to put her out of his mind all night. He only hoped that was because he'd been in here where she worked, and not because of the way she distracted him and heated his body all too quickly with little more than a glance. 'See you later, boyo.' He brushed a kiss on his son's head. He was the luckiest man alive, having Jordan in his life. Thankfully everything had gone well yesterday, and they'd soon be back to normal.

The sound of Anna laughing reached him as he walked to the lift. Certain muscles tightened and his mouth tipped up into a cheerful smile. Her laughter made him light-hearted and it hadn't even been directed his way.

The lift pinged and the door slid open.

Stepping inside, he pressed the floor for Theatre and turned to lean back against the wall.

'Wait.' Anna flew through the closing doors and tapped floor two before spinning around and colliding with him.

Eli grabbed her to keep her on her feet. 'Careful.'

She looked up at him. 'Oh, Eli, sorry.'

'Where are you off to in such a hurry?' He didn't remove his hands from her arms, just absorbed the warmth in his hands and gazed down into those suck-him-in eyes that had followed him into sleep last night.

'Pharmacy.' She sounded surprised, as if she'd forgotten what she was doing. Her eyes widened, but she didn't pull back.

He could feel himself falling into her gaze. 'Anna.' Her name roared through his head. Dropping his hands, he stepped back, bumped up against the wall. Anna was beautiful inside and out. And waking him up fast. Too fast considering it was only yesterday Jordan had his surgery and he hadn't had time to think about what was going on. Yet his body was zinging with lust. It took all his self-control not to reach out and haul her against him, to kiss those sensational—

Ping. The doors began sliding open.

He straightened instantly, and drew a lungful. What the hell had he been thinking? They were at work. Nor were they an item. Anna might be out-of-this-world attractive but hell. He slammed fingers through his hair.

Get back on track, go see some patients, forget the heat firing you up.

That easy? Hardly. Worse, now he knew she was even more kind and generous than he'd realised. Remember he had a son to protect, as well as a heart to keep safe.

Anna charged out of the lift without a backward glance.

'See you later,' he said under his breath as she disappeared along the corridor and other people stepped into the space she'd vacated. No one took his breath away as Anna suddenly did. No one. Pulling on his professional face, he leaned against the wall and waited impatiently for the lift to drop another level so he could get on with his day without any distractions of the bewildering, taking-over-his-rationale kind.

Damn you, Nurse Anna. You're something else, and I'm getting rattled by how easily you're undermining my strength to remain aloof when it comes to women.

Ping.

Thank goodness for something. He stepped around people who weren't budging and made his way out of the lift and along to Theatre, to work, his go-to place when he couldn't cope with problems.

Anna's not a problem.

Too right she was if she could trip him up so easily.

'Morning, slow coach.' Phil, the anaesthetist he was working with, tapped the computer screen when Eli joined him in their theatre unit all scrubbed up. 'Millie Lewis is prepped and ready to go nigh-nigh soon as you're ready.'

'It was hard to leave Jordan.'

'You're fine. Millie was only brought in two minutes ago. Just like winding you up.' Phil was looking at him as if there were a wart growing on his chin. 'How is the wee lad?'

'Bouncing around too much but Anna seems to quieten him down easily enough.'

Phil laughed. 'No surprise there.'

Seemed Anna's reputation as a superb nurse was well known. Time to focus on the operation and forget her. 'I'll talk to Millie now.' The teenager was having a thyroidectomy and was lying on the table a few feet away, no doubt already dozy from the sedative she'd have been given after Phil talked to her. 'Morning, Millie.'

The girl dragged her eyes open. 'Hello, Doctor.'

'Looks like you're ready for this. Any last-minute questions?' Always a tricky one but he liked his patients to feel confident about going under the knife. As much as possible anyway.

'None. Just get it over, will you?'

'Phil, I think that's your call to give Millie something stronger. I'll talk to you later, Millie.' He waited until the anaesthetist gave the nod that she was properly under and then picked up the scalpel. 'Everyone ready?'

Nods all round gave him the go-ahead. 'Right, let's do this.'

Prescription in hand, Anna took the stairs back to the ward to avoid bumping into Eli again if he decided to check on Jordan before going to Theatre. Knowing her luck he'd be in the same lift if she pressed the button and right this minute he was the last person she needed to see. He'd already pressed her buttons, which was left-field considering how, until now, she'd always managed to keep a lid on the flare of excitement she often felt when he was around. And all the moments when he annoyed the hell out of her with his aloofness.

Yet back in the lift, she'd wanted to lean into him, to touch him, feel that amazing body against her. Talk about losing her mind.

Now what? It wasn't as if she could avoid Eli. She couldn't spend her shifts watching out for him and then hiding in the linen room until he left the floor. So back to ignoring the way he got her in a tizz and carry on as though he didn't interest her one little bit. These sensations he caused meant nothing. Just focus on the fact they were doctor and nurse in the same hospital. Doctor and nurse! Ha. Sounded like a line for a romance novel.

Except her romance couldn't include falling for a man who had a son because of her history of two relationships going pear-shaped when the man involved learned about how she gave up her baby. Neither of them had accepted she'd had no choice. She had no doubt the same would happen if she got close to Eli and told him her story. Losing Eli if they were involved would be bad, but it would be dreadful to hurt innocent little Jordan, who'd have no say in the matter. Of course, she was getting ahead of herself, something she didn't normally do. They weren't in any type of relationship, but this was a big indicator that she was already caught up in his aura. She hadn't had thoughts like this about any man in a long time.

'You look like someone stole your lunch out from under your gaze.' Leanne laughed when she reached the ward.

The problem with best friends was they knew her too well. 'If only it was that simple.' She said that? Once more it showed how much Eli got to her. 'I had to come up the stairs as the lifts were busy.'

'Try again. You take the stairs at least once a day, usually more often.'

Anna said nothing, instead picked up a file and pretended to read it.

'Nothing to do with Dr Delicious by any chance?'

'Why would it be?' she snapped, a dead giveaway if ever there was one.

Leanne laughed again. 'Knew it. You'll have to work harder at keeping a straight face if this is going to continue.'

Dropping onto a chair, Anna huffed out the air stalled in her lungs. 'It's not.' Another giveaway. Talk about losing grip on her sanity. All because of a sexy man in boring scrubs with the most intense grey eyes that saw far too much for his own good. Or hers. 'He's too aloof for me.' That intense way he'd looked at her in the lift gave her the shivers. Hot shivers full of need.

'Eli keeps everything close to his chest. We've all commented over time about how he never gives anything away about himself. I reckon it's because we had Jordan in here that he's let go a little,' Leanne commented. 'How good you were with his little boy did get to him and probably helped him relax a bit. It was obvious he liked how you made Jordan feel comfortable. He's been watching out for you ever since.'

She did not need to hear that. It only intensified her thoughts about him. 'I'll have whatever you're on, Leanne, because that sounds like a load of drivel even to me.' But if she was right, then she might be willing to look a bit deeper into what made the man tick. Take a risk? When it could, and most likely would, turn to rubbish and make life very awkward here. Because no matter what happened in her personal life she was not leaving this job. She loved it, loved helping other people's children get better, loved making them laugh when all they wanted to do was cry. It went a little way to atoning for letting her son go.

'He's a great guy.' Leanne was still laughing but there was sympathy in her eyes. 'Why not get to know him better? You deserve a break, Anna. You should have someone to go home to at the end of the day. Someone to share more than work with.'

Another problem with besties was they didn't know when to shut up. 'Stop right there. I'm not ready.' Which was a lie. She was past ready, but hadn't found a man who'd accept her for who she was, and not what she'd done. Throw in that she didn't believe she deserved such happiness when she'd let her son go and a happy ever after was never going to happen. But could it be time to move on? Could she do it? A picture of Eli as he'd gazed at her in the lift filled her head. Why not try? Simple. Getting hurt again wasn't an option. There were only so many times her heart could take a hit, and she'd already done them.

'You're well and truly ready.' Leanne picked up the prescription from where Anna had plonked it. 'Now, let's get back to work.'

Relieved, Anna headed over to see an eleven-year-old girl who'd had a plate attached to a broken ankle yesterday. 'Hey, Jenna, how's things?'

'Sore. The physio made me do exercises and they hurt.'

Back to normal. This she could deal with. Way better than spending minutes in a lift with Dr Sexy. Damn it all. Because she did feel disappointed that nothing could come of these new sensations Eli caused. Nothing. It was too risky.

CHAPTER THREE

ON FRIDAY A loud bell buzzed indicating an emergency. Eli leapt up from the computer where he was going through patient notes. 'Room four,' he said loudly as he sped down the ward so anyone around might hear and come to help.

Leanne was right beside him. 'We put an eleven-year-old boy in there two hours ago after he came back from Theatre where he had fluid drained off his lung. But there are two other boys in that room too.'

When he entered the room the first thing he saw was Anna desperately holding down a boy fighting to get off the bed. 'What's going on?'

'Adverse reaction to something,' Anna said through gritted teeth. 'He's been fighting me for a few minutes and I had to get one of the other boys to press the call button as I needed both hands here,' she gasped.

He moved to the other side of the bed and placed his hands on the boy's shoulders. 'Here, let me take over.'

'Anthony, can you hear me?' Anna asked, still holding down the boy. 'He won't answer any of my questions. I'm not even sure he *can* hear me.'

Typical for a seizure, which was what this looked like. 'What analgesic was administered after the procedure?' Pain killers didn't usually have this effect but he knew it wasn't always the case. The boy's breathing was shallow and rapid.

Anna told him and added, 'He's also on another medicine for hyperventilation.'

Great. 'Leanne, get the defib just in case.'

'Onto it.'

Anna placed a hand on Anthony's wrist, tried to take his pulse. 'Not easy when he's pulling and shoving. Calm down, Anthony. We're trying to help you.'

'Sweat's pouring off him. Oof.' An elbow slammed into Eli's side, knocking the air out of his lungs.

Anna reached for the boy's arm, grabbed it and held tight. 'He has no idea what's going on, does he?'

'Afraid not. This is severe.'

'I didn't get a proper pulse reading but it's rapid.'

'Exactly as I expected. Damn.'

Anthony had suddenly gone limp. His mouth hung open and his chest was still.

'No pulse,' Anna reported calmly.

Clenching his hands together, Eli placed them on the boy's chest and pressed hard. One, two. 'Where's that defib?' Three, four.

'Coming through the door.' Anna stood ready to breathe into the boy's lungs when he reached the number of compressions required.

'Here we go.' Leanne placed the machine on the stand and handed Anna the leads to place on Anthony's chest.

'Twenty-nine, thirty,' Eli called calmly.

Quickly setting the leads aside, Anna drew a breath and exhaled into Anthony once, then again before straightening up and placing the tabs from the defib on the exposed chest. Nodding at Leanne, she said, 'Ready.'

'Stand back,' Leanne replied.

Eli stopped the compressions and moved back one step, ready to go again if the electrical current didn't start Anthony's heart. 'Ready.'

The boy's body jerked upward, dropped back onto the mattress. The defibrillator showed a green line moving up and down.

Relief poured through Eli. 'That was close.' Having to continue compressions on a kid was awful. Their ribs often cracked under the pressure and instinct said go lightly even when medical training said the opposite. 'Right, let's see where we're at with this guy.'

Anna was already taking his pulse, and there was a relieved look on her face. She didn't mess around for sure. When she saw him looking at her, she nodded. 'Steady and stronger than it was. Still fast but nothing like before.'

'His chest's steadier too. His skin's hot.' He took the temperature gauge Anna held in her free hand and placed it in Anthony's ear. 'Thirty-eight point three. Who's his specialist?'

'Hillary. She's got appointments at Outpatients now.'

'I'll give her a call.' It wasn't his place to take over treating Anthony now that they had him under control. 'He needs sedating and no more of the drugs he's had.'

Anna's nod was sharp, but he didn't take offence. She'd know all that but accepted it was his place to point it out. 'I'm not leaving his side for a moment. Fingers crossed he doesn't have another seizure.' Her smile was sad. 'The poor kid. That was scary.'

'You all right? He fought hard when you were trying to hold him down. You didn't get a whack too?'

She shook her head, making her ponytail swish across her back.

His fingers tingled as he imagined those red curls spilled over her skin. *Down, boy.*

'No. You were the unlucky one there.'

'It wasn't too hard. I got more of a surprise really.' There'd probably be a bruise to remind him to be careful around out-of-control patients. 'I'll be back once I've talked to Hillary.' Heading out of the room, he refrained from turning around for another look at Anna. He was at work, and the emergency might be over, but there were still things to be done for Anthony. The kid could have another seizure any time. Though he doubted it would happen, this was the medical world and no one knew exactly what was coming at any moment.

When he returned to room four and saw Anna gently wiping down Anthony to remove the sweat, a flutter of longing caught at him. This was how she'd been with Jordie the other night. So gentle and caring. He wanted a part of that. Pulling up sharply, he smothered a groan and said, 'Hillary's on her way up.'

'Good.' Anna lifted her eyes from Anthony and looked directly at him. 'He's a lucky boy.'

Because you helped save him.

'Yes, he is.'

Rubbing her lower back at the end of night shift over a week after she and Eli had worked to save Anthony's life, Anna sighed. 'Glad that's over.' It had been a busy night on the ward with a boy coming from emergency surgery to his abdomen after being in a car accident, followed by another boy being admitted with both his arms badly fractured after falling out of a second-floor window. All a bit much to cope with.

'Get out of here while you can,' Gabrielle said. 'I've read your notes, and don't need any further explanations.'

Anna gave the other nurse a tired smile. Thank goodness for something. Throw in that it was Saturday and she had two days off and things could start looking up. 'Hope your shift's not too stressful.' She'd say break a leg, but was afraid of tempting fate. 'See you. I need some food to shut up my grumbling stomach.' She turned and almost walked into Eli. Jerking backwards, she said, 'Oh, hello.'

'Hi.' He caught her arm to steady her, then drew her away from everyone else. 'Glad to hear you're hungry because I'm here to suggest you join me for breakfast at the café down the road.'

Why would he do that when he'd been all but avoiding her since that awkward moment in the lift last week unless a patient was involved? 'Are you sure?'

His mouth twitched in amusement. 'Wouldn't ask if I wasn't.'

Fair enough. But did she want to spend time with him outside work, or anywhere? Sitting at a table together could be tricky. There again, it might help thaw the chill between them and they could get on with being friendly. So, 'I'd like that. Be warned, a piece of toast won't fix what's upsetting my stomach.'

His laugh was light and sensuous, not what she needed if she was going to eat. 'Nothing like a full breakfast to do the job.'

As they rode the lift down to the ground floor, she aimed for light conversation. 'Why are you here this early?'

'I had a patient in General to check on.'

'You knew I was on nights?'

'That's why I'm here to ask you to join me.'

It was starting to sound like a date, except it wasn't one. Couldn't be. Not after how stilted they'd been around one another recently. 'You don't have my number. But then why would you?'

'No reason except I'd like it now. Who knows when I might get the urge to give you a call?' He looked a little surprised at himself.

She definitely was. She'd never have believed Eli Forrester would say something like that if he hadn't thought it through first. Good sign? Had she rattled him a little? Cool. Because he'd done more than rattle her so it was only fair he should suffer too. 'I'll give it to you over breakfast as long as I get yours in return.' Not that she could imagine calling him without good cause. But who knew what that might be? Could be she just wanted to hear his deep, husky voice. Oh, yes.

He smiled at her. 'Deal.'

Now Anna laughed, freely and happily. She was sharing breakfast with a man she'd never have believed would want a bar of her. He was so polished and kept to himself so she couldn't imagine she'd be his type in any way. She might be exhausted but this was giving her new energy.

'I want to thank you for that dinner you gave me the other night,' Eli told her, dampening her excitement a tad.

'You don't owe me for that.'

'It's an excuse, all right?'

An excuse for what? He didn't need one. But then she didn't exactly put it out there how attracted to him she was. That would be beyond stupid. Back to feeling happy, she said, 'Fair enough.' That wasn't giving anything away about how she truly felt, if she even knew.

'How is Jordan? Back up to speed?'

'Pretty much. He's excited to be going to preschool today.'

'I bet he is.'

'In here,' Eli indicated the café they were going to.

'Morning, Eli,' the woman behind the counter called as they walked in. 'Grab your usual table while you can. I'll bring the menu over for your friend.'

'Cheers, Margaret.' Eli pulled out a chair at a table for two set by the window. 'Here you go.'

A gentleman too. But then she'd have been surprised if he wasn't. He seemed to look out for people in many ways without giving anything away about himself. Sitting down, she asked, 'So Jordan's back on his feet?' He'd gone home the day after his surgery when Eli had finished work.

'There's been no stopping him since he got home. Almost too energetic at times. It worried Mum he might do some harm to himself but you can't keep a pup down for long.'

'Are you a solo dad?' No mother had turned up to be with Jordan in hospital. Might as well gain what info she could while she had the chance. Unless he changed his mind about sharing breakfast. She shrugged mentally. Too late to be worrying about that.

'I am.' He sat up even straighter. 'Mum and my sister Liz help out a lot. I owe them big time. Dad too.'

Lucky you.

'Do they look after him when you're on call?' Would he carry on with this?

'He stays over with Mum or one of my sisters then. Everyone's so helpful, but then they adore Jordie.'

'Nothing like a good family.' If only. Not only had her family not given her any support when she was pregnant, they'd been infuriated when she'd managed to put herself through nursing school without asking for a cent. Working at supermarkets filling shelves when not studying had been hard but a good lesson on life.

'You winced then. Your family not close?'

Guess she deserved to be asked personal questions when she hadn't kept her mouth shut about his, but that didn't stop her speaking sharply. 'Let's just say that my parents haven't always been there for me when I've needed them.'

A menu appeared on the table in front of her.

'Here you go. What would you like to drink?' the woman asked.

Saved from further questions about a tricky subject, she smiled at the woman. 'A pot of tea, thanks.' After quickly scanning the menu she glanced up to find Eli watching her. 'I'll have the full breakfast with eggs scrambled.'

He nodded. 'Way to go. Make that two, Margaret. Plus the usual coffee.'

'Done.'

'It must be difficult at times raising your son on your own.'

'It has its moments but I wouldn't change a thing. I have full custody of Jordan. My wife left when he was two.' Eli looked away, swallowed hard.

She felt bad for asking now. 'You're a very caring dad.

Spending the night with him in hospital to make sure he wasn't frightened whenever he woke and found himself amongst strangers in a strange place was lovely.'

'Thanks.'

'I'll shut up now.'

'Good.' Eli looked at her, and a tiny smile emerged on his sensuous lips. 'I might as well finish the story then your mind can rest. Melissa wanted to move to New York to further her career in fashion design. Though the idea of living in such a huge city didn't appeal I was prepared to back Melissa in her choices, and thought we'd go as a family as people do. Turned out I wasn't wanted. Nor was Jordan.' He didn't sound sad or upset. More relieved, if anything. Not such a great marriage in the first place?

'I'm sorry to hear that.' For his sake. Maybe not hers. *Settle.* They were having breakfast, not on a hot date.

'What about you? Been married?' He'd flipped the conversation back on her.

Damn him. 'I've had two serious relationships.' She could talk about those without giving too much away. 'The first man was Danny. When we met he was a trainee doctor and I'd been qualified for a year. We were together about two years before we began to drift apart. No argy-bargy, nothing awful.' Apart from the fact he was appalled that she'd given up her son, though he'd tried to accept it for a while. His reaction had made her believe she didn't deserve to have a happy family life after putting her son up for adoption. 'We were spending more and more time apart, doing our own things, and finally went separate ways.'

Their drinks arrived and she took a moment to pour a mug of tea. 'I've seen Danny a couple of times since and have no regrets. He's happily married with two toddlers hanging around his feet.' If only she'd been so lucky. But there was still time. Thirty-four wasn't too old to have babies, or to raise them into something resembling decent young adults. 'The second relationship was no better.' A lot worse. 'I wasn't good enough and that was that.'

'I'm sorry to hear that.' Eli was regarding her with something like compassion, which didn't please her.

He didn't know the whole story and if she told him there'd only be disgust in those beautiful eyes. She'd seen it often enough to know what to expect.

Move on before he asked something she'd refuse to answer. 'Does Jordan's mother keep in touch with him?'

His mouth flattened. 'She phones for his birthday and Christmas, and a few other times. Whenever she returns to New Zealand, which isn't often, she'll drop by for a brief visit.'

I haven't met her and I don't like her.

'That's so not fair.' It seemed there were more ways than one to lose a parent. Which was worse? To never have known your birth mother, or to have spent two years with her and still lose her? Tea slopped over the rim as she picked up her mug.

Eli handed her a paper napkin. 'You're right, but then there's no knowing when someone will put themselves before their child.'

More tea sloshed out of her mug. She put it down fast. Eli would definitely be appalled to learn what she'd done. He wouldn't listen to the reasons, would only hear that she'd left her son. 'You're right,' she said, instantly regretting her reply. This man was too astute for her to be saying things like that. He wasn't right though. Her boy had deserved better than she'd been able to give him.

'You okay?'

No, she wanted to run out of here, get away from Eli and his questions. But it was her fault he'd asked since she'd talked about Jordan first. Anyway, if she was going to start looking for the life she really wanted, she had to stay, face up to whatever came next because if she found a man to love then she'd have to tell him everything. Did she want that? Looking at Eli, she knew she did. Not why, only that it was time to turn her life around. Starting now. 'Sorry, I get upset when I hear about parents doing awful things with their children.'

A frown appeared on that handsome face.

Her reaction had been strong, too strong for what she'd said. Warning—Eli wasn't a pushover. Again she lifted her mug and this time didn't spill a drop—probably because the top half had already splashed onto the table. 'The reason behind that is something I don't want to talk about.' She couldn't be more honest than that. Not yet. He didn't need to know her history until she knew him way better, until he understood more about her so he might accept why she'd done what she did.

Slowly his frown disappeared. 'Fair enough.' He sipped his coffee, looking worried. 'We have opened up pretty quickly.' Then he smiled and she knew everything was all right for now. 'I'm not used to doing that, and I suspect behind that regular smile you're much the same.'

He understood that while she talked a lot, she didn't often say anything about what really held her back from a normal life. Dredging up a smile in return, she admitted, 'True.'

'Relax. I'm not going to push for answers.' He stood up. 'But I am going to get a cloth to wipe away that tea.'

Just then Margaret appeared with two laden plates. 'I'll do that. You sit and enjoy this.'

Anna stared at the plate. 'I'm going to be here half the day.' There was enough food to feed the kids in room one on the ward.

'We do doggy bags.' Margaret laughed.

'I haven't been known to leave anything on my plate,' Eli said as he ground black pepper over his. 'Not even here.'

Where did he put it all? There wasn't any sign of over-indulging on that amazing body. 'Is that a challenge?' Yeah, and she knew where the result would show on her figure.

'Could be,' he said through a grin, looking relaxed again, as if their tense conversation had taken a back seat.

Hopefully it had because she wasn't prepared to tell him about her baby. Very few people knew and that was how she liked to keep it. 'You're on.'

For a while they focused on eating and not talking, which was fine with her. She could talk the tail off a donkey but not when it came to personal subjects.

When Eli placed his cutlery on his empty plate and pushed it aside she knew he had something to get off his chest. He wore a studied look. Something serious was going on behind those grey eyes. For the life of her, she could not think what it was, and her stomach knotted.

Then he pulled an envelope out of his pocket. 'This is for you.'

Nurs Ana was written on the front in a young child's wobbly style. 'From Jordan?'

'Yes.'

'That's sweet.' Sliding her finger under the flap, she opened the envelope and withdrew a card. Warmth stole through her. 'An invitation to a party?' Then she remembered something about him starting school soon. 'Jordan's birthday?'

'Yes.'

She opened the card and read her name again, spelt properly this time. The party was on Sunday afternoon. Tomorrow. If she accepted, that meant a shopping trip after she'd grabbed some sleep this morning. Why was she invited? She didn't know the boy other than his time in the ward. He was adorable, but she wasn't part of his life, though it was tempting to accept because she did like the little guy, *and* she'd get to see Eli outside the hospital. As she was doing now. She glanced at him, her heart sinking. The worried look she was receiving said he didn't want her to accept. 'What's the problem?'

Leaning back in his chair, he asked softly, 'Do you want to come?'

Put it back on her, why didn't he? She'd go with honest. 'I'd love to but I'm not sure why I've been invited. Was it your idea, or Jordan's?' She thought she knew the answer but wanted to know for sure.

'Jordan's.'

Got that right at least.

Leaning forward, Eli added, 'I'll be truthful. I tried to talk him out of it but he refused to listen.'

'You don't want him getting too close to me and then me not being around any more. He'll be hurt.'

'Correct.'

'So you want me to turn down the invitation and hurt him

anyway.' She did understand. Better now than later when they'd had a bit more time together, but Eli wasn't giving her a chance to show she could be reasonable and keep the barriers up.

'No, I don't.' So Eli could surprise her on more than one thing. 'I'm between a rock and a hard place but then my dad always says I overthink things, that sometimes I should let them unfold as they're meant to and deal with the consequences later, if there are any.'

She stared at him. 'I have no idea where this leaves me. He's a great little guy and I'm thrilled to be asked to come to the party, but I also don't want to be the cause of any problems for either of you.'

Eli sat quietly, as though thinking it through some more. Finally, 'Tick yes on the reply card and I'll give it to him when I get home.' There was a wobbly smile on Eli's face that gave her no clue to what he was really thinking.

'Are you sure?'

'I'm very protective of my son, and don't ever forget that, but yes, I'm sure.'

'Can't say I blame you about looking out for Jordan.' His mother had done a bunk. A few phone calls and rare visits didn't make up for that. 'His heart must've been broken when Melissa left.'

'I don't think he'll ever understand. Why would he? I don't.'

There was a depth behind those words she didn't quite understand. Anger at what his wife had done, sure, but she sensed more to it. The pain over losing the woman he loved too would have something to do with it. Not that she'd be asking. She did know when to keep her mouth shut sometimes. So why was she laying her hand on top of his? 'He's a very lucky boy to have you for a dad.'

Eli's hand turned over and his fingers wrapped around hers, squeezed ever so lightly before he pulled back as though he'd been stung. 'Thank you.'

Despite his withdrawal she liked this man a lot. He was genuine and caring and adorable. Her kind of man, if she had a kind. So far she'd always been wrong about the men she'd had anything to do with romantically and that had made her believe even more that she didn't deserve to be happy. She dug in her bag for a pen. 'I'll answer the invitation now.'

'When's the last time you went to a kid's party?' he asked with a crooked grin.

'Another challenge?'

'Could be.' He laughed, totally relaxed again. This man could go from hot to cold and back again pretty quickly.

'It was two months ago. Leanne's a close friend. She and her husband have two youngsters and I spend quite a bit of time with them.' They were the children she let most into her heart, believing they'd always be in her life in one way or another.

'Damn, I think I've lost that one before we've even started.'

Not quite, Anna thought the next afternoon when she walked around Eli's house with a plate of chocolate-chip cookies she'd baked that morning, following the excited shrieks coming from the back lawn. It wasn't the kids that were giving her butterflies, but meeting Eli's family. They were the unknown, and must wonder why Jordan had invited her. Hopefully they'd accept it for what she presumed it was—a result of spending time with him when he was hurting from his surgery. She'd briefly met Jackie, Eli's mother, when she'd come to visit Jordan in hospital, but as they'd been flat-out busy and her shift had been about to end it had only been a passing hello.

'Nurse Anna, you came.' Jordan charged at her like a bull on steroids.

She braced for the impact, caught him as he banged into her. 'Happy birthday, Jordan. Thank you for asking me to your party.'

'You had to come. I wanted it. Is that for me?' He was reaching for the brightly wrapped parcel in her shoulder bag.

'Steady, Jordan. Remember your manners.' Eli strode towards them. 'Howdy, Anna. Glad you made it.' He looked genuinely pleased as he took the cookies from her hand.

'I wouldn't not come after saying I would.'

'I figured. Now, Jordan, what do you say?'

'Thank you, Anna. Can I open it now?' He was already tearing at the paper.

'Of course you can. It's yours.' She smiled at the excitement on his face. Fingers crossed elephants were still the flavour of the month.

'Yippee,' Jordan shrieked as he stared at his gift with big eyes. 'Look at this, Dad. Grandma, look. I've got a elephant.'

'*An* elephant,' Eli corrected through a smile. 'Thank you, Anna. You've really made his day. Now come and meet the tribe.'

'Glad I got it right,' she admitted. 'Kids change their minds about what they like all the time.'

'Dad, this is Anna Passau. Anna, meet Kerry Forrester, and mum, Jackie, who you've already met.'

'Nurse Anna, lovely to meet you. Jordan hasn't stopped talking about you since he came out of hospital.' Kerry gave her a brief hug. 'You rock, apparently.'

Wow, talk about making her feel comfortable in an instant. 'He's a great wee guy. Nice to meet you, and hello again, Jackie.'

'Hi, Anna. We are thrilled you've joined us for the party.' Another hug came her way.

Thrilled? A bit OTT, surely? But then again, she could get to like the family after a welcome like this. Down, girl. It was only a birthday party for their grandchild, nothing more. 'Glad to be here.' Even when it did seem a little strange being invited to a patient's party, even if his father was a colleague and getting a little closer. As a friend or more? No idea. 'I really am.'

Jackie flicked Eli a smile before saying to her, 'You have to meet the sisters and their better halves. Come on.'

Eli shrugged exaggeratedly. 'I've been made redundant.'

'You get to run pin the tail on the horse,' Jackie said.

'Great. I had Anna down for that. From what I've observed she's good at keeping kids under control.'

'I'd far rather watch you do it,' Anna said.

'You're returning my challenge, aren't you?' His shoulders lifted and he winked. 'Just watch and be warned.'

'Hi, you must be Anna.' A woman dressed in jeans and a black and white striped shirt held out her hand. 'I'm Liz, Eli's big sister.' Nothing big about her, all slim and short.

'Hello, Liz.'

'Bossy sister,' Eli called over his shoulder as he knelt down to sort out the game.

'No, that's my role. Hi, Anna. I'm Karen, the best sister.' Another hand to shake. This time getting a thorough once-over.

Suddenly Anna felt almost shy, which was unheard of. 'Hello, Karen.' Why were these women checking her out so thoroughly? She was here for Jordan's birthday, nothing else. Except she had been looking forward to spending some time with Eli as well, when and if he had any to spare given it was his son's party.

'Feel like a wine?' Liz asked. 'It might be Jordan's party but adults are allowed to relax too. It might help you deal with all of us. We're not known for being aloof.'

Unlike your brother?

'I'd love a small one.' She followed Liz to the table set up on the veranda. 'Which are your two?'

Liz looked surprised she knew that. 'Over there by the bouncy castle is Mackenzie. She's six, and Thomas is the boy in a green T-shirt giving his father a hard time about cooking the sausages on the barbecue. He's seven.'

Anna felt a familiar tug at her heart. She'd missed out on so much with her boy, especially the simple things like sharing a barbecue. 'They're lovely.'

'They're hell on legs, is what they are.' Liz laughed. 'But I love hell when it comes packaged as my two. What about you? Any children?'

'Not yet,' she said. It was her standard answer to save having to go through the story that could never be changed. 'But who knows what's around the corner?'

'Always fun taking a peek. Here, Sauv Blanc or Pinot Gris?'

'Pinot Gris, thanks.' When she took the glass Liz handed her, her first instinct was to swallow the lot and get a refill. She needed to calm down, and stop thinking everyone wanted to learn all there was to know about her. This was Eli's family. Of course they were being chatty and asking what for most people were perfectly normal questions. Looking over at Eli, she said, 'I'd better go see what I can do to help.'

'No need. That's not why you're here.'

'Old habit to the fore.' Keeping busy meant staying away from difficult questions.

Eli clapped his hands. 'Okay, kids, over here. We're going to put blindfolds on you and then you have to stick a tail on the horse. The one who gets closest to the right place gets a parcel. Let's do this.' He glanced at Anna. 'Want a turn? Or would you prefer to take a tumble on the bouncy castle?'

He really was different away from work. Because he was with his family and could relax completely as he didn't have anything to hide from these people? There was a thought. But what would a man like Eli need to hide? He was always calm and confident. And aloof. Of course.

Stop with the questions and get on with enjoying yourself.

Good idea, Anna admitted. 'Not if you want that castle to stay in one piece. Even pinning the tail on could have dire results. My sense of direction isn't flash, and that's without a blindfold.'

'You're hardly going to get that confused,' he said happily. 'From what I've seen you're always aware of where you are and what you're doing.'

She could take his compliments any time. He'd obviously been taking notice of her at work, which made her feel good. Desperate to be noticed by an attractive man, by any chance? 'Come on, the kids are impatient to get started.'

Eli just laughed. 'What's new about that?'

'True.' She'd dealt with enough kids of all ages through her job to know he was right.

By the time all the children had had a couple of turns sticking the tail on the horse they were eager to know who'd won while demanding food and sodas at the same time. Eli studied the stuffed horse and scratched his chin. 'I think this tail is closest to where it should be. Whose is that one?'

'Mine,' shrieked a little girl.

'Mine's best,' Jordan yelled.

'Hey, buddy, Alice's is closer and it's only fair she wins. You won the dunking doughnut competition.'

Jordan calmed down and took the small parcel from Eli to hand to Alice. 'It's yours.' He gave her a hug.

Aww, he was so cute. Anna blinked once and looked to Eli. 'Dunking doughnuts?'

'Don't ask. It was messy. One of Liz's not so brilliant ideas for a game.'

'Nothing wrong with a bit of stickiness,' Liz retorted. 'You've got to get messy at these parties, Dad.'

Eli just laughed. 'Didn't see that in the rule book.'

Anna took a step back, trying to breathe normally. Eli really was different from the man she'd known prior to today. Couldn't fault either version of him. Though previously at work there'd been plenty of times when she'd wanted to tell him to stop being a jerk, she wouldn't be thinking that today. As her lungs slowly returned to normal she wondered how far she could take this. How far he might be interested in going.

'You know how to handle kids.' Liz appeared beside her.

'I guess that's because you spend so much time nursing them when they're at their most vulnerable.'

'Yes, I do seem to be able to manage children. I've always had an affinity to them,' she added thoughtlessly, then gasped. Eli wasn't the only member of this family who had her talking too much. Must be something in the Forrester genes that made them able to suck her in without realising until it was too late. She hadn't let out anything important but it was a warning to be careful.

'Why wouldn't you? They can push every button you've got and some, but there's something wonderful about children.' Liz grinned. 'I'd better go sort the food problem before someone throws a tantrum because there's no cake on the table.'

Anna watched Liz stroll across to the house and felt a moment of loneliness, which was out of character. Eli's lot were easy to be around, and obviously got on well. Suddenly she wished she and her parents could bury the hatchet. She'd lost more than her son, she'd lost the two people who should've always been there for her, no matter what mistakes she made. While they did sometimes call her on special occasions she was never comfortable. The past hung between them like a fence too high to climb, and probably always would. She'd once tried to breach the gap only to be told she'd wasted her intelligence becoming a nurse.

'You look like you're about to run away,' Eli said quietly behind her.

Spinning around, she stared at him. 'Not likely. I'm having fun.'

One dark eyebrow rose as he locked his gaze with hers. 'You can do better than that, Anna.'

True, she could. 'Your family's lovely.'

'What's wrong with yours?'

'We don't get on at all. I did something many years ago that changed everything.'

'That's tough. Everyone makes mistakes along the way. What did you do? Or would you prefer I didn't ask?'

Tell him and Eli would have her out of here before Jordan cut his birthday cake. Funny thing though, she did want to tell him the truth and get it over and done with so she'd know where she stood. But this wasn't the right time or place. 'I don't mind that you asked, but now's not the time to give you an answer. This is Jordan's day.'

He continued to watch her for a long minute, then finally nodded. 'You're right, but if you ever want to get something off your chest, you only have to nudge me.' Then his gaze dropped to her chest and his eyes widened. Hadn't he noticed she had breasts before?

She had to laugh, because otherwise she was going to leap into his arms and hold on tight. She hadn't known a man quite so refreshing and understanding as Eli. 'I just might do that.' How understanding would he be if he knew the truth? She shivered, already believing she knew the answer.

'Come on, it's feeding time at the zoo.' He took her elbow and led her across to the deck where a laden table was surrounded with excited children and parents trying to make them behave.

'Who made all this food?' Anna asked. Ten kids were never going to eat everything.

'Mum and Liz. What's not eaten today will go to day care with Jordan tomorrow.'

'I thought he'd be starting at school tomorrow.'

'It's mid-term break this coming week so he's starting the following Monday, which gives more time to getting over the op. Not that it's been holding him back much so far. He's been back at preschool since Wednesday, only for half days. They've been very vigilant but there've been no problems. How I'm going to keep him from getting over-excited during the intervening days I have no idea.'

'You'll manage. I saw you calm him when he was frightened in hospital and when he was hurting. You're a great dad.' Hadn't she told him that once before? Nothing but the truth was the way to go.

Eli looked at her again. 'Thanks.' He ran a finger down the side of her face. 'I like you.'

A scream rent the air before she could answer.

They both spun around, searching for the child making the racket. Eli raced across the lawn to a girl near the hedge. 'Sarah, what's happened?'

'A bee got me,' she gasped. Her eyes were wide and her breathing was slowing. 'It—' she tried to breathe '—stings.'

'Here, I'm going to take you inside.' Eli had Sarah in his arms and was striding back to the house as a woman rushed up to them.

'What's wrong? Sarah, are you all right?'

'Jane, has Sarah got any allergies?' Eli asked as he laid the crying girl on a couch.

'Not that I know of.'

His mouth tightened before he said, 'She's been stung by a bee and I want to check her over thoroughly.' He said no more but Anna had seen the swelling beginning around Sarah's eyes and noted how her breathing was getting more laboured with every breath she took.

'Want me to call for help?' she asked him quietly.

'Yes, definitely. Jane, we're calling the ambulance. I think Sarah's having a reaction to the sting and it's better to have the medics here.'

'In case something goes wrong? Is that what you're saying?' Jane slumped against Anna, then straightened to reach a hand to her daughter. 'Sarah, you'll be all right. Jordan's daddy's looking after you.'

Anna had her phone pressed to her ear. 'Ambulance,' she told the man who answered her call. Then she explained to the call base operator. 'We have a young child who's been stung by a bee and appears to be having an anaphylactic reaction. No known allergies.' She gave the address, Eli nodding when she got it right. 'Thank you.' Hanging up, she moved closer to Sarah and Eli and watched him counting the breaths. Taking Sarah's wrist, she timed the girl's pulse.

'What's happening?' Kerry asked from the doorway. 'I heard Sarah screaming. Has she hurt herself?'

Looking around, Anna realised the room was filling with anxious-looking parents. 'Sarah's having a reaction to a bee sting. Could someone wait on the footpath for the ambulance and show the medics the way in when they arrive?'

'Can everyone else move back to give us some space while we look after Sarah?' Eli said in his no-nonsense voice Anna knew from hospital.

Liz came to stand by Jane, put an arm around her waist as she stared at her daughter, her teeth biting into her bottom lip. 'She's in good hands.'

'But—' Tears trickled down her cheeks. 'What if—?'

'Don't go there. Be brave for Sarah.'

Anna spoke quietly to Eli. ‘Pulse’s weak.’

‘Fits the picture. She’s not reacting to my touch now.’

‘How far away is the local ambulance base?’ Surely they wouldn’t have to wait for one to come from the city centre. No, there was one at Wigram, not far away at all, she recalled.

‘Ten minutes max.’

‘I’m ready if we have to do CPR.’

‘Me too.’ His face was grim. Then he drew on a smile and looked up at Jane. ‘She’s doing well. Has she ever been stung before?’

‘Yes, often when she’s gone to her grandparents’ farm. But this never happened. Are you sure it’s anaphylactic?’

No doubt about it. Anna had seen this often enough to know. ‘Some people don’t react the first time they’re stung or eat a food item they’re allergic to. It can build up slowly.’

Jane looked at her with a question in her eyes.

‘I’m a paediatric nurse.’

A bleak smile touched Jane’s face then disappeared. ‘Thank you for helping.’

‘No problem.’ Sarah’s wrist was limp in her hand. She glanced at Eli, saw worry reflected back at her.

Ten minutes felt like an hour, but finally the sound of an approaching siren filled the air.

Sarah gasped. Her eyes closed. Her chest stopped moving.

Eli joined his hands and pressed down hard on the frail chest in front of him. ‘One, two, three.’ On he went, paused at thirty presses.

Anna breathed into Sarah’s lungs.

The little girl coughed, sucked in air, opened her eyes, and cried.

The air shifted and two uniformed men appeared beside them with a large bag and a stretcher. 'Hi there. Is this Sarah?'

'Yes, this is Sarah, and her mum, Jane, is right here too.' Eli stood up and filled the medics in.

Anna got out of their way and went to stand with Jackie and Liz. 'Her breathing's improving a little but the medics will put a mask on to give her oxygen.'

'She looks so little,' Jackie whispered. 'I can't believe this is happening.'

Anna gave her a quick hug. 'She'll be fine now. But it is a huge fright for everyone. How about I go put the kettle on?'

'Good idea,' Liz said. 'I'll do that. I need to be busy.'

Anna understood. 'Fair enough.' Crossing to Eli, she said, 'That was a bit of a shock for Jane.'

His arm went around her shoulder, drew her closer. 'Sure was.'

'Sarah's lucky we were here.'

His arm tightened around her. 'Yes.'

CHAPTER FOUR

'ONE HELL OF a shock for any parent,' Eli said again a couple of hours later when the party had wrapped up and Jordan was tucked into bed, sound asleep after Anna read him two stories. He was cuddling his new elephant tight, which had to be uncomfortable since it was made out of wood. What a day. Asking Anna to stay on for a wine had only added to the awkwardness. She fitted in too well.

'I can't begin to imagine how Jane felt. I mean, she was terrified but no one expects something like that to happen to their child.'

'At least we were around to help.'

Her smile was brief. 'Sarah's going to have to be vigilant from now on. I bet Jane will be watching over her closely for a long while to come.'

'Hopefully Sarah's old enough to understand it could happen again and that she needs to carry an EpiPen everywhere she goes.'

'Poor kid.'

'Yeah. No child likes to be different from their mates.' Eli looked around the kitchen and dining area, and sighed. Once again his family had come to the rescue by helping clean up after everyone had headed away. 'Where would I be without them?'

'Your family? Busy scraping plates and storing leftovers in the fridge and freezer.' Anna looked a little sad. She'd told him her family weren't on good terms so her feelings on that were probably coming to the fore.

'You did your share too. Thanks, Anna. You got more than you bargained for coming here today.' She did seem to have enjoyed herself. 'Jordan was thrilled with his present, and your presence,' he added. His son thought the world of Nurse Anna. But he was more than a little concerned about how attracted he was to her. She was adorable. And sexy beyond reason. He still couldn't believe how he'd managed not to get too interested before now, but they'd only known each other at work where both of them focused on patients, not each other.

'I suppose I'd better head away,' she said, looking anywhere but at him.

'You haven't finished your wine.' She'd been taking her time over it. 'I can get you a taxi if you don't want to drive. We can also heat up some leftovers if you're hungry. Or I could order something in if that doesn't suit.'

Slow down. You're sounding desperate.

Maybe he was. It had been a while since he'd felt so interested in a woman. Since Melissa he'd given women a wide berth other than the occasional one-night fling to ease some of the tension that arose every now and then.

That long curly red hair slid across Anna's shoulders as she shook her head, making his fingers itch. 'Don't go to any trouble. There's heaps of food stacked in containers in your fridge.'

'Does that mean you'll stay a bit longer?' He wasn't sure

why her answer was important but his breathing was on hold as he waited.

'Yes, I think I will, thanks.' Her enthusiasm levels weren't overwhelming but her smile seeped into him like a slow-heating oven, getting warmer by the second.

'Good.' Leaning back into his seat, he asked, 'There isn't someone else who could pick you up later?'

'I'm single and live alone in my own town house out in Lincoln.' Sounded as if there was something she needed to get out of the way underlying that.

Did that mean she wanted to spend more time with him? Did he want to see more of Anna outside work? Unfortunately he did. So he shouldn't have invited her to share leftovers because he couldn't afford to get caught up in a relationship that might harm his boy. He dug for a smile. 'I take it no other patient has invited you to their party?'

'Never.' She studied him as she sipped her wine. 'I'm glad I came despite your concerns that Jordan will have expectations about me being around on and off.'

'The thing is, Jordie's been hurt big time by his mother, and I can't bear to watch him go through that again so I'm very cautious about who I let into my life.' That didn't come out well. 'What I mean is I'm single for a reason.' He still got angry about Melissa putting herself before her son. He'd never understood how his birth mother could've given him up, and then he'd married a woman who'd done a similar thing.

Anna looked stunned. 'Me too.'

He wasn't the only one talking about things best kept to himself. 'Which is?' Never let an opportunity go by.

Putting her glass aside, she began to stand up. 'I'd better go now.'

Leaping to his feet, Eli put his hand out to stop her. 'Anna, no, please stay. I promise not to ask any more personal questions.'

Her eyes were full of sadness as she looked at him. 'I enjoy your company, Eli. I really do, but I'm not prepared to talk about my past. Not yet,' she added so quietly he wasn't sure he'd heard right.

'Then I won't mention it again. Let's see what we'd like to eat, and get it warming up.' And forget this moment. For now anyway. Without thinking, he reached for her hand and was surprised when her fingers tightened around his. Talk about mixed messages. Was she as insecure as him when it came to relationships? Guess he wasn't about to find out any time soon since he'd keep his word. 'I can still order in something more exciting than party leftovers.'

Stepping away from him, she laughed softly. 'I'm sure you can but I'm more than happy with some of those yummy whitebait patties and a bit of salad.'

'Shouldn't have invited you. Whitebait's one of my favourites.'

'Tough. Hope there's plenty left or you'll have to go without.'

So she could tease him. He kind of liked that. It meant she wasn't tiptoeing around him as some women he'd dated off and on had. He knew he was a bit remote at work, but he also didn't want women fawning over him to get his attention. Anna didn't, which was refreshing. 'I'm in luck. There're quite a few left. The kids didn't touch them and even the adults didn't get stuck in.'

'Let's do this. I'm starving.'

Within minutes they were sitting at the counter, enjoying their patties and other leftovers. Eli had brought their drinks across and he lifted his glass to tap against Anna's. 'Here's to the end of a rowdy day.'

'To a fun afternoon.' She tapped back and took a small sip.

'I'm still happy to get a taxi for you if you're worried about finishing your wine.'

'It's all right. I haven't had much so a few sips won't hurt.' Looking around the room, she grinned. 'I love the artwork.'

Jordan's paintings were on the fridge door and the wall by the table. 'He gets a kick out of using a paintbrush.'

'He must be shattered after today but he still managed to keep his eyes open while I read stories.'

'He's got preschool in the morning too so any hour spent asleep has to be a bonus for everyone.'

'Is he a good sleeper?'

'On and off. Sometimes he wakes nearly every hour, then there'll be nights when he doesn't wake until dawn.'

'That must make it hard for you some days.'

'All part of being a solo parent. Probably not a lot different for couples with kids. There'll always be sleepless nights for one reason or another.'

'Imagine his first date. What's he doing? Is he safe? Behaving?' Anna chuckled.

Warmth stole through him. He liked that she didn't talk about Jordan as though he was different. 'Even though they're some time away I am not looking forward to those years. Yep.' He laughed when she glanced over at him. 'I'm already worried.'

Her eye roll was cute. 'Why am I not surprised?'

'Because you already know I like being in charge.'

'At work, yes. I'm only beginning to find out how you do things in your private life.'

It stung that she thought he liked being in charge at work, even though he'd said it in the first place. Had he been looking for a compliment instead? 'It's not so much about being in charge as making sure what's necessary for a patient gets done properly.'

Anna blanched. 'I understand that.' She shoved her empty plate away and picked up her glass. 'The only problem with that is we all know what we're doing and do it well.'

'You'll get no argument from me there. It's just that I am a perfectionist, which goes against the theory of medicine because there's no such thing as being perfect when every person's symptoms vary according to their physical details.' Enough of being serious and defending himself. It was a tad boring. 'You never wanted to be a doctor?'

'Not at all. Too many years' study required for that.' Her hair swung over her shoulders. Dang, he loved that intense red shade that reminded him of the Christmas roses his mother grew. 'I couldn't wait to leave school and get out in the real world. Except I didn't do that. I'd always dreamed of becoming a nurse so I stuck with it to get my leaving certificate before enrolling for nursing school.'

He wasn't surprised. Anna came across as dedicated to whatever she believed in, whether it was looking after young patients or turning up to have fun at a kid's party. He had no doubt she'd be the same in a relationship. Except she wasn't in one and didn't want to talk about her past so he presumed something had gone more badly wrong for her than she'd said. 'Nursing is more hands on, isn't it?'

'I love that intensity, getting to know a patient a little bit and trying to help them by talking or not, whichever they want.'

If only she'd talk to him about what had happened to her. But was he ready to tell her about the woman who gave birth to him and then gave him away? How he'd been angry with her for many years? How, despite all that, he'd grown up in the best family possible. Too soon by far. If there'd ever be a right time, now wasn't it. As he turned around on his stool his knee bumped up against Anna's. Stayed there. 'I was going to be a fireman, then a policeman, and a horticulturist.'

Her eyebrows rose at that last one.

He relaxed some more. 'Finally medicine called. I loved science at school, especially biology, and here I am. A no-brainer, really.'

'Isn't it a great feeling when you realise you've got it right for yourself? I used to think I wanted to be a nurse because my grandma had been, but the dream never left, and when I walked into the nursing school for the first time I knew I'd made the right call.'

Did she know she'd moved her hand to lie on his knee? Placing his over hers, he waited to see if she withdrew. When she didn't he lifted it and brushed his lips over her knuckles. 'I've enjoyed having you here today. I know I was hesitant about you accepting Jordie's invitation but I am glad you did.'

'So am I.' Heat crept up her cheeks.

It was as though she was shy when she wasn't being Nurse Anna. Not so confident in other aspects of her life? There was so much to learn about this wonderful woman, and he wanted to know it all. Now. Impatience was another of his characteristics, though one he kept on a tight rein. Leaning closer to her tempting mouth that was curved into a small smile, he kissed her lips lightly. At least it was a soft kiss until Anna pushed closer and her mouth covered his and then it was intense, filling him with a longing he hadn't known in years. Not only for a physical release but for a depth he'd spent most of his adult life looking for. A depth that could lead to understanding—and eventually love.

Standing, he pulled Anna onto her feet and into his arms, and went back to kissing her blind. Or was it him who was going blind with passion? It certainly felt like it as he gave in to all the hot sensations filling him.

Anna's hands were on his back, rubbing softly, hard, then soft again. Her mouth was warm as he tasted her. Her scent teased him, wrapped around him, drew him in deeper than ever.

Suddenly Anna jerked back. 'Oops. Think we'd better stop.'

'Why?' he croaked through the desire filling his throat.

'Daddy? Where are you?' Jordan called from his bedroom.

Dragging his fingers through his hair, he pulled his other hand away from Anna's waist, and tried hard not to be cross with his son for interrupting the most amazing few minutes he'd had in a long time.

'Daddy!'

'Coming,' he called back.

Anna was already picking up her handbag.

'Anna, I'm sorry.' He probably should be thanking Jordan

for interrupting them before it got too far out of hand. He wasn't ready to take this any further. Too much to consider, like the wee man down the hall demanding his attention.

'Not a problem.'

Her wry smile nearly undid any thoughts of not grabbing her and dashing to his bedroom after he'd seen to Jordan. *Jordan.* He came first. 'See you at work.'

'Sure.' Now she sounded annoyed, as if he'd said the wrong thing.

Tough. He was looking out for his own.

And then Anna was gone, taking the heat out of the room but leaving desire swirling through his overwrought body and tightening him with longing.

Anna got into her car and slammed shut the door. Leaning her head back, she closed her eyes and breathed deep, then deeper. What had she nearly done? That kiss was a start-up button for sure. If they hadn't been interrupted, she felt certain they'd have made their way to Eli's bedroom. Unless he'd woken up to the fact his son was in the house and then she knew he'd have poured cold water on the desire filling her. And him. His erection had been hard as it pressed against her thigh.

'That kiss finished far too soon.' Opening her eyes, she sat forward and started the car. Eli knew how to push all her buttons and some she hadn't known were there. Just the feel of his back under her hands was a turn-on. As for his kiss—she'd easily lose her mind over more of those. He was something else. He'd often had her looking twice when he was on the ward, but then he'd be abrupt and she'd immediately get over the mild attraction. Only to feel it all over again next time he turned up to see a patient.

A quick glance at the house and she pulled away. Time to go home and have a cold shower. She was roasting hot with need for Eli. She hadn't really realised until these past weeks since Jordan was admitted to the ward and she'd seen another side to Eli that attracted her in ways that she didn't usually feel with the men she sporadically dated nowadays. There was a lot to him she hadn't noticed before. Not in an open and finite way.

He had a big heart. Seeing him with his son made it so obvious, but it didn't go away when around his family or friends. Since Jordan had spent a night on the ward and Eli had been a patient's parent, not the doctor on the case, he'd opened his mind to the staff and seen them in a different light. He'd also been wonderful to her at times when normally he'd have treated her with some aloofness.

'Where to from here?' she asked the darkness in the car. What did she want from Eli? A fling? Friendship with benefits? Or something deep and meaningful, long term and permanent? That idea felt good. But did she deserve him? So far she hadn't been successful in finding the ideal man to spend the rest of her life with. She didn't deserve to since she'd given her son away to be adopted at birth. What right did she have to be utterly happy when she'd done that?

At first Danny had made her believe she might get a second chance. They'd lived together, talked about getting married, and had been happily in love. So she'd believed—until he'd changed his mind. As for Jock, he'd gone ballistic, calling her all sorts of names, and told everyone she was a bitch. The only thing she'd been grateful about was he'd never mentioned her baby to anyone. She had no idea why when it would've played into his ego.

Despite Danny and Jock, she still wanted to find that passion she'd always hoped was out there.

Like you felt when Eli kissed you?

Exactly like that. Legless. Hot. Tender. Loving. Heady. How to work with him, day after day, and ignore those sensations? It wasn't going to be a picnic. Not now that they'd kissed, and she'd felt his need for her as much as hers for him. But she would not quit her job to put space between them. That would be the craziest thing she could do.

Ahead, red and blue lights were flashing. A police car had pulled up behind a ute and the cop was standing at the driver's window. A timely reminder to focus on driving and not Eli.

She managed not to think about him too much for the rest of the drive home, but he was fully back in her head the moment she slid between the sheets and turned out the bedside light.

Minutes later her phone pinged. Eli. Really? Yep.

His message read: Wow.

She stared at the screen, certain she was seeing things. But no, she wasn't. It was for real.

Wow? Yeah, it had been that all right.

Never in a million nights would she have believed Eli Forrester would send a message like that. Another warning to tread carefully.

'Afraid so,' she admitted before tapping her phone and replying to his wow.

Goodnight.

* * *

Eli knew he shouldn't have sent that message to Anna the moment he touched send. It spoke volumes about how screwed up he was. Hopefully she would think it was normal for him.

Sitting in his lounge with a bottle of icy water in hand, he laughed at himself.

Dream on, man. Anna ain't stupid.

If anyone was, that would be him. Pouring water down his throat wasn't doing anything to cool him down either. Anna had been gone forty-five minutes and he was still hot for her. As in on fire. Not even Jordan's tears over being told he had to stay in bed and go to sleep so he wouldn't be tired for school had dampened anything going on inside his head and body.

Anna Passau hadn't just tweaked his interest; she'd grabbed him around the throat and wasn't letting go. Not even when he knew he had to put Jordan first.

So he wasn't allowed a life that included a sexy woman and maybe one day love? As long as none of that hurt Jordan, then yes, he was. But how could he guarantee Jordan wouldn't get let down badly if Anna left his father after they'd become more deeply involved? He couldn't. His family kept saying he had to let go the past and make a life for himself and Jordan would be as happy as ever. They were right. But when Melissa had walked away from her son as his mother had him, not quite the same circumstances but close enough, he'd got angry for Jordan. With his history of being given up by his birth mother he'd have thought he'd have seen Melissa for who she really was before they married and had Jordan.

None of this meant Anna was anything like her, but he couldn't trust himself not to make the same mistake. But there was only one way to learn to trust and that was get out there and start taking some risks. Slurping down more water, he swallowed hard when his phone beeped. He smiled, heated right back up.

Anna had come back.

Goodnight.

His smile dipped. Not wow. And here he was, acting crazy all over a kiss. A couple of kisses. Not enough. He wanted more. Lots more. Followed by something deeper and sexier—if that was possible because Anna's lips were to die for. She seemed to be pulling back. That alone should quieten his racing pulse, but not at all.

Holding the water bottle over his shirt-covered chest, he squeezed it empty in an attempt to cool off. Didn't work.

Pacing around the house did nothing to help either. Jordan was out for the count. His own bed looked empty and lonely. He could hardly mow the lawns at this time of night and remain on good terms with the neighbours. What was a man supposed to do when his mind was out of control?

Think of somewhere to take Anna on a date. A date? As in pick her up from her place and go for a meal or the pub and take her home again? What else did people do on dates? Kiss Anna again. That was his pick. She hadn't come back with a happy text, just goodnight.

So show her you're more than a kiss or sex.

Grabbing his phone, he found the ad for a rock concert at a vineyard in Waipara next Saturday Phil had been talking about in Theatre during the week. He'd ask Anna if she'd like to go. Or he could buy the tickets now and talk to her about it later on. He could also arrange a picnic with wine and roses—no, forget the roses. They suggested more interest than even he was willing to admit. But great food would be in the basket. If Anna declined the invitation he'd give the tickets to one of his sisters. And pretend not to care.

On Monday Eli came onto the ward as Anna was getting up to speed with patients for the three to eleven shift. 'Hi, Anna. What'd you get up to this morning?'

Warmth spread through her. His friendly approach was continuing despite the abrupt end to last night. Would he continue to be friendly to everyone here or only her? Surely not that. He wasn't stupid and wouldn't want staff noticing his attention was only on her if it was. Then again, she was probably looking for something that didn't exist. After his kiss and text? The warmth was turning hot.

Thought you were pulling back?

'Digging part of my veggie patch to plant more chillies and capsicums for a later crop. Hopefully this fine weather will help out.'

'What else have you planted?' The surprise in his question made her smile.

'It's a long list. Nothing like fresh vegetables from my own garden.'

'She brings half the crop in here for us,' Leanne piped up from her desk. 'A person can only eat so much lettuce in one sitting.'

Anna ignored the look in her friend's eye that suggested

she knew darned well she'd seen Eli over the weekend. 'That's not what you say when I give you a couple at a time.'

'Put my name on the list, will you?' Eli said as he reached past Anna to pick up a file. 'I've seen Andy, Leanne. You're right. There is an infection in his abdominal wound, which seems internal as well. I'll fill out a prescription for stronger antibiotics.'

'Talk to Anna about Andy. She's taking over. I'm off to pick up my kids and take them to swimming lessons.' Leanne nudged Anna none too gently as she stepped around her. 'We missed you yesterday.' Her grin was more than cheeky.

'I was busy.'

'I figured. See ya tomorrow.'

'How long have you two been mates?' Eli asked.

'We went through nursing school together. Now, is there anything I need to know about Andy? I've seen the case notes.'

Hopefully getting down to business would settle her racing heart. Who'd have thought she couldn't even stand near Eli any more without getting in a pickle? All because she'd gone to a kid's party.

Try again, Anna. All because he's kissed you and smiles like the devil.

'He presented in ED this morning with severe gastric pain caused by a bowel infection. I've gone in and removed the source, cleaned up the site as best as possible, but infection was a given.' He'd know he was repeating what she'd read but then he did like to be careful. 'Septicaemia is of concern. I'm watching closely. I want bloods taken every two hours for a CBC.'

Anna had the file back up on screen. 'Right. That'll be done. Anyone else in here who's your patient?'

'Not at the moment. I'm doing a tonsillectomy on an eight-year-old girl in the morning, which should be straightforward.'

'Careful.' Anna grinned without thought.

'True. Tempting fate is not usually my thing.' He turned for the door. 'See you later maybe.'

She gave up trying to stay focused only on work. 'I'm not going anywhere till eleven.'

Eli waved over his shoulder and left without another word.

Not that she could think of any answer to her comment—other than 'Come visit me when you leave here. We can pick up where we left off last night.' If only. The chances of that happening were zero with Jordan at home. The man was super protective of his boy and she couldn't see him being happy if Jordan were to find him in bed with a woman. Then again, this was only supposition, going on what little she knew about Eli. She could be totally wrong.

The next time Anna saw Eli he'd returned to check on his patient. 'Andy's slept a lot,' she told him. 'He was given antibiotics and light pain relief earlier because apparently he said it was hurting a lot. Otherwise all good.'

'Just as I expect,' Eli answered as he read the printout from the monitor, looking pleased with the result.

'Then I'll get back to my desk.' The ward was quiet other than the sound of chatter and laughter as parents boosted their sick children's moods. It would be dinner time soon and that would change as kids either gobbled down their meal or grizzled that they didn't like it.

'Got time for a coffee?'

'I have.' When they reached the staff kitchen dining room she was happy to see it was empty. Sharing Eli wasn't her idea of a good time together, even at work when either of them was likely to be called for at any moment. She held up the coffee plunger that was full and hot. 'Someone's beaten us to it.'

Eli placed a hand on her arm and turned her to face him. 'I'm sorry we were interrupted last night.'

'Me too.' She watched his mouth coming closer to hers and caught her breath. He was going to kiss her. There was singing in her veins. So much for staying in control of herself.

Eli's mouth covered hers. His tongue slipped inside and touched hers. Her knees softened. She grabbed his shirt to stay upright as she returned the kiss with all the pent-up frustration that had been knocking at her since she'd driven away from his house last night.

'Eli,' she murmured against his mouth.

His mouth pressed harder, driving her insane with desire. Then he stepped back, shoved his hands in his pockets and looked around as a nurse walked in. 'Hey, Gabrielle, did you make the coffee?'

He sounded so in control it bothered Anna.

Was he having her on? Was this not a real deal for him?

'Hope you don't mind sharing,' Eli said to Gabrielle, before turning and mouthing 'Phew' to Anna.

Had he heard the other nurse coming? She wouldn't have heard a bomb blast, she'd been so engrossed in kissing Eli. 'I agree,' she said quietly.

'There's enough for all of us. I'm taking mine back to the

desk as I've got some notes to enter about the kid who's just been brought up from Theatre,' Gabrielle told them.

Anna had to shake her head to remember she was talking about coffee. 'Thanks for that. I'll join you shortly.' Grabbing her mug, she sank onto a chair. Work had never been so entertaining. But then she didn't usually take a lot of notice of the males who worked here. Nothing like how Eli had her attention. 'That was close,' she said to him when Gabrielle was well gone. 'Have you got extrasensory hearing or something?'

'Just a sixth sense that someone was coming.' He stirred sugar into his coffee and joined her at the table.

'Glad it worked.' She sipped her coffee thoughtfully. It would've been awkward to have been caught out. That particular nurse wasn't known for keeping quiet about just about anything.

'Relax, Anna. We got away with it.' Eli looked ridiculously comfortable, as though he couldn't care two tosses if someone had interrupted their kiss.

'Something you're used to?' she asked before putting her brain in gear. Then again, so what if she spoke her mind? Only way to know what was going on.

His mug banged on the table. 'No, Anna, it is not. As you have pointed out, I haven't been known for getting friendly with the staff in any way.'

Guilt made her grimace. 'I'm really sorry. I am a worry wort about these things.'

'You don't like people knowing you're having fun?'

'I don't want the nurses I work with giving me a hard time about you. It wouldn't feel right. Not that I'm spending time with you but— Oh, hell, I don't know what I'm trying to say.' She stared at Eli, resisting the urge to throw herself into his arms and never let go. Which wasn't how she acted any time with anyone. She'd learned eighteen years ago it didn't get her anywhere other than mess with her relationships.

Eli turned his hand over to encase hers and stood up. 'Come here. Believe it or not, I understand what you're trying to say. You seem as cautious about getting close as I am so let's enjoy each other's company and see what happens.'

What a man. She could love him already if she were open to the idea. Which she wasn't sure she'd ever be after trying to let love in before and having it fail. She did want to fall in love with the right man and the scary thing here was Eli felt as though he could be that—if she allowed him in. If he allowed her in. But first she needed to know what held him back other than his ex and Jordan. Or was that more than enough? 'Done. Now I'd better take my coffee back to my desk before someone comes looking for me.'

'Not before we finish that kiss.'

Before Anna had time to think she was in Eli's arms and his mouth was covering hers, cranking up her hormones all over again.

Then he was walking out of the door as though he'd just had the perfect cup of coffee. Then he turned around and came back. 'I meant to ask if you're free on Saturday night to go to the rock concert out at a vineyard in Waipara. We'd take a picnic dinner and get some wine there.'

He was asking her on a date. A real date. 'I'd love to go with you.'

'Thank goodness or I'd have to decide which sister to give the tickets to.' His grin was mischievous. 'Talk later about details.' This time he did leave the ward.

Her eyes followed him, as did her heart. No doubt about it, Eli was special. She skipped back to the desk and sat down, only to realise her coffee was still on the table back in the kitchen.

CHAPTER FIVE

ANNA LOOKED BEAUTIFUL in her butt-hugging jeans and low-cut emerald-green blouse. Her hair was free of any ties and fell over her shoulders to her breasts, accentuating their wondrous curves. Eli was beyond happy as he returned from the wine stall and stopped to watch her surveying the crowd. Hard to believe she'd always tickled his interest but only recently had she tripped him up with her sexuality and looks. And delightful personality.

Getting in a bit deep, he thought, and shrugged. He was here to have fun with Anna and that was what he'd do. He'd let reality back in tomorrow. A guy was allowed to have some fun.

'I see you've got the glasses out ready.' He laughed as he uncapped the bottle. Laughing came easy around Anna. 'They're doing a big trade in the wine tent.'

'Hardly surprising considering whose wine it is. Plus the fact we weren't allowed to bring our own.'

Sitting in the outdoor chair beside her, Eli filled the glasses and handed Anna one. 'Here's to a great night.' Who knew how it would unfold? All he could think was that he was with a lovely lady, and feeling so relaxed he had to keep pinching himself to make sure this wasn't a dream.

Rock music split the air as the first band for the night

started up, silencing the audience all around them. Anna's fingers began tapping the rhythm on her thigh. 'Cool.'

At least that was what Eli thought she said. It was impossible to hear himself think, let alone whatever Anna said. Taking her hand in his, he settled back to enjoy the music, and the company, which couldn't be better. To think Anna had been there, right in his daily life at the hospital, and until recently he hadn't taken a lot of notice of her. Not quite true, but he'd deliberately ignored the flare of interest and the spark of heat she'd often provoked with little more than a glance or a shrug. 'Seems I can't ignore this any longer.'

Anna leaned closer. 'Ignore what?' Her hearing had to be sharp if she'd heard him.

He hadn't realised he'd spoken out loud. Seemed to do too much of that around Anna. 'The hamper full of food?'

'Try again.' She wasn't buying it.

Being so close to her brought that vanilla scent to his nose. 'Having fun on a date with a woman I am coming to like more every day.'

Jerking away, she stared at him, surprise lightening the green of her eyes so they looked like emeralds in the sun. She shook her head. 'I must be hearing things.'

I wish you were.

He'd shocked himself by being so open. Showed how out of practice he was when it came to dating. Tugging her close, he said, 'It's true.' Might as well stick with honesty. It wasn't as though he'd told her he'd fallen in love with her so he didn't need to retract his words and spend the rest of the night hoping the bands would pack up and go back to their hotels early.

'You never stop surprising me,' Anna told him.

'Until Jordan's op you'd only known me as a surgeon, nothing else. There's more to me than scalpels and vinyl gloves.'

'I guess.'

'You guess? I can't be doing a good job at showing you who I am.'

'So tell me more.'

'Later when I'm not competing with the band.'

And have had time to think where I'm going with this. With Anna.

She unfurled from her chair and took his hand. 'Come on. Let's boogie.'

'Me? Boogie?' Now she'd get one answer to learning more about him. He couldn't dance or boogie to save himself. Looking around at the crowd now on their feet, he shrugged happily. Nor could half the people here and no one seemed to care less. 'You're on.'

An hour later the band members hung up their gear and headed off stage, making way for the next band.

Anna sagged against Eli. 'I need water and food, in that order.'

'Me, too.' They hadn't stopped moving since they'd stood up. He wouldn't call either of their moves by any dance name, but it had been fun. Anna had been as sexy as all get out. But then he suspected she could be swimming in mud and he'd find her hot. 'Our wine didn't survive the moves.' The glasses lay empty on the grass between their chairs.

'What a waste. That's a tasty wine.'

'We can have some more with our food.' He opened the hamper. 'But first you wanted water.' He handed her a bottle and then unpacked the appetisers.

'These look delicious.' Anna picked up one and bit into it.

He tightened as he watched. So fast, so easy with this woman. Something to be wary about. If she could upend his world biting into a pastry then she could cause a lot of damage with a kiss or sex. Right now he was ready to ignore the signs and have a fabulous time. Tomorrow he might regret everything, but tonight he'd enjoy being with Anna.

'Do you want to come in?' Anna asked Eli when he pulled into her drive hours later. She was putting herself out there with Eli, taking a chance that they'd continue the wonderful time they'd been having without him pulling back and leaving her wondering what he really wanted. The thing was, she wanted him. Badly. Not only in bed but in her life. So far they'd got along a lot better than she'd have believed not so long ago. She wanted that to continue.

'I'd love to.'

That was easy. 'Great.' Was he the man for her future? She had no idea. There was only one way to find out and that meant spending more time with him. The odds on him dumping her sooner than later were high. He'd said he'd do anything to protect his son. Because she didn't deserve happiness she always managed to cool off with any guy she dated, but Eli was different. Walking away wouldn't be easy. His caring side touched her deeply along with his sense of fun, his loyalty to Jordan and his family. But more than that, it was how he understood her, or, when he didn't, how he tried to. Of course he had no idea what she'd done, and if he did would probably move on from her. He made no bones about his feelings towards his ex over how she'd abandoned Jordan. He'd think the same if not worse about her giving her baby up for adoption.

'You seem to be deep in thought,' Eli said as he followed her up to her front door.

Shaking away the errant thoughts, she spun around to kiss him. 'I'm right here with you.'

Eli's mouth took over hers, kissing, tasting, turning her into a puddle of desire. Hot, wet need. Falling into him, she held him tight and gave back as good as she got.

'Anna,' he groaned against her. 'Open the door, will you?'

It took three attempts to get the key to work but finally they fell through the gap and she slammed the door shut again with her hip as she placed her hands on Eli's cheeks and stretched up to continue kissing him.

He was hard, pressing into her abdomen as his hands moulded around her butt. Damn it, but he was sexy, and turned her on without a blink. 'I want you.'

'Patience, Anna. We've got all night.'

'Patience, my ass. I won't be able to wait five minutes, let alone all night.'

He growled out a laugh. Then swung her up in those strong arms. 'Which way?'

'Straight ahead,' she said before pressing her mouth to his neck and licking up a storm. He tasted divine. Smelt even better. His skin was smooth and hot.

'Anna, slow down or I won't last the distance.'

She was already well on the way to combusting. 'Me either. In here.'

The moon lit up her bedroom like a hundred-watt bulb. Eli laid her on the bed and she held onto him, pulling him down on top of her quaking body.

'Clothes.'

Always something to get in the way. She tugged at his shirt, but it was stuck between them.

Eli was slipping her jeans down over her hips as he lay against her.

Pushing her hand between them, she found his erection and took it in her grasp.

'Anna… Wait.'

'Can't.'

'Have to.' He sat up, dug into his pocket for a packet and then shoved out of his trousers and pulled his shirt over his head. 'Condom.'

'I'm on the pill.'

Pulling a packet from his pocket, he said, 'I always make sure I'm covered.' He began undoing her blouse one agonising button at a time. Slowing them down while the urgency grew and grew.

'Better safe than sorry?'

'Absolutely.'

She couldn't blame him for that. No one wanted to find they were unexpectedly going to be a parent, especially when they were having a fling, not a full-time relationship. Taking him in her hand again, she slid her hand up and down, up and down.

'Stop.' Eli took her hand away, then covered her nipple with his mouth, running his tongue over and around it, sending her into another world, full of sensations that wound her up tighter than ever, bringing her to a climax without touching her sex.

Grabbing his hand, she placed it on the hot spot between her legs, and cried out when his fingers moved over her. Her body bucked against him, again and again. Then she exploded with heat and desire, with need for this amazing man.

Eli knelt between her legs and lifted her up. His throbbing sex slid into her slowly, gently, and pulled back.

She cried out. 'Eli, please, more.'

He obliged. In, out, the tempo increasing with each move until she thought she was going to fall apart. 'Eli, now.'

He drove into her, hard and fast, and called out as he came. 'Anna, oh, Anna.'

Her name on his tongue was sensual, sexy, alluring. As he fell away he took her with him, held her close, wrapped in those arms she was coming to adore. His chest rose and fell rapidly. Like hers as she struggled to regain composure. 'Eli, that was beyond wonderful.'

His arms held her tighter.

Snuggling against his chest, she let her eyes fall shut. Every other sense was wide awake. It felt as though they were in a little world of their own. Tuned into each other, not needing to say a word, their bodies touching was enough. Wow. She'd been waiting for ever to feel like this. Hadn't known it was even possible, yet now Eli had set a benchmark there'd be no ignoring.

'Anna,' he whispered. 'I don't know what to say other than I'm more than happy.'

'That's enough. To try adding to it will only undo the wonder you've just given me.'

His lips brushed her forehead. 'You're amazing.'

'Takes two to tango.'

'I think we did way better here than with our dancing.' His laughter was low and light. And as sexy as it was possible to be.

When Eli began tracing circles on her thigh she knew they were going to make love again. This time they took their time discovering each other's body from top to toe and back to the centre where they both throbbed with need. After Eli made her pause so he could put on a condom Anna rode him hard, gazing down into his adorable face as they came together.

Snuggling up close afterwards, she slipped into sleep, her heart full of wonder at what had gone down between them. She woke as Eli was getting out of bed. 'Eli?'

'I'm heading home. Liz is bringing Jordie home first thing as she's got to be somewhere. Thanks for a wonderful night.' He leaned down and kissed her gently. 'I have seriously enjoyed our date.'

'Me, too.'

'We'll have to do it again.'

Try stopping her. 'You're on.'

Eli looked stunned, as though he hadn't meant to say that.

Anna ran a hand over his chin. 'No rush.'

'You're right there.' He was withdrawing. Pulling on his clothes fast.

Within moments of getting out of her bed. 'Thanks, Eli. You certainly know how to kill the moment.'

He hesitated. 'Anna, I didn't intend that. I've had a wonderful night with you. An amazing time.'

'But?'

'Reality's kicking in. I can't spend lots of time with you. I have other commitments that come before anything else.'

'You think I don't understand that? Stop treating me as though I expect you to put me first all the time. We're not even seeing that much of each other.' So much for a wonderful night. It was going up in smoke fast.

'Fair enough. I'd better get going. See you at work.'

Anna stared at her empty doorway until she heard the front door close, then she got up to make sure it was locked since there wasn't a hope in hell Eli would come back tonight. He was on a mission that didn't involve her.

Thank goodness she was on nights for the first three days where chances of bumping into him were remote. Her heart was heavy. So much for getting to know him better. The biggest message she got was he didn't want to allow her into his life if it meant Jordan could be upset. Fine, except it seemed that boy ruled his father completely. Or was Eli hiding behind him? Now there was something to think about.

Night shift worked. Anna didn't see Eli at all for the first half of the week, though she couldn't stop herself from looking out for him. She had it bad. After making love, she felt she'd found someone so special that she was willing to risk everything to be with him. Apparently she hadn't affected him half as much, which highlighted the fact she didn't deserve to find true love.

On Thursday she was on morning shift with Leanne.

'Feel like checking out the sales for some summer clothes when we're finished here?'

Not really. What was the point? Come on. Don't let Eli wreck everything. 'I could do with a spruce up,' she said half-heartedly.

Her friend laughed. 'Nothing to do with a certain surgeon by any chance?'

Not at the moment. 'Whatever makes you think that?'

'The fact you're always keeping an eye out for him between patients.'

'We're not seeing eye to eye just now.'

'So I gathered, which is why shopping is a good idea.' Leanne glanced at the computer screen. 'You'd better grab a bite to eat while it's quiet.'

Standing up, Anna stretched her back. 'I'll be in the canteen if you need me.'

Leanne looked past her and grinned. 'I'll try not to call you.'

Instantly Anna felt Eli's presence. He'd got to her so much she always seemed to know whenever he was around, but not this time. 'I'm off. Hi, Eli. Have you come to see Laurie? She's doing well today. No more pain, and the infection's abating.'

'I've just seen her. She's improved a lot since yesterday.' Eli had his serious doctor face on.

'Problem?'

'No. Mind if I join you for a coffee in the canteen?' Still serious.

Why would there be a problem? 'Of course not.' She headed for the lift, not waiting to see what he'd do. When the door opened and he stepped in beside her she sighed with relief. He had her stirred with worry over a simple question, and that demeanour that had been absent lately. 'Everything okay?'

'Yes.'

Sounded more like no to her. 'Any plans for the weekend?' He hadn't mentioned them going on another date. Had she got it all wrong and he'd only been there for one night's pleasure. If that was the case she'd toughen up and get over it. Better to find out now and not weeks down the track when chances were she'd be right into him. *Aren't you already?* Pretty much, she admitted silently.

'Jordan's got another party to go to. His best friend's turning five and will start at the same school on Monday.'

'How's Jordan enjoying school so far?'

'Loves it.' Eli's mouth flattened. 'It's one of my concerns that he'll get teased for being different.'

'He comes across as quite tough.'

'You haven't seen him when he's been bullied by kids who think they're perfect.'

No, she hadn't, but she could imagine Jordan's little face screwed up with tears pouring down his cheeks as he tried to work out why kids teased him. 'Hard for you both.'

'Are you working this weekend?'

Was he going to ask her to join him at some point? 'I'm rostered for Sunday night, otherwise I'm free.'

'I'm sure you'll be busy with something.'

The hope lifting her heart fell away. So they weren't getting together. Stepping out of the lift, she headed for the canteen. Not that she was hungry any more but she'd do her best to eat something so he didn't see how hurt she felt.

'I'll get you a coffee.'

'Thanks. I'll grab a table.'

Something definitely wasn't right. He hadn't called her since Saturday. Not that she'd tried to get in touch either. Yet here he was, wanting to talk to her. Nothing added up. When she sat down with her lunch and two coffees he gave her a warm smile, confusing her even more.

'Cheers, Anna. Jordan was asking after you last night. In fact he does just about every night.'

Light-bulb moment. 'Is that a problem?'

'I hope not.'

Another punch to her heart. 'I can't see how it would be.' Unless he didn't want his son to have another woman in his life.

'After what Melissa did I am probably overprotective but I do not want him hurt again. I still struggle to understand how she could walk like she did. How any mother can leave their child for that matter.' He raised his hands in a futile gesture. 'How does a woman give up her baby for adoption after carrying him, nurturing him, for nine months? It's beyond me.'

Anna's stomach lurched. There was the answer she'd been dreading all along. They were over before they'd started, if that had been on the cards. No need to explain that she'd given up her son, and why, and that it wasn't as easy as he seemed to think to keep a baby when you were sixteen and no one was there for you. Because she got the sense that she was included in that general statement about women because he didn't trust any female who might get close to him.

'You think I might hurt your son? Well, Eli, if we were to get any closer—' obviously they weren't but she couldn't let this go '—it would be both of us involved and we would talk about Jordan and how to keep everything shipshape for him.'

He leant back in his chair, looking baffled, as if he didn't know how to deal with her. 'You know what I like about you? You don't hold back. You're not into trying to get on my best side by saying what you think I want to hear, you just get on with speaking your mind.'

That was a surprise. Very honest. Hope he liked how she made love to him too, though right now that would be the last thing on his mind. 'Only way to go.' Though there were things she had no intention of telling him now unless they progressed further. He'd find every fault with what she'd done and wouldn't understand she'd had no choice if her son was to have a good life. He'd return to being aloof Mr Forrester, which would hurt almost more than anything else.

'Yes, it is. Anna, I don't want to stop seeing you.'

Then she'd better tell him. Get it over with. At least she'd know where she stood. She already did though. Seeing his reaction, hearing what he'd have to say, would only underscore what Danny and Jock had said and she didn't need to hear that again. Except she wasn't going to be a coward. Big breath. 'Eli, I—'

'I hate that Jordan's so vulnerable. It's one thing for me to worry about where I'm going with our future but it's quite another to think he could get close to someone I bring into the family and then be hurt badly.' He paused, drumming his fingers on the table. 'Anna, I need to take things slowly. If that doesn't work for you then I guess we remain solely friends.'

Doubt that would be the case when he heard what she had to say. 'I hear you but first—'

His pager interrupted.

Was she ever going to be able to finish a sentence? Though relief was taking over. It wouldn't be pleasant telling him about her past. Besides, doing that here in the cafeteria, surrounded by people, wasn't the wisest idea.

He stood up. 'Got to go. A patient in ED requires my attention.'

'Catch up some other time.' That sounded as if she was going with the go-slow option, and maybe she would give it a try, even if it meant her heart might take a hard knock in the end. As she watched him walk away her head spun. Eli really had got to her and she couldn't imagine not getting along with him as more than friends.

'Hello. Are you Anna Passau?' A young man stood beside the table, watching her warily.

'I am.' She stared at him, not knowing who he was yet feeling as though she should. 'Do I know you?'

'I'm Charlie.'

Her mouth fell open. She *had* to be hearing things. 'Who?'

'Your son.'

'They named you Charlie?' The name she'd chosen even when knowing she had no say in what her boy was called or that she'd likely ever see him again.

'Mum and Dad did it for you. And for me.'

She was still staring at him, drinking in the sight of her son. Her son. Charlie. No. Couldn't be. What was he doing here? How had he found her? What was going on? 'Charlie.'

'Can I sit down?'

'Yes,' she all but shouted.

Don't go anywhere.

'I don't know what to say. I mean, I'm stunned, surprised, happy, scared. Every emotion possible is racing through me. I can't believe this is you. Why are you here? I mean, why at the hospital and not at my house? Or don't you know where that is?'

Slow down, Anna. Give the kid a chance to speak.

Pulling out a chair and sitting down, he blushed.

Her heart swelled.

'Um...it's like this. When my brother, adopted like me, approached his birth mother the first time it was at her house where her husband and other kids lived. She screamed and yelled, saying he had no right turning up in her life. I didn't want that and kind of figured you'd be quieter if there were lots of people around.'

She closed her eyes, counted to ten, opened them. 'I'd never say that. I've wanted to see you ever since you were taken—' Her mouth dried. Reaching for her mug, she swallowed cold coffee and tried again. 'Since the day you were born. I am thrilled you're here.' More than thrilled, but she couldn't find another word to describe the feelings rolling through her.

'Did you ever try to find me?'

'I had nothing to go on. The adoption papers included a no visit edict.'

'You signed that.' He wasn't giving anything away.

'I had no choice.'

'You could've kept me.'

'Again, I had no choice.' Again, she closed her eyes and drew a long steadying breath. Locking eyes with Charlie, she tried to explain. 'I turned sixteen two weeks before you were born. I was still at school. I would've left and got a job, two jobs, to support you but I wouldn't have earned enough to put a roof over your head, let alone feed and clothe you.'

'You lived with your parents. Mum and Dad told me,' he snapped.

'They said they'd kick me out if I kept you. I'd have dealt with that if I could've managed on my own.' Hesitantly she reached for his hand, felt a stab of love when he didn't pull away. 'I really would have. I wanted you. I did not want to adopt you out. You are my son. No way did I want strangers raising you.' He felt warm, but he was shaking. Or was that her? 'It was the most difficult time of my life. All I could hope was that one day you'd understand I put you first. You had to have a good life. That was the most important thing.'

He jerked his hand away. 'You don't think growing up with my birth mother would be more important?'

'Yes, I did. I do. At least I think I do but I'm not in your position so I could be wrong.' Clenching her hands in a knot in her lap, she stared at this young man who'd approached her. She had no doubts he was her son. None whatsoever. Even if he didn't have the same green eyes she saw every morning in her mirror she'd know. He was tall, unlike her. His hair was fair, not red. But there was something in the way he sat, back straight, mouth firm, that spoke of her at times when she was stressed or worried.

'I have always dreamed of meeting you, of telling you that you did me a favour because I did not want to have anything to do with a woman who could give me away.'

Pain sliced into her. Hot and hard, and deadly. She slumped in her seat. 'I can't explain how sorry I am, but I believed I was doing the right thing for you.' He'd never understand, or believe her if the angry look in his eyes was anything to go by.

For a moment Charlie was silent and Anna wondered if he'd walk away, never to see her again. She waited, swallowing the words that threatened to spill across her lips. There was so much she wanted, needed, to know, and was afraid to ask for fear he would disappear out of her life again.

Then he stunned her once more. 'In some ways you did. Mum and Dad have been the best parents I could've wished for. They love me so much, as I do them. They've given me a fabulous life, supported me through everything, including trying to make me see you had to do what you did.'

'I didn't ask for that clause that said I'd never get in touch to be included.'

'They told me your parents did that.'

'Yes.' She'd never forgiven them, which probably got in the way of at least having a family-friendly relationship.

'You're a nurse.' He'd changed the subject fast.

'I am.'

'I'm in my first year training to become one.' For the first time there was a glimmer of a smile coming her way.

Not a big one, but, hell, did she feel so, so much better. 'We have something in common,' she told her son, hoping that wouldn't send him running out of the room.

'That's what I thought when I found out.'

'Where are you training?'

The smile switched off. 'In Wellington where I've been all my life.'

'Wellington? I had no idea that's where you grew up.'

'No, of course not.' The anger had returned.

'How did you find me?'

'I didn't.' He was watching her with wariness. 'Mum did. She won't tell me how, only that she knew your family lived in Christchurch at the time, and she went from there. I think she knew your father was in business of some sort and started asking around.' His shrug was tight. 'She understood I needed to know who you are, and that I also didn't want to know.'

Again pain slammed into her. Yet she thought she understood where Charlie was coming from. It still hurt. From the moment he'd been taken out of her arms she'd hoped for this day. Now he'd turned up she wasn't going to wish him away. No way could she. He was her son whatever he felt. 'You'll never know how glad I am you decided to see me.'

'I've often been angry at you, while still wanting to find out about you.' He stood up. 'Time I got going. I've been in Christchurch at a general practice doing some training and I've got a flight back home at five.'

Leaping to her feet, she cried, 'Charlie. Don't go. Not yet. Please.'

'I have to.' He hesitated. 'Can I have your phone number?'

'Absolutely.'

He pulled a phone from his pocket. 'What is it?'

So he wasn't ready to give her his. 'Can I have yours?'

'No.' Then he muttered, 'Not yet.'

'Fair enough,' she supposed aloud, but what if he never got in touch again? She'd be heartbroken for ever. But she had finally seen him, knew what he looked like, how his voice sounded. It wasn't anywhere near enough. She gave him her number. It was better than nothing.

What name did he use for her number? It wouldn't be Mum.

Charlie glanced up from his phone, suddenly looking like a little boy who'd lost something monumental, instead of having found it. Had she failed him? What had he expected?

'Charlie?'

'I'll see you around,' he said and walked away. No hug, no last look over his shoulder. Nothing.

Anna stared at his retreating back until he left the cafeteria, and then she stared some more but he didn't come back. Sinking back onto the seat, she put her head in her hands and cried.

CHAPTER SIX

'HERE, GET THIS into you.' Leanne placed a fresh mug of coffee on the table in front of Anna and pulled up a chair to sit beside her.

Anna raised her head slowly, feeling utterly ravaged. Her cheeks felt puffy from crying and tears were still pouring down them. 'I doubt I can swallow a thing.' Leanne had come looking for her when she hadn't returned to the ward, and when she'd told her Charlie had turned up, her friend had sat down beside her, ordered more coffee and held her hand.

'Give it a go. It'll perk you up.'

Coffee splashed over the table when Anna tried to lift the mug. Banging it back down, she stared at it as if it were a monster. 'I can't believe it. All Charlie's life I've waited and hoped I'd get to meet him and now it's happened.' Tears splashed on the backs of her shaking hands.

Leanne's smile was understanding. 'You've wanted this for so long. It's going to take time to absorb it all. You'd better sign off for the rest of the day. You're in no shape to go back to work.'

Staring at her hands, she whispered, 'I am so glad he found me, so amazed, yet I feel all over the place, like there's another bombshell to come.'

'Of course you do. It's only natural.'

'Thanks, Leanne. Where would I be without you?'

'You'd manage. You're tougher than you think.' Leanne hugged her. 'I'd better get back to the ward. We'll talk tonight. Be patient with yourself, girlfriend.'

'Me?'

'Yeah, you. Ring me later.'

'Will do. Think I'll go for a walk in the park. I need to get my head around this.' If it was even possible. Charlie had walked back into her life. Charlie.

Anna wandered around Hagley Park for endless hours, not taking a lot of notice of where she was going, just walking and thinking, and thinking and thinking.

Charlie. Her boy. Impossible to believe he'd come to find her. But there was no denying the vision of him standing beside the canteen table looking at her as though she was an apparition. He was for real. Charlie. Her boy. Not her boy. Yes, her son.

Her heart was all over the place. Happy, bewildered, sad, full of love for the young man she'd brought into the world eighteen years ago. There'd been moments when he'd looked ecstatic to see her, and others when doubt would darken his face and he'd looked disappointed. That was to be expected. He must've grown up wondering why she'd left him, and no doubt would've hated her at times for that. Did he regret finding her? Did she measure up to his expectations? What were those? He wouldn't understand how hard it had been for her too, and that if only she'd known where he was she'd have sent him birthday cards and presents. Would've banged down the door to his home to see him and hold him in her arms.

Now he was here. And she still hadn't held him. No, he'd gone. Back to Wellington and his parents. Mum and Dad. That hurt. Sure, it shouldn't. She had no right to keep him here, to demand he spend time with her. She wouldn't do that to him. It would be unfair and would only lead Charlie to believe he was better off not being a part of her life.

Now that he'd come to her, she could not let him walk away again. She had to be more patient than she'd ever been, let him make the decisions about what he wanted and when. And hope like crazy that included her. She wasn't asking to become part of his life twenty-four-seven. No, just to have some phone calls, visits, talk about what he was up to, all the general goings-on of a family life—part removed.

Family life. Eli.

Anna tripped, straightened, continued walking. Eli. She'd come close to telling him about her son. Charlie. Her son, Charlie. His adoptive parents had given him her chosen name. That said a lot about the couple, said he'd been very lucky getting them for parents. They cared, not only about him but about her.

What would Eli think now that she could add to her story that her son had found her? Would he still walk away because of what she'd done? Or would he stop and think it through, realise she'd only done what couldn't be avoided, and that Charlie had been fine?

She had to stop tormenting herself. There was already too much going on in her mind about Charlie to get wound up about Eli right now. Nor could she let him go completely.

As she turned for the car park there was a light spring

in her step, as if a huge rock had fallen away to leave her filled with hope. Maybe she wasn't so undeserving of love as she'd believed.

'Hey, my man, how's things?' Eli swung Jordie up in his arms and hugged him tight.

Jordan wriggled to get down. 'I learned to write your name, Dad. The teacher said I'm good at writing words. Want to see?'

'Of course I do.' This was one reason why he loved being a dad. He got to share all Jordan's excitement over small things like learning to spell. Though it wasn't so small for Jordie.

'Here.'

Eli unfolded the piece of paper he'd been handed and saw his name in lower case and erratic capitals and his heart squeezed with love. Bending down, he kissed the top of his son's head. 'That's awesome. I'm going to put it in a picture frame and have it by my bed so I know my name when I wake up in the mornings.'

Jordan laughed. 'Silly Dad. You know your name.'

Scratching his chin, Eli asked, 'What is it?'

'Eli Forrester. Like my name. Jordan Forrester.'

'Have you written your name on a piece of paper? Because then I could put them both in the picture frame.'

'You know my name too.'

Sometimes his kid wasn't as slow as people thought. 'You're right, I do.'

'How do I write Anna?'

Crunch. Eli's mouth dried. This was what he'd been dreading. Jordan getting too involved with her.

'Dad, tell me.'

There'd be no avoiding this. Don't show him how to spell Anna and Jordan would throw a paddy. On the other hand, show him and he'd have more to worry about. Right now he did not need a tantrum. Giving in too easily? Giving into Jordan or the lift of his heart that usually came when he was with Anna? Though he had managed to put a dampener on that over the past few days, there were cracks appearing in his façade. He did want more to do with her, despite holding out about Jordan. It could work out if he let go of his caution and put everything he had into a relationship with Anna. 'Here, give me your pen and paper and I'll show you.'

As soon as Jordan had finished copying Anna's name he said, 'I'm hungry.'

It was hard to keep up sometimes. 'Let's see what Grandma's made us for dinner.'

Where would he be without his mother? She provided so many meals it got embarrassing, but whenever he suggested she take a break she'd look sad and say she loved being able to help out. She'd always been there for him and his sisters, helping wherever needed and loving doing so. A big-hearted woman who knew no bounds when it came to her family. He'd been incredibly lucky to be adopted by her and Dad.

'I want beans on toast.' Jordie leapt up and down in front of him, Anna forgotten for now. 'I don't like shepherd's pie.'

'You loved it last week.' Eli flicked the oven on and slid the pie inside to warm through. 'You had two helpings.'

'Did not.'

One of these nights, just when he didn't need it. Eli sighed. Did any parent ever need them? Loud shouting came from the TV where the home side was playing the Aussies in a cricket one-day match. 'Go, Barker.' A fielder had caught the ball and Aussie was down another wicket. The run rate was ten an over. The Aussies needed to lose a few more wickets.

'I want beans.' Jordie banged a tin on the bench.

Eli didn't have the energy to argue. Today had been hectic and seeing Anna had tightened those places he couldn't control around her even when their conversation had been stilted. When he'd explained why he didn't want to rush things he'd sensed she was holding back on something important. He needed to know what it was and, being him, wouldn't be able to let it go until he did.

They'd been talking about keeping their budding relationship—his word, not hers—moving slowly because of Jordan. He'd also said he didn't understand Melissa leaving her son and that was when Anna had pulled back. It didn't make sense, when he'd been honest about how he felt.

Anna, Anna, Anna. She was dominating his thoughts too much.

He'd slept with her. That had been beyond amazing. She was wonderful and had woken him up to all sorts of possibilities, along with increasing his wariness. So wary that he'd walked away without a backward glance, without hugging and kissing her goodnight and promising more to come.

Was he afraid to give in to these feelings she engendered in him?

Was he using Jordan as an excuse to protect his heart?

The ward was busy when Anna arrived at six forty-five the next morning after lying awake thinking about Charlie—and Eli—all night. 'Wow, what happened?'

'A three-year-old with appendicitis was admitted from

surgery at four this morning. Then there's a seven-year-old girl with fractures and severe bruising who came in late last night,' Jacob told her. 'She'd been beaten but of course no one knows when or by who.'

Anna shivered. Some people didn't deserve children. 'That's hideous.'

'It certainly is. Jossy is being kept under sedation. She was beyond distressed when she was brought in.'

'Who's her surgeon?' Eli? She wasn't sure she wanted to see him this morning. His comment about women giving up their babies still hurt despite Charlie turning up in her life and making her happy. While Charlie appeared to have had the good upbringing she'd hoped for, she wasn't ready to explain everything to Eli and hear how wrong she'd been in the first place. This might mean that once more she was alone, single. Harder to swallow than before Eli came along. But she did have a son who'd made contact. Not everything was bad.

'Duncan saw her during the night but I don't know if he's following up today or Eli will take over.'

The way things went, Anna figured she already knew the answer. Sitting down at the computer, she updated herself on patients who'd been admitted since she'd left yesterday. Getting back to work would help settle her overactive mind and get her back on track. It was amazing that Charlie had approached her and she would wait to see what came next, feeling confident that he would get in touch again. As for Eli, she was worried, and had spent time thinking about him during the night when Charlie hadn't been ruling her mind. Did that make her a bad person? Depended who she asked.

Eli said they needed to go slow. That she got, but Jordan couldn't rule the relationship if there was any chance of continuing once she did pluck up the courage to tell him everything.

So you still want him in your life despite what he said?

If he listened to her and accepted how it had been for her, then yes. If not, then no.

First she needed to know they were still on good terms. They'd got on so well. Hopefully they still did and she was exaggerating everything.

Two hours later, when she was dressing a wound on a boy's leg where he'd fallen onto a garden stake, she felt a thrill of anticipation run up her spine. Totally out of place.

'Morning, Anna.' Eli stood at the end of the boy's bed, watching her closely.

'Have I got jam on my chin?'

'No, shadows under your eyes.'

'Not enough make-up obviously.' She couldn't make him out. Not overly friendly but neither was he being aloof Mr Forrester. 'Are you taking over Jossy's case?'

'For today anyway. Duncan rang me earlier about her. It doesn't sound good. I've read the notes and am on my way to see her now.'

So he'd stopped in here to say hello. All was not lost. She had been getting in a stew over nothing. 'I'll be there as soon as I've finished this dressing.'

'It's all right. Leanne's already there.' Leanne. Without her, Anna wouldn't know where to turn. They'd talked for an hour on the phone last night and Leanne had said she shouldn't be so quick to judge Eli. He might be venting about his past, and not really serious about what he'd said.

Anna wasn't so sure, but she was already smitten with him and didn't want to walk away too quickly. Honestly? Yes.

Eli headed out of the room without a backward glance.

She didn't cover all the cases, and not even all the new ones, but that felt like a deliberate snub. Couldn't be when he'd dropped by to see her. She was still looking for trouble. She was falling for Eli, was what she was really doing.

Ten minutes later Eli was back. 'Anna, I've ordered a prescription for different antibiotics for Jossy. The ones she's been having aren't doing a lot of good for that wound in her chest.'

Glancing up at him, she nodded. 'I'll see that it's collected.'

'She also needs bloods done.'

'Okay.' The request would've been emailed to the lab downstairs and a phlebotomist would come to the ward on her rounds, unless Eli had marked it urgent. 'What are you checking?'

'CBC, liver function, non-fasting glucose, CRP.' Run of the mill tests.

'Her grandmother will be here soon to sit with her.' Not her mother. But then no one knew what or who was behind the beating Jossy had received. 'I hate these cases.' They brought tears to her eyes and wound up her anger levels. Why were some people so cruel as to hit a child? It was beyond comprehension. She'd be grateful for ever that Charlie obviously hadn't had any abuse growing up. It would've been in the back of his eyes, behind the few things he'd told her. She'd have known. Wouldn't she?

'Don't we all?' Eli muttered before heading away again.

Nothing about seeing her for a coffee or lunch. Nothing

personal at all. The fact they were at work had nothing to do with it. He'd moved on from being reticent when it came to spending a few minutes with her here. Watching that straight back and those long legs eating up the distance to the lift filled Anna with sadness. They were back to square one.

The lift opened and an orderly pushed a bed out and along towards the desk. 'Molly Hebberd to see you,' he joked.

'Hello, Molly. I'm Anna, one of the nurses who's going to be looking after you.' Molly had had pins inserted in her right tibia, which was fractured in two places.

'Hello, Anna.'

'Room three,' she nodded to the orderly and led the way. 'You've got two roommates, Molly. Both are your age.' Fourteen going on twenty judging by the chatter and giggles coming from the room when she'd arrived on the ward earlier.

'Cool. How long am I here for?'

'I'll have to ask your specialist. Didn't he tell you?'

'Dr Duncan said I'd have to wait and see how soon I get used to crutches.'

'There you go. We've got a physio coming to see you this afternoon. She'll be starting you on easy moves.'

'Anna, can I see you for a moment?' Eli was back.

For a second, hope flickered, but one look at his serious face and she knew whatever he needed it had nothing to do with them. 'I'll be right back, Molly.' As she followed Eli out into the corridor, Anna's heart was tight. How she wanted to wind her arms around his waist and hold him close, breathe in his scent, feel his warmth under that plain blue shirt. Instead she slipped her hands into her pockets and asked, 'What's up?'

'I want to ask that you keep a close eye on Jossy and any

visitors she might get. Her grandmother has talked to me and implied that not all the family should be allowed anywhere near Jossy.'

It was good the girl was in a room on her own. The last thing anyone wanted was trouble in front of other sick children.

'Has anyone contacted Social Welfare?'

'That was done as soon as she was brought in. They'll be here soon.'

'Thanks for the heads up. The problem being we won't have a clue as to who should be allowed to visit and who shouldn't.'

'I'll speak to Security but there's not a lot we can do. The grandmother wasn't very forthcoming with names, only that Jossy would be distressed if certain people visited. It's not what any of us want a patient to have to face. Keep me posted if anyone causes trouble.' Eli was on his way again, not a smile in sight.

'Of course,' she replied to his back. She was glad she had two days ahead where she wouldn't be bumping into him and wishing for more than a medical discussion about one of his patients. What was his problem anyway? He hadn't been there when Charlie turned up. Had he decided going slow meant going nowhere and hadn't got around to mentioning it? They might be at work but five minutes in the staffroom would suffice. It was busy around here though. She shrugged. She had no idea what was going on with Eli, or herself. Focusing on patients was the only answer for now.

The weekend wasn't going to be a barrel of laughs. She had no plans other than the usual routine of housework, shopping and maybe catching up with friends on Sunday for lunch. And probably cooking meals to put in the freezer for night shifts as that was always a go-to when she needed a distraction. Being creative in the kitchen was a balm to her soul and filled in lots of hours, and the deep freeze. Funny how that had never bothered her until Eli came into her life. Now she wished they could get together and have fun, whether it was taking Jordan somewhere or getting between the sheets for some hot sex, and enjoying her cooking.

This playing cautious was driving him nuts. Eli's hand tightened on the steering wheel. Waiting till he'd figured out whether he wanted to pursue the relationship they'd begun was all very well—if it was a relationship at this point—but it was damned hard to keep on with doing it. One kid's party, one date with unbelievable sex. Did that add up to a relationship? Add in coffees and lunches and chit-chat on the ward, and it sounded a little better.

The fact was, Anna was special. He wanted more time with her. Wanted to get to know everything about her. To enjoy her company regularly. Unfortunately he had said they needed to go slowly, something he struggled with. It would be easier to stop altogether because then he wasn't building on the level of happiness she made him feel. He did care for her a lot, to the point it wouldn't take much to fall totally in love with her and that was downright scary. The fact she'd held back on something the other day suggested she could hurt him. He couldn't abide being kept in the dark by someone important to him. He'd suffered the consequences of that before. Yet his heart wanted to open up and be free.

Jordan already thought Nurse Anna was the bee's knees, always asking when he could see her again. That Anna could let him down frightened the daylights out of his father. He didn't want Jordan growing up thinking all women were selfish when it came to children.

Anna's not selfish.

She was big-hearted and generous with her time and self. He couldn't see her putting herself first over anyone in her life. But he had to look out for Jordan because if Melissa could do what she did, then anyone could.

Was he being unfair? Possibly, but he knew what it was like to be put aside by a parent. When he'd tracked down his birth mother only to be told she really didn't care if she saw him again or not, he'd felt as though a spear had been slammed into his heart. That was behind his feelings about any woman who gave up their child, no matter why. Call him narrow-minded, but he'd grown up longing to meet his birth mother only to be rejected. While struggling to forget that, he also acknowledged how lucky he'd been with his real family. His birth mother hadn't wanted him. When Melissa had left him he'd known more pain, but when she'd said Jordan wasn't going to be a part of her life in New York his anger had exploded and he'd said a lot of things that could never be taken back, and nor had he wanted to. He'd meant every single word. Still would if Melissa ever changed her mind about raising Jordan. Chances of that happening were remote, and legally she'd have a battle on her hands given how he was raising their son perfectly well with the help of his family.

Pulling into the school car park, he switched off the motor and leaned his head back. Anna was awesome. Within a short time she'd sneaked under his caution radar and made him start thinking about the future. A future with a woman he loved and a brother or sister for Jordan. Possibly one of each. He grinned. As if he'd get a choice. He hadn't thought too much about finding another woman to share his life with, then along had come Anna. Wrong. Anna had already been there. He'd refused to take notice of her other than as an excellent nurse. Oh, and a woman who made his skin tighten and his toes curl. Now he knew better. There was a lot to her. She had a big heart, cared plenty for others, never complained about anything, gave as good as she got in bed. At least he hoped she got as good from him, because he'd certainly had an amazing experience.

The screen on his phone lit up.

You going to sit there all afternoon?

Followed by a grinning emoji. Typical. His sister Karen always gave him cheek, and had done pretty much most of his life.

He headed for the gate and the school playground where Jordie was trying to throw a basketball through a low hoop. 'Hey, man, how're you going?'

'The stupid ball won't go in.'

'Here, stand like this.' Eli stood with one leg back, and held his arms above his head. 'With the ball in both hands.'

Jordie tried to copy him, then threw the ball and missed. 'Stupid, stupid ball.'

'Try again. You've got to watch the hoop, not the ball. Look where you want it to go.'

The ball banged on the side of the hoop. 'Yes!' Jordie fist-pumped the air. 'I want to do more, Dad.'

'Just a few. I've got to get back to work soon.' He'd take

Jordan home to his mother's and have a few minutes with him over orange juice and cake.

'He's had a good day.' Karen stood beside Eli. 'He mentioned Nurse Anna a couple of times when I saw him at lunch time. Says he hasn't seen her for ages.'

Eli tried for nonchalance. 'She's not a regular visitor.'

'And you're not happy about that.'

So much for thinking he could fool his sister. 'It's my choice, not hers.'

'Aah, so Anna would be happy to pop by occasionally. Or even more often.'

He wasn't so sure about that. They weren't exactly best buddies at the moment. He missed her though. It wasn't the same seeing her on the ward. That didn't give him the warmth he got whenever they were alone. And he wasn't thinking about sex. Just being with her, talking and laughing, was more than enough to make him happy. 'Jordie, come on. Time to hit the road.'

'You like her a lot, don't you?' Once Karen started there was no stopping her until she'd got whatever was on her mind out there.

Might as well be blunt. 'Yes.'

'So what's the problem?'

'You know I'm waiting until Jordan's a lot older before I get into a serious relationship.'

'What I know is you're avoiding one because you're afraid you'll get hurt. It's not all about how Jordan copes if a relationship doesn't work out. He'll cope, as he's done before. He's a tough little guy. Like his dad. That's all I've got to say.'

'Which was too much anyway.' Eli laughed, because there

was never any dodging the bullets his sisters fired when they thought he needed putting in his place. 'I hear you, but you're not going to change my mind.'

'No, but Anna might.'

The problem with that, Eli thought, was Karen might be right. Which was one reason he'd been a bit remote with Anna at work this week. He was trying to be sensible. 'Don't you have work to do, headmistress?'

'It's not as much fun as ribbing my brother.'

'Come on, Dad. I'm hungry.'

He ruffled his son's hair. 'When aren't you?'

He'd missed Anna so much over the past days, and it was all his fault. He'd been the one withdrawing, not Anna. The resignation that had filled her face when he'd spoken to her as he used to before they'd become friendly made him sad. Also guilty, but not guilty enough to do something about it. It was very apparent there was something bothering her. He should talk to her, ask if he could help her with anything, not avoid involvement.

It's not too late.

Or was it? Only one way to find out.

'There you go, Lucy. You're all set to go home as soon as Dr Eli says so.' Anna finished taping the bandage in place around the ten-year-old's thigh where she'd had surgery to remove an embedded metal stake.

'Yippee.'

Yippee. Yes, exactly how she felt too, after talking on the phone for an hour with Charlie last night. He'd rung as she was about to go for a walk. At first he'd sounded nervous, but slowly he'd relaxed and they'd chatted about themselves and a whole load of ordinary everyday stuff. As a mother and son would normally do, except it wasn't normal and Anna felt it was going to take a lot more talking before it was for either of them. She could understand Charlie had trust issues, and all she could do was wait and give him the time he needed to get to know her.

'What do you say?' said Lucy's mother.

'Thank you, Nurse Anna.'

'No problem. You've been a great patient.' No complaints at all. She grinned. 'I'll go and fill in your paperwork. It's the last thing to do other than wait for the doctor.' Hopefully Eli turned up sooner rather than later as Lucy was more than ready to be on her way. 'Any sign of Eli?' she asked Leanne at the desk.

'No.' Her friend looked up at her. 'Mr Forrester is back. Eli seems to have fallen off the planet.'

Anna couldn't argue with that. In the days since he'd walked out of the cafeteria before Charlie turned up in her life, he'd become remote again. He always said hello and asked how she was, but there was no real warmth in his smile when he did. 'You're right. Everything's gone back to the way it was.' The rest of the staff were also paying for something that had nothing to do with them.

'Hello, ladies.' Eli spoke from behind them.

Anna slowly turned around. 'Hi. Lucy's impatient to go home.'

Eli was watching her, looking a little taken aback. He must've overheard her and Leanne talking. 'I'll deal with her in a moment.' He stepped closer. 'My apologies to everyone for being subdued lately. Rest assured, I'll stop being so quiet from now on.'

Why now? What did that mean for her? Anna wondered. Was he going to start talking again as though nothing were off balance between them?

Leanne looked at her, and when she didn't say anything turned to Eli and said, 'Good, because it's so much easier working with you when you're being cheerful and friendly.'

Go, girl. That was her friend sticking up for her, as well as the rest of the staff. Giving her a knowing smile, Anna said to Eli, 'I'll be with Lucy when you're ready.' Then she walked down the corridor with a bounce in her step. Nothing Eli could say or do right now could dampen her happiness over hearing from Charlie.

'Anna,' Eli called. 'Wait.'

She slowed, but didn't stop. 'Lucy's fairly pain free, but will need some analgesics to take home.'

'Anna, wait, please.'

She did as asked, leaning against the wall and glancing around to make sure no one was in sight. 'I owe you an apology, Anna. I shouldn't have closed down on you like I did.'

'You're dead right there. I know you worry about Jordan, but that doesn't give you the right to judge me without getting to know me properly first.'

'You're right. I am sorry.'

Lucy appeared in the doorway of her room. 'There you are, Dr Eli. I can't wait to get out of here.'

End of that particular conversation. For the first time ever Anna wished the ward were much longer and that Lucy's room were furthest away. But it wasn't, and now she had to focus on work, not the man playing with her heart. 'Don't think you can play tennis for a while yet, missy.'

Lucy giggled. 'You're like my mum. Don't do this, don't do that. Bet you tell your kids not to jump off the deck too.'

If only she had kids to tell off. 'Not saying.'

'Lucy, Nurse Anna tells me your pain is light but I still want you taking painkillers every four hours for another two days.' Eli used his doctor-to-patient voice, calm, kind and not to be messed with.

'Why?'

'Because they build up in your system and if you stop now they'll wear off and then you will be in real pain.'

'Okay.'

'I'll see she does what's necessary,' her mother reassured Eli.

'Good, then I'll go and sign a prescription to take with you. You'll get a follow-up appointment in about two weeks' time.' He didn't rush away to do the prescription, as if he was waiting for something. Someone? Her?

Anna shrugged mentally and helped Lucy onto her feet. 'Look after yourself, young lady.'

Back at the desk, she tried to appear busy but it was impossible with Eli taking up space and air at the computer next to her. 'I'll go and check on Rosie.' The tiny tot had had a hernia removed that morning and they were keeping her heavily sedated for a few hours.

'Isn't Kay with her?' Eli asked as he pressed the print button. Of course he'd know that. He'd done the surgery and would've popped in to see the child before coming to the main desk.

'Yes, but I still like to keep tabs on everything.' It was her job after all.

'Feel like a coffee?' He swished his signature across the bottom of the script.

'That depends.'

'I'll be nice, promise.' No cheesy smile with that. He must be serious.

'Go on,' Leanne piped up from the office next door. 'I'll check on Rosie. You're due a break.'

Thanks, friend. You're making it too easy for Eli.

'Fine.' She stood up and went to her locker to get the muffin she'd brought from home and hadn't had time to eat. 'Want half?' she asked Eli when they sat down in the cafeteria with coffees.

'No, thanks.'

'Good, because I'm starving.'

'You're looking tired again. Something causing you problems? Someone?'

The muffin tasted gluggy. This was not the place to open up about Charlie. Or them. 'I'm fine. A few restless nights, that's all.' Not an answer, but she was looking out for herself here.

'I'm here for you, Anna, if you want to talk about whatever's bothering you.'

Anna had to grip her hands together to prevent herself from reaching across and grabbing his. It would be so easy to let go what was holding her back, but again, wrong place, wrong time. If there ever was a right time with Eli. 'I will say I think you're overreacting about me and Jordan. It's as though you've got more to protect than you're letting on.' Like her.

Surprised grey eyes locked on her. 'You read me too well sometimes, Anna. I'm not sure if I like that or not. You're just like my sisters in that respect, though somehow it feels different coming from you.'

She stared at this man, being so open and honest as he was prone to do when she least expected it. What had come over him? 'How?'

'I guess because you're not a sister. You haven't known me since I was swathed in nappies and crying all night to be fed.' Now he gave her a full-blown grin. 'Apparently I wasn't an easy baby. I think when Jordan was born, Mum was hoping he'd give me a hard time, but he was an angel. At first, anyway. Now he's a troublesome but gorgeous boy.'

Unable to stop herself any longer, she reached for his hand. She had to feel his warmth, his skin against hers. 'Eli, he's lovely.' *So are you.* 'He's lucky to have you, too.'

He held her hand lightly. 'Like I said, you're different. But that's not why I suggested coffee.' He took a mouthful of his drink. 'I have let you down. I suggested we go slow, then backed off totally.' When she went to answer, he held his hand up. 'Hear me out. Obviously I have a lot of issues with people who won't share with me what's bothering them. Those I care about anyway. You're doing that at the moment.'

Pulling her hand free, Anna sank back in her chair, and picked up her coffee in shaky hands. Where was this going? Was there a massive but coming?

'I might not always see things your way but, like I've said before, you won't always see it my way either.'

'So why the cold shoulder since Thursday?'

'I'm trying to get my head around some things bothering me.'

'That doesn't explain why you withdrew from all the staff

as well.' Did it matter? He'd given her an answer to her question she couldn't refute.

'I don't know. It seemed easier to fall back into the old mode of not talking to everyone about anything but patients.'

'I don't understand why you do that. You're so different outside the hospital it's like you're two different men.' But she also knew he wasn't the only doctor who did that. It was often a way of coping with very ill patients and not letting the nurses see their emotions. She shrugged as she drained her coffee. 'I'd better be getting back or Leanne will send the squad out to find me.' As if, but she couldn't sit here all afternoon talking to Eli. 'As for you being there if I need someone to download on, that's great.' About Charlie? Not so sure, but it had to be done, and the sooner the better.

He stood up, too. 'Who knows? You might be good for me, too.'

She had no answer for that. 'See you tomorrow.'

'Actually, Anna, how about we go out for a meal tonight?'

'What about Jordan?' He didn't like asking his family to babysit any more often than necessary.

'I can twist Karen's arm. She'll grizzle and growl and do it anyway.'

She answered without overthinking it. 'Then I'd like to go out with you.' She was going on a proper date. The second one with Eli.

'I'll pick you up at six, if that suits. Put your glad rags on.' There was a bounce in his step as he left the cafeteria. Surprised she'd said yes? So was she. Did she regret it? No.

CHAPTER SEVEN

ELI SMILED NON-STOP. It had felt so good when Anna said yes to coming out to dinner, especially as there'd been some hesitancy about her throughout their conversation. He was buzzing. It had been a long time since any woman made him feel so full of anticipation. A date with her was a good, exciting thing to be doing.

Anna was gorgeous. He took her elbow as they strolled into the top-end restaurant he'd chosen because if he was going to date Anna then he wanted to give her the best possible night out.

'Mr Forrester,' the waiter said. 'We've reserved your favourite table for you.'

Anna glanced up at him with a comical look on her face. 'Your favourite table? Blimey, I am being honoured.'

Cheeky wench. He laughed. 'Only the best will do for you.'

She blinked, and looked away.

He'd gone too far, but that was what she did to him. He lost control of his emotions whenever he was with her. Forgot he needed to be extra careful because, no matter how he felt about her, he was not ready for a full-on relationship, though it was getting harder by the day to believe in his reasons for holding back. 'I rarely come here. I know the waiter from when he had surgery on his shoulder after a rugby accident and I'd say he was being cheeky. Come on. Over here.' He led her to a table by the window overlooking the Avon River.

Anna sat down and stared out at the green river banks and tall trees. 'Wow. That's pretty.'

Eli stared at the beautiful woman opposite him. Her short, thin-strapped emerald-green dress highlighted her stunning body and creamy skin to perfection. Her make-up was light and becoming, and that satiny hair fell over her shoulders in shiny waves. His heart began pounding. Easy, man. The night was only beginning.

'Have I got egg on my face?'

'On your chin,' he replied and reached over to run a finger over her skin.

'Glad you noticed.'

Sitting back, he struggled to get back on track. Touching her chin with his fingertip sent his hormones into overdrive. If he wanted to back off he'd made a big mistake by asking her out when he knew she'd do this to him. Was she even aware of how she wound him up? 'Would you like a glass of wine?'

'I'd love one. Pinot Gris if that's all right with you?'

Why wouldn't it be? 'You can have whatever you prefer.' He turned to the waiter and ordered two glasses of the same wine. 'Likewise with the menu.' In case she was thinking she had to be careful about what she chose, though why she would he couldn't understand.

'I was thinking that if you didn't like Pinot Gris and were going to order a bottle of wine it would be a waste.'

'I'd have taken it home for you.' This wasn't going quite

how he'd hoped. 'Anna, let's start again. We're having dinner together and nothing else matters.'

She blushed. Cute and unexpected. 'I'm not usually so obliging about menus and drinks.'

'Why with me?'

Her forefinger drew circles on the table. 'I'm not sure what you expect of me, I guess.'

That stung. 'To be yourself is all I ask.'

'I have been, but there might be a few surprises along the way you aren't comfortable with.'

'True. Isn't that the case whenever we start seeing someone?'

'Of course it is.' Her stunning eyes locked on him, sucking him in as if he were about to dive deep into the unknown, something he might even like.

Leaning back in his chair, he tried to gather his wits, and did okay. 'Let's decide what we want for dinner.'

Once their orders had been placed and the wine brought to them, Eli picked up his glass and held it out to tap Anna's. 'Here's to getting along and having fun.'

'I agree.' She tapped back.

Relief soared. He hadn't realised how worried he was she'd ignore his gesture. Incredible how much Anna had got to him so fast. He hadn't been looking for another partner, but it seemed he mightn't have as much say about his feelings as he'd thought. 'Where did you do your training?'

'Here in Christchurch. I've lived here all my life.'

There was a seriousness behind that he couldn't quite put his finger on. He dug a little deeper. 'Not interested in moving around to other cities or small towns?'

Her finger was doing that circle thing she often used

when she was thinking. 'I've never had any desire to dash off around the world like so many do. This is home and I'm comfortable here.'

So she hadn't gone anywhere else. There was more to this than she was letting on but he'd wait until she was ready to tell him. That was something he'd decided to do—wait, not push Anna and risk everything.

'It's odd that we didn't bump into each other a long time back. I've spent most of my time as a doctor here, apart from one year in London specialising in paediatric surgery.'

'I did work in ICU at St Clair's for a while. You were doing surgery there then.'

The private hospital in the city. 'Five years ago. I was married then.' Wouldn't have been taking a lot of notice of other women. When he'd loved Melissa so much.

The waiter arrived, bearing plates of delicious-smelling food.

'Thank you, Sebastian. That looks wonderful.'

'Enjoy.' He smiled widely and left them to themselves.

They talked about work and friends as they ate, relaxed, comfortable with each other. Just how Eli liked it, and how he'd wanted it from the moment he'd invited her to dinner. Thanks to Karen looking after Jordan, he'd been able to bring Anna somewhere special. So much for always being organised. He didn't do making sudden plans, liked to be in control of everything so there was less chance of something going wrong. Yet he'd hoped Anna would say yes without any forewarning. And she had. 'Thank you.'

She frowned. 'What for?'

'Coming out tonight. I'm enjoying this.'

'I can't imagine you being turned down often.' Her wink was cheeky.

He grinned. 'No comment.' The fact was he didn't ask many women out these days. They always wanted more than he was prepared to offer, and the ones who were happy with a one-night stand weren't his type. He was hard to please. Except when it came to Anna, and even with her he had some problems. 'How come you're single?'

Her back straightened and she placed her knife and fork down on her plate. No cheeky winks in sight now. In fact she wasn't even looking at him. Not like Anna at all. 'It's how I choose to be.'

'I don't believe you.'

Looking around the restaurant, she appeared to be gathering her thoughts.

He could be patient when necessary.

Finally she looked at him. 'I told you I'd had two serious relationships and that they went wrong. I ended up believing maybe I don't have staying power.' She shrugged. 'Who knows?'

Be warned, Eli.

That was exactly why he hadn't got into deep and meaningful relationships since Melissa. He couldn't bear to be left again.

Anna obviously didn't like the silence that hung between them because she continued. 'I haven't been hiding in the cupboard ever since. There've been a few brief flings but that's it.'

'Sounds lonely.' He understood how that felt.

'It has been.' She picked up her glass and took a mouthful of wine. 'Have you been with anyone since your marriage finished?' She obviously wasn't ready to tell him any more, might never be.

'No. Like you, the occasional fling, nothing more serious.' Was that what this was? It didn't feel like it. Anna had him thinking beyond the next week to considering what might be out there for them if he could get past his concerns that dominated everything.

Understanding filled her eyes. 'A lot easier that way.'

'You're making me feel bad. As though I treat women as objects. I assure you I don't. It's only that I don't want to get too involved.'

Her mouth flattened. 'That was not what I was thinking at all. When we're getting along you're kind, caring and considerate, to mention a few things. I understand how you mightn't want to get involved with anyone yet, but I don't see that lasting for ever. You have too much to give.'

Knock him down. He hadn't seen that coming. He picked up her hand and kissed her palm. 'Thank you.'

She shrugged. 'Just saying it how I see it.' There was a worried expression crossing her face.

'Anna.' He still held her hand. 'I want to keep seeing you, going on dates and having some fun. I can't promise any more than that for now.'

Her fingers wound around his hand as the worry slowly disappeared. 'I like your honesty.'

He waited, because this was Anna and he'd learned she didn't leap in to say things she might later regret.

'I'd also like to spend more time with you whenever possible.' Finally a beautiful curving of those sumptuous lips he remembered all too well tracking kisses all over his body.

'You're on.'

* * *

The way her blood kept pounding through her body, Anna thought she might have to see her GP for some blood-pressure pills to slow it down. Or she could just let go and have a hot session with Eli. She wasn't thinking about the days when he'd barely talked to her, wasn't even going to consider how he'd feel about her when she told him about Charlie. This was about them, and how he turned her on so easily. This was now, and the rest could wait for later.

He pulled up outside her house and switched off the motor.

'Coming in?' she asked, the pounding getting louder in her ears.

'I was hoping you'd ask.' He was out and striding around to her side before she took another breath. Feeling as wound up as she was?

She hoped so or she was going to look stupid. Once out of the car, she took his hand and almost ran to her front door.

Eli was laughing as he swooped her up into his arms the moment they were inside. 'I'll take you out to dinner every night if this is the result.'

'You're on.' His neck was right by her mouth, and she had to kiss his skin, taste him as he headed for her bedroom.

Within moments they were naked and touching, kissing and feeling each other everywhere. Desire shot through her. She reached for him, held him and rubbed up and down.

Eli pushed her back. 'Wait.'

'I don't want to. I'm ready.'

'Thank goodness because I can't last either.'

Then they were on the bed, together in the most intimate way, moving in unison, crying out as they came.

'Anna.'

'Eli.'

Then she was free falling, taking Eli with her, not wanting to let him go ever again.

If only, was her first thought as she came to, curled up against Eli, his arm around her waist. He was amazing. Certainly knew how to tick her boxes when he made love to her.

'Hey, you,' he whispered against her neck.

Rolling over, she kissed him lightly. 'No messing around, was there?'

'No, straight down to it.' He grinned. 'You're incredible.'

'Thanks.' She'd take all the compliments she could get. It wasn't often she got this close to a man. Sex was one thing, but with Eli it felt like making love. Love. There was that word again. It was occurring more and more whenever she spent time with him. Even when she hadn't over the past week she'd felt something for him and tried to deny it. It could be a one-way ride to hell if it didn't work out but she wanted to try and make it happen. Yes, she was beginning to accept she might deserve some happiness in the love department. 'You're not so bad yourself.'

He gave a mock groan. 'Seems I need more practice.' He rolled over and covered her with his sexy body. 'How's this?' He touched her nipple with his tongue. 'And this?' The other nipple tightened. 'What about this?'

Intense desire spread throughout her, following every touch Eli made, setting her alight again. So fast, so soon after the first time. Unreal. Incredible. Sliding her hand over his backside, she made to find his sex.

'No, Anna. This is my time to give you pleasure.'

Keep this up and she wouldn't have the strength to return

the compliment when he'd finished. 'Together?' she croaked through the heat in her throat.

He raised his head from her breast briefly. 'Nope.'

She lay back and absorbed every sensation, every touch, kiss and more. Way more. This time she was free falling without a parachute.

And when she finally landed and caught her breath, she straddled Eli and gave to him what he'd given her—touches, kisses, and lots more.

Less than ten minutes after Eli had left Anna's phone rang. Her heart bumped hard. Charlie's name was on the screen.

'Hello, Charlie.' It was quite late to be phoning, wasn't it? Was he ringing to tell her he wanted nothing more to do with her?

'Hi, Anna.'

That was it? 'How's things?'

'Good. I'm back at polytech at the moment. My next secondment is a month at Wellington Hospital in Theatre.'

The tightness around her chest eased off. He hadn't gone silent on her. 'How do you think you'll cope with that?' She'd fainted at the first operation she'd been assigned to observe. All that blood.

'Not sure, but we've been told it only gets better after the first day.'

'True, it does.' It was pretty cool how they'd both chosen nursing as a career. 'Did you always want to be a nurse?'

'Not really. It was only when my granddad got hit by a bus and spent two months in hospital that I began to think I'd like to be one. Everyone was so amazing to him.'

Granddad. That should've been her father's role. Would've

been if her parents hadn't been so determined she get rid of her baby. 'My grandmother was one too. Seems it runs in the family.' Anna winced. Charlie mightn't like that comment.

But, 'That's kind of neat.' Then there was another silence. This time Anna waited it out.

'Um…is it okay if I come down and see you again in a couple of weeks?'

Her heart swelled. 'Of course it is. Any time.'

Stop. Don't overdo it or he might back off.

'Um…good. Um…what about if Mum and Dad come too?'

'They want to meet me?'

'Yes.'

Wow. That had to be good, didn't it? 'Then tell them yes, I'd like to meet them too.' Would she? Of course she would. These were the people who'd raised her son to be a great young man. And a nurse. She smiled to herself. 'When you know when you're coming, I can pick you up.' She presumed they'd fly down.

'Dad's going to hire a car. We'll only come for a day, depending on your shifts.'

They weren't planning on spending too long with her. Guess that made sense. It was a strange situation for everyone. 'I'll text my roster to you.' Charlie's number had been in her phone from the first time he'd called her. 'I can meet up with you anywhere it suits.'

'Thanks, Anna. Bye.' He didn't mess around making small talk, then.

Staring at her phone, Anna felt a bubble of excitement expanding in her chest. Her son was bringing his parents to meet her. Strange as it was, it was also beyond what she'd hoped for so soon. Yippee.

* * *

At work on Friday, Anna saw Eli enter the ward and look around until he spied her.

Smiling, he came across. 'Afternoon, Anna. How's things?'

'All good.' Great was the real answer, but she downplayed it at work. Other staff members had exceptional hearing at the most inconvenient moments, especially Leanne. Her date with Eli had been nothing short of magic and she was constantly recalling every moment of it. 'Which patient are you here to see?'

'Benjamin. How's his wound?'

'It's clearing now that the antibiotics are kicking in.' The teenager had had a splenectomy after a cycling accident where the handlebar rammed into his abdomen. The infection was a result of pathogens on his skin from another medical problem he had.

'That's good.' He looked around, saw they were alone. 'Would you like to join me in taking Jordan to swimming lessons tomorrow morning? It's Saturday, I thought we could go to the beach afterwards, take a picnic with us.'

'I'd love to.' Eli was seriously asking her to go with him *and* Jordan? That was progress. He was normally very protective when it came to his boy. 'Let me sort the picnic. Anything Jordan doesn't like?'

'Easier to tell you what he does like.' Eli grinned. 'He's a picky little blighter.'

One of the other nurses was heading their way. 'Let's go see Benjamin. His dad's with him at the moment.'

Eli nodded. 'Right. I'll be there at nine-thirty,' he added quietly.

She presumed he meant her place as she didn't have a clue

where the lessons were held. 'Everything will be ready.' Especially herself. She was already thinking about the new bikini she'd bought a few weeks back. Sky blue with splashes of white, it fitted her perfectly. Her feet were all but skipping as she entered the room where Benjamin was sprawled over the bed, talking to his father. 'Hey, Benjamin. Dr Eli's here to give you the once-over.'

'You already did that.'

'Yeah, but nothing like the real deal from the doc.'

'Anna will have done exactly what I'm about to do, and I totally trust her observations, but I'm a bit of a control freak and like to take my own notes.' Eli was still grinning.

As her feet were dancing? Were they becoming an item without realising it? Without setting out to do so? Whichever, she was happier than she'd been in ages. Happier in a different way. She had met a man who touched her in so many ways. She laughed. Touched her? Fingers and hands on her overheated skin. Funny how since Charlie had turned up out of the blue, she felt more worthy of a love life. What if this time she could follow through and fall so deeply in love that she wouldn't walk away from it—from him? Something chilly ripped down her back. It wasn't possible. She hadn't been lucky so far and she was thirty-four, so why would it happen now that she'd met Eli?

She had no idea whether Charlie had forgiven her but he was staying in touch so far, which had to be a good sign. During their phone conversations he hadn't come out and said she was a terrible person for giving him up, but there were moments when she thought she heard anger in his voice. Hopefully that was because he was coming to terms with everything she'd told him about why she'd done what she had. But she did feel more at ease now that her son had found her and hadn't fled to the hills afterwards. That ease seemed to be flowing into other aspects of her life, such as her starting to let Eli into her heart.

'Anna, can you put a new dressing on this?' Eli interrupted her musings. 'There's been some seepage.' There was a question in his eyes when he glanced at her.

'I'll get the tray.' He really had disrupted her usually orderly mind if she was thinking all that while standing at a patient's bedside with a surgeon.

When she returned with the required equipment Eli and Benjamin's father were animatedly discussing cricket, a game that bored her silly. 'Here we go, Benjamin. You're not into cricket either?'

The boy was on his iPad. 'Rather watch paint dry.'

She laughed. 'Know what you mean. Okay, lift your top up and lower your pants. I'll get this sorted as fast as possible.'

'Hang on, not so quick,' Eli interrupted. 'I want to have another look at the wound.'

Hadn't he already done that before requesting her to change the dressing? She stepped back to allow him room to move without bumping into her. Not that she didn't mind the odd nudge but not here with patients and parents.

'Change the dressing every hour, Anna. Apply cream to the other infected sites each time too. The sooner we knock this on the head, the better.' Eli straightened and looked right at her. 'That's it.' There was a slight twist to his lips as though he'd read her mind earlier and was having a good old laugh at her.

But she knew she was safe. He had no idea what she'd

been thinking other than maybe something about him. It wouldn't do for him to know she was contemplating getting closer to him. His guarded manner would step in and put the brakes on her faster than it took him to make her orgasm the other night. 'All under control,' she said, tongue in cheek.

Benjamin didn't wince when she cleaned his wound and pressed the new dressing on. Nor did he move when she cleaned and creamed the other messy sites on his body. 'You're a toughie,' she told him as she finished up.

'Nah, you don't hurt like the last nurse did.'

She'd take the compliment and carry on as usual. 'There, all done. You can get back to that game you're trying to win. You might like to click on the bottom left-hand picture and I bet you'll get a great score.' She recognised the game that many teens who came into the ward enjoyed playing.

Benjamin stared at the screen for a moment, then grinned. 'You're right.'

'Of course I am.'

'How did you know that?' Eli asked on the way back to the desk.

'I spent a whole eight-hour shift with a girl who played it non-stop in an attempt to ignore the pain in both her fractured legs. Seemed to work too as she became zoomed out.' The things she did as a nurse weren't all about bandages, injections and blood pressures. 'Does Jordan have apps for games?'

'Unfortunately, yes. I try to keep him off his tablet as much as possible but it's hard when nearly every kid has one these days. There are time limits though, which I insist on, and they often lead to tantrums, which lead to more time off the tablet.'

'The joys of parenthood, eh?' What she wouldn't have given to experience them.

'I'll see Ollie now and then head to the clinic.' Eli peeled off into the next room and Anna followed. 'How's that tummy?' he asked his patient, who'd had a splenectomy that morning.

'Sore.'

'Ollie's last analgesic was less than two hours ago,' she told Eli.

'Give him another dose at the four-hour mark.' Eli was examining Ollie's sutures. 'Everything looks all right.'

'A placebo might be a good idea,' she told him on the side. She doubted Ollie, who was only nine, knew what a placebo was, but kids these days were quick to look up on the internet to find out anything, so she'd best not let him hear what she'd suggested.

Eli's eyes widened in acknowledgement. 'I'll write up a prescription.' Not necessary, there were some in the drug cabinet, but Eli was onto it in that he was acting as though Ollie were getting a different painkiller.

'I'll make sure we give him the tablets soon.' Ollie was complaining non-stop about his pain and discomfort. He'd had his mother demanding more drugs last night and from the moment she'd arrived to see her son that morning. She'd gone off to get something for Ollie's lunch, hospital food not being good enough for her son.

'Ollie, your wound is looking good. It will start healing soon.'

'But it hurts.'

'Any surgery hurts a little bit. Best thing you can do is

not to get too active for a day or two. I'll see you again tomorrow.' Eli headed for the door.

Anna tucked Ollie's pyjama top down and pulled the blanket up. 'I'll be back with some pills soon.'

'I want them now.'

Eli came back into the room. 'You'll have them when it's the right time, and not before, otherwise you'll get sleepy and that's not good for your recovery. Understand?'

'Yes, Doctor.' The boy looked more annoyed than repentant.

Anna knew she was in for some attitude later on, but she had broad shoulders. 'Thanks, Eli,' she said as they left the room.

'I probably was a little harsh on him. It would've been a shock having an operation today.'

'You're right but it doesn't help when his mother fuels his ego.' She glanced around, saw no one close, and said quietly, 'You weren't too tough on him. Sounded to me more like a dad trying to do his best.'

Eli laughed. 'Yeah, right. Might need to rethink how I deal with my patients.'

'No. Keep on doing what you do best, being kind, considerate and good at surgery.' With that, she went into the nearest room to see any patient that could distract her from Eli. She said too much to him these days. Almost as though she was stroking *his* ego, and probably giving him the wrong idea about what she thought of him. Not that she'd said anything she didn't mean, but she didn't want to appear as a simpering female who'd do or say anything to get his undivided attention.

'Anna,' he called from the doorway.

So much for getting away from him. 'Yes?'

'Nine-thirty, tomorrow. Your place.' Then he was gone.

She'd be ready and waiting, most likely at eight-thirty. She wouldn't want to be late for her date. Grinning widely, she crossed over to Jessica. 'How you doing, sport? Your hand feeling any better today?' One thing for sure, Anna thought, *her* heart was feeling lighter than it had for a while.

CHAPTER EIGHT

'DID YOU HAVE to wear that bikini?' Eli groaned as he watched Anna slather her fair skin with sunscreen. The bikini left nothing to his imagination, but then his imagination needed no help. His mind knew her body very well. A tightening in his groin suggested he should go take a dive in the sea right now.

'I could go naked.'

'That wouldn't be much different.' Taking the tube of sunscreen lotion from her, he rubbed cream on her shoulders and over her back, swallowing hard as another part of him hardened.

She laughed. 'Jordan, come here and let me put some more screen on your face. You're going pink.'

'Pink's a girlie colour.'

'Exactly.' Anna rubbed some cream on his skin.

Eli moved to hide his reaction to Anna's smooth skin, thankful Jordie was engrossed in whatever Anna was telling him. His heart was expanding with love for his boy, and for Anna. No, he wasn't in love with her, but he was letting go of the things holding him back and letting her in. She was so special it hurt to think he might not follow up on these new feelings. Glancing at Jordan, he felt a moment of panic. Jordie thought Nurse Anna was the best. Which was good.

It was also a worry. They hadn't established a relationship, were only dating occasionally. Yeah, so, wasn't that a relationship of sorts?

Jordie laughed at something Anna said.

Eli couldn't help thinking that was lovely too. His boy did deserve a mother figure in his life. But was Anna the one? Only way to find out was to keep seeing her and go with his gut instinct.

'You've gone awfully quiet.' Anna nudged him. 'Something not right?'

'Not at all.' Not entirely true, but near enough. 'Let's go get wet.' He stood up and grabbed Jordie, tucked him under his arm and began jogging down the beach to the water. He didn't look to see if Anna followed them, just ploughed into the water with Jordan squealing in his ear and jiggling fit to bust as the water crept up their bodies.

A slim body in a blue and white bikini went splashing past, tightening him some more. Anna stopped and rolled onto her back. 'This is good.'

'Anna, watch me.' Jordan began dog-paddling towards her. 'I'm fast.'

Paddling beside him, Eli held back a laugh. Fast as a snail. 'You're doing great, Jordie.'

'Come on, you're getting closer,' Anna encouraged.

Jordan disappeared under the water, popped back up coughing and spluttering. 'Yuk. That tastes horrid.'

'You're not supposed to drink sea water.' Anna laughed. 'Not frightened, is he?'

Eli wanted to grab him and hold him close, but that would be OTT. He had to give Jordan space to be a boy, no matter what the ramifications—up to a point. 'Unfortunately not.'

'Come on, Dad. He's happy, and we're right here.' Anna was laughing at him, but there was also understanding in those beautiful eyes.

'I know.'

'But.'

'Always plenty of buts. No wonder people go grey. It's all about raising children.'

'Remind me to check how many grey hairs you've got later.'

Later? When he took her back to her place with Jordan in the car? Not happening. Jordan was not going to get used to sleeping at Anna's house. That was getting too close to being like a family unit for comfort. 'One hundred and twenty-three,' he told her.

'You've missed some at the back of your head.' She flipped onto her back. 'Come on, Jordan. Race you to the beach and then we can have our picnic.'

Jordan tried to swim on his back but all he managed to do was sink.

'Try paddling,' Eli suggested. He could see Anna was going as slow as possible so Jordie would pass her. 'Hey, I'll hold you around the waist and you start running. Once your feet touch the sand you do it for real.'

'I'm gonna beat Anna, Dad.'

'You bet.'

When he did, he fell about laughing, before asking, 'Are you coming to my swimming next week, Anna?'

'I'll have to see if I'm working first.'

'Say you can't.'

'If only it were that easy.' She grinned.

The picnic was great, something for all of them to enjoy,

and more points for Anna from Jordan when he found chocolate fish in the chilly bin.

'What treat do I get?' Eli asked her.

'You'll have to wait and see.' There was a sexy twinkle going on in her eyes.

'We're not staying the night at your place,' he warned. Disappointment struck. He wanted to be intimate with her again. To hell with it. 'But you could come back to my house for the evening.'

'That was the plan,' she admitted. Then her face dropped a little. 'I'm not being too presumptuous, am I?'

So unlike the Anna he knew that again he wondered if she wasn't as strong as she made out to be. 'Not at all.'

'Sorry.' She fidgeted with the edge of the towel she'd wrapped around her waist when they returned from the water. 'It's only that I'm not really sure where we're at. I know you don't want me getting too close to a certain little man, but then we have an explosive time together and that takes over my thinking.'

She was trying to fit in with his requirements when it came to their relationship—yes, it was one even if he'd been denying it—which meant not letting Jordan take her presence for granted. He could love her for that alone. But he didn't, wouldn't. Not yet. If only he could drop the worries and be free to do as he wished. It was so tempting, and yet so hard. His ex really had done a right number on him by taking his love for granted until she no longer wanted it. Add in his birth mother turning him away when he found her, and it was very difficult to give his heart to anyone else. On the other hand, Mum and Dad and his sisters had never let him down, and that was how he was with them and Jordan. Could he do it with Anna? Did he want to?

Short answer? Yes. Longer, sensible one? Still yes if he could be absolutely certain she wouldn't let him down. No one got that card. It was a wait and see situation.

'Ahh, hello, Eli? Is this where I get up and go find a taxi to take me home?'

Gees, man, get a grip. Stop this procrastinating and make the most of your time with Anna.

'I was off in doo-doo land. I know what you mean about not knowing where we're at. How about we carry on as we are and see where it goes from there? I'm not one for rushing into anything, especially relationships.' Funny how he was so upfront with Anna at times. He didn't have it in him to hide everything he felt or thought from her. Just some things. Nor was it funny; it was disturbing and said a lot more about where he was at with her. He wanted more, lots more, and the only way for that to happen was to trust her not to let him down and give as much of himself as he was comfortable with.

'When we're finished here you can drop me off at my place and I'll shower and change, and drive over to yours afterwards.' Her uncertainty made that sound like a question.

'I—I'd like that.' Gulp. He'd nearly said he loved the idea. What would be wrong with that? It was a normal thing to say. Yeah, but he was afraid of the love word at the moment. It had a lot of meanings, and therefore repercussions. 'Really like it.'

Later that evening, after they'd made love—the love word again—Eli sat up in his bed and reached to hold Anna against his chest. She was warm and soft, and limp after falling apart under him when she climaxed. Intimacy with Anna was something else. Unbelievable. Of course there hadn't been a lot of sex going on in his life lately but he was sure that making out with Anna would always be mind-blowing. The sensations she caused in him had him feeling as though he'd found something magical. Something he didn't want to let go ever again. 'You're amazing,' he said as he brushed a kiss on her cheek.

She snuggled closer, sliding her arms around him. 'I quite like you, too,' she murmured through a laugh.

He heard a cough coming from Jordan's room and swore. 'Sorry, but I think Jordan's waking up.' Coughing was a common start to him coming up out of a dream. 'That means we have to get out of bed. The last thing I want is for him to find us together in this state.'

Her smile disappeared as she sat up and put her feet on the floor, ready to get up. 'Seriously, Eli, I got the message the very first time you told me how worried you get about Jordan being hurt.'

The look on her face suggested it didn't make her happy either. Well, she'd have to accept it or they were over. He leapt out of bed. 'Jordan's too young to understand what we were doing. Plus I'm not ready for him to see you in my bedroom. That's suggesting you're going to be here a lot.'

'Eli, give it a break. I'm not stupid. I get what you're saying. I was thoroughly enjoying being held by you and didn't want to move away. That's all.'

Tugging on some shorts, he leaned over to cover her mouth with his. 'Thank you.' He hadn't apologised to any one half as much as he seemed to with Anna.

'I'll head home now.'

'Fair enough.' Not that he wanted her to, but it was the best option with Jordan waking up.

'Daddy, where are you?'

'This is always the result of a bad dream.'

'Does he have many?' Anna shoved into her T-shirt, apparently not worried about her bra and more concerned about Jordan walking in.

Thankfully he'd remembered to close the door when they'd made their mad dash down to his bedroom. 'Not really. He'll settle down again after I've heard what he was dreaming about.'

After zipping up her denim shorts, she grabbed her bra and opened the door. 'Right. Time I was out of here. See you on Monday, unless you're going in to check up on a patient tomorrow.'

'You're on tomorrow?'

'Yep. Nights for the next four shifts.'

There went any idea of getting together soon. Might be a good thing as there was a bit going on in his head that needed sorting before they went too far. Another kiss and he opened the front door for her. 'It's been a great day, Anna.'

'It has. Thanks for everything.' And she was gone, no lingering looks or glancing over her shoulder. Leaving him bereft when he had no right to feel that way.

Thank goodness for night shifts or she'd be beating down Eli's door to be allowed in to make love, Anna thought. She reached for some pills from the drug cabinet for a young patient with nausea after surgery for three fractured ribs that had pierced the lung. There was no such thing as too much sex. Not with Eli. The man was incredible. He seemed to read her like a book with a size twenty font. He knew what she wanted and when.

She hadn't seen him since Saturday as he was gone by the time she signed on at eleven in the evening, and she was home tucked up in bed by the time he was turning up on the ward. Bed. That word had taken on a whole load more meaning lately. He had phoned every night before she'd started her shift to see how her day had been and what she'd been up to. She liked talking to him and felt they were getting more relaxed with each other about everyday issues and learning more about each other as time went by. There was still the problem about Jordan. Where she didn't mind having to step back for his son, Eli was still overprotective at times, and she believed he felt she was getting too close to the boy.

That made her cross. No way would she ever intentionally hurt Jordan. Of course, if she and Eli did get into a full-time relationship there was always the chance it would sour and then Jordan might be upset, but that was a risk Eli had to decide was worth taking or not. At the moment, she suspected he wasn't ready to commit to much more than they already had, and yet he mightn't be ready to back off entirely either if the way he kept asking her out or phoning her meant anything.

There was also the other elephant between them. Charlie.

In her pocket her phone vibrated. Pulling it out, she sighed. Eli.

Goodnight. xxx

Okay, that was a move in the right direction.

She replied.

Sleep tight. xxx

The simple things made her happy, and loving. In love a little. Or was that getting to be a lot? Who knew? Not her, and she was over trying to work it out. It was early days and for now she'd run with the flow and make the most of the good times.

But on Saturday when she got a call from Eli saying he'd catch up with her later in the day after Jordan's swimming class, her happiness deflated a little. It stung a bit that he hadn't asked her along, but then she couldn't really expect him to ask her along every weekend. They weren't that close yet. 'How about you come here? Leanne and her husband and kids are coming round for a barbecue on the back lawn at about four. Bring Jordan,' she added carefully. 'He can play with Leanne's youngest, who's five.' Going on twelve some days, but she wouldn't mention that.

'You don't mind if Leanne knows we're seeing each other?' Surprise lifted his voice.

'She's one of my best friends and has known for a while that we're spending a bit of time together. If it bothers you, then rest assured she doesn't gossip. You'd have known by now if she did.'

'What can I bring?'

Guess that's a 'Yes, we'd love to come' then.

'I've got it covered, but if there's anything you think you want feel free to bring it along.'

'See you later, then.'

With or without Jordan? Anna shrugged. Men. Sometimes they could be difficult, but worth putting up with for the good times. Eli was anyway.

Jordan was happy as a kid in a candy shop playing with Leanne's son, Luca, Eli thought as he watched the boys chasing each other around the lawn, laughing their heads off and shouting like crazy. 'Your neighbours will be calling in the noise control at this rate,' he said to Anna.

Craig, Leanne's husband, just laughed. 'They're used to it. There's another young lad along the road who often comes along to play with Luca when we're visiting.'

Anna added, 'Can't have too many friends at their age.'

It was getting too easy to fit in with Anna. Jordan was happy. *He* was happy. Her friends accepted him, especially Leanne. But then why wouldn't she? It turned out Craig was a GP and he'd met Leanne when he was doing his training in Dunedin. Doctors and nurses falling in love everywhere. A pathologist once said to him, if a doctor qualified without finding the love of his life in the medical world then there was something wrong with him or her because there were so many wonderful people working in the system to choose from. Maybe the pathologist was right. He should've gone for another medic. They'd at least understand the long hours required, something that Melissa had constantly complained about.

'Time we hit the road.' Craig stood up. 'These kids have got sports day tomorrow.'

Eli glanced at his watch. Seven o'clock. Where had the time gone? 'Guess I'd better make tracks too. Jordan should be tucked up by now.' He could blame Anna for sidetracking his usually controlled mind, but for once he would just go along with the fact he'd been having a wonderful time and forget about worrying about running late getting his boy home. But first, 'Want a hand clearing up, Anna?'

'Where have you been? Leanne and I did that a while ago.' She looked amused. Pleased that he'd been so at ease with everyone?

'Guess I got that wrong.'

'I bet Craig was keeping you occupied talking so he could pretend he didn't know what we were doing,' Leanne retorted as she gathered up her kids' gear. 'He's allergic to doing dishes.'

'Best allergy to have if you're going to have one,' replied Craig. 'Thanks for a great afternoon, Anna.' He planted a friendly kiss on her cheek. 'Always good to get out of the house.'

She laughed. 'You're never in it. If not at work, you're digging the garden.'

'True. Keeps me out of mischief.'

'Oh, come on.' Leanne laughed. 'Glad you joined us, Eli. We'll have to get together again soon. At our place next time.'

'I'm glad Anna invited us along. Jordan's had a blast with Luca.' Another friend to talk about. Where was he anyway? Looking around, he couldn't see him anywhere. 'Jordie?'

'He's curled up on my bed with a book,' Anna informed him. 'He asked if he could go in there and I couldn't see why not.'

'Not a problem.' That meant they might stay a few more minutes, and he could briefly have Anna to himself.

'See you both tomorrow,' Leanne called from the door before closing it behind her family.

'Want a coffee before you go home?' Anna asked.

'Love one. I'll just check on Jordan, make sure he's not getting into mischief.'

Not a chance. Jordan was sound asleep, hugging one of Anna's pillows to his face, looking completely at ease. Something his dad should take note of and try harder to become so relaxed, thought Eli when he returned to the kitchen. 'He's out for the count.' When Anna started to smile wickedly, he held up his hand. 'Be warned, he can wake up just as quickly as he went to sleep.'

'Then I'd better kiss you while the coffee's brewing.' Her arms were around his neck and she was pulling his face down to meet hers. Her mouth tasted of fruit and heated him instantly.

He groaned as he returned the kiss, deep, tightening him, as she always did with little effort. She really was so damned sexy and attractive that he couldn't remain calm around her. 'Is there a lock on your bedroom door?' he joked.

'If only.' She went to pour the coffee. 'Let's sit in the lounge. We can share the sofa.' Her wink was saucy. 'Who knows? We might get lucky.'

'Daddy. Where are you? Come here.'

'There goes that idea.' Eli said. He placed his hand on Anna's cheek. 'All part of being a parent.'

'Not a problem,' she replied. 'I didn't really believe we'd have a chance of getting too close tonight.'

He couldn't help asking, 'You're not disappointed?'

'Duh. Of course I am, but I totally understand that when Jordan's with us things are different.'

He should be glad she wasn't causing trouble or demanding time alone with him, instead of overthinking what she said. Her mouth beckoned, and it was hard to resist so he stepped away. 'I'd better get Jordan before the trouble starts. As in I keep kissing you and forget what I'm supposed to be doing.'

'I can't see you doing that.'

But then she had no idea how much she tipped his world upside down. Best she didn't find out either. Not yet, anyway. He had a way to go before getting fully involved. He went to Anna's bedroom and lifted a sleepy Jordan into his arms to carry him out to the car.

Anna picked up Jordan's bag and Eli's chilly bin that he'd brought beer and nibbles in and followed him outside. At the car, she leaned over and kissed Jordan's cheek. 'Goodnight, little one. See you again soon.'

'Nigh, nigh, Anna. Love you.'

Eli jerked back, pulling Jordan away from Anna, shocked. That was not meant to happen. His heart was thumping. How had he got to this point? Now Jordan really could be hurt.

Anna placed her hand on his back. 'It's what kids say all the time. Don't take it too seriously.'

Damn it, Anna. I thought you understood my concern?

'Jordan doesn't, and even if he did, it worries me that he's looking for something that's not there.'

'Thanks a lot, Eli. I know you're very protective of your son, but I don't deserve to be shoved aside willy-nilly when something happens that you're uncomfortable with. A few minutes ago you wanted to get into bed with me. Don't say you didn't,' she snapped when he stared at her. 'If you're not going to be open-minded about how your son and I get along then I suggest we stop seeing each other as of now.'

The problem was he didn't want to. He was halfway in love with Anna and wanted to find the other half. Wanted to give it a chance. Most of the time that was. There were all the questions he kept putting to himself, but deep down where it mattered he cared for her a lot. A hell of a lot. 'Please be patient with me. This is new for me and obviously I'm not doing a good job of getting it right.'

She stared at him. 'You'd let me spend time with him?' She nodded at Jordan who was nodding off again, unaware of his role in this uncomfortable conversation.

'I'd better put him in his seat.' His bundle was getting heavier as they stood beside the car.

'That's hardly an answer, Eli.'

He waited until he'd clipped the seat belt in place around Jordan and closed the door before answering. 'You're right. It's not. You have no idea how much I want this to work out for all of us.' There, he'd put his heart on the line. 'I'm not saying you'd deliberately let him down but if we get more involved then decide it's not working he is going to be hurt.'

So am I, he thought, but he'd keep that to himself. He was nowhere near ready to tell Anna how he felt about her.

Her sigh rippled through the warm air between them. 'Low blow, Eli. You'd better get going. I'll see you at work tomorrow.' With that, Anna turned around and strode up her drive to the front door where she went in and closed it behind her without a backward glance.

He stood by his car, staring after her, feeling ill as sadness engulfed him. Had she just pulled the plug on their burgeoning relationship? Or did she need time to think about how to come back from what they'd both said? Because she wasn't happy with him. Not at all. An enjoyable few hours had gone belly-up in a matter of minutes. Minutes he'd do almost anything to retract. Anything but set Jordan up for a fall. Or was he protecting himself here? Using Jordan as an excuse? Hardly. Jordan came first.

But if he listened to his sisters, and his parents, he was wrong. They all said if he found happiness then Jordan would be a happy boy and would have a normal life. And if it went wrong, he'd survive because he had a loving dad and a great family.

CHAPTER NINE

'THAT WAS DANDY,' Anna muttered to herself as she leant back against her front door and listened for him to drive away. 'As if I want to upset Jordan in any way.' Surely Eli was being oversensitive? He was a good dad, but this was getting out of hand.

Damn him. It was like taking two steps forward, one, sometimes two, back. On again, off again. He'd kissed her as if there were no tomorrow, then gone all weird on her. Did she wind him up that much he lost control of his serious side?

She laughed bitterly. Good. Because that was what he did to her when she was with him. She didn't want to be alone when it came to feeling hot and horny. So was she willing to spend more time with him? Sex-starved brain says yes. Serious brain? Same answer because she believed there was something very special developing between them. She had to accept she'd fallen for him, but there was more to it. When they were getting along they jelled well, understood each other, sometimes read each other's mind without a word being spoken. They liked doing similar things and eating the same foods. Neither of them spent all their spare time rushing around trying to look busy when all they wanted to do was relax.

But there was a huge monkey in the room and she had to deal with it.

Finally she heard the car drive off. What took him so long? Thinking about coming back to give her some more grief? Or to apologise? No, he didn't seem in the right frame of mind to do that. Was he expecting the same from her? Should she be sorry for speaking her mind? She had been blunt, but that was her. Take it or leave it.

He's left.

But he did have a child to get to bed. They'd see each other tomorrow on the ward and then she'd see where things lay. 'Goodnight, Eli.'

Next morning Eli strolled onto the ward as though nothing had gone wrong between them. 'Morning, Anna. Sleep okay?'

Hardly, when she'd been thinking about his sexy body and what they might've got up to if Jordan hadn't been there. 'Like a log.' She'd got over her funk by the time she'd switched her bedside lamp off, and had started imagining Eli lying beside her. She had it bad. She could no longer put off having that talk with him. 'Did Jordan go back to sleep when you got home?'

'He was up and down every hour. Wanted a drink of water when there was already one by his bed, a story, which he didn't get, then to climb into bed with me. Again, that didn't happen. Then something to eat. He got a banana.'

'No wonder there're shadows under your eyes.' Eli looked even more tired than she felt.

'Yeah, it was a long night.' He looked at the screen she

had up with notes on one of his patients. 'No change in Hayley's readings, I see.'

'There was a spike in her temperature around midnight but it's dropped a little since. The wounds on her thigh are still inflamed, and she's feeling some pain despite the drugs we're administering.' The girl had been knocked down by an angry ram on her father's farm two days ago and suffered external and internal injuries from the animal's horns.

'No surprise there. If only I could sedate her for longer but it's not a healthy thing to do. She's coping very well for a nine-year-old, though. A tough wee thing.'

'Her mother's struggling this morning. She needs a good night's sleep, too.'

'I'll see if she wants something to help with that.' Eli sat down at the computer next to her. 'How about Mason? Did he manage to eat anything this morning?'

'Guzzled down porridge and stewed peaches like he hadn't eaten for a week. He says his throat's still sore but a lot better.'

'A normal result for a tonsillectomy, then.' Eli looked relieved.

'Do you worry about every patient?'

'It's hard not to when they're children.'

'Fair enough.' She stood up. 'I'll be with Hayley unless you need me for anything else.'

'I'll be right behind you.'

Not watching my backside in the horrible scrubs, I hope.

'I think Leanne has a patient she wants to talk to you about.'

'Where is she?'

'Grabbing a coffee while she can.' It had been hectic so

far. Anna walked away feeling happier about Eli than when he'd left her place last night. He didn't seem to have any problems he wanted to deal with this morning, but that was also annoying because it was as if he believed he didn't have to explain anything else. Did she need to? Definitely. He had to learn about Charlie. However, they were at work, not the place for that conversation. But she'd been expecting Eli to have returned to his aloof manner, not be so friendly as he'd done before. No doubt about it, he was good at confusing her.

'Anna, up for a coffee when I'm done here?'

Like she said, confusing. Was he about to talk over things he'd refused to last night? This was the last place she wanted a personal conversation, even if they were the only ones using the staffroom. 'Sure.'

'I only have one muffin again,' she told Eli when they were sitting at the tiny table with coffees in hand.

'I'm not hungry as I had a big breakfast.'

Good, because she was starving. Having slept through her alarm, she'd had to dash to work to get here for the start of shift, forgoing breakfast apart from the banana she'd grabbed on the way out of the house. Drinking her coffee, she waited for Eli to say what was on his mind. If there was something bothering him, that was. He seemed serious enough for there to be some issue.

Eli rinsed his mug in the sink, and took hers to do the same. 'Can I drop by later when you're at home?'

The look in his eyes said this wasn't about lovemaking. Well, the time had come for her to say her piece and tonight would be it. 'Of course.'

'I'll come round after I'm done here. Jordan's at Mum's for dinner tonight.'

'I'll look out for you.' So he wasn't taking a hike yet. She'd stop by the supermarket to get some cheese and crackers to eat while they sat on her deck with a wine or beer. Or she could heat the zucchini pie that she'd made yesterday. Somehow she doubted she'd be able to swallow anything but she had to try.

In the meantime she had a wee patient to nurse and take her mind off Mr Forrester, who knew how to wind her up fast and confuse her big time. Was she so out of practice when it came to dating that she didn't know what was happening? The few guys she'd dated over the past couple of years hadn't intrigued her half as much as Eli did so it was possible she was looking for too much, and not accepting what was on offer because she couldn't see it for the mess in her head.

One thing she was certain about was that tonight she had to do what she should've done weeks ago. And most likely lose Eli for ever because of it.

Eli grabbed the bottle of wine he'd bought on the way and strode up Anna's pathway. He couldn't stay away from her. Yes, he was here to find some answers to what she wanted from them but he had to spend more time with her for his own sake. If that wasn't falling in love then he had no idea how to explain his actions.

'Hi there,' Anna called from the vegetable garden against the side fence where she was getting a sprinkler sorted to water the plants. She looked as confused as he was, though he didn't know if the same reason was behind that.

Holding up the bottle, he asked, 'Where do I find some glasses?' He hadn't needed to look for any last night as

Anna had had everything required on a table handy to the barbecue. And he hadn't helped with the dishes afterwards.

'Cupboard above the fridge. I'm nearly done here.'

'Don't rush. I'll bring the wine over.' Her gardens were in good condition with early cauliflowers and broccoli coming on. A zucchini plant was still producing at one end, with another coming up to speed. His mother always said those were like weeds, but weeds he loved when she made chocolate zucchini cake.

'There're some nibbles on a plate in the fridge if you can grab them.'

'Onto it.' Anna made him feel quite at home despite how he'd been towards her last night. Another reason to wake up to the potential he was trying to ignore. They did get on well when he wasn't looking for reasons not to. He found her already sitting on a deck chair when he went outside with their glasses and the platter, and laughed to himself. She obviously didn't feel the need to check to see if he'd found his way around her kitchen. He liked that. There wasn't much he didn't like. 'Here you go.' Placing one glass on the small table between the two deck chairs, he sat down and looked at her. 'This is a good space. Open and light, and your gardens enhance the yard.'

'Even the roses have done well this year, if I may say so.'

'It's a lot quieter tonight than it was yesterday.' He laughed. 'The kids know how to make a racket, don't they?'

'It's what they're good at. I love it when they're here. They don't hold back at all. Jordan fitted right in.'

'He was talking non-stop this morning on the way to school. Luca this… Luca that.' He'd wanted to know when he could come back to Anna's again.

'Leanne's kids are here quite often so if Jordan's free he can always come by.' The wariness in her voice told him she was questioning whether he was prepared to allow his son to visit again.

'He'll be rapt. Making friends is big with him at the moment. I think he still misses those from his preschool and is afraid he won't make enough at the new school.'

'That's understandable.'

'Would you like to have children one day?' He had no idea why he asked, but now that the question was out there, he was eager to hear what she had to say.

'I'd love to. The biological clock is starting to tick quietly. I know I'm only thirty-four, but I can't help thinking about the women I met when working on the gynaecology ward who hadn't been able to get pregnant in their late thirties.'

'You've got time, though I see where you're coming from.'

'I'm not going to leap into a relationship just so I can have a baby. It's got to be all or nothing.'

'You're looking out for yourself. It's the right way to go.' Which he was doing when it came to getting close to Anna, looking out for himself. Except he was beginning to see that it might be the wrong thing to do. He was falling deeper in love with her by the day. Time for a change of subject. Except he couldn't think of one to distract him from those long, tanned legs stretched out in front of him. Damn, but she was sexy. Heating him up faster than he'd once have believed possible. Not even a gulp of chilled wine did a thing towards cooling him down. Talk about being all over the place with Anna. Last night he'd been cross with her, and now he wanted to carry her inside and make wild passionate love to her, instead of discussing serious things.

She was looking out over her tidy lawn, seemingly far away from where his mind was going. But then she turned to face him and he knew she wanted him here. 'I'm tired of looking out for myself. I'd just like to let go and have some fun, to hell with the consequences. Except I know it doesn't work like that. Things tend to come back and bite me on the butt if I don't keep control on my emotions.'

'Seeing you out of control isn't new. Not when we're between the sheets.' There was fire in his veins. Anna did that to him too easily. It was her way and it was his to fall into the blaze and try to make her feel the same. If she didn't already.

A rare blush turned her face pink. 'How long before you have to go?'

He placed his glass on the table and stood up. 'Long enough.' Once again he'd gone off track, and once again he couldn't wait to get into bed with her.

'You haven't stopped smiling all week,' Leanne said as she sat down beside Anna at the desk. 'He's that good?'

'Nope.' Anna grinned to herself. 'Better.' Eli had woken her up in ways she'd not believed possible. In bed, that was. When he'd asked if she wanted children the other night, she'd known what she had to tell him, but then he'd looked at her with such heat in his eyes that everything had gone out of her head except getting down and dirty. Her grin faded. She couldn't hold that against him.

'Afternoon, Anna, Leanne.' The man himself strode into the office. 'How's things?'

'All good. None of your patients are causing problems,' Anna replied as she breathed in the sight of that gorgeous body she now knew very well.

'Good, because it's been a long day in Theatre and I have one more patient to operate on when she's been prepped.' Eli dug into his pocket and pulled out his phone. 'Sorry, got to take this. Hi, Mum, what's up?'

Anna shut down the files she'd been looking at. Nearly time to head off and go to the supermarket to deal with the long list of groceries she'd made that morning.

'Don't worry, Mum. I'll sort something out.' Eli dropped his phone back in his pocket, a worried frown forming.

'Got a problem?' she asked.

'Mum's stuck in a traffic jam due to a truck and trailer unit rolling just this side of Kaikoura and won't make it back to pick up Jordan from school.'

'And you've got surgery to deal with.' Anna shrugged. The groceries could wait. 'I'm out of here shortly. I can pick him up and take him to my place. Or yours, if that's what you'd prefer.'

'I'd get Karen to look after him in her office but she's got parent-teacher meetings this afternoon.' Eli looked around, then returned his gaze to her. 'Okay, thanks. That would solve the problem.'

'Your place or mine? If mine, I can make dinner for all of us to have when you're done here.'

'I'd prefer mine. Jordan has a routine after school that I like him to stick to.'

'All right.' She wouldn't admit he'd hurt her a little. What harm could it do for Jordan to spend a couple of hours at her house? But then Eli was always over-careful when it came to his boy. 'How do I get in?'

He rattled off the security code for the keypad. 'I'll try to get home as soon as possible.' He turned to go.

'Hang on, Eli,' Leanne called. 'What about the school? They're not going to let Anna take Jordan away without your permission.'

He shoved a hand through his hair. 'It's not a problem with my sister being the headmistress, but you're right, I'd better phone and tell her what's going on.'

Anna tuned out as he explained to Karen she'd be picking up Jordan. Time with him would be fun. He was such a busy wee guy and they got along fine.

'Sorted,' Eli said from behind her. 'Ask for Heather Brown, Jordan's teacher, Anna. She'll take you to his room.'

'Go now,' Leanne told her. 'It's nearly three and the next shift's starting to arrive.'

'I will. It'll take some time to get to the school at this hour. Does Jordan know I'm collecting him?'

Eli was watching her. 'Karen's gone to tell him.' Then he surprised her by stepping close and touching her shoulder. 'I really appreciate it.'

'No problem.'

Just don't overthink it, she begged silently.

'It's no big deal.'

Wrong thing to say, if the way his hand on her back tightened was anything to go by.

She added hurriedly, 'I had nothing else on.' Nothing important anyway. Her pantry wasn't bare. Except she realised she'd probably made matters worse because it sounded as though she wouldn't have offered if she did have something else to do. 'I mean, I'm happy to do this. I'd better get going or Jordan will think I've forgotten him.'

Eli's smile went a way to lifting her spirits. 'You're right about that.'

It took longer to get to the school than Anna had expected with traffic banked up all over the town. When she parked outside she sighed with relief. Mums did this all the time. Talk about stressful. Out of the car, she spied Jordan kicking a ball around with another boy. 'Hey, Jordan, I'm here.'

He raced across and threw his arms around her. 'Hello, Nurse Anna. You're taking me home.'

'Yes, I am as soon as I see your teacher.'

'Here I am,' said an older woman behind her. 'No need to ask who you are. Jordan's reaction is all the proof I need, though for legal purposes I need to see some ID.'

'No problem.' Anna tugged her phone from her pocket and found her driver's licence.

'You're good to go, Jordan. See you on Monday.'

'Okay, Mrs Brown. Anna, can I have an ice cream on the way home? A big one in a cone. Chocolate with sauce.'

She rolled her eyes. 'You're setting me up to get in trouble, young man.'

'Dad always buys me one when he picks me up.' The impish look on Jordan's face suggested otherwise.

But she might give him a treat. It wasn't as if she'd done this with Jordan before and once couldn't hurt. Could it? Would Eli see that as trying to win him over? Too bad if he did. It was what she did with Leanne's kids. There was no difference as far as she was concerned.

Her phone played a tune. 'Hi, Eli. Thought you'd be operating by now.'

'There's been a hold-up as the previous operation went beyond expected time. How's Jordan?'

'He's good. Want to talk to him?'

'Sure.'

'Jordan, Dad wants to say hi.'

'Dad, Nurse Anna's going to get me a ice cream. Okay, *an* ice cream. Yes, she is. She told me.'

Um…that wasn't quite how it had gone, but still.

She took the phone back. 'Hope that's all right?'

'Make it a small one or he won't eat dinner. Right, got to go. We're on.' And he was gone.

An hour later when she was playing hopscotch with Jordan on Eli's back lawn, Eli rang again. 'Just checking everything's all right.'

'Of course. Why shouldn't it be?'

'You might've forgotten the code to get into the house.'

'I didn't need it as Jordan spouted it off numerous times when I turned into your drive.'

'He knows it? I didn't have a clue.'

'He's not silly. Want to talk to him again?' To make sure she hadn't beaten him or tied him to the bed?

Calm down, Anna. Eli's a caring dad.

Of course he'd ring to check all was okay.

'Not at the moment. My patient's coming round and I'm needed in Recovery.' Gone.

This was starting to become annoying. Two calls to check up on Jordan when he'd often said that she was good with children. Bet he didn't phone his mother or Liz to check on how they were doing all the time. 'Bye, Eli,' she muttered as she banged the phone down.

'Was that Daddy?'

'Yes, he's still working.'

'That's okay. I've got you to play with.'

Therein might lie a problem, if Eli's wariness had anything to do with it. In the meantime she'd get on with keeping his son happy and if he didn't get home soon, she'd make Jordan some dinner. The kid was hungry despite the ice cream he'd gorged on earlier.

When Eli called again at six o'clock she snatched the phone up and growled, 'Jordan's fine. He's had a bath and I'm about to feed him. Anything else bothering you?'

Silence. Then, 'I was calling to see if you'd like pizza for dinner.'

The air left her lungs in a rush. Closing her eyes, she counted to ten in her head. 'Sorry, Eli. Really sorry.'

That's enough. You don't have to grovel.

'If that's still on offer, then I'd love one. Seafood if possible.' She was going to stay after that? Sit and eat pizza as if nothing were wrong? Actually, it was a good idea. She'd have it out with him and finally learn where she stood.

'See you soon.' Gone—again.

Why had she reacted so fast and not given Eli time to say why he'd rung?

Because I'm afraid he'll find me wanting, that I'm not good enough to look after his son. Not good enough for Eli to love me.

Just when she was feeling she might be able to move on she went and blew it. The doubts that had haunted her for eighteen years were still there. But then, were they ever likely to disappear? Maybe after forty years in a stable relationship?

'Seafood pizza as requested.' Eli placed a box on the table in front of Anna, noting the stress in her face. They'd talk shortly. He swung Jordan up in his arms and hugged him. 'I see you've been having stories read to you.'

'Yes, Daddy. Nurse Anna reads all my favourites.'

'Cool. Now it's time to clean your teeth and go to bed. It's already past your bedtime.' He glanced at Anna. 'That's not a dig at you. I knew he'd insist on staying up until I got home.'

'I have no idea what time he usually goes to bed, and wasn't asking.'

'Good thinking. He'd have said ten o'clock.'

A small smile lifted her face, but whether it was for him or his son he didn't know. 'That's what I figured.'

'Give me ten? And pour us each a glass of the wine that's in the fridge?' The situation was awkward enough so he'd try to be relaxed and casual.

Without waiting for an answer, he carried Jordan to the bathroom and supervised the teeth cleaning and the other requirements before getting into bed. After a few minutes listening to how his day at school had gone, Eli kissed him goodnight and went out to face Anna.

She was twisting her glass back and forth in her hands, looking thoughtful and not happy.

'Thank you for looking after Jordan. It's much appreciated.'

'I enjoyed it.' She sipped her wine and put the glass down. 'You thank me and yet you kept ringing up as though you expected something to go wrong.'

He put plates and serviettes on the table, opened both pizza boxes, and sat down. 'Call me paranoid.'

'Distrustful, more like.' She picked up a piece of pizza and took a large bite.

'That, too.'

She flinched. 'Great.'

The wine didn't taste so wonderful tonight, but he swallowed a large mouthful anyway. 'It's not you personally that I have trouble with. In fact I've got further with you than any other woman since Melissa.'

A puzzled expression came his way. 'I'm not sure how to take that.'

'Damn it, Anna. This is ridiculous. We get on so well, and yet here we are arguing like kids.' Another gulp of wine and he pushed the glass aside. Wine wasn't going to solve a thing. 'You know why I worry.'

Her eye roll was exaggerated. 'You tell me so often I wonder if this isn't more about you not trusting me not to hurt *you*.' She locked formidable eyes on him. 'Actually, forget Jordan. This *is* about us. You and me.' Her finger tapped the table with each word. 'You're afraid of being let down again. I get that because I have fears about being let down too.'

That was a slap around the head. It had never occurred to him she'd think that with him. 'What's behind those fears?' Would whatever was worrying her explain those days when he'd believed she was hiding something?

A solitary tear rolled down her cheek.

His heart was breaking for her, but he remained where he was. It was for Anna to make the next move.

The piece of pizza she held hit the bottom of the box. 'Easy said. The thing is, I'm not even certain I can be trusted to stay in a relationship. I've got a bad track record. Even with family. So I don't have a lot to offer in the way of guarantees.'

That concurred with all his worries. 'Then we're in a deeper quagmire than I'd thought.'

'Want to keep trying to sort this out, or is it time to bail before it gets too difficult?' More tears filled Anna's eyes.

His heart dropped—hard. She was hurting. He was hurting. He wanted to leap up and haul her into his arms and never let her go. But if he did, it was a commitment he wasn't ready to make until he knew what was behind those tears. She might not want to be there for him for ever. She was right in that this was as much, if not more, about his feelings as Jordan's. If he committed it had to be for ever and he wasn't sure she could reciprocate.

Her glass was going round and round in her hands. 'When I was fifteen I got pregnant.'

He hadn't seen that coming. Everything in him stopped as he waited for Anna to continue.

'I turned sixteen two weeks before my son was born.'

What did that have to do with anything? She'd had a baby. Where was he now?

'My parents refused to help or support me.' Imploring eyes lifted to look at him. 'I was still at school. If I kept the baby they'd have kicked me out on the street and I wouldn't have been able to support him.'

'There are social services that'd do that.' Bile soured his mouth. Why hadn't she told him before? It made all the difference to his decisions to stay with her.

Her head moved slowly from side to side. 'I talked to them. Was offered accommodation in a home with other girls in similar situations but I was sixteen and totally out of my mind about what had happened. Friends talked about drugs and other things that terrified me. I couldn't see how I'd ever be able to give Charlie everything he needed.'

The bile got stronger. 'So you gave him up for adoption.'

'I had no choice. It was the best I could do for him.'

He could not believe what he was hearing. Anna was so

good with kids. All the pain from his own mother's abandonment filled him, making it difficult to breathe, let alone think straight. Yet she was also very good with Jordan. Jordan. Deep breath. Thank goodness they hadn't got too deeply involved. This was the end of anything between them.

'But not for me. I have lived with guilt and sorrow every day since they took him away out of my arms.' Her face glistened with tears.

He went to get a box of tissues. 'Here.' Sinking onto his chair, he shook his head. 'I don't know what to say, Anna. You've shocked me.'

Her head shot up and there was anger in her glare. 'You don't have any right to judge me, Eli. I didn't walk away from my boy because I had better things to do. I gave him up for his own good.'

'Yeah, well, maybe, but you don't know what he will have gone through in the intervening years wondering about you and who you are and why you did what you did.'

'And you do?'

'Yes, I damned well do. Mum and Dad are my adoptive parents.'

Her mouth fell open. Her eyes widened. All colour drained from her face. 'I see.'

'No, you don't. I was six months old and my birth mother didn't want me any more. She had better things to do than raise me.' He stood up and paced around the lounge. 'She told me that when I tracked her down six years ago.'

'Charlie found me. Last week.'

'Last week?' That explained a lot. 'You didn't think to talk to me about him then?' They were never going to get close and involved. She'd kept this huge piece of information from him.

'I wanted to. I tried.'

'I offered an ear when I thought you were worried about something. That's not how it works in a good relationship.'

'The thing is, I wasn't sure if we had one of those, or were even starting out on one.' She was getting stronger by the minute. 'I knew once I told you there'd be no chance of you wanting to have anything more to do with me.'

'Are you saying you intended to hide it from me for ever?'

'Never.' She swallowed hard. 'I—' Another swallow. 'I have a lot of feelings for you. I stalled. I know that was wrong, but I couldn't lose you so soon. I kept fooling myself that you might fall for me and understand why I did what I did. Of course, I didn't know about your adoption.'

'Anna, I'm sorry, but I've taken two hits in the heart. I can't take another.'

Her face crumpled. Then she said so softly he had to strain to hear the words. 'Charlie and I are talking. He's beginning to understand why I gave him up and that I've always loved him.'

What could he say? It hadn't worked out like that for him, but he was pleased for Charlie. Anna had such a big heart. The young man deserved no less.

Anna stood up slowly, as if hoping he'd stop her before it was too late. He couldn't. When he didn't, she shook her head sadly. 'Goodbye, Eli.'

His heart was already aching. There'd be more of that to come. Tomorrow he'd be back to being Mr Forrester. He'd bet his next salary payment on that. 'Goodnight, Anna.'

CHAPTER TEN

'I'VE FILLED OUT a prescription for Tobias.' Eli stood up from the desk and moved away as Anna came into the office. 'See that he starts the antibiotics immediately.'

'Onto it,' she said, nurse's head firmly in place as she dropped into the chair he'd vacated.

'Thanks.'

Anna watched him stride away as though he hadn't a worry in the world. If she hadn't seen the sadness in his eyes she'd believe that to be true. It had been the week from hell. They'd dodged each other as best as possible, and when they couldn't they had exchanged only the bare minimum of words. He was never going to forgive her for not telling him about her son right from the start of their relationship. She might not forgive him for being so cold about it all either. He hadn't shown any compassion, probably too busy protecting his own feelings. 'Thank goodness for Fridays.' She had the whole weekend to bury her head under her pillow and wait for her heart to get over itself.

Make that most of the weekend. Charlie and his parents were flying down to see her tomorrow afternoon. It would be exciting if she didn't feel so wound up about how the meeting would go. Charlie had tried to reassure her his mum and dad were happy he'd met her and only wanted to get to know her a little. But she'd lived with the idea of this moment for so long she couldn't relax. Dealing with the bust-up with Eli as well didn't help. It was too hard. If only he were around for her to curl up against and talk about her fears. But that was never going to happen.

'What's going on?' Leanne asked after looking around to make sure they were alone.

She hadn't told Leanne what had happened. It would make it even more real. 'Nothing's going on. We're done and dusted.' Except she doubted she'd get over Eli in a hurry, if at all. She hadn't loved a man as she loved him. It had really come home to her during the night as she tossed and turned while trying to accept they were through. He hadn't made any attempt to stop her leaving, had sat there watching her walk away, while her heart was crumbling, filling her with pain unlike anything she'd known except for the day they'd taken Charlie away from her.

'I don't believe you, Anna.' Leanne had turned to look at her, worry covering her face. 'You were getting on brilliantly.'

'Were being the operative word.'

'You're going to give up that easily?'

'Nothing easy about it.' Her sigh was filled with pain. 'I love him, Leanne.'

'I know you do. It's been obvious from the get-go. You've been more you: happier, bubblier, laughing more if that was possible.'

How was she going to cope? Her heart was shattered. The phone rang and she grabbed it for the distraction. 'Paediatric ward. Anna speaking.'

'Pete from the pharmacy. I've got an urgent prescription for one of your patients ready.'

'On my way.' She stood up. 'Don't say any more, Leanne. I have to think about what comes next.' All she knew was that whatever she came up with, it wouldn't include the man of her dreams.

'I'm your buddy. You don't get away with that. But it will have to wait until later tonight when you come round for dinner with the tribe.'

Thank goodness for besties. 'I'll bring chocolates for the kids.' There was no way she wanted to go home to her empty house. Funny how she'd never had anyone else living with her and the house had never felt empty. It didn't feel like home any more. Home would be wherever her heart was, and that was with Eli now.

'Do that and you'll have a bed to use if required.'

'I might do that and all.'

In the end Anna didn't stay with Leanne and Craig, instead drove home around midnight and crawled into her own bed to pull the pillow around her neck and try to go to sleep. But all she could think of was Eli and how he was back to being aloof. She hated that. She deserved better now that they'd been intimate and had enjoyed being together. Especially now he knew about her past. She did deserve better. She did. Charlie had muttered he could see why she gave him up. Why couldn't Eli understand her reasons? His mother hadn't wanted him. But she had wanted her son and she'd told Eli so.

Throwing her pillow at the wall, she cried, 'I love you, Eli.'

She was ready to commit for ever? Not to back off after

time? Yes, she was more than ready, but Eli wasn't. He never would be. Not with her.

She'd pulled away from her parents after they'd put the pressure on her over Charlie. She'd let Danny go when she should've grabbed him and marched down the aisle on his arm so she could prove she wouldn't let him down. There were other men she'd let slip through her hands all too easily because she hadn't believed she deserved to be happy.

Then along came Eli. The one man who'd got past her barriers, had made her realise she was capable of love and ready for the whole shebang, and now she wanted it more than anything. With Eli.

Why had she walked out of his house without putting up a fight? Was that a habit? Or was fear the reason *he* didn't reciprocate her love? And that he'd never get past what she'd done to Charlie?

She had no idea how he felt about her. Apparently she'd been a breath of fresh air for him, and he'd liked how she talked openly about most things, but he didn't trust her not to leave him. Forget Jordan. He was one of Eli's concerns, but she'd swear nowhere near as big as his own fear of being let down. That she could understand, feeling much the same.

Since she couldn't promise to be there for him for ever, he had probably done the right thing by not asking her to stay any longer. Throwing a second pillow after the first did nothing to calm her distress. 'I love you so much it's painful, Eli. Do you even love me a little bit?'

Eli groaned as he rolled over in bed when Jordan bounced under the sheet. No such thing as a sleep-in these days. 'Hey, little man, go easy on my old bones.'

'Wake up, Dad. I want to do something.'

Like what? He'd learned not to ask. 'Starting with breakfast.'

'Can we see Anna today?'

His heart crunched. 'Afraid not, Jordie.' If only they could bowl around to her place and sit on the deck.

Why don't I? Just go, do it.

He should ignore all the noise in his head and listen to his heart. Talk to her about her son, and really listen to her as she talked about him. If Charlie could accept what had happened, then why couldn't he? Anna was nothing like his birth mother. Not at all. She loved her boy.

Could it be that easy to move past this? Was he making it harder than necessary? He knew what his family would say. Which didn't make it any easier. They weren't the ones who had to front up to his gremlins. 'Come on, let's get up and ready for swimming class.' Something to keep him busy for a couple of hours at least and then he'd think of something else to do with Jordan.

It was a long tedious day that brought only more questions and no answers. Despite what she'd told him, he missed Anna like he couldn't believe, yet they'd never spent a whole weekend together. This felt final. They weren't going to work through it and start over. Nor would they carry on with what they'd already had. Everything was different now.

What are you doing today, Anna? he asked silently again and again. *Missing me? Cursing me for being stubborn?*

Finally he gave up trying to fill in the hours until sunset and packed Jordan into the car and headed around to Liz's where Jordan would have someone to be busy with.

The first thing he said when he walked into her house was, 'Don't say a word.'

She studied him for a moment and nodded. 'Fine. Beer's in the back fridge and Gary's in the garden picking peas. Take him one, too.'

He gave her a hug. 'Thanks.'

After roast lamb and vegetables, and an apple tart with cream that Eli barely tasted, Jordan crawled into the spare bed in his cousin's room and fell asleep.

'Guess that means you're staying the night,' Liz said.

'Might as well,' he agreed and reached for the wine Gary had poured them after dinner.

He didn't sleep any better than the night before at home, tossing and turning until finally at around five o'clock he got up and went for a walk through the quiet streets, Anna with him all the way. He couldn't let her go, didn't want to let her go.

He loved her. Yeah, he could admit that to himself. He was head over heels in love with Anna Passau. Which left him with little choice. He had to follow up, to expose his heart and tell Anna how he felt about her, and then ask her to believe in him. He needed to accept her history so they could go forward *together*. It shouldn't be hard to do.

It was a huge weight holding him down, preventing him from opening up. 'Why?' he asked the sun peeking over the horizon. 'Why can't I do this?'

Because of Jordan.

Not true. Eli tripped. Stared around, barely seeing where he was, the realisation in his head blinding him to everything else.

He *was* hiding behind his son. Using his son as an excuse

to protect his heart. He didn't want to be hurt again. He knew that, had always known that, but he hadn't realised how deep his need to do it had become. He needed to be shaken awake so he could focus on reality and drop the what-ifs. There was only one way to live and that was to be open about his feelings with other people. Most of all, with Anna. As he always was with his family.

Turning back the way he'd come, he thought about where to go from here.

Placing the baguettes in the oven, Anna turned to the fridge to get some zucchinis to make fritters. Nothing like zucchini and parmesan together, she thought as she began grating the vegetable.

After the Zoom call with Charlie and his parents she'd hit the kitchen. It had been another disappointment to get over when Charlie had phoned to say the weather in Wellington was so bad most flights had been cancelled and could they have an online meeting instead.

The meeting had gone better than she'd expected. She even found herself liking Charlie's parents and at the end they'd all agreed to get together some other time. Charlie had given her a cheeky smile that had really lifted her spirits.

Until she closed down her laptop and Eli flooded back into her head, taking over all thoughts.

The oven timer beeped. Removing a cake and placing it on the wire rack, she groaned at herself. 'Who's going to eat all this?' Her appetite had disappeared along with any chance Eli might decide they should be together. Looking around the benches where a lasagne and two bacon and egg pies sat cooling, she shrugged. She'd find someone to give it all to. Leanne and Craig were always happy to receive her cooking.

She'd been filling in hours here in the kitchen, trying her damnedest not to think about Eli. And failing completely. He was there with every egg she broke into the bowl, every piece of pasta she placed in the pot, every punch of the dough that was now baking and filling the air with a delicious fragrance. Face it, Eli was in her heart and head and wasn't going anywhere else any time soon.

She loved him. He didn't know that. She hadn't told him.

Would it have made a difference to how he'd let her walk away if she had? Would he have leapt up and hauled her against that strong chest, never to let her go? Not likely. He'd more likely have shaken his head and told her to get a life.

Only one way to find out. Which meant laying her heart out for him to see. Was she brave enough? Could she afford not to be? People said nothing ventured, nothing gained. They didn't say what happened if it failed. She had to know. Though after seeing his shock when she talked about Charlie, she knew he would never let her in his front door.

To hell with the bread. She flipped the oven off as she untied her apron. Same for the fritters. She shoved the bowl of batter into the fridge. She had to do this. Had to. If Eli never knew she loved him, then she had only herself to blame for whatever came next.

Knock, knock.

Someone was at her back door. 'Bad timing, because I'm outta here.' Pulling the door open, she gasped. 'Eli?' Who else did she know who was so good-looking and sexy and kind and caring and—? She slumped against the doorframe. 'I was just coming to see you.'

He took her hands, held them tight. 'Anna.' His eyes looked haunted, and his face was so sad it brought tears to her eyes. 'I—' He swallowed, hard.

Noise from the street made her straighten up. 'Come inside.' She forced her lungs to breathe, and, still holding one of his hands, pulled him in and closed the door on the rest of the world.

'Anna, it's been a long weekend and it's nowhere near over. We need to talk.'

She kept moving, not wanting to have this conversation in the entranceway.

Eli moved with her, as though he never wanted to let her go again. That had to be good, didn't it? But 'we have to talk' sounded quite the opposite. They sat at the table, watching each other warily. After a laden minute, Anna bit down on the words her heart wanted to put out there, and said, 'Go on.'

'I'll be blunt. I love you, Anna. I've fallen hard and deep and I never want to let you out of my life.'

'You what?' Her heart was pounding, her head spinning. Never had she expected that. If anything she'd thought Eli would've given her a hundred reasons why he was reticent about telling her his feelings, not come straight out with the words.

'I love you,' he repeated, looking relieved. As if getting the words out had lifted a huge weight off him.

Standing up, she moved around beside him and took his stubbly face in her hands. 'What about my past? What about Charlie?' She didn't want to spend time with Eli only for him to decide again he couldn't deal with it.

'I've done a lot of soul-searching, and I talked to Mum

and Dad about this. I hope you understand I had to hear their perspective as adoptive parents. Anna, I haven't been in your shoes. I can't criticise you for what you did. Bottom line, you didn't have a choice if you wanted your son to have a good life. I admire you for that.'

Her heart cracked wide open. Not once had she expected Eli to tell her that. 'Thank you. It means everything to me to hear you say that.'

His smile was tentative. 'I mean it with all my heart, Anna.'

The last knots around her heart broke away. She was free at last. 'Eli, I love you with all I've got. I have for a while now.'

She didn't get any further as he pulled her down onto his knees and placed his mouth over hers. His kiss was gentle and loving and told her more than his words had. Eli Forrester loved her. Her heart was safe. She kissed him with all she had, and more.

When they finally pulled apart and regained their breaths, Eli smiled. 'I've been fighting with myself for a while about how to approach this. Do I tell you? Don't I tell you? Until in the end it was a no-brainer. I had no choice if I wasn't going to go mad. I'm sorry I visited my fears about Jordan on you, Anna. You didn't deserve that.' He paused, then drew a deep breath. 'But I'm even more sorry that I used my concerns over Jordan being hurt to hide behind. You were right. I was, still am a little, afraid to commit my heart. But I'm doing it. I can't not when you mean so much to me.'

Tears began streaming down her cheeks. 'Neither of us is perfect. I always believed I didn't deserve love because of what I did, and then I met you and thought I might be able to change that. Charlie turning up when he did helped me see I could be totally happy, but really it all comes down to you. I've been waiting for you to come into my life. When you did, you chipped away at my fears bit by bit without me understanding what was going on until I was in so deep there was nothing else to do but tell you I love you. That's what I was coming to do when you knocked on the door.'

'Mum and Dad support you one hundred per cent, by the way.' Brushing her cheeks with his fingers, he kissed her again, a loving, heart-sharing kiss that spoke of their future together, for ever. Then they sat holding each other tight, not saying anything, absorbing the love that bonded them together.

Anna in his arms was the best feeling in the world, Eli thought as he brushed a kiss on the top of her head. She loved him. He was still getting his head around that. He believed her, of course he did, but it was hard accepting that he'd found a woman who meant so much to him and seemed to think the same of him. It was the most wonderful thing to happen in a long time.

Looking over at the kitchen benches, he chuckled. Typical Anna. 'I take it you've been cooking up a storm as a way to shove me out of your head?'

'That's only this morning's efforts. I baked some cakes late last night too.'

'What are you going to do with it all?'

Green eyes met his grey ones. 'Give it all away, I guess.' Then she blinked and smiled. 'Or, we could ring your lot and tell them to get their butts around here for lunch so we can share our news. Along with Leanne and Craig.' She got up and switched the oven back on before returning to Eli.

His heart swelled even further when he didn't believe it was possible. 'Why not?' Then he asked, 'What are we saying? That we're in love?'

'Isn't that enough for now?'

'There'll be endless questions about what we're going to do about it.' He had to warn her, though she probably already knew.

'Leanne will be no different. They'll all have to wait and see.' Anna grinned, then grew serious. 'What are we going to do?'

'Spend as much time together as possible. Make plans for our for ever future together.'

'Plans that include Jordan.' She smiled.

'Yeah, and maybe add to the tribe?' Eli knew Anna wanted to become a mother again, this time to go the distance, and who better for his son to have as a stepmum? Anna would never let his boy down. Never.

'Did I say I love you, Eli Forrester?'

'Once or twice.' Damn, his heart felt good. Full and happy and ready for anything.

EPILOGUE

Twelve months later, at the beach

'MUM ANNA, I want a juice.' Jordan flopped down on the beach towel beside her.

'Help yourself.' Sometimes she still had to blink away the tears that his name for her brought on.

The moment Eli had explained that she was moving into their house to live with them, and that Dad loved Anna, Jordan had leapt into her arms shouting, 'Mum Anna, I love you too.' Her heart had imploded with love for the little guy.

Glancing across at the other Forrester male who did unbelievable things to her heart, she sighed with happiness. Life couldn't get any better. Her hand sat on the baby bump under her singlet top. She was too big for a bikini at the moment.

'Mum Anna, I want a beer.' Eli sat down on the blanket she'd spread on the sand and gave her one of his heart-stopping smiles.

She could never get enough of those. And his kisses. And their lovemaking. 'Help yourself. I'll have a water while you're at it.' The only downside to being pregnant was not being able to share the occasional wine with her man. It wasn't a biggie. Their baby was far more important. She could barely wait for Rose to pop out so they could all get to know her. But she'd have to. Ten weeks to go.

'How's Rose this afternoon?' Eli handed her a bottle of sparkling water.

'She was snoozing since I went for a swim.' Made a nice change from all the energetic kicks that had been going on earlier. Leaning back in her beach chair, she watched the man she loved so much. How lucky she'd been to find him. 'I could almost thank Jordan for getting appendicitis.'

'It was the tipping point for us, wasn't it?'

Her eyes dropped to the emerald ring on her finger. The colour to match her eyes, Eli had said when he'd held it out after proposing. His favourite colour, he'd added. 'Yes, it was. When I called you a jerk that night, I'd never have believed that I'd fall in love with you, even though I was already feeling the heat whenever you were around.'

'Little hot blasts that made my toes tight,' Eli said with a sideways glance at Jordan. 'If you know what I mean.'

'Not at all.'

He grinned. 'Bet you didn't expect to be having *my* baby and getting married once she's here.'

'Never crossed my mind.' Though she had hoped for something like that once she'd accepted she'd fallen for him. 'Nor did I know how much effort goes into planning a wedding.' But now the venue had been booked, the caterers lined up, and a dress was being made with allowances for a change in her figure after Rose was born. The invitations had gone out a week ago and already most people had answered. Including her parents. They were coming. It had been tense the day she'd taken Eli to meet them, but he had been at ease with them and soon they had all been talking. It had almost been like old times for Anna. Since then they'd made an effort to see more of her and had met Charlie too.

Which reminded her. 'Charlie's got a partner for the wedding.'

'I'm surprised he didn't already have one. He's such a cool dude.'

'He's choosy.' He was also adorable. They got on really well nowadays, and he and Eli seemed to have a natural bond together.

Eli. The love of her life. Reaching across for his hand, she gripped him tight. 'Have I told you lately that I love you?'

'Over breakfast this morning.' He lifted her off the chair and onto his thighs. 'I love you too, soon-to-be Mrs Forrester.'

'As in aloof like Mr Forrester? I don't think so.' She chuckled.

'Okay, then, soon-to-be Mrs Anna Passau-Forrester.' He grinned, kissed her.

'Yuk. I'm going for a swim,' Jordan shouted, and charged down the beach to the water, bringing their kiss to an end as they kept an eye on him.

* * * * *

If you enjoyed this story,
check out these other great reads
from Sue Mackay

Paramedic's Fling to Forever
Marriage Reunion with the Island Doc
Resisting the Pregnant Paediatrician
Fake Fiancée to Forever

All available now!

MILLS & BOON®

Coming next month

FESTIVE FLING WITH THE SURGEON

Karin Baine

'You don't want me to talk? I thought some women liked that sort of thing?' he teased her, whispering low in her ear, knowing the effect it had on her.

Her knees buckling, goosebumps rippling over her skin and a little gasp emitting from her lips were all things he remembered from their last time together, and he wasn't disappointed.

'Hmm, I'm of the opinion your mouth could be put to better use…'

The growl that came from deep inside his chest spoke of those caveman urges Tamsin appeared to waken in him. He'd never let himself get so wrapped up in thoughts of a woman that he'd brush aside all of his long-held reasons for avoiding commitment for something as basic as sex. Yet that was exactly what Tamsin did to him. All he could hope for now that he was lost to this chemistry was that things between them remained strictly physical. With any luck, a short fling over Christmas would give them both what they needed and they could move on in the New Year without fear of recriminations.

The knowledge that he didn't have to curtail his needs, that they'd gone into this together, eyes wide open, unleashed a part of Max he usually held back. Tamsin was getting more of him than anyone ever had.

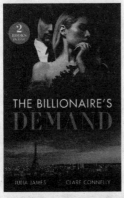

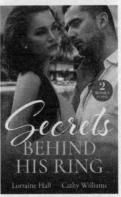

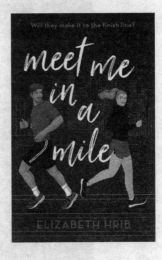

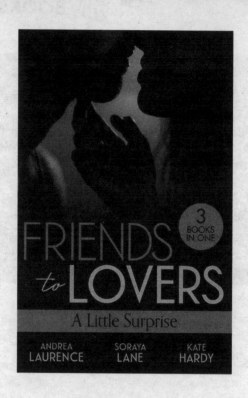